OPERATION THUNDER CHILD

Nick Pope

SIMON & SCHUSTER
A VIACOM COMPANY

Also by Nick Pope

Open Skies, Closed Minds
The Uninvited

AUTHOR'S NOTE

Numerous experts have provided me with much valuable assistance in my research for this novel. Nevertheless, some of the technical details about weapons systems, defensive capabilities, military doctrine, strategy and tactics have been altered, for obvious reasons of national security.

First published in Great Britain by Simon & Schuster UK Ltd, 1999
A Viacom Company

1 3 5 7 9 10 8 6 4 2

Simon & Schuster UK Ltd
Africa House
64-78 Kingsway
London WC2B 6AH

Simon & Schuster Australia
Sydney

A CIP catalogue record for this book is available from the British Library

Although this is predominantly a work of fiction, some of the events
featured or referred to in this book relate to real incidents or are based on
actual occurrences. The locations used in this novel are real, as are the
political, civil, scientific and military posts featured. However, the
characters associated with these locations and posts are fictitious, and any
resemblance to actual persons, living or dead, is purely coincidental.

ISBN 0-684-85160-1

Typeset in Garamond 3 by SX Composing DTP, Rayleigh, Essex
Printed and bound in Great Britain by
Butler & Tanner Ltd, Frome and London

To Seb, Laura and Jared
With love

CONTENTS

Acknowledgements   viii
Glossary of Abbreviations   ix

Prologue   1

Chapter 1: Intruder Alert   6
Chapter 2: Investigation   26
Chapter 3: Escalation   47
Chapter 4: Connections   67
Chapter 5: Exposure   86
Chapter 6: Thunder Child   104
Chapter 7: Surprise Attack   124
Chapter 8: Diplomatic Manoeuvres   144
Chapter 9: Fallen Angel   165
Chapter 10: Predators and Prey   182
Chapter 11: Politics   197
Chapter 12: Revelations   213
Chapter 13: The Eve of the War   230
Chapter 14: The Battle of Britain   249
Chapter 15: Endgame   272

ACKNOWLEDGEMENTS

This book owes its existence to the dedication and efforts of a team of people, whose many and varied contributions have been beyond value. I would particularly like to thank my agent, Andrew Lownie, for his tireless efforts on my behalf, and Martin Fletcher at Simon & Schuster UK for having faith in me and the project. The entire Simon & Schuster UK team have been marvellous, and I am eternally grateful to them all for working so hard.

My family and friends have rallied around, offering encouragement and sound advice when it was most needed. It would be impossible to pick out all those who helped, but I should mention specially Brigitte Barclay and Georgina Bruni, whose support has seen me through the darker moments and whose friendship is beyond value. I should also like to pay special tribute to Michèle Kaczynski, whose assistance has been priceless and without whom this project would never have got off the ground.

Finally, but perhaps most crucially, there are those who, for a number of reasons, I am not able to name. I was helped with this book by a wide range of experts from various different agencies, who supplemented my own knowledge with their insights into the worlds of politics, science, military doctrine and much else besides. Their generous assistance has brought authenticity to this book, and any remaining errors are mine alone. Our country is blessed to have such loyal and able servants.

GLOSSARY OF ABBREVIATIONS

ACC	Air Control Centre
AD	Air Defence
ADGE	Air Defence Ground Environment
AEW	Airborne Early Warning
AFBSC	Air Force Board Standing Committee
AFOR	Air Force Operations Room
AMRAAM	Advanced Medium-Range Air-to-Air Missile
AOC-in-C	Air Officer Commanding-in-Chief
APS	Assistant Private Secretary
ASRAAM	Advanced Short-Range Air-to-Air Missile
ATC	Air Traffic Control
AWACS	Airborne Warning and Control System
BMD	Ballistic Missile Defence
BMEWS	Ballistic Missile Early-Warning System
BOI	Board of Inquiry
BVRAAM	Beyond Visual Range Air-to-Air Missile
CAA	Civil Aviation Authority
CAP	Combat Air Patrol
CAS	Chief of the Air Staff
CBDE	Chemical and Biological Defence Establishment
CDI	Chief of Defence Intelligence
CDS	Chief of the Defence Staff
CE 3	Close Encounter of the Third Kind

CE 4	Close Encounter of the Fourth Kind
CGS	Chief of the General Staff
CIA	Central Intelligence Agency
C-in-C	Commander-in-Chief
CJO	Chief of Joint Operations
CO	Commanding Officer
COBR	Cabinet Office Briefing Room
COG	Current Operations Group
CRO	Community Relations Officer
CPO	Chief Press Officer
CSA	Chief Scientific Adviser
CTR	Close Target Recce
DA	Defence Attaché
DCMC	Defence Crisis Management Centre
DERA	Defence Evaluation and Research Agency
DIA	Defense Intelligence Agency
DIS	Defence Intelligence Staff
DISN	Director of Information, Strategy and News
DUS(S&T)	Deputy Under-Secretary (Science and Technology)
ECM	Electronic Countermeasures
ETH	Extraterrestrial Hypothesis
FCO	Foreign and Commonwealth Office
FSC	Field Standard C
GCHQ	Government Communications Headquarters
GPMG	General-Purpose Machine-Gun
HCDC	House of Commons Defence Committee
HMS	Her Majesty's Ship
HQSTC	Headquarters Strike Command
IFF	Identification Friend or Foe
IMINT	Imagery Intelligence
JARIC	Joint Air Reconnaissance Intelligence Centre
JIC	Joint Intelligence Committee
JTIDS	Joint Tactical Information Distribution System
LMG	Light Machine-Gun
MACA	Military Aid to the Civil Authority
Min(AF)	Minister of State for the Armed Forces

Min(DP)	Minister of State for Defence Procurement
MOD	Ministry of Defence
MPA	Maritime Patrol Aircraft
NASA	National Aeronautics and Space Administration
NATO	North Atlantic Treaty Organisation
NATS	National Air Traffic Services
NBC	Nuclear, Biological and Chemical
NLW	Non-Lethal Weapon
NOTAM	Notice to Airmen
NRO	National Reconnaissance Office
NRPB	National Radiological Protection Board
NSA	National Security Agency
NVG	Night-Vision Goggles
OP	Observation Post
PJHQ	Permanent Joint Headquarters
PLB	Personal Locator Beacon
PS	Private Secretary
PSYOPS	Psychological Operations
Q/QRA	Quick Reaction Alert
RAF	Royal Air Force
R&D	Research and Development
RIC	Reconnaissance Intelligence Centre
RN	Royal Navy
ROE	Rules of Engagement
RPV	Remotely Piloted Vehicle
SAM	Surface-to-Air Missile
SAR	Search and Rescue
SAS	Special Air Service
SATCOM	Satellite Communication
Sec(AS)	Secretariat (Air Staff)
SETI	Search for Extraterrestrial Intelligence
SHORAD	Short-Range Air Defence
SIS	Secret Intelligence Service
S of S	Secretary of State
SOP	Standard Operating Procedure
THAAD	Theatre High-Altitude Area Defence

TIALD	Thermal Imaging Airborne Laser Designator
UAV	Unmanned Aerial Vehicle
UFO	Unidentified Flying Object
UKADR	United Kingdom Air Defence Region
U/S	Unserviceable
USAF	United States Air Force
US of S	Under-Secretary of State

PROLOGUE

It had started as an adventure, but it certainly wasn't living up to expectations. Throughout their initial training it had been drummed into them, time and time again, that they were on foreign soil and that they were not to go off base in uniform – and certainly not armed. But that was precisely what they were doing now, on the instructions of their officer. That had made it all right because, young though they all were, they still realized that the officer would carry the can if anything went wrong. They had been told nothing, although the smarter ones guessed they were on some sort of short-notice exercise designed to assess their readiness. There had been some serious questions asked about their security when a couple of SAS men had managed to infiltrate the Weapons Storage Area a few weeks ago – something they were entitled to attempt, as part of an ongoing programme to test security. A bemused member of D Flight had found them sitting atop one of the nuclear weapons, drinking tea, and it was a reasonable assumption that this unexpected departure from a standard operating procedure was somehow connected with the fallout from this embarrassing incident.

As they moved through the trees, a sense of creeping unease spread throughout the group. All were agreed that their location was spooky enough in the light of day, and the drab, lonely area was one of the most unpopular postings in the Air Force. But at night it was even worse, and the young airmen could not help but recall some of the stories told by the old hands; stories about ghosts, witchcraft and other unspeakable horrors. The pine trees seemed to possess a life of their own, planted so close together that they looked like they were pressing in on the path, as if trying to overwhelm those who trod the narrow and muddy track.

Some of the men carried torches. But they had been aware of another light in the forest ahead of them for a while and, after a few minutes, the torches were unnecessary. As they emerged into a clearing, they saw several other groups ahead of them, bunched around two massive light-alls. These mobile floodlights had been the source of the light that had drawn them to this location but, even as they arrived, they could see that something was wrong. One of the light-alls wasn't working, and the other was clearly in trouble. They heard the whine of its generator, struggling to maintain sufficient power and clearly losing the battle. The light flickered. And died. At the same moment there was a flurry of activity from beyond the clearing and a young airman burst into view, ran straight through the newly arrived men without uttering a word and disappeared down the path they'd taken to get there. People shot questioning glances at each other, looking for some clue about what was going on. There had been a look of terror on the face of the man who'd just run through the clearing, and the group he'd pushed past could sense that something was badly wrong. At the edge of the clearing, two of the senior commanders were having a whispered conversation and although nothing could be heard it was clear that an argument was taking place. A few moments later, one of the men came over, instructed the new arrivals to leave their weapons and led them out of the clearing. Five minutes later, they turned off the track and arrived at the edge of the forest. Climbing over a gate, they emerged into a field and moved towards another light that was coming from a dip about fifty metres away. They assumed it came from a Land Rover. They were wrong.

The air in front of them was glowing. It was is if they were looking at a thick, luminous and extremely localized area of fog – and that was what some of them believed it was. Their officer instructed them to surround it and look at it. Most of them were confused, while a few were terrified. But all obeyed the order. There were twenty of them, and as they encircled the strange mist they gave dimension to it. Each man stood some three or four metres from the two men on either side, and the area covered by the fog was around thirty metres in diameter. They stood like that for around ten minutes, nobody daring to say a word. The only sounds came from farm animals, about a mile away but clearly audible and in a state of frenzy. Suddenly the officer's radio crackled into life and, although there was a lot of interference, most of the men caught the crackly message.

'It's coming.'

The men looked around, but could see nothing. Then they noticed that their officer was looking upwards, scanning the skies. They followed his gaze, some of them expecting to see a helicopter heading towards their position. A moment later, a pinprick of red light appeared in the distance before rushing towards their position. It was over the field in an instant and the bemused men could not make out any details as it hovered over the luminous mist. With a breathtaking turn of speed the redness plunged directly into the fog, and this movement was accompanied by a flash of light and a sharp sound accompanied by a shock wave. The men fell back as one, their arms raised in front of their faces to shield their eyes from the glow. They were momentarily dazzled by the intensity of the flash but there was no lasting damage to their eyes and as their vision returned they could see that the mist had gone.

In its place was a metallic object that was very definitely not a helicopter nor an aircraft. This craft was triangular in shape and covered in various strange markings. At first it seemed as if it was resting on the ground, but on closer inspection it appeared to be hovering half a metre or so above the field, the air shimmering and crackling underneath the main structure. There was a smell of ozone in the air and another smell, as if something was burning. There was a low humming sound coming from the craft, but it was not constant and it cut out from time to time – not unlike the way in which the light-alls had cut out, as if the power was being drained from them.

A group of three officers emerged into the field from another part of the forest and approached the craft. They waved at the men surrounding it to back off and this they did, willingly. Although they all had questions they were desperate to ask, they were glad to be leaving. They filed back into the forest and, as the last man scrambled over the gate, he glanced back over his shoulder.

The officers had reached the craft and one of them had approached it, his arm extended as if to shake hands with someone. For a moment the curiosity of the man on the gate overcame his fear and he tried to see what was happening. It was difficult, because the craft was bathed in light that made everything else hard to see. But there was a dark patch on one side of the object, as if there was an opening. In front of it, he could see the officers. But there were other shapes there too – smaller figures he hadn't seen before. At that moment his officer grabbed him, swearing at him and pulling him roughly off the gate and towards the rest of the group, who were standing motionless and silent among the trees. Nothing further was said, and the group trudged back towards the base.

The days that followed brought more confusion. First the young airmen were told they'd seen a new holographic weapon being tested, then they were told they'd been drugged and had been hallucinating. Somebody even suggested they had seen the light-house through the trees. They were subjected to numerous debriefings, during which their interrogators would move seamlessly from polite suggestions that they keep quiet because it was their patriotic duty, to threats of imprisonment – or worse.

'Bullets are cheap,' one of them had drawled.

'Yeah,' his companion replied, 'and they're a dime a dozen.'

The base itself was a hive of activity, with unmarked aircraft flying in and out, and various smartly dressed civilians arriving to confer with the senior staff. A few people complained, but the smart ones kept their heads down, and peer pressure soon ensured that people toed the party line. Assignments were changed, and people were moved from shift to shift and from room to room so that they found themselves working and sharing rooms with strangers. Somebody was hoping that they'd keep quiet about what had happened, and most of them did. Most of them held their tongues – but none of them ever forgot what they'd seen that night.

Chapter One

INTRUDER ALERT

RAF Neatishead, Norfolk

It was either the best job in the Royal Air Force or the worst, depending upon your viewpoint. To be a Fighter Controller nearly two decades after the end of the Cold War struck some as deadly dull, with little more to do than stare at a radar screen for hours on end, looking for hostile aircraft that never came. Alan Whitfield disagreed. The twenty-six-year-old Flight Lieutenant had wanted to become a Fighter Controller from the moment some eleven years earlier when his Air Training Corps squadron had visited RAF Portreath, the Control and Reporting Post on the north Cornish coast. He'd sat in a controller's cabin and marvelled at the way in which aircraft could be tracked and directed from hundreds of miles away.

Whitfield had been in the RAF for just five years, having joined up after completing a degree in computer studies at Durham University. The RAF seemed the ideal place for him to put some of his knowledge to practical use. He was a serious-minded individual who wanted to make a contribution to society, not simply drift from job to job in the private sector, explaining the benefits of new IT systems to bored-looking executives who regarded computers as a necessary evil that their staff needed to master in order to increase profits. Whitfield had already done a tour of duty in Kosovo, in command of a mobile radar, and had also served on one of the RAF's Sentry E-3D Airborne Early Warning aircraft. He was very much the new boy at Neatishead, which was one of the RAF's east-coast Control and Reporting Centres. But although he'd arrived just four weeks ago, he was already making friends and involving himself in a whole range of social and sporting activities. He was skilled at chess and an enthusiastic new recruit to the base's football team. His tall, lean figure was a familiar sight to those early risers who started the day with a jog, and his stamina and pace suggested that he would be a force to reckon with in the forthcoming station road race.

He bitterly resented the implication that Fighter Controllers – and indeed, virtually all other specialists in the RAF – were failed pilots and navigators who had been re-streamed into other jobs. While it was true that some people were guided away from a flying tour into an area where aptitude tests suggested they would be more effective, most people were doing the job they wanted to do in a Service they loved. He certainly was.

Whitfield's radar was a Siemens Plessey Systems AR327 Commander air defence radar. But this was a bit of a mouthful and, so far as the RAF was concerned, the system had simply been designated as Type 101. It provided long-range, three-dimensional surveillance and target detection, and comprised part of the Air Defence Ground Environment. If any unauthorized penetration of the UK Air Defence Region took place, Whitfield and a few colleagues at the other Control and Reporting Centres would be the first to know – and to react. They were the eyes and the ears of Britain, in the words of one of Whitfield's instructors at the RAF School of Fighter Control at RAF Boulmer. Despite the complex nature of the RAF's radar network, the basic principles were straightforward. Few people realized that, although now recognized as a word in its own right, 'radar' had started out as an acronym, standing for 'radio detection and

ranging'. At its most basic level little more was involved than
devising a system that emitted a constant stream of radio pulses
and then calculated the position and distance of any interacting
object by measuring the time taken for the pulses to be reflected
and returned.

The night shifts were usually quiet, as there was very little civil
or military traffic in the air. Even the latter had dwindled to
virtually nothing as part of a public relations drive aimed at
dealing with complaints about the noise from low-flying aircraft.
The American statement that this was 'the sound of freedom'
made for a fine catchphrase, but was not deemed suitable for the
more prickly British public. Whitfield was just mulling over the
debate about low flying when something happened that would
change the world forever.

Ping! *What the hell was that?* Whitfield peered at the radar
screen intently. There it was again, a blip that simply should not
have been there. Whitfield did some rapid mental calculations and
failed to come up with anything that made any sense. He had an
uncorrelated target on his screen, way outside of any flight paths,
and on a night when nothing was booked to fly. He told himself
to be cautious and to think things through. Nobody would thank
him for requesting an aircraft launch on a whim, and it wouldn't
be the first time that a controller had been fooled by a spurious
return. He punched a code into his computer system, initiating
the newly-designed program that would filter out some of the
clutter that appeared on the screens from time to time and
enhance the image. The return was still there. He grabbed his
telephone, intending to call his boss and inform him that he was
launching two Eurofighter Typhoon interceptor aircraft on his
own authority. Before he could make the call his screen went
blank. The target had disappeared.

The Norfolk Broads
The three men stared intently at the water. Had there been any
movement? The youngest of the men thought there had been,
tapped his colleagues on the arm, and shot them a meaningful

glance. It said much for his skill that he had avoided pointing or speaking. This was the second night they'd spent at this particular spot, and each hoped that this time their quarry would not give them the slip. They had nicknamed the fish 'Nessie' and estimated its weight at around fourteen pounds, which was nowhere near a record weight for a pike but was still sufficiently exciting to justify the flak that they had got from their wives. They crouched low on the river bank and squinted at the floats bobbing in the water. Would any of them be lucky tonight? Bob Jennings certainly hoped so. Newly married, and more than twenty years younger than his companions, he needed some sort of triumph to sweeten the blow of the night he'd spent on the sofa following his wife's discovery of a tub of maggots in the refrigerator. He was still struggling to understand why his assurance that the tub was tightly sealed had only made things worse. Still, he was learning more about fishing from his two wily companions than he'd learnt in years with his regular fishing partners. Some of the new baits they were trying were so unlikely that he'd wondered at first whether his new friends were winding him up. That suspicion had lasted no longer than the night when he'd landed a ten-pound carp that had taken a hook baited with a piece of curried luncheon meat. Just as the middle float twitched again, all three men caught sight of a light reflected in the water. Whether it was a bailiff or someone else going night fishing, the timing could not have been worse. The idiot would lose them the fish, for sure. Three heads spun around to confront the intruder, and saw . . . nothing. But the light was still there, and there was only one other place it could be coming from. The men looked up.

'*What the fuck . . . ?*'

RAF Neatishead, Norfolk

'I hear you had some excitement last night?'

'Unfortunately not, sir. I was on duty!'

Both men laughed at the double entendre before getting down to a serious discussion. Squadron Leader Mike Maddox was Alan Whitfield's boss. An experienced Fighter Controller, he had been

at Neatishead for the best part of two years and was perceptive
enough to have spotted that the younger man was a rising star. He
had already made some suggestions about altering some of the
software and, although such a move was unlikely to be approved
by the chain of command, Maddox had run the program himself
and had been impressed. He recognized that Whitfield had a
genuine passion for his work and had already come to the
conclusion that he was a lucky find. Maddox's own special skill
was as a trainer, and most of his twelve years in the RAF had been
spent at Boulmer, Buchan or Neatishead, teaching newly-
qualified controllers. He had successfully guided numerous keen
young men and women through their first level of qualification
and then on to the more advanced courses that would lead them
to their qualification as supervisors. He was a good talker but, like
all good trainers, he wasn't afraid to listen to his students and
either correct their ideas or sometimes learn from them. So when
Whitfield had written an account of the previous night's events
into the log, Maddox had noticed. He had been about to call the
man when Whitfield beat him to it and asked to see him. Good.

'OK,' said Maddox. 'Talk me through what happened.'

'At 0330Z last night I picked up an uncorrelated target on the
Type 101,' Whitfield began. 'It looked pretty solid, but there was
no civil or military activity booked to fly, and, well, it's in the
middle of the North Sea. So I ran the new filter program, thinking
it might be anaprop.'

The discussion turned highly technical for a while. Few people
realized that radar was sometimes more of an art than a science. Two
radar systems could interfere with each other, causing a return to
appear on a screen when no object was present. Flocks of birds
sometimes played havoc with Air Traffic Control radars, showing up
on the system and then disappearing suddenly if the flock dispersed.
Anomalous Propagation was the worst culprit when it came to the
business of ghost returns. Under certain meteorological conditions
a layer of dense air could reflect radio waves and cause them to
bounce off features on the ground. Such 'ground clutter' was a
problem around certain radar heads, and a number of tall trees and

church towers gave the RAF occasional problems. It could get much worse and both Maddox and Whitfield knew of the occasion when, at the height of the Cold War, a target had been detected over the skies of East Germany, near the border, heading west. Panic had ensued, and senior military commanders had been unsure whether they were witnessing an attempted defection or something much worse. Jets had been scrambled, and nothing was seen until the pilot was right on the target and was able to tell relieved controllers that the culprit was a train, directly below his position! But the filter programs on modern AD radars were designed to deal with such problems. They screened out signals that showed the characteristics of a spurious return, leaving only those that behaved like aircraft. The program was the logical extension of a concept developed for air-to-air combat that filtered out any object not travelling at speeds of around four hundred knots – although this could be adjusted according to the type of aircraft you were facing. It helped clarify the picture for pilots by ensuring that they weren't distracted by irrelevancies.

'There was no IFF signal,' Whitfield continued, 'and I've made preliminary checks with the CAA and NATS, but come up blank. It was only a brief signal, sir, but it looked good to me. I'd like permission to try and run this one down.'

Maddox thought about that for a moment. They were busy, and he didn't want everyone chasing their tails on this matter. On the other hand, Whitfield was good – the best new controller he'd seen in a while. He was young, bright and keen, and knocking him back now, so early in his tour, might take the wind out of his sails. On the basis of that, he made his decision.

'OK, run with it.' Maddox leaned back in his chair. 'See if any of the other east-coast stations had anything on their radars, both AD and ATC. But I want you to take down the radar, get your team to run a full diagnostic, and go to the secondary system. I don't want us to rattle everybody else's cages just to find that the problem's here. And have a quiet word with someone in Intelligence to make sure we're not poking our noses somewhere they don't belong.'

'Yes, sir. Will do.' Whitfield had already considered the possibility of a transitory return from a stealth aircraft. 'I'm also planning to go back through some of the old logs, just to see if anything stands out.'

Whitfield shifted awkwardly in his chair, and Maddox understood why. Checking the old logbooks implied that his predecessor had missed something. Whitfield was enough of a professional to realize the checks had to be made, but was loyal enough to feel uneasy at the implied criticism. Maddox understood the situation and defused it with the sort of casual remark that came easily to an experienced officer.

'Good idea, but everyone gets ghost returns from time to time. This is pretty thin, and I wouldn't blame anyone for ignoring it.'

The discussion over, Whitfield made his way back to his own office. He had a lot of calls to make.

RAF Coltishall, Norfolk

Flight Lieutenant Steve Parry was having a good day. His job as Community Relations Officer was one that he enjoyed, and he had just received a batch of thank-you letters from a group of schoolchildren whom he'd hosted on a tour of the base the week before. He had one other school visit to arrange, and after that he could concentrate on putting together the programme for a group of local business people keen on the idea of forging closer links between the base and the local community. All CROs had been ordered to adopt a more proactive policy but, from what he'd picked up from friends and colleagues at other stations, he was having more success than most. He'd already interested *RAF News* in doing a small feature in the near future, and that would be another feather in his cap.

The other contents of Parry's in-tray consisted of letters of complaint about low-flying aircraft – Coltishall was home to three squadrons of ageing Jaguars – and a couple of UFO reports. The flying complaints were all from regular correspondents, and Parry noted with a wry smile that all of them had moved to the area long after the base had been built. He wondered about the competence of some of the solicitors and the morals of the estate agents – he'd heard stories about people new to the area being shown houses at weekends, when there was little or no flying, and then getting the shock of their lives on the first weekday after they moved in. Parry shrugged. It was becoming one of the biggest issues affecting the RAF, but what could they do? Military jets were noisy, and they still had to train, even if the public didn't see the need for low-flying sorties.

The UFO reports were almost a pleasant distraction. Standard Operating Procedures required Parry to send them to Sec(AS)2a in the MOD, but the SOPs allowed him the freedom to make some preliminary enquiries to see if he could come up with an explanation for what had been seen. After all, in many cases the answer to the mystery was that aircraft from the base itself were the culprits. And, in any case, Sec(AS) were generally happy to let him deal with the matter locally, bringing them in only if the person making the UFO report wasn't satisfied with what was, generally speaking, a standard response about how easy it was to misidentify ordinary objects and phenomena under certain conditions. Parry thought the line was patronizing, but generally true. But he'd come across a few genuinely odd cases over the years, and one of the items in his tray looked interesting. Written up on the standard UFO report form by the duty staff in the ATC tower, it was a report from the police, who'd taken a call from some men who'd seen something strange last night. The report said the men had sounded truly scared. Apparently they'd seen a triangular craft firing a beam of light down at the ground. That got Parry's attention, because like most CROs he'd heard about the night back in 1993 when a similar event had been witnessed by personnel at RAF Cosford and RAF Shawbury. He resolved to make a few enquiries. But before he could reach for his phone, it rang.

RAF Neatishead, Norfolk
Whitfield had been having a busy day, and the hastily arranged briefing was the result of his work. The audience was not a large

one, but the three people he would be briefing were the key personnel in this matter. Maddox was there, as Whitfield's immediate boss. Also present were Squadron Leader Mark Winter, an intelligence specialist from the Operations Support Branch, and the Station Commander, Wing Commander Bob Spink.

Whitfield received the nod, and began to deliver his brief. He ran through the events of the preceding night, and then moved on to explain how his investigation proceeded.

'I noticed a regular pattern of uncorrelated targets had been showing up. They were only transitory, and I can quite understand how they were written off as ghost returns. I'd probably have reached the same conclusion myself by now, were it not for what happened next.'

Good man, Maddox thought. *He's still being very careful not to drop his predecessor in the shit.*

'My next step, sir, was to phone around a whole bunch of other fighter controllers and ATC personnel. I rang people at Buchan and Boulmer and, although they didn't have anything last night, both bases have been having quite a few odd readings over the past few months. But it's all been transitory, so no action has been taken. It makes me wonder what we've been missing.'

'So what makes you think we're dealing with anything other than anaprop, or a choice from a host of other standard things?' Spink asked. He was sure this had been checked out, and Maddox was certainly backing up his man's assessment, but he wanted to put Whitfield under some pressure, if only because he had a feeling that this could go rapidly up the chain of command. He liked to think of himself as a laid-back boss, but there were some people at Strike Command or in MOD Main Building who would doubtless give Whitfield a hard time if he was called upon to brief them. *Then again*, he thought, *I'll probably have to do that brief*. It was another reason to turn up the heat. He wasn't going to take this any further unless he was convinced and he hadn't been won over yet, although he was curious.

'We've taken the radar off-line and cranked up the secondary system,' Whitfield continued. 'Everything looks fine so far, and there's no reason to suggest any fault with the radar head or with the computer. Also, I've spoken to Met Officers at all the east-coast stations, and none of them thinks there's any chance of it being anaprop.'

Spink nodded. This was getting more interesting.

'My next call was to Fylingdales,' Whitfield explained. 'They had something on their screens barely two minutes before my return showed up. They tracked it at four thousand miles per hour, so wrote it off as a fireball.'

'*Wrote it off* as a fireball?' said Spink, somewhat sharply. 'What the hell else was it going to be, at that sort of speed?'

'Well, sir, five minutes after I noticed the return, three men night fishing on the Norfolk Broads were scared half to death by something they saw in the sky. It was a large aircraft of some sort. Flat, sort of like a slice of pizza, if you get my drift, sir.'

'And how much had they had to drink?'

'Nothing, sir. At least, not according to the police officer who took their stories. Two of them are actually quite well known – in the national team, so I was told. The sergeant who interviewed them said they were very shaken. The police phoned it through to ATC at Coltishall, who passed it to the CRO. He's treating it as a UFO report, sir, but here's the clincher.' He handed a sheet of paper to Spink and gave a copy to Winter.

Whitfield began his explanation, but none was needed. The paper was a visual record of his radar return, the 'meteor' data from Fylingdales and the UFO sighting, and it was obvious at a glance that the three events had occurred on a straight line. What was more, the timing of each event suggested an object that had travelled rapidly from the north-east to the south-west. Extremely rapidly.

'And I take it from Mark's presence here that you've followed up the idea of this being some experimental aircraft we're not supposed to know about?' Spink glanced at Winter, but then turned his gaze back on the younger man. He was a demanding boss who believed in putting pressure on subordinates, believing it to be one of the best ways to bring out the best in people while weeding out those who couldn't hack it. He also believed in letting those who'd done the work take the credit. *And leaving those who fucked up to carry the can.* This was Whitfield's ball, and he'd let him run with it for the time being.

'That's right, sir. I asked Squadron Leader Winter whether either we or the Americans might have had something a little . . . *exotic* . . . in the area at the time. He checked through the usual channels, but nobody knew a thing. There's precedent for people running prototypes or UAVs through our patch without giving us all the details, but normally they would tell us *something*, even if it was just a "suggestion" that we look the other way. So that's all we know at present, sir. We're continuing to run more detailed diagnostics on the radar and the computer, and I plan to go back even further in the station logs to see what else I can tease out. I conclude there's a distinct possibility that we *are* dealing with a structured craft, and what worries me is that, given the direction it came from, it could be a new Russian UAV. I do have some recommendations.'

Spink was pleased with that, and Maddox felt a surge of pride. There was nothing worse than a briefing that tailed limply off and simply dumped the problem in the lap of the next person up the chain of command.

'I'm listening.'

'I wonder if we haven't been missing a trick here, and I think it's time to bring in the rest of the ADGE. I propose we signal the other Control and Reporting Centres, suggesting they look out for transitory signals and pay them more attention than usual. If and when we get something else like this, I think we should send up the QRA aircraft. They haven't had an operational scramble for months, and they might as well substitute a practice session for one based on data from us – however flimsy it looks. We have nothing to lose.'

He was wrong.

'OK, let's do it.' Spink had made up his mind rapidly, which tended to be a characteristic of either a good or a bad commander. 'Nice briefing. I'm not sure I buy into it all the way, but I accept it looks like one hell of a coincidence. And we're not supposed to believe in them, are we, Mark?'

'No, sir.' Winter smiled. 'It's the first thing they taught me at spook school.'

RAF Leeming, Yorkshire

The crewroom looked like any other crewroom in the RAF. It was a shambles. But to the men and women of 11 Squadron it was something to be proud of. Pride was something that came easily to them all, but it was a pride that came from ability and hard work rather than from any misplaced sense of arrogance. They were one of only five squadrons in the RAF who flew the new Typhoon Air Defence jet that was gradually replacing the old Tornado F3s – which had been loved by few.

The Typhoon – or the 'Eurofighter' as it had been known before being formally named – had been a collaborative project and was now in service with the Germans, Italians and Spaniards, as well as with the RAF who would ultimately have 232 of the aircraft when the final delivery was made in 2014. The Typhoon was a unique aeroplane, designed as the RAF's primary air defence fighter but also having a ground attack and tactical reconnaissance capability. This had worried some pilots, who had initially felt the plane would turn out to be a jack of all trades, hence master of none.

These fears had turned out to be unfounded, and the Typhoon had proved immediately popular. There had been the inevitable difficulties resulting from requiring pilots to retrain on a different aircraft type, but the problems had been small ones and had been more than outweighed by the pilots' sheer enthusiasm for the new machine. It handled well and, now that the old Sidewinder and Skyflash missiles had been replaced with ASRAAMs and BVRAAMs, the pilots felt they had an aircraft that would give them the advantage over just about any other type of combat plane that they might conceivably have to engage. Most of them had been glad to see the back of the F3s, nervous of their chances in a straight fight with Mig 29s. Indeed, many had supported the idea – which had been seriously considered by the RAF – of actually replacing the F3s with Mig 29s purchased from the currency-hungry Russians. It was only question marks over spares and, of course, the political angle that had put paid to this idea.

'I hear you boys might be going for a spin tonight?' The question had been shouted across the room at the two men, fully suited up, who were peering intently at the wall map.

'That's right,' one of them replied. 'And we even get to sit in the aircraft first, twiddling our thumbs.'

That got people's attention. A few heads turned and looked with interest at the two young Flying Officers. Mark Sanders and John Gooding were a popular pair and always seemed to be at the centre of social and sporting events. The two were both unmarried, and were enjoying the bachelor lifestyle to the hilt. Both lived on-base in the Officers' Mess, and neither had any difficulty getting an attractive partner for the various dining-in nights and other Mess functions. But both men were hard workers who took their RAF careers extremely seriously. They were both bright and had worked hard to get the jobs that each had cherished since their schooldays.

'What gives?'

'We've been told to expect a possible scramble tonight,' Gooding explained. 'Apparently there's been some strange stuff showing up on a few screens. It's been written off as fireballs or anaprop, but now somebody thinks it may be for real.'

He had everyone's attention now, and the half-dozen members of the squadron who were present gathered around the two pilots.

'The CO called us in about an hour ago, as we've got the duty slot tonight,' Gooding went on. 'The rest of you will be briefed shortly, but we're on in a few minutes.'

'What's the best assessment?' somebody asked.

Sanders shrugged. 'They don't know. Maybe it's something, maybe not. If it's for real, probably a new Russian RPV. All I know is that for the first time in a long while, we're gonna be sitting in the aircraft during our Q shift, not in the crew room.' He pulled a silly face, and leered at his colleagues. 'Exciting, isn't it?'

The other pilots weren't sure if it was exciting or not, but they were certainly going to have some questions to raise at the next briefing. Each of them had their own thoughts, but all were asking the same basic question. *What was going on?* Quick Reaction Alert had once been one of the best things about flying an AD aircraft in the RAF. Even though most of these pilots hadn't joined up until the Nineties, all of them had heard the stories. The Q aircraft – F3s and, before that, Phantoms – had been on constant alert. At least two pilots were always suited up and ready to go. The aircraft were fuelled and armed and the ground crew ready to move at a moment's notice. Depending upon the seriousness of the alert state, pilots were either in the crewroom or, sometimes, in the aircraft themselves. The Soviets had kept everyone on their toes and frequently sent aircraft to test the UK ADGE. They would send Badgers, Backfires or, best of all, one of the huge, lumbering Bears. There were some marvellous photos of aircrew waving at their RAF counterparts from the cockpits of the massive Soviet bombers. The Soviets wanted to see how good the UK's aircraft, radars and personnel were, while British Intelligence specialists always tried to vary the intercept times so as to deny the Soviets firm data on RAF capabilities. A game of sorts but one that could have turned frighteningly real at any moment. Few people realized just how close it had come to that on a couple of occasions.

The room was quiet for a few moments as each pilot thought things through. *Were the old days back?* Surely not. Resource constraints meant that there were very few practice scrambles these days. And as for the Russians, with their economic problems it was debatable how many fully operational aircraft they really had. Problems with spares and maintenance meant they tended to stick to short sorties, and it had been a long while since they'd probed the UKADR.

'Wish us luck, boys and girls,' Sanders hooted, as he and Gooding strolled out towards their aircraft, helmets tucked under their arms. 'Try to stay out of mischief.'

Gooding picked up the theme. 'I might be home late from the office today, so sleep well and don't have nightmares.'

It was the usual nonsensical banter that most of them indulged in at times like this. It always got a laugh, and it did on this occasion. But the laughter was not quite as loud as it might have been.

RAF Buchan, Aberdeenshire

Flying Officer Sue Harding had been briefed as thoroughly as was possible, given how little anyone knew. She was on the night shift at the RAF's northernmost Control and Reporting Centre, and as such was very much in the front line. Although Fylingdales would pick up anything at really high altitude, her unit would be the first to pick up anything on a more conventional track. Or it should be, if she was on the ball. She was a competent officer, but she didn't like this new turn of events. It had started with a call from the new guy at Neatishead who'd quizzed her about ghost returns. *Well, we all have those, don't we?* But now it seemed someone thought they'd been duped by some new piece of kit, probably stealthy. So she was supposed to pay more attention to ghost returns and pass the details to the rest of the ADGE. And if anyone thought there was the slightest chance, they'd scramble. If they were wrong, they'd lose some fuel out of their monthly allocation, but that just meant less routine training. *But if they were right?* For about the tenth time since the briefing she looked at the text of the signal she knew had been sent to her counterparts.

```
FROM:      HQSTC
TO:        RAF BOULMER
           RAF BUCHAN
           RAF NEATISHEAD
COPY TO:   MODUK AIR
           MODUK
SUBJECT:   UNCORRELATED TARGETS
TEXT:      FOLLOWING POSSIBLE DETECTION BY RAF
           NEATISHEAD OF UNCORRELATED TARGET
           AT 0331Z LAST NIGHT, POSITION 554908N
```

033901E, ALL SIGNALS UNITS AND CON-
TROL AND REPORTING CENTRES ARE TO
PAY PARTICULAR ATTENTION TO TRAN-
SIENT SIGNALS, AND ARE AUTHORIZED
TO LAUNCH QRA IF RETURN LOOKS
SOLID.

Harding was not pleased with this signal, nor with the briefing
she'd received. There were too many unknowns, and trying to
evaluate transient radar signals was notoriously difficult. She had
a nasty feeling that everyone would take a better-safe-than-sorry
attitude, and launch aircraft at the tiniest blip. *We're chasing
seagulls*, she thought to herself. She thought she'd be able to tell
the difference, but with an order that gave her so much leeway
she'd find it difficult to hold back. She told herself to be cautious
but decided that if it was a borderline decision she'd have to go for
it. Better to launch on nothing than miss something.

RAF Leeming, Yorkshire
The voice came over loud and clear on Gooding's headset.
    'John, I need a piss.'
    'Go in the bag, you stupid bastard.'
    'Yuk!'
The exchange was light-hearted but served two purposes. It
confirmed that the radios were working and also kept both men
alert. Conversation stimulates the mind, however pointless the
discussion – another lesson from training. Sanders had been
joking, and both pilots had been very careful not to take in too
much liquid in the hours before their stint in the aircraft. There
were facilities for that particular onboard emergency: bags were
available. But it was best to avoid using them at all, if only
because a smelly cockpit was not a pleasant environment. And
nobody forgot the case of the American pilot who'd actually
crashed his A-10 whilst fumbling with his waste bags after having
been caught short. They'd become entangled with the control
stick and, despite a desperate attempt to retrieve the situation, the

aircraft had been lost. The pilot had survived, but the jokes from his colleagues had been merciless.

The exchange had provided some light relief for the fliers. Much of a military career was spent just waiting for something to happen. The trick was to fill the huge gaps that often occurred between events of any significance.

RAF Buchan, Aberdeenshire
Ping!

Harding looked at her screen, then pressed some buttons on her computer, running a few programs, and trying to make sense of the signal. In the normal course of business she'd have waited a few seconds to see whether the signal persisted. If it didn't, it would be ignored. (This was not sloppiness, it was standard practice.) But not tonight. The return looked solid enough and although it disappeared after just five seconds she had calculated a location, height and track. The speed was impossibly high, but if Leeming could get their aircraft up quick enough, the target – if it was a target – would come pretty much straight to them if it continued on its present course. Her decision made, she grabbed the red telephone on her desk, and spoke a line that had been spoken many times before – though never with such unimaginable consequences.

'We've got visitors.'

Over the North Sea
The aircraft were climbing steadily now and had just passed through a layer of cloud that had its ceiling at around twelve thousand feet. It was a clear, cold night, and the blue-white twinkling of the stars illuminated dimly the dark waters of the North Sea below. The jets' cockpits were twin islands of warmth in the icy bitterness of the night: the two pilots were securely wrapped up in cold-weather flying suits, G-suits and life jackets.

Gooding and Sanders had received the order to scramble only a few minutes ago and were now racing towards the point where an interception of the target might be possible. Both aircraft had been equipped with gun cameras, and their primary aim was to validate the contact and to get some film footage. Although both aircraft carried a mix of ASRAAM and BVRAAM missiles, this was standard practice for aircraft on QRA and the normal peacetime Rules of Engagement applied, meaning they could only fire if attacked. Radio silence was to be maintained unless absolutely necessary, and there had been a minimum of instructions from the fighter controller at Buchan. If there was a craft there at all, it was coming towards their general location very quickly. Indeed, operational control would be passed to Neatishead if the object came much further south. There was little to go on. A return that might or might not indicate the presence of an object travelling at thousands of miles per hour. The Typhoons had an impressive – and classified – top speed but, if the analysis was correct, even this wouldn't be sufficient to catch the object. Instead, they'd be vectored to a point in its path so that the object came to them. *If there is an object. If it is flying in a straight line*, both men were thinking.

As the aircraft levelled out at around twenty thousand feet, both pilots activated their interceptor radars, housed in the nose cones. The radar doubled as a threat receiver, not that any such role was anticipated for this particular mission. This was strictly a 'look but don't touch' job. As it turned out, they didn't have long to wait. There had been no word from any of the fighter controllers and it had been agreed that there would be none, unless the object was detected. But while the ground-based radars clearly had no further information, aside from the initial contact that had led to the scramble, the airborne radars were having better luck.

'Eagle One to Sector Control, I have a contact ahead of our position. Distance is eighty-nine nautical miles, I say again eighty-nine nautical miles. Position is fifty-six, fifty-one, eighteen North, zero one, forty-two, twenty-five East. I say again, fifty-six, fifty-one eighteen North, zero one, forty-two, twenty-five East. Speed is estimated at . . . Mach four, I say again Mach four. There is no, repeat no IFF signal. Over.'

Gooding's report was concise, and the reply he received from

Buchan was equally brief, indicating that the controller knew her stuff and was leaving them free to get on with things.

'Sector Control to Eagle One, I copy that. We have nothing, repeat nothing on our systems. Over.'

'Acknowledged. We'll let you know what happens. Over and out.'

Gooding activated the night-vision goggles mounted on his helmet. At the speed the object was travelling he'd have a visual fix on the target within the minute and the goggles would enhance any reflected light, giving him a better chance of spotting it. At the back of his mind the possibility of a collision lurked, and he had no way of knowing whether the object had a pilot who was picking up their aircraft on radar. If it was an RPV it might be coming in blind, and he cautioned himself to be ready for an evasive manoeuvre. The chance that it would come to his exact position was slight but there remained a possibility – and no experienced pilot left anything to chance.

Little more than ten seconds after activating his NVGs, Gooding picked up the object. A glance at his airborne radar showed that it was slowing down. *What the hell was happening?* As the object decelerated, Gooding watched in absolute amazement, reaching for the switch that would again activate his radio. It was a move he was not to complete.

RAF Buchan, Aberdeenshire

Harding stared in absolute horror at her radar screen, scarcely able to believe what she was seeing. There were two blips on the screen, but there was no lateral movement. Both blips were descending steadily. There was no doubt in her mind about what she was seeing. The two Typhoons were going down. She reached for her phone and initiated a Search and Rescue operation, calling out a Sea King HAR3 helicopter from RAF Boulmer, and a Nimrod from RAF Kinloss.

RAF Neatishead, Norfolk

Whitfield had been following events intently. Although not under his operational control, the ADGE was an integrated system and so he had access to exactly the same data as Harding. Spink, Maddox and Winter were watching too, and the men exchanged looks of disbelief as the blips on their screen passed below the level of their coverage. They knew that the next few hours would be frantic, with a mass of signals traffic and flash calls to Strike Command and the MOD. This had to go up the chain of command fast, and their desperate lack of knowledge about what had happened would serve only to make matters worse.

Whitfield felt as if somebody had punched him in the stomach. He wanted to be sick, and he felt a sense of grief and rage that was only made worse by the fact that his anger had no target. He prayed that the pilots had survived. But he feared the worst: the lack of any distress call was an ominous sign, and there was no word yet to indicate that a personal locator beacon had been activated. He turned the matter over in his mind, asking himself if he'd missed anything. So far as he could see, he'd done everything right. But, nonetheless, two people were probably dead because of his actions.

Chapter Two

INVESTIGATION

Rowledge, Surrey

The second hand on the clock reached the mark indicating twenty minutes past the hour and then stopped. She always knew when *they* were coming but could never stop them.

Jenny Thornton was thirty-five and a divorcee. Although her marriage had lasted five years, the truth was that she'd realized the union had been an error little more than two months after the church wedding that had delighted both sets of parents and surprised her friends. She'd met her ex-husband in the housing department of the local authority where both worked in junior managerial positions, handling casework concerning benefit claimants. Their liaison had been noted with approval by others in the office, who regarded both of them as somewhat shy and introverted individuals whose shyness made finding partners difficult. But what should have stayed just a friendship had evolved into something more, with neither of them quite knowing how and neither being sufficiently perceptive or brave to back off. They had enjoyed each other's company, and found the prospect of regular sex a pleasant change. Neither of them had experienced many previous relationships, and both were scared of being alone again. It was this same attitude that had resulted in the relationship drifting on for so many years, long after any love had died. Children might have saved the marriage but none had come, and neither Thornton nor her husband had seriously considered fostering or adoption. The house had been sold and she had moved, with some help from her parents, into the small village where she'd been brought up. Doubtless a psychologist would have had something to say about this, but she'd always liked the place, despite what had happened there.

As usual, she didn't know whether to be frightened or angry about *them.* She had long given up on the idea of sleeping with a kitchen knife on the bedside table and, although she determined to switch on the light, she realized that the paralysis had already set in. The room was illuminated by a familiar blue-white light and, although she couldn't turn her head towards its source, she already knew where it was coming from. She was lying on her back, and although her main view was of the bedroom ceiling, her field of vision included the wall directly in front of her. And the three small, grey figures that had just walked through it.

Egerton Gardens, Knightsbridge

Martin Blackmore, Under-Secretary of State at the Ministry of Defence, was furious with himself. The time was just past three-thirty in the morning and as the fifty-three-year-old member of Her Majesty's Government splashed water onto his face he wrestled with his conscience, looked in the mirror and wasn't entirely sure he liked what he saw. The unremarkable lined and slightly chubby face of a middle-aged man stared back at him, but the eyes – red from lack of sleep – were unfocused, as if even his reflection couldn't bear to look at him. He blinked several times, ran a comb through thinning grey hair, and tried to clear his head.

The ringing telephone had awoken him ten minutes ago. The MOD Resident Clerk had told him that two RAF aircraft had been lost over the North Sea and that the pilots were missing, presumed dead. His first thought was that this was a problem.

Not a tragedy, but a *problem*. With cuts in low-flying activity the
RAF's safety record had improved, and crashes were now
extremely rare. This accident was the first in two years, and the
fact that it was the first loss of a Typhoon would mean a whole pile
of work, including a statement to Parliament that he would
probably have to give. It was the need for this statement that had
prompted the Resident Clerk to place the call and awaken the
Minister, suggesting politely but firmly that he might like to
come into MOD Main Building where he could discuss the matter
with the Air Staff and work up his statement to the House of
Commons. *A problem. An inconvenience*. His initial attitude had
shocked him, filling him with a mixture of guilt and self-loathing.
Two pilots were probably dead, and his first thought had been
concern about his workload. Where had his humanity gone, and
what had happened to the bright, keen MP who'd entered
Parliament less than ten years ago, and climbed to junior
ministerial rank through hard work in the Whips' Office? The
long hours had cost him his marriage, and this in turn had allowed
himself to throw himself more vigorously into work. He was an
able man, and honest enough to acknowledge that his idealism
had been tempered by the realities of life in Government. That
bothered him, and he knew that the day it didn't would be the day
he should retire from public life. As he waited for his official car
to arrive he wondered if that day might not have already arrived,
unnoticed.

Rowledge, Surrey

She was floating now. Floating off the bed and towards the
window, with the three hateful creatures drifting alongside her.
Although there were all sorts of questions in her mind, she knew
that the next few minutes would be predictable. It had been a cold
night, and the window had been closed. Now, as she approached
it, she braced herself for a sensation that, though familiar, was
nonetheless almost impossible to bear. She was able to see her bare
feet in front of her, and winced as they approached the window. In
the next instant she was passing *through* the solid glass, fighting

down a wave of nausea as she did so. It was like passing through an enormous jelly filled with burning embers. The analogy was ridiculous, but how else to describe an experience that was like being cut without bleeding, or being submerged in water without drowning? Her biggest fear was that something would go wrong and she'd be stranded halfway through the glass. It was the same terror she'd felt as a child when watching *Star Trek* and being scared that somebody would materialize within a solid object such as a pillar when they were 'beamed down'.

A moment later a wave of cold air struck her and she realized she was outside. She was wearing a nightdress but it provided scant protection against the chill wind, and although she was bathed in a beam of blue-white light there was no accompanying warmth. A feeling of weightlessness followed – and it was clearly more than just a feeling, because she felt herself rising into the night air. She was still incapable of any independent movement but could see at the periphery of her visual field that the three beings were still with her, accompanying her on her journey and actually guiding her upwards towards their destination. She was actually in an upright position, as if she were standing up, and she bobbed around a little, like a leaf caught in a sudden whirlwind. Every time she approached the edge of the beam, one of the creatures nudged into her, keeping her on a steady course. She was not going particularly fast, but the sensation was decidedly unpleasant – a bit like travelling in one of those fast lifts that took you rapidly to the top of a building while all the time your stomach struggled to catch up. *Why doesn't anyone see me? Why doesn't someone come and help me?* Her thoughts were a mixture of self-pity and rage, but they were familiar thoughts and ones that she knew were pointless. *Nobody can stop this.*

MOD Main Building, Whitehall

As the car swept into the secured parking compound, Blackmore had allowed his thoughts to drift, contemplating irrelevancies rather than the matter in hand. He'd noticed that, despite the hour, numerous lights were on in the Department's nine-storey headquarters. He'd turned this over idly in his mind, wondering whether the illuminated offices indicated the presence of duty officers on the night shift or were merely evidence of the small army of cleaning staff who serviced the building in the silent hours. Then again, had someone simply forgotten to turn the lights off when they'd left, hours earlier? He'd noticed that a lot of the lights were burning on the sixth floor, which was the domain of Ministers, Chiefs of Staff and a host of other senior officers, both service and civilian. Perhaps some of these people had been called in for the same reason that he had. Perhaps one of those offices contained staff who were working up a brief for him.

'We're here, sir,' the driver said, mistakenly thinking that Blackmore had nodded off during the short drive.

'Thank you.'

Blackmore saw the familiar figure of his Private Secretary, Susan Farthing, at the top of the steps at the South Door. She moved down towards the car, annoyed that the driver seemed to be leaving it to her to open the car door, but too preoccupied with the business in hand to let the minor irritation linger in her mind for more than a moment. Her boss was out of the door and moving before she got there and the two greeted each other warmly. Blackmore rated his PS highly, recognizing that the high-flyer was a dedicated professional already well on her way to the senior ranks of the Civil Service, despite her youth. He'd taken the trouble to get to know his Private Office staff well, especially his PS on whom so much depended. On first taking up his position it had amazed him that the key personnel in the Civil Service seemed to have the most junior-sounding titles. Calling Farthing a Private Secretary made it sound as if she did the typing. And it got worse the higher you went. The civil servant heading up the entire department was referred to as the Permanent Under-Secretary. It was the same with ministerial appointments, and he sometimes felt that his own title of Under-Secretary of State made it sound as if he made the tea. It was the sort of anachronism that he'd thought of rectifying, before he'd realized, sadly, that there was never the time for such 'nice to have' initiatives. He'd only been

in Government for a month or so before realizing that although
the old comedy series *Yes Minister* had been exaggerated, it was not
too far wide of the mark in places. He had *some* power, but not as
much as people supposed. And much of the work of Government
was crisis management, as distinct from policy making.

Blackmore noticed Farthing's red Fiesta in the official car park,
and realized that they'd both probably been telephoned by the
Resident Clerk at about the same time. She lived in a small flat in
one of the numerous new developments in Vauxhall, and the
location was clearly one that she'd chosen. Her boyfriend worked
in the City, and the Minister doubted whether Vauxhall had been
his idea. The car was dirty, he noticed, realizing that they were
both too busy for such chores.

'Good morning, Minister.'

'Good morning.'

'Sorry you had to be called out at this hour, but we need to say
something before the morning television and radio news
broadcasts – especially *Today*. As far as the papers are concerned,
the crash happened too late for the nationals but we do need to
think about the *Evening Standard*, since their lunchtime edition
goes to press in a few hours.'

It was distasteful to both of them, but the sad fact was that
media management was becoming increasingly important. Two
people lay dead, and their first concern was with formulating the
defensive lines that the Press Office would deploy to try and
ensure that the media reports were not critical of the Department.
It was a sign of the times.

'Who else is in?'

'CAS is already here, and the Press Secretary is on her way.'

'Preliminary assessment on the crash?'

'When we heard, we thought it was a mid-air collision. But
CAS thinks there may be more to it than that.'

'Oh?'

'I don't know yet, Minister. I've only been here fifteen minutes,
and when I came down CAS was still speaking to Strike
Command.'

The two of them entered the building via a small side door to the left of the massive steel door that would not be opened for another few hours. They were waved through by the guards and took the lift to the sixth floor. As they swept into his office they saw that CAS was there, frowning as he glanced at two military signals.

'Good morning, Minister. I'm afraid we've got real problems.'

'What happened, Bob?'

Air Chief Marshal Sir Robert Pickering waved at one of the duty clerks, who promptly handed the Minister copies of the signals that he'd been reading and passed another set to Farthing, who had just instructed one of the other clerks to fetch coffee for the assembled group.

'We've just received a flash signal from Strike Command,' Pickering explained. 'It confirms that two Typhoons have crashed into the North Sea. The pilots are missing, presumed dead. There's a Nimrod on station now and, although it will stay there until its fuel state forces it to break off its search, there's no real hope of finding the pilots alive. We've detected no signal from either man's personal locator beacon, and it seems clear that neither pilot had time to activate them. There are helicopters on the way, but I'm afraid that they're looking for bodies and wreckage. We're in touch with the Navy. The Type 23 frigate HMS *Lancaster* is heading for the area now and will be able to help recover wreckage. Anything we find will have to go to DERA at Farnborough for analysis.'

He paused, as much to gather his own thoughts as to allow the Minister a chance to ask a question. But the Minister was an astute man and, realizing that the RAF officer was building up to something important, he decided not to distract the man with questions. Farthing, too, knew the value of silence.

'The two aircraft that crashed were on Quick Reaction Alert. In the normal course of business the Q aircraft would be on the ground and only scrambled in the event of an intrusion into the UKADR. These aircraft were scrambled in response to some anomalous radar returns that had been noticed by Air Defence staffs. The other signal you have is an earlier one from Strike

Command to the Control and Reporting Centres, alerting them to these radar returns and authorizing launch action if appropriate. The radar evidence is . . . confusing, but there are some indications that there was another aircraft in the area.'

'Whose?' demanded the Minister.

'Unknown,' replied Pickering, only too aware of the inadequacy of his answer and angry at having to give it. 'Chief of Defence Intelligence is on his way in, but the threat board is clear. We're in the process of setting up a video conference with the key people from Strike Command. They're still collating information, but I've told them we'll run with what we have and schedule a briefing for 0500. Hopefully, they'll have some more information for us by then.'

Blackmore turned matters over in his mind. There was no point in bombarding CAS with questions to which he clearly didn't have the answers, and it seemed prudent to wait until the briefing, after which they all might know more.

Coffee arrived and was gratefully received. It was going to be a long day, and they'd all need to stay alert. A thoughtful sergeant had located some biscuits, and these too were accepted with appreciative nods. It was unlikely that any of them would have the time for regular meals for quite a while.

'Sue, what action do we need to take?'

'First step is the news brief – a press release and the defensive lines to take. The Press Office are drawing up something now, based on briefs for earlier crashes. This one's going to get a lot of attention, for three reasons. First, it's a quiet news day; second, this is the first crash we've had in a while, and third, these are the first Typhoons we've lost. And I'm not even factoring in the unusual circumstances of the loss.'

'What can we say about those?'

'Not much, but we don't really have to. The RAF have already called a Board of Inquiry, which is standard practice with an aircraft crash. It's normal policy to say that we don't speculate on the cause of an accident, on the grounds that it might prejudice the inquiry.'

Blackmore thought about that. It was a reasonable position and not unlike the policy on legal affairs, where the Home Secretary was forever stating that she was unable to comment on this or that because there was a court case under way. But he had an uneasy feeling about deploying such a line, worried it might be a hostage to fortune.

'We may need to say a little more this time.'

Farthing and Pickering nodded. Clearly neither was going to disagree with the Minister and if either of them had their doubts they were keeping their own counsel. But that was an issue which they had tacitly agreed to put on one side for the time being.

'There are some other things we need to do,' Farthing continued. 'Sec(AS) are the division with the lead on aircraft accidents. The head of division has been called in and is working up a brief that will go to Ministers, Chiefs of Staff and others with an interest. Again, this is a fairly standard procedure. We'll brief the key players by telephone this morning; those most directly involved have been told already, and some – including the PM and other Defence Ministers – will be briefed once they're awake. We've also informed the Palace and the leaders of the main opposition parties. A call and then a letter will also have to go to Lisa Parkinson. RAF Leeming – where the aircraft were based – is in her constituency and as both pilots lived locally she was also their MP. This is all in hand, although the text of the press release and the briefing will need to be firmed up in the next hour or so. What we need to give more thought to now is the statement to Parliament.'

Politics, Blackmore thought. It always came down to politics, and he wondered whether the Opposition would try to make capital out of this.

'I'm working on a statement that you'll need to make to the Commons this morning,' Farthing explained. 'Earl Sutton will deliver the same statement to the Lords. Normally we wouldn't be doing this but, although it's a Ministerial decision, this is going to be so high-profile that I think we *have* to make a statement.'

Farthing paused, offering her Minister the option of overruling her judgement call.

'Agreed,' Blackmore nodded. 'Please continue.'

'I'll be contacting the Speaker's office in the next few hours, briefing them in and arranging a time for your statement. It will probably be fixed for as soon as possible after morning prayers, say at around eleven-fifteen. As to the text of the statement, I suggest something short and very much in line with the press release. We'll sit down with the Press Secretary, Head of Sec(AS) and the key players in the Air Staff after the 0500 brief and firm up the wording. When S of S gets in you'll need to agree who gives the statement. It's within your purview, of course, but S of S may feel he should take the lead. In either event, we'll be pretty much tied up with this all day, so I'll ensure that your diary is cleared. There's nothing that can't be postponed.'

'Thank you, Sue. Good work.' Something suddenly occurred to Blackmore. 'Have next of kin been informed?'

'Yes, Minister,' Pickering replied. 'Neither man was married, but both sets of parents have already been visited.'

Blackmore's first thought was that this had been premature. Why wake them in the middle of the night? The day that lay ahead of them would be the worst day of their lives, so why not give them a few extra hours of sleep? The answer struck him immediately. It was because there was no guarantee they'd actually be asleep and, while the media didn't have the story yet, they might get hold of it at any time. Waking the parents was a precaution against the nightmare scenario of them finding out about the death of a loved one from the media: information about the names of casualties should never be made public before next of kin are informed. But the press were always after the human angle in such stories, so the RAF would have to be careful here and would leave nothing to chance. *Neither man was married*. That meant no wives and children would be bereaved but it also meant that the parents would be even more alone, with nobody to be strong for and no grandchildren in whose young lives they might find some comfort. *Neither man was married*. Blackmore was unable to decide where the balance of advantage lay, and was still turning things over in his mind when Pickering spoke up.

'It's nearly time for the brief. I suggest we make our way to the DCMC.'

Rowledge, Surrey

As usual, she knew nothing about how she'd actually got inside and remembered no doorway or hatch, not even a sensation of passing through the hull of the craft. All she knew was that she was flat on her back on a cold, hard surface. She was still paralysed but could see her immediate surroundings and seemed to be able to move her eyes from side to side. She was in a round, white room that appeared to be featureless. It was extremely bright, although there was no visible source of illumination. It seemed as if the walls themselves were giving off light.

Despite the brightness, she couldn't see clearly and wondered whether the haziness was due to her own state of mind or was another feature of the place in which she found herself. All she could do now was wait for the inevitable. One of three distinct things would happen next, and she wondered which it would be. Two were tolerable, but the third involved agony beyond comprehension. Even the memory of it was painful, so as she waited she allowed her mind to drift back instead to the day when her life had changed forever, the day when she'd realized that adults didn't know everything and that there were some things from which even grown-ups couldn't protect her.

She had been eight years old and she'd been playing in Alice Holt Forest with her parents. (Back then she'd called it the Magic Forest, and it had been very special to her. It had been a fun place, and a good place. Once.) Although she couldn't see her parents, she could hear them, and they could hear her. She was running through some fern, and every now and then she had jumped up above it and shouted 'Boo!' at the top of her voice. Her parents had shouted back at her in the same way, and the game had continued.

It was then that she noticed a fire tower. She knew it was a fire tower because her parents had told her about them. If there was ever a forest fire, the rangers could use the towers to pinpoint the blaze and coordinate the fire-fighting. To her, it was a strange-looking thing, with its wooden (*metal*) legs and its sides (*hull*) made from rounded planks (*yttrium-coated bonded polycarbonate*). Although her father had told her about these things, there was something that didn't seem quite right about it, nagging away at the back of her mind. She hadn't realized it at the time, but looking back on the incident in later years she'd seen the absurdity of the situation when it came to her that the structure had been located in a small gully with a limited field of view – which probably made it the worst possible location in which to build a fire tower. But stranger still had been the cub scouts (*entities*) she'd met up there, who had asked her if she wanted to play a game (*'We want to see how you interact socially with strangers and how bonding occurs, especially under stressful circumstances'*) with another little boy. He'd been about her age and she'd never seen him before, although she was somehow sure that she would see him again. They'd had such fun there (*'Don't be afraid; please don't be afraid'*) and although she couldn't remember much about the game (*'You will remember nothing of this experience, and if recollections begin to surface you will classify them as dreams or the product of your childish imagination'*) she knew it had been great fun (*'Please stop this. Leave us alone. Mummy, Daddy – help!'*). Eventually she had climbed down from the fire tower, leaving her new friend with the cubs. Although she'd left of her own will (*'Go now'*) she'd felt a little bit sad that she couldn't play with her new friend any more. The village was small and she didn't have that many friends. Her watch had stopped, but then it seemed to have started again, so that had been all right. She had found her parents. They had been frowning, although they had seemed particularly pleased to see her. She had had that annoying feeling that she sometimes got when she was about to say something but forgot what it was. It had been something important, but in an instant it had slipped away to be replaced by talk of orange squash and biscuits when they got back. The moment had been lost, and her world moved on. It had been months later when the lost thought finally returned. Why had the cubs all been wearing sunglasses when it hadn't been sunny? That was when she realized they hadn't been cub scouts at all. They'd been fairies. But they hadn't been the mischievous fairies of cartoons or children's stories. They'd been bad fairies. *Very* bad fairies.

MOD Main Building, Whitehall

The Defence Crisis Management Centre always managed to focus people's minds on the serious nature of the business conducted within its walls. Located deep beneath Main Building – just how deep was still classified information – it was a secure and entirely self-contained environment that had been designed to survive even a direct hit by a nuclear weapon on the structure above it. The current DCMC had replaced an earlier one that, laughably, had been located on the fifth floor – a glaringly obvious location, since passers-by could hardly fail to notice that at night, during a crisis, just about every light on that floor was turned on, in contrast to the darkness of the rest of the building. This had been one of the main factors contributing to the approval of the project to place a new DCMC deep underground. But it was ironic that, while it had been approved in the early Eighties during a particularly frosty part of the Cold War, it had become operational only when the old Soviet Union had broken up and the threat of nuclear conflict had all but disappeared.

In the normal course of business the DCMC was staffed by a skeleton team of about half a dozen, who served mainly to deal with out-of-hours incidents. In conjunction with the Resident Clerk they would decide whether or not an incident merited calling people during the silent hours, or even – as with the case in hand – actually summoning them to Main Building to deal with something in person. The DCMC's other functions were as a centre for periodic Crisis Management Exercises and as the coordination point for the Department's responses to real crises, such as those that arose from time to time in the Gulf or the Balkans.

It was an austere environment, and the lack of windows meant that the place always seemed to carry a faint smell of sweat and stale air, despite the state-of-the-art filtration unit. In truth, the odour was probably psychosomatic in origin, reflecting a natural

human aversion to enclosed spaces. The addition of a few paint-
ings and pot plants did little to dispel the sense of gloom that
descended over most people who worked there. Unsurprisingly,
submariners found the DCMC a familiar environment: astute
personnel managers often looked to them to fill any naval duty
slots that arose there.

As they entered the complex of rooms, Blackmore noted that
there were a few more people around. He recognized a few of them
by sight, though not by name. They were middle-ranking
officials, mainly Squadron Leaders and Higher Executive Officers.
They were the briefers and staff officers whom he'd seen at various
meetings but who never said more than the occasional sentence.
Their jobs were to back up their principals, furnishing them with
the appropriate facts and figures and ensuring that their bosses
had any relevant documentation to hand. That they'd arrived later
than the senior staff simply meant that the Resident Clerk who
had called them in was working her way down a list compiled in
order of seniority. Also, of course, only the most senior people had
the luxury of being picked up in official cars. Those arriving in
what Blackmore thought of as the second wave had clearly had to
make their own way in. Nobody was saying much since the 0500
brief was about to start and there was little point in speculating
on matters that, for all they knew, were about to be clarified. Duty
Clerks were offering cups of coffee and copies of the two signals to
all those present. About half those present accepted a hot drink,
while everybody took the signals.

The assembled group were ushered politely into the main
briefing room, the largest room in the DCMC. It was dominated
by what looked like a glorified television set but was actually an
interactive and totally secure video conferencing system that
linked the facility not only with Strike Command but also with
the Permanent Joint Headquarters at Northwood and a number of
other key sites.

Blackmore saw that Farthing had dutifully located both the
Press Secretary and Head of Sec(AS). These people, together with
CAS, were very much the key players and Blackmore knew that

whatever came out of the brief, they were the ones who would have to thrash out the text of the press release and the Parliamentary statement. But before any of that could be decided, they had to know whether they were dealing with a mid-air collision or something far more serious. The RAF crest had just appeared on the screen and an expectant silence descended as the assembled group awaited the briefing. Abruptly, the picture changed, and those present saw the face of Air Chief Marshal Sir Charles Warburton, Air Officer Commanding-in-Chief at Headquarters Strike Command. His brief began with military precision at exactly 0500 hours.

'Good morning. I wish we were here under more pleasant circumstances but that is not the case. As you all know by now, we have lost two Typhoons, with their pilots missing, presumed dead. I will outline what we know about the events surrounding this tragedy, with particular reference to the circumstances that led to the aircraft being launched in the first place. Once I've completed this initial brief, we will move to a discussion of what action we now need to take.'

The first part of the briefing took just ten minutes. Most of those present already knew some of the story, even if it had been gleaned from little more than a quick reading of the two Strike Command signals and a hurried consultation with some of the other assembled personnel. But, judging by their reactions, many had been unaware of the detailed background. Most people were making notes, and there were a few whispered conversations as they tried to make sense of matters.

'The problem,' Warburton said, beginning his concluding remarks, 'is that we are faced with inconclusive data that points to one of four mutually exclusive scenarios. Number one, the radar data is spurious and the aircraft simply collided. Number two, the radar data is spurious and one aircraft exploded – possibly as a result of a catastrophic failure in its engine or fuel tank – with the fragments taking out the second aircraft. Number three, the radar data is solid, and there was an unidentified aircraft or RPV present that collided with the Typhoons. Number four, the radar data is solid, and an unidentified aircraft shot down the two Typhoons. My tentative conclusion is that we are dealing with a straight-forward mid-air collision, but I freely admit that at this early stage this conclusion is based on little more than a personal view that the other scenarios are unlikely – especially scenarios three and four. This concludes the first part of the briefing. I'd now be happy to take any questions, and indeed would ask if any of you have anything to add to my statement.'

Etiquette demanded that the Minister was given the opportunity to speak first, if he so wished. He felt there was pressure on him to make some sort of response, especially as the way forward was so unclear. Blackmore's position as a Minister in Her Majesty's Government gave him certain privileges but, although much of the work was more routine than many would suppose, there were still hard decisions to be taken and tough choices to make. This was a moment when a degree of leadership was called for, and Blackmore thought it fortunate that he actually did have a question.

'Thank you, Sir Charles,' he started. 'We're all grateful to you for putting together the brief so quickly. You've encapsulated things nicely. Before I throw things open I'd like to ask what action can be taken to clarify the radar data. Who's looking at the tapes?'

It was a perceptive question and one that had occurred to most of the assembled company. Still, the Minister was a relative new-comer to military matters and it always gave service personnel confidence when they realized their political bosses were on the ball, as clearly seemed to be the case here.

'Copies have already been made of the key segments,' Warburton replied. 'We've transposed onto one tape the anomalous returns that first alerted us, together with the radar data from last night's incident. Copies are on their way to the Chief Scientific Adviser and the Defence Evaluation and Research Agency experts at Malvern. They'll analyse the data inde-pendently, then get together later today to pool data and see about drawing up some firm conclusions.'

There were appreciative nods from around the table. It had been the first mention of the scientific staff whose technical expertise would be the key factor in interpreting the data already available. CSA was on leave in Italy but she had been contacted by her staff and was even now arranging to cut short her holiday and return to London. In the meantime, the Deputy Under-Secretary (Science & Technology) would deputize for her. He was yet to arrive, being one of those who had not been called in specially. Doubtless the Defence Intelligence Service and the Air Staff would also have a view, but nobody doubted that DERA would be the key players and the ones who would best be able to decide if the Typhoons had been chasing ghost returns or the real thing.

The discussion broadened out and others spoke up. CDI confirmed that the threat board was blank and said that there were no factors that would indicate any hostile intentions towards UK military interests, whether from the Russians or from anyone else. There was some debate over whether the Typhoon fleet should be grounded, but this was dealt with firmly by CAS.

'That's Controller Aircraft's call. He's not in yet, but I've spoken to him and he recommends against it. With his agreement we've already signalled all operating bases and ordered checks on each aircraft, with particular reference to engines and fuel tanks. We've also contacted the other nations flying Typhoons, appraised them of the situation and recommended that they make precautionary checks themselves.'

Blackmore was grateful both for this information and the fact that the military were moving at their usual speedy pace. They had thought of everything and had taken what action they could at this early stage. At least it was something he could draw upon in his statement to Parliament. However, after a few more minutes of discussion it was clear that there was one fundamental question that had not been asked. Blackmore promptly asked it.

'What about the instructions to the Control and Reporting Centres? Do we change them, or do we stick to them and scramble aircraft if the same situation crops up again? Thoughts, please?'

It was CAS who provided the answer. 'I believe we have to carry on, Minister. After all, we have a responsibility to watch over the UKADR. If there's any evidence suggesting there's unauthorized or unidentified traffic on our patch, we can't ignore it.'

'Agreed,' Blackmore replied immediately. There could be absolutely no compromise on the territorial integrity of the United Kingdom, but he'd needed to ask the question so any dissenters could speak up. Politically, he'd need to be able to show that due consideration had been given to the way forward. Politics again – but it was also a sign of the sophistication of those present that most understood the real reason the Minister had raised the issue.

The formal part of the briefing came to an end and those present split into a number of sub-groups, ready to implement various related but separate actions. Blackmore sought out the Press Secretary and together with a few others looked through her draft news brief, made a few minor changes, and then authorized its release. Copies would go out to the media on a standard distribution list that ensured that all the major players were swept up. Although it was bad news, a proactive strategy had been adopted on the understanding that it was always best to be up front with such announcements. The media were like the Inland Revenue – always better to contact them than to leave it, giving the impression that you had something to hide, and have *them* contact *you*. The news brief would form the basis of Blackmore's statement to Parliament, and Head of Sec(AS) was duly tasked with expanding and adapting this material into something Blackmore could use in the House.

Things were beginning to happen, but the trouble was that they were happening too quickly. The problem with living in a democracy in a multimedia age was that there was simply too much to do and too many people to consult. The result was that the system contained a large degree of inertia. Important announcements generally had to be cleared with a plethora of civil servants, not to mention the political apparatchiks and spin doctors who had to ensure that everything was 'on message'. It occurred to Blackmore that the Typhoons had been lost only a couple of hours ago, and already half the RAF seemed to be responding to the tragedy.

It had been agreed that there needed to be a further meeting later in the day, probably at 1300 hours. This would serve two purposes. It would give the key players nearly eight hours to explore some of the issues raised by the loss of the aircraft and it would also serve as a useful forum to discuss the various unexpected questions that would inevitably be raised by Parliament and the press, despite everyone's valiant attempts to anticipate every possible query. Another problem was that nobody could agree quite who should meet to discuss matters. Normally the Air Force Board Standing Committee might have been the appropriate forum, but the AFBSC was not best suited to discuss some of the technical radar data that needed to be analysed in the next few hours. It had been decided to leave that question for the time being, and reconsider it later in the morning, by which time – with luck – things would be clearer. It was most likely that an ad hoc group would be put together, with various specialists attending as required. There was only one certainty, Blackmore mused, and that was that a lot of people in the MOD were going to be very busy. He was right.

Rowledge, Surrey
They were just memories, and they couldn't hurt her now. Memories were like dust in the mind and could blow away on the slightest of breezes. There were no more thoughts of cub scouts or bad fairies because she knew the true identity of her tormentors and, although she was afraid of them because of the pain that they could inflict, she had seen through the deception and knew who they were. They were aliens. But there was nothing magical or noble about them, and the only mystery they engendered was a kind of low deception – like the sort of nasty lowlife that posed as gas board officials and stole from pensioners. They were dirty, lying creatures and her secret aim, insofar as it was possible to have secrets from them, was to kill one of them. Maybe then they'd think twice about taking her and doing these things to her. And if they killed her in retaliation, well, it would be the end of a nightmare and a final release from the years of fear, pain and that sense of helplessness that came from being used and then

discarded like some limp, dirty piece of kitchen rag.

She was jolted out of her thoughts by the realization that the procedure was about to begin. She knew what to expect because she had heard the nightmarish sound of something metallic being removed from a tray. She knew these noises well after so many years and, through a mixture of half-glimpsed events and lucid deductions, knew that her captors operated to a fairly set routine. So, today it was to be a medical procedure – the most physically painful of the three things that they did to her. *But the easiest to deal with.*

She closed her eyes and allowed her mind to drift away. She was on a beach, and a warm breeze was blowing over her body. At her side was a paperback and a long, cool drink. She was alone, and no sounds disturbed her restful state. This was her strategy and although the pain came, as it nearly always did, it was short-lived and soon receded. *Little shits! I know you have the power to use anaesthetic, so why don't you? Is pain part of the deal? Are you studying how I respond to it?*

She articulated her thoughts clearly, unsure whether the beings could really read her mind in any other than the most general sense but hoping they could read *this.* She formed a vivid mental image of her hands around the scrawny little neck of one of the beings and smiled to herself as she imagined its huge, almond-shaped eyes bulging outwards as she strangled the life out of the loathsome creature. *I hope you can understand this.* Clearly it could.

'Why do you hate us?'

'If you really don't know, you must be incredibly stupid.'

'We are helping you.'

'I don't want your help.'

'But you *need* it.'

'I haven't consented to this.'

'You *have* consented.'

The unexpected nature of the last reply, with its obvious falsehood, had the effect of a verbal slap and was so effective that she gasped in astonishment. But then she put that thought aside and pondered what had just happened. It was by no means the only conversation she had had with her captors, but it was one of the most interactive. Usually she got little more than platitudes about how the experience would not hurt, or how it would soon be over. It was the sort of nonsense that nurses spouted to small babies in a clinic, and as often as not it was an outright lie. But this had been, by their standards, a detailed exchange – a conversation of sorts, as opposed to mere one-way communication. Were it not for the total helplessness of her position she might almost have believed that she had been talking to them as equals.

A few minutes later she was back in her own bed and it was only then that a realization dawned upon her. They had not given her any instruction to forget her experience. She turned this perception over in her mind. It would not have been the first outright mistake they'd made – she remembered once waking up in a nightdress that was not hers. But *was* this a similar mistake, or had her conversation with what she thought of as the leader-being somehow distracted them from their normal routine? The fact that they were fallible was a great comfort to her, not least because it gave her hope of fighting back. She could not fight against gods – but against demons she might stand a chance.

Her recollection of her experiences normally came to her though dreams, flashbacks or hypnotic regression, but for this experience she would need none of these tools. She snatched a lined exercise book from her bedside table, picked up a pen and started making some notes. She had some important calls to make the following day and she wanted to get down all the details. It was only when she had finished that the enormity of the situation struck her. Before, there had always been some uncertainty at the back of her mind about the reality of her experiences, and she could hide intellectually behind doubts about the validity of regression hypnosis, allowing herself the possibility that her experiences were what psychologists called False Memory Syndrome. But not now. This was final, unequivocal confirmation that the things that happened to her occurred not in her mind but in the real, physical world. The realization struck her that her final defence had been stripped away. It was then that she began to cry.

Chapter Three

ESCALATION

RAF Coningsby, Lincolnshire

News travels fast in the RAF. Even though the loss of the two Typhoons had occurred only a few hours ago there could have been few people who had not heard about the tragedy by midway through the following morning. The story had broken on the TV breakfast news shows but, as ever, the story had already circulated to most members of the small community of fast-jet pilots in the RAF, each of whom felt the loss in ways that few outsiders would have understood. While the MOD bureaucrats in Main Building grappled with their press releases and what defensive lines to take, those who actually flew the aircraft had to mourn the loss of friends and wonder again whether, one day, their own luck would run out.

Flying Officer Isabelle Bentley hadn't known either of the two dead pilots, but a couple of her fellow fliers had served a tour or two with them and apparently they had been extremely popular. Being a fast-jet pilot in the RAF meant that she was part of a small and very exclusive club and, like all its members, Bentley grieved the loss of two comrades-in-arms. Five squadrons at just three separate RAF bases flew the Typhoon and although all Tornado F3 pilots had undergone conversion training, no squadron yet had its full complement of the new aircraft. This meant that some F3s were still flying, albeit very much as the poor relations of their glamorous replacements. Bentley was one of the lucky ones. She was a relatively new recruit into the RAF and had therefore missed out on the F3 altogether. She'd been one of the first to have been taught exclusively on the Typhoon once she'd been streamed into fast-jet flying in an air defence role, which was exactly what she'd always wanted to do.

Bentley had always wanted to fly, and could even remember the exact moment when she'd made the decision. She'd been about twelve when she'd seen a feature on the television news about one of the first women pilots to get an operational role in a fast-jet squadron. She'd thought this was great, and had resolved to become a pilot herself. Her father had dismissed the idea as a childish whim, but her mother had sensed the determination in her daughter and had fuelled her interest by taking the family to air shows. Bentley had gone to university and had come away with a First in Classics. But the real thrill for her had been the chance to join the University Air Squadron where she'd absorbed the basics about the RAF and learned to fly in the wonderful but unappealingly named Grob 115D training aircraft. As soon as she'd graduated she'd applied for a Permanent Commission and had sailed through the Officers and Aircrew Selection Centre with one of the highest marks on her course.

Basic training had been tough, but Bentley had done well and had duly started her flying training. She'd renewed her acquaint-ance with the Grob before working her way through the Tucano and then the Hawk, once it had been decided that her talents were best suited to fast jets rather than multi-engine aircraft or helicopters. Her instructors were impressed and recognized that she was a natural who had a genuine love for flying. She'd flown on Harriers for a while before being re-streamed into the prestigious Typhoon training programme.

Bentley was popular with the other pilots because of her

outgoing personality and mischievous sense of humour: she was often to be found at the centre of social and sporting activities. She was tall, with shoulder-length blonde hair and an athletic figure. Early in her career one of her bosses had suggested that she'd be a suitable subject for the recruiting brochures but she'd turned him down at first with a terse comment about being a pilot and not a model. But she actually quite liked being the centre of attention, so had sought out the nonplussed officer later and told him she'd changed her mind. Pictures of her in a flying suit and standing next to a Typhoon had duly been included in various pieces of recruiting and publicity literature, leading to a few profiles of her appearing in the media. It was something that she thought of with a mixture of pride and amusement.

Now, like all the Typhoon pilots, Bentley was waiting for news of whether the fleet was to be grounded. Urgent checks had been ordered, and even now dedicated teams of engineers and technicians were checking each airframe for signs of a design fault. In the main they were looking for hairline cracks in the engine and fuel tanks, but she knew that the procedure would go much further than this and that nothing would be overlooked. She felt herself to be in a sort of limbo, unsure of quite what she should be feeling. Grief, certainly, for the two dead pilots, but fear too: had she been flying an aircraft that might have blown up at any moment, and had she escaped death simply because somebody else's plane had been the first to explode? She felt physically sick at the thought that she might so easily have been assigned to fly in one of the doomed airframes.

Bentley made her way to the crewroom and sought solace in the company of other Typhoon pilots wrestling with the same thoughts. They were a gregarious and proud bunch, but their mood today was subdued as theories were put forward and rejected in the cut and thrust of debate. Like all RAF pilots they had a built-in bias against the idea that pilot error might be a factor in any crash. Such an attitude only made their apprehension worse, of course, because while each of them was confident of their own ability to avoid making a fatal error they knew that there was nothing they could do about a design fault once the aircraft was in the air. Once you were up there, it was just a matter of luck, God, fate or whatever it was you chose to believe in. Which wasn't a pleasant thought.

House of Commons, Westminster

As Blackmore rose to his feet, having been called by the Speaker, he noticed how few MPs were present. It was only then he realized that the events that had occupied almost all of his time since he'd been awoken were not as crucial to everyone else. It was a big issue to him, to the MOD and to the RAF but the world went on, and other problems demanded the attention of the Government. The Minister counted around thirty people in the chamber, most of whom he recognized. The opposition Defence spokesperson was present, having been briefed over the phone earlier. His own Secretary of State was also there. There had been some discussion about who would deliver the statement, but Blackmore's own desire to see the matter through had carried the day. He glanced at his papers and began his speech.

'Thank you, Madam Speaker. It is my sad duty to inform the House of the loss of two Typhoon air defence jets in an incident last night that, tragically, has almost certainly cost the lives of the two young pilots. The aircraft were based at RAF Leeming in Yorkshire and were on Quick Reaction Alert.'

Blackmore paused briefly and looked up. His statement was being received in silence, which was rare for the House of Commons but understandable, given the sombre nature of what he had to say. The usual political point scoring would have been crassly inappropriate. However, what he had to say next might just provoke comment. The wording had been discussed at great length between all the key players who knew that they couldn't avoid the issue of the radar returns but who also knew the dangers inherent in premature disclosure.

'I want to say a few words about the circumstances leading up to the incident. It's standard practice to launch these aircraft to investigate any radar contacts not immediately identifiable to

Fighter Controllers. However, radar systems are susceptible to certain meteorological conditions and other technical factors that sometimes mean blips are often seen when no aircraft are actually present. In normal circumstances planes would only be scrambled if there was clear evidence that an aircraft was intruding into the UK Air Defence Region. But it's useful training to scramble under realistic conditions, and Fighter Controllers are within their rights to launch jets even if they think a radar return may be spurious. Last night's launch was a result of such a borderline call, and the jets were tasked to check out an indeterminate contact which is still the subject of analysis.'

These were weasel words, Blackmore thought to himself and, judging by the expressions on some faces, his statement seemed unlikely to be accepted without comment or question.

'Fighter Controllers tracked the Typhoons as they moved out over the North Sea but lost radar contact shortly thereafter. An immediate search-and-rescue operation was launched, but nothing has been found thus far and no signals have been detected from the personal locator beacons that both men carried. Although the search continues as I speak, the pilots are presumed dead, and next of kin have been informed. A Board of Inquiry has been called in the usual way, and although it would be premature of me to anticipate its findings in any way, I can assure the House that immediate checks on all Typhoons have been ordered as a precautionary measure. Authorities in Germany, Italy and Spain – whose air forces also fly the Typhoon – have been informed of events, and we have suggested that they check their own fleets. I am sure I speak for the entire House when I express my sadness at this tragedy and say that our thoughts are with the families and friends of the two pilots.'

Blackmore sat down and, as he did so, the Speaker called Gordon Bannister, Shadow Defence Minister, who rose to his feet to reply on behalf of Her Majesty's Opposition.

'Madam Speaker,' he began, 'may I first thank the Minister for his statement, and for coming to the House so quickly to inform us of this tragedy. I too should like to express my sincere condolences to the families and friends of the two pilots, coupled with the sincere hope that even now, against all the odds, we may yet receive good news. I am sure that the search operation will not cease until all hope is lost.'

Bannister paused. Blackmore gave an exaggerated and visible nod from his sedentary position to indicate that this was indeed the case.

'May I press the Minister on a couple of points, though,' Bannister continued. 'Whilst appreciating the need not to prejudice the Board of Inquiry, I should like to know whether the Typhoon fleet is to be grounded for the time being. I should also like to know more about this business of the radar return. Can the Minister dismiss the possibility that another aircraft was involved, and if not can he say what steps are being taken to resolve the mystery?'

There were nods from some of the other MPs present, and Blackmore knew that he had not managed to deflect the House on this issue. There had been little hope of doing so, but right now Parliamentary pressure was a distraction he could do without. He wanted to get back to Main Building to take this forward. But there was no getting away from the matter of the radar return and, while it had put him in an awkward position, the consequences of omitting the information would have been dire. However well-intentioned, it would have been viewed as misleading the House – a matter that would have ended his political career in an instant. He rose to respond.

'Madam Speaker, may I first say to the House that a decision on whether or not to ground the fleet has not yet been taken. As I have said, checks are now being made on each and every aircraft, and on the basis of these detailed and professional examinations informed decisions will be taken, probably later today. With regard to the radar returns, the analysis is continuing, and further data is being gathered. Until this process is complete it would be premature to dismiss any possibility.'

Blackmore noticed that a number of MPs were trying to catch the Speaker's eye and were rising in their seats. This could go on for a while yet. *Damn.*

RAF Neatishead, Norfolk

'Sir, why is the data we developed being ignored?'

Whitfield had asked for the meeting with his boss and the Station Commander the moment he'd heard about the Parliamentary statement on the news, even though he'd not seen the text. It was Wing Commander Spink who replied.

'It isn't. It's being considered as we speak by DERA's experts at Malvern, who will go over the radar tapes frame by frame, I promise you.'

'Then why is everyone playing down the fact that we had a solid return and describing it in such vague terms?' Whitfield continued. 'Every time I listen to what the radio news says, there's speculation about a mid-air collision or a design fault, and hardly a mention of the radar evidence that all but eliminates these two possibilities. When it does get a mention it sounds as if we launched those aircraft on a whim, because we didn't have anything better to do. But we all know that's not true. We *all* looked at the data and we *all* agreed there was a solid object there.'

Squadron Leader Maddox raised his hand to cut the younger man off, as he was getting increasingly agitated. 'Look, we all know how you feel—'

'With respect, sir, you don't.' Whitfield interrupted. 'I was the one who brought this matter to everyone's attention, and I'm the one who has to live with the fact that two people died as a result.'

Maddox didn't like to be interrupted, but he sympathized with Whitfield. God only knew what was going through his mind, but he had to get him away from the idea that he was personally responsible for the deaths. His boss had the same idea, and beat him to it.

'We all have to live with it, because we all had a part in the decision. You noticed the anomalous returns and recommended a course of action, but I endorsed that action. Am I responsible for those deaths?' Spink asked.

'No, sir.'

Spink was being harsh, but it was a situation he'd encountered once before and he knew that unless he snapped Whitfield out of his current line of thinking, the younger man would descend even further into despair and guilt. Maddox saw what his boss was doing and approved, although he knew it would be a painful process.

'Strike Command authorized the operation and someone at Buchan actually initiated the scramble. Are they responsible? No, of course they're not. They were doing exactly what you were doing – their jobs. These deaths are tragedies, but they were the end result of a long chain of events and even if there is blame – which I very much doubt – I'm satisfied it can't be attributed to you in any way.'

'Then what about the UFO sighting, or the fireball reported by RAF Fylingdales? I haven't heard any mention of them, and yet it was the straight line we plotted linking these two events with the radar data that led to the decision to authorize a scramble in the first place.'

'They haven't been ignored,' Spink replied patiently. 'Everything will be considered by the Board of Inquiry and, if it looks to me as if anything is being overlooked, I'll make sure it's examined properly. That's a promise.'

'Then, sir, I have a suggestion,' Whitfield began. 'Let me interview the three guys who saw the UFO. I understand that the CRO's planning to speak to them, but I want to talk to them as an AD man. If there's a connection between their sighting and the loss of our aircraft – and I firmly believe there is – they may have seen something that might be useful. I'm thinking about aerodynamics and propulsion system. Did they see anything that might give us a clue about this thing's capabilities? Did they hear anything that might tell us how the thing's powered?'

Spink thought for a moment. The Board of Inquiry would have to go over this ground, but it couldn't do any harm to follow up a report that had already involved the RAF in some work. It would certainly help the Inquiry if this particular point could be cleared up. And it might help Whitfield to deal with his misguided sense of guilt. At times like this, people needed to be busy. 'OK.'

MOD Main Building, Whitehall

'I'm glad that's over,' said Blackmore, smiling briefly at his PS. 'Now, what's been happening while I've been at the Inquisition?'

Farthing glanced briefly at some notes she'd been making over the last hour, recording the key events. It was little more than a list of names and telephone numbers, but it was a valuable aide-mémoire for the hard-pressed civil servant. 'Actually, Minister, not much. We're at the stage now where everybody's gone away to think about what's happened and to make further checks. People are gearing up for the big meeting this afternoon, and some of the specialists are on their way as we speak.'

'What about arrangements for the meeting itself?'

'All in hand, Minister. 1300 still seems the best time, and as all the experts will be present there's no need to have the meeting in the DCMC. I've booked one of the historic conference rooms, arranged for coffee and biscuits, and told everyone that the meeting will go on for as long as necessary. You'll be in the chair, of course.'

Blackmore nodded appreciatively. 'Excellent. Anything else?'

'Here's a copy of the draft agenda, which I've been working up with Head of Sec(AS) and the Air Staff. It may change, but it's the best we can do at the moment. The key point will be a technical analysis of the radar tapes leading up to the crash.'

The Minister scanned the piece of paper carefully, and raised his eyebrows as he noticed the final agenda item. 'UFOs?'

'Yes, Minister,' Farthing replied warily. 'Head of Sec(AS) felt it was important to give a background briefing, given the circumstances. It's helpful, by the way, that Sec(AS) is the lead division on UFOs as well as aircraft accidents. Of course, when he talks about UFOs he doesn't mean flying saucers – he simply means anything that can't be readily identified. If the radar data isn't spurious, that's what we're dealing with, in a literal sense. Politically, of course, we need to cover all the bases, so that we can truthfully say that we are considering every possibility.'

Blackmore nodded his agreement, pleased that his PS was thinking like a politician as well as a civil servant – a difficult balancing act but an essential one for all senior Private Office staff.

'There are some other reasons why a briefing on UFOs is appropriate,' Farthing continued. 'Firstly, there was a UFO sighting that just might tie-in with what happened to the Typhoons reported to RAF Coltishall. It's being looked at now, but there does seem to be a straight line that can be drawn between the place that the UFO was seen, the area where the aircraft were lost, and some earlier activity – originally classified as fireballs – picked up by RAF Fylingdales.'

'Why wasn't I told?' Blackmore was astounded at this latest revelation.

'We didn't know, Minister. Information is coming to us in fits and starts, and this has only just been mentioned. Nobody is really paying that much attention to UFOs and fireballs, but again, we have to show that we're covering all the bases. In any case, the other reason why a UFO briefing is appropriate is because the Press Office are beginning to get a few calls. They've been swamped with enquiries from the media, and while most have focused on the possibility of a technical problem with the Typhoons, one or two have picked up on the business of the radar returns, even though we downplayed this in the press release. The term "UFO" has been mentioned a few times already, and this can only increase once the apparently rather excitable UFO lobby get involved. That's a firm prediction from Head of Sec(AS), by the way.'

'Great,' commented the Minister, sarcastically. 'As if we haven't got enough on our plates. OK, what else do I need to know?'

'Three main points,' Farthing replied, glancing again at her notes. 'First, HMS *Lancaster* is still searching the area but has found nothing to date. Second, checks on the Typhoons are continuing but so far everything looks fine. Controller Aircraft sees no reason to ground the fleet but has said that we'll not fly a particular airframe until it's been checked. It'll take another day or so to check each one: although things will be tight, we should have enough cleared aircraft to carry out scheduled tasks. There's no word yet from any of the other operating nations. I'll chase that up later, but I think it's a fair assessment that no news is good news: we did ask them to let us know immediately if they found any problems.'

Farthing paused for a moment since the Minister was making notes of his own. When he'd finished, she continued her update.

'The final point is the trickiest. It's to do with the possibility that the Typhoons collided with a Russian RPV. As was said earlier, the threat board is clear, but CDI says we do need to raise it with the Russians, if only to satisfy ourselves that we're checking every possibility. The problem is that the FCO are a bit twitchy about asking them. It might help if you placed a call to your opposite number.'

'Agreed. I'll do it now,' said Blackmore. *Bloody typical of the FCO to be more worried about upsetting the Russians than helping us out.*

'That's about it for now, Minister. I'll be in the outer office and will update you as and when any fresh information comes in.'

'Thank you, Sue. Good work.'

Farnham, Surrey

It was fortunate that Jenny Thornton lived so close to a man who was generally considered Britain's leading expert on UFOs and alien abductions. Richard Cody was a retired barrister whose own interest in UFOs had started with a personal sighting as a child. By his own admission, the sighting had been unspectacular – a brief flash of green light in the night sky, which his subsequent research suggested was almost certainly a fireball burning up in the atmosphere. But it had fuelled something in him that had never gone away and that, if anything, had intensified over the years. A widower, the dapper sixty-seven-year-old now devoted much of his time to researching UFOs and was the author of four books on the subject.

The media thought of ufologists as bobble-hatted, anorak-wearing train-spotter types or as barking-mad conspiracy theorists. While an unfair generalization, it was not without its grain of truth. So Cody was someone to whom the media turned when they wanted a serious figure to comment on the issue. Eloquent and articulate, he was a publicly recognized personality who put the case for an extraterrestrial presence on Earth with an air of quiet authority that had won over many and that had also led to a lucrative sideline for him as an after-dinner speaker. He was seen by his peers as being the grand old man of British ufology, and he scrupulously avoided the political infighting that bogged down most of the established UFO societies in the country.

Most recently Cody had specialized in investigating reports of alien abduction, the subject of his latest book. He ran a small support group from his house, where abductees could come and share their experiences with each other and gain some measure of comfort from the knowledge that they were not the only ones experiencing such things. He was a tall, well-built man who had a real presence about him, together with a rare combination of strength of character and compassion. So he was someone with whom people felt comfortable, and with whom they shared their secrets. He had known Thornton for nearly two years and had appeared with her on a couple of television shows. A chapter of his last book had been devoted to her case, and the two had become friends. When she had telephoned him in a state of anxiety, earlier in the morning, he hadn't hesitated in inviting her over.

Thornton had clearly been upset when she arrived, and the two of them had exchanged small talk over a cup of coffee before turning to the reason for her visit. When Cody judged that the moment was right, he asked Thornton to relay her latest experience. With her permission, he taped the conversation, making a few notes as he went along. His experience as a successful and highly regarded barrister was central to his technique, which was based on the principle that, at first, he should say as little as possible. It was his listening skills that put people at ease and made them think – correctly – that he was genuinely interested in and concerned with what he was being told.

Over the next forty minutes Thornton explained what had happened to her the night before. Cody interjected just twice, and then only when the frightened woman seemed to have lost the thread of her thoughts. It was certainly a remarkable story, and

Cody was quick to see that the key element in her account was that the entire experience was consciously recalled and that no attempt to induce amnesia had been made. Cody was a qualified hypnotherapist and had been criticized by sceptical researchers for his reliance on regression hypnosis to draw out the memories of people who claimed to have had alien contact. But Cody was the first to admit that the technique was not foolproof and he was careful to put warning markers on any of his information that had come to light through the use of hypnosis. He thought for a moment.

'Jenny, I'm so very grateful to you for sharing this experience with me. I know it's been deeply traumatic but, if I may, I'd like to suggest that this empowers you a little. Unsettling though it is, you have a degree of control that you lacked before; you have absolute command over your own memories.'

Thornton smiled. Cody had a way with words, and while he was clearly doing his best to put her at ease, there was no denying that what he said was true.

'I'd like to suggest something,' he continued. 'With your permission, I'd like to put a bulletin on various Internet news sites. Most of the key players in ufology are on-line and this would be a way of getting details of this development to people as quickly as possible. I really believe we may have something very important here and I'd like to see what other experts think. Most of all, I'd like to see if anyone else has experienced the same thing.'

'Yes, that's OK with me. I just want to get to the bottom of it all and if it can help anyone else along the way, then great. Use my real name if you like – I've gone public already, so it can't hurt.'

'Thank you, Jenny. I'll work up a short piece now and show it to you before I circulate it, in case you have any suggestions.'

Fort Meade, Maryland

The headquarters of the National Security Agency was a vast, sprawling complex of buildings within which numerous analysts toiled at making sense of intercepted communications from all around the world. This was the NSA's primary mission, one that kept them increasingly busy as more and more information was

traded on the Internet and on cellular phones. But on the basis
that the best place to keep a secret is amidst other secrets, the
NSA's vast budget hid other missions, some of which had never
seen the light of Congressional scrutiny.

Director Edwin Van Buren was tall and thin, with grey hair and
piercing blue eyes. A man of few words, he was respected and
feared by his subordinates. He seldom raised his voice because he
didn't need to. He operated with a sureness and confidence
grounded in the absolute knowledge that he wielded the sort of
power that few possessed. Pale-complexioned, he stalked the
corridors of the NSA in a way that more than one of his staff
privately thought was like the tread of a vampire. It was a testament to his standing that nobody had dared voice such insights to
a colleague.

There were three other people in Van Buren's small but
elegantly furnished office, all waiting expectantly for their boss to
speak. Each of the three section heads had been curtly summoned
by Van Buren himself since he'd sent his secretary home.

'I've received a disturbing report from Menwith Hill, which has
now been confirmed by open-source media. The British have lost
two air force jets in what is being presented as a mid-air collision.
However, it seems that the aircraft were scrambled in response to
what some people clearly felt was a solid radar return. The Royal
Air Force are actively investigating this possibility.'

The faces were impassive. Nobody asked questions, although
they all had plenty.

'We shall follow this up immediately,' Van Buren continued,
'with our friends at RAF Feltwell. We shall cross-check with
Cheyenne Mountain. I'm sure I don't have to tell you what this
may mean.' He stared at the three other men, looking each briefly
in the eye. 'It means that after decades of play and counter-play,
we could now be approaching the denouement.'

RAF Buchan, Aberdeenshire

It was perhaps fortunate that Sue Harding was not on duty. The
sudden *ping* of the signal that had just appeared on the radar screen

would have chilled her to the bone. Another young Flying Officer had the duty watch and although, like all Fighter Controllers, Michael Chow had been briefed on recent developments, he did not carry the emotional baggage that came from authorizing a launch and then watching the aircraft disappear from his screen. His heart rate quickened, though, as he struggled to evaluate his orders. He plotted the position and calculated which was the nearest base with Typhoons. *I'll give it three more sweeps, just in case.* The return was remaining stubbornly on the screen, moving laterally in a way that looked pretty normal to him – except that it was travelling at Mach 2 and carrying no IFF. *Three, two, one. Oh, shit.*

Chow lifted his phone and punched in the code that connected him instantly with the duty controller at RAF Leuchars. He instigated a launch of the Q aircraft, then began making a series of follow-up calls to inform a long list of people about what he'd done. The list was a standard one, although it had virtually doubled in length in the last few hours. First to receive a call was Chow's boss, who was at his side within minutes. The other links in the ADGE chain would be watching events in real time, but Chow would be the one actually communicating with the Typhoons and plotting the intercept, at least until the pilots acquired the target themselves on their airborne radar. It was a task that nobody envied him.

MOD Main Building, Whitehall

The meeting had been going on for about twenty minutes and had not yet touched on any new material. The reason for this was that several of those present – particularly the specialists – had not previously been given an overview of the incident. This was essential, although frustrating for those present already familiar with events. Blackmore was chairing the meeting but after a short introduction had called upon Head of Sec(AS) to give the initial briefing. Although familiar with the material, Blackmore was listening intently, evaluating not just the information but the man who was imparting it to the assembled audience.

Nick Templeton was young for a Grade 5, and his relative youth was the first thing one noticed about him. Just thirty-six, the short, slender fast-streamer had obviously leapfrogged over colleagues with more seniority. Templeton was fairly new in the post, which Blackmore had felt would be a disadvantage. The Minister had asked his PS about the man and had been told that he was highly regarded and much tougher than he looked. Blackmore felt this was a fair assessment, even though he was sure Farthing would be loyal to her Civil Service colleague.

The Minister looked hard at Templeton who was wearing a smart dark suit. His hair was black, although it was going completely white at the temples. Slim and bespectacled, he looked at first sight as if he might have been overwhelmed by his taller colleagues in the military. His voice, however, was the confident one of a man who knew his subject and was well briefed. His rapid promotion was another indicator that this rather mild-looking individual possessed hidden strengths. *He'll need them.*

Once Templeton had completed his part of the brief, Blackmore turned to Mark Fox, DUS(S&T). The Chief Scientific Adviser was still on her way back from her holiday so Fox, her deputy, had been pulling together the various analyses that had been carried out by the scientific staff. At his side was Mahmood Nahar, a senior scientist from DERA's site at Malvern.

'I'll give you the raw data,' Fox began. 'But first I'll give you our initial assessment. The radar returns do *not* appear to be spurious; on the basis of the available information, we believe there *was* another craft present.'

Fox knew that his dramatic opening had caused quite a stir, just as he had intended. It was a pre-planned remark designed to grab people's attention, so that the non-scientists would pay as much attention as possible to the technical part of his brief. Blackmore cut him off. He knew how the Civil Service couched everything in cautious terms – this *may* be the case and that *might* be the case. But Fox was a scientist as well as a civil servant, and Blackmore wanted something more precise.

'How sure are you of this assessment? I know it's early days, and

I won't hold you to this, but on a percentage scale, how sure are you that your initial analysis is correct?'

Fox thought for a moment. He didn't like being put on the spot when there were so many variables, but he appreciated the skilful way in which the Minister had phrased his question so as to shield him from any blame if the assessment proved incorrect.

'I'm eighty per cent sure, Minister. Dr Nahar here did much of the analysis, and I think it only fair to ask him to answer the same question. Anything to add, Mahmood?'

In the normal course of business, deputies wouldn't be expected to speak at a meeting at this level, and they certainly wouldn't be invited to disagree with their boss. But the scientists had a different way of doing business, and Fox was keen to acknowledge Nahar's contribution. Nahar was a strong-willed character who would have no difficulties in disagreeing with his boss in front of the assembled dignitaries if he had a different view. That was precisely the reason why Fox valued him.

'I concur with the assessment, although I should say that we have had some intellectual difficulty in divorcing the data from the account that went with it. In other words, our lack of knowledge about any craft with the characteristics suggested by the radar tapes has been the main argument against the validity of the tapes themselves.'

'Thank you,' Blackmore responded. 'There are many things we do not yet know, but it seems to me that what we are saying, if this assessment proves correct, is that we are dealing with either a horrendous mistake or an act of outright aggression.'

There were nods from around the table: nobody could disagree with the Minister's analysis, even though none present could see quite how such a situation had arisen. At Blackmore's bidding, Fox began to give a more technical analysis of the radar returns, which were on videotape and could therefore be played on a large television positioned at one end of the room. Fox gave a clear brief that was understandable to those who lacked technical knowledge but that contained enough details for those who could understand the raw scientific data. When this section of the meeting had been completed, Blackmore turned, predictably, to the Chief of Defence Intelligence.

'The threat board's blank, as we all know, but I'm afraid I'm going to have to put you on the spot, Sir Charles. If the assessment is good, who are we dealing with?'

Sir Charles Crompton was an Army General known to most of his colleagues as CC. He'd spent much of the day talking with his various key section heads and desk officers, trying to come up with any facts that might explain what was happening if the radar data was not spurious. Like everyone else, he wanted to believe that the Typhoons had collided, simply because the alternatives were more frightening. But it was these alternatives that needed to be explored more fully now, as the possibility of collision or structural failure receded.

'The starting point for the DIS analysis is that the radar returns do show a solid craft. And on that point I should add that my own experts concur with the DERA assessment. Assuming there was an object present, it was either an aircraft or an RPV of some sort, although not one that any of my staff recognize. The speed and manoeuvrability are way ahead of anything we are aware of. It's cutting-edge stuff: stealthy, hypersonic – at least ten years ahead of anything we know about.

'There are three possibilities as to the operating nation. First, and least likely, it's ours, but a project none of the DIS know about. This *is* extremely unlikely, because some of us around this table would *have* to know about such a craft, and I find it inconceivable that the operators wouldn't have owned up, given that people have died. Second, it belongs to the Americans. Almost as unlikely. We have asked through channels and have received assurances that it wasn't them. Now, as you know, the Americans – like us – keep their most highly classified projects on a strictly need-to-know basis, and information is extremely compartmentalized, so it's possible that the channels we went through were not in the picture themselves. But again, people have died; the Americans are our allies; we would have heard *something*. So the only viable possibility is that the Russians are involved, and I should stress that even this is assessed as extremely unlikely.'

One or two of those present leaned forward. Blaming it on the Russians was at least something they could understand.

'The following scenario is therefore the only one that stands up to scrutiny. It is just conceivable that a small faction within the Russian Air Force has developed and is testing a hypersonic RPV, and that this accidentally collided with our aircraft, bringing them down.'

'You talk about an RPV,' interjected Blackmore. 'Could we be dealing with a manned aircraft?'

'No, Minister, I think not,' Crompton replied. 'The development of a new manned aircraft would involve far too many people and far too much industrial activity to have escaped our attention. An RPV of the type envisaged, although still involving a quantum design leap we haven't detected, would be on a much smaller scale. As such, it's just possible, although I'd ask you to bear in mind that the FCO has now formally asked the appropriate Russian authorities and has received what seem to be genuine expressions of surprise and regret.'

'And what about the possibility that our aircraft were brought down deliberately?' Blackmore asked.

'Virtually impossible,' Crompton retorted. 'Such a move would serve no political or military purpose, and would not have been undertaken in isolation. Other things – detectable things – would be happening right now.'

'This could all be cleared up quickly,' Fox suggested. 'Our number one priority must be to locate the wreckage. It'll tell us whether the aircraft collided, whether one blew up and took the other out, or whether "something else" collided with them. We may even find that something else, if it exists. All we have to do is locate and recover a significant part of the wreckage and take it to the DERA site at Farnborough for analysis.'

'The latest report from HMS *Lancaster* states they have found nothing yet,' offered Templeton. 'But we do have word from the crew of a fishing vessel who saw what they thought was a bright meteor. Later the captain heard about the Typhoons, put two and two together, and contacted us. We're collating the information, but hope to be in a position to signal HMS *Lancaster* within an hour or two, suggesting a new – and, with luck, more accurate – search area.'

'Why is this proving so difficult?' Blackmore asked. 'We were tracking the aircraft even after the disaster. Surely they fell into the sea at a point almost directly below their last known position?'

'It doesn't quite work like that, Minister,' Templeton explained, before anybody on the Air Staff could reply. 'The aircraft were travelling at around Mach 2, and so did not simply fall vertically. The possible impact area is therefore huge.'

'OK, thank you,' Blackmore said, holding his gaze on the young civil servant. 'Perhaps we can now move to the final item on the agenda, which is your background brief on the UFO issue. We are discussing this because of a report received by the CRO at RAF Coltishall shortly after our aircraft went down. Nick?'

'Thank you, Minister. First, may I ask that you set aside any preconceived ideas about UFOs. We are *not* talking about flying saucers or little green men, but about the six or seven hundred reports investigated each year by my staff. Ninety-five per cent can be explained as misidentifications of—'

At that moment there was a knock on the door. It opened, revealing a smartly dressed man who some immediately recognized as a Squadron Leader in CAS's office. He entered the room and looked briefly at the Minister and his boss, clearly wondering to whom etiquette dictated that he should speak first. The two men were sitting together so the officer kept his gaze fixed neutrally between them as he leaned over them and whispered a few sentences. Both men's faces betrayed the fact that it was bad news. CAS deferred to the Minister to make the announcement.

'It's bad news. We've lost another Typhoon.'

Chapter Four

CONNECTIONS

North Walsham, Norfolk

'Bob Jennings?'

'Yes?' replied the rather shabbily dressed young man, hesitantly.

'I'm Steve Parry, the Community Relations Officer at RAF Coltishall. This is my colleague Alan Whitfield from RAF Neatishead. We spoke on the phone; may we come in?'

'Oh, yeah. Sorry, I thought you'd be in uniform. Come in.'

Jennings led them through a hallway that was cluttered with fishing rods and other angling gear and ushered them into the living room.

'The wife's out at work,' Jennings explained. 'I'm self-employed; removals, van hire, that sort of thing. Do most of my fishing at night now I've hooked up with a real couple of old pros. They're happy to meet you, if you want, although Tom was a bit suspicious of you Government people showing up on his doorstep. You know, Men in Black and all that.'

Parry and Whitfield smiled with Jennings, as much to put him at ease as anything else. Jennings was clearly nervous, and the two

RAF officers had resolved to chat to him about his fishing before getting down to serious business, in an attempt to break the ice. Both knew that they would get far more of the story if Jennings was relaxed, so for the next ten minutes they talked to him about his hobby, getting him to tell them the story of the quest for the pike that he and his friends had dubbed 'Nessie'. As this was the reason for the three men's presence in the Norfolk Broads on the night concerned, it led logically to the account of their UFO sighting. Both RAF officers knew the story, of course, but neither had heard it first hand.

Jennings outlined the situation for his visitors who – with his permission – were taping the conversation and making occasional notes. By mutual agreement they held back from asking any direct questions, so as not to interrupt the flow of Jennings's narrative. Jennings was not the most articulate of men but he had an admirable directness about him and the useful habit of differentiating between what he saw and what he thought. In Parry's experience this made him an excellent witness – far better than those who thought they knew it all and who tried to impress him with their knowledge or theories about UFOs. When Jennings described the craft, Parry began to draw a rough sketch on his pad.

'It was shaped like a triangle, with equal-length sides,' Jennings explained. 'But it seemed to be flat. Like I said to the police, almost like a slice of pizza, you know? It was big, like an aeroplane, but quiet. There was this low hum, though. That was creepy, like you could feel it going through your body. Then it fired a beam of light down at the water, ahead of where we were. Frightened Nessie away, that's for sure! Then, after a moment or two, the beam was switched off and the craft shot away – whoosh!'

There followed another ten minutes during which Parry and Whitfield sought further details of the craft, in some cases going over ground that had been covered before in a deliberate attempt to see if the witness could be made to contradict himself. He didn't: it was clear to both men that Jennings clearly believed what he was saying. Whitfield really didn't know what to think, but Parry had come across descriptions of craft like this before, sometimes from military witnesses. Parry handed Jennings his notebook and showed him the sketch he'd made.

'Is this a good likeness of what you saw?'

'Yeah, not bad at all. But listen, if you wait a couple of days I can send you the photos I took of the thing, when they've been developed.'

Parry and Whitfield stared at each other, astonished, and then turned back to their host.

'The *photos*?'

Farnham, Surrey

Richard Cody had been at his computer for several hours. He was a skilled user of the Internet, to the surprise of some prejudiced souls who doubted that anyone over the age of fifty even knew how to switch on a computer. In fact, Cody had his own website that served not only to promote his books but to give an overview of his work.

One of the benefits of being on-line was very quick access to new and important information, usually posted as newsflashes on various different sites. Cody's account of how Jenny Thornton's latest abduction experience had been recalled in its entirety, without the use of hypnosis, had been widely circulated in the last twenty-four hours and now he was checking his e-mail for any responses. He had over seventy bits of new mail but, as ever, much of it was dire nonsense that came his way simply because he was on the standard distribution lists of some of the more frequent – and barking mad – users of the Internet. Much of it he could recognize from the originator and he deleted it unread. Other messages he set aside for later, as ever cautioning himself to give the benefit of the doubt to anything where the source or subject was not obvious – one never knew when an important piece of information might crop up unexpectedly.

One particular piece of new mail caught Cody's eye: it was from a respected American researcher. He moved his cursor to the appropriate point on the screen, clicked once – and recognized immediately that he was looking at something of enormous importance.

FROM: DR ELIZABETH KRONE
TO: RICHARD CODY
RE: CONSCIOUS RECALL OF ALIEN ABDUCTION
MESSAGE: MANY THANKS FOR YOUR POST. I HAVE A
            SIMILAR CASE THAT CAME TO ME TODAY
            (DETAILS ATTACHED AND POSTED TO
            SAME NEWSGROUPS AS YOURS). LET'S
            TALK. EK.

Cody quickly went to the attachment, downloaded it, printed it out and began to read the hard copy. A sense of excitement was building within him. Krone was a professor of psychology at one of the more prestigious American universities. Although criticized by some of her academic colleagues for getting involved in abduction research in the first place, her position as a recognized scientist lent much credibility to the subject and her views on the phenomenon were always listened to by the UFO lobby and the media. Cody had met Krone four times when their paths had crossed at conferences and had corresponded with her from time to time, exchanging data and ideas.

Cody read the report twice before setting it aside. If it hadn't been for the time difference between the UK and the USA he would have telephoned Krone immediately. As it was, he made a mental note to call her later in the day. In the meantime he decided to go into some of the more popular newsgroup sites to see whether his original message or Krone's response had provoked any useful comment. There was quite a lot of debate, as it turned out, although no new facts had come to light.

Once Cody had collated all the available material he started to make a few notes, including a list of calls to make. After his call to Krone he'd update Jenny Thornton on developments and speak to a few other abductees who weren't on-line, just to see if they'd got any views. Then, perhaps, he'd contact a journalist he knew on one of the nationals. They liked to run the occasional piece on UFOs and abductions, so perhaps they would be interested in this latest development.

MOD Main Building, Whitehall

The only advantage – if it could be considered such – in the loss of the third Typhoon was that most of the key players had already assembled to discuss the earlier disaster. In the minutes that had passed since the news had been brought to the meeting, frantic calls had been made between Main Building, Strike Command and the various military bases involved in the latest incident. Eventually the meeting felt that they had all the facts that they were going to get for now.

Apparently the downed aircraft had been one of two scrambled in response to another uncorrelated radar return. But the other jet had had to return to base with mechanical problems, leaving the remaining one to carry out the interception alone. The pilot had reported a fleeting contact on his airborne radar before his plane had disappeared from the Fighter Controller's screen altogether. In this respect the incident was almost a carbon copy of the original tragedy.

There was a macabre sense of déjà vu as the meeting discussed and agreed the various actions that would need to be taken. Informing the next of kin was the first priority but the second, as ever, was the speedy production of a press release to ensure that the Department wasn't beaten to the draw by the media. There was much debate about the problem that had forced the surviving aircraft to turn back. Although initial indications suggested it had been a comparatively minor software glitch, the issue of grounding the fleet arose once more.

'I just don't think it's warranted,' came the view of the man whose decision this was. Air Vice-Marshal Colin Swann was Controller Aircraft and addressed his comments to the meeting which had reassembled after half an hour during which what information was available on the latest incident had been collated. 'Aircraft have to return to base all the time in the middle of training flights, and until we know the details I wouldn't recommend such action.'

Swann's use of the word 'recommend' was a deliberate one. Although grounding the fleet was technically his call, he recognized that political concerns would be a factor and that the decision might effectively be taken out of his hands. *Not without a fight, though*.

'Grounding the fleet is absolutely the move of last resort,' Swann continued. 'It should only be considered when there is strong evidence that an endemic and potentially catastrophic fault is present in each individual airframe.'

'Doesn't the fact that we've lost three aircraft suggest that there *is* such a fault?' asked Blackmore, a trace of anger detectable in his voice.

'No, Minister,' Swann retorted. 'Not least because the aircraft was checked thoroughly after the first tragedy.'

Blackmore turned his gaze to CAS. 'Bob?'

Pickering looked uncomfortable and paused for a moment before replying. 'I tend to agree that grounding the fleet would be premature. We should know more about the problem that forced the surviving aircraft to turn around very soon now, and I suggest we wait for that information. But I have to say that it looks like the sort of software glitch that happens all the time. And although this shouldn't be a factor, I must point out that grounding all our Typhoons would leave us very short-handed. Of course, the programme to replace F3s with Typhoons is ongoing and won't be complete until 2014, so we can attempt to plug the gap with the F3s and perhaps bolster things up by reassigning some other jets fairly quickly. But the bottom line is that we depend heavily on the Typhoons so far as the AD role is concerned: our ability to police the UKADR would be degraded at a time when, if anything, we need it upgraded. And, as an aside, pilot training would suffer very quickly. People simply wouldn't be getting the necessary hours on the Typhoons, and that could set us back a lot, very quickly.'

'I'm sorry to raise the political angle, but there's no getting away from it,' Blackmore said, moving the discussion on. 'The Government will come under intense pressure from the Opposition, maybe even from our own backbenchers; the HCDC are also bound to express an interest. Nobody will accept that the loss of three aircraft in such a short period of time is coincidence.'

'It almost certainly *isn't* coincidence,' Pickering retorted. 'But it's very unlikely that the aircraft itself is at fault. It's reasonable to assume that the two incidents are linked, and that in itself makes the idea of the first one being a mid-air collision less likely. That brings us back to the radar returns. Minister, I think we need to get the FCO in here. If something brought our first two aircraft down, it could conceivably have been a horrendous accident. But for it to happen again . . .'

Pickering left his sentence unfinished, but Blackmore felt it needed to be said. 'Then it's an act of war.'

RAF Leuchars, Fife

Stuart Coultart sat on the end of his bed in his quarters in the Officers' Mess, his mind a turmoil of confused thoughts. He had just attended a debriefing and had been told that he would almost certainly be required to answer further questions at a moment's notice. What he actually wanted to do was to go to the bar and drink himself senseless.

Just an hour ago the young Typhoon pilot had received orders to scramble. Coultart and his colleague Mike Quinn had raced towards what their Fighter Controller had told them was a possible contact. He'd been nervous, having being formally briefed on the incident that had led to the earlier loss of two aircraft. But he'd been excited, too, and curious to find out whether there was a target there or not. He'd been absolutely furious when a warning light came on in the cockpit, indicating a situation which – while not immediately dangerous – demanded an immediate return to base.

It was only after Coultart was safely down that they'd told him that Quinn hadn't made it. His first thought had been that he'd had a brush with death and had narrowly escaped whatever fate had befallen his colleague and friend. Then he'd felt a pang of guilt, and wondered whether Quinn had run into trouble that had proved too much for one pilot but which two might have tackled successfully. This had led to a moment of panic. Might some of his colleagues think he'd bottled it, and mark him down as what was known as a Lack of Moral Fibre pilot? Coultart realized that all this was selfish introspection in the circumstances and his thoughts soon turned back to his dead colleague – he felt the normal mixture of grief and anger that aircrew feel when one of their number is lost. Mostly it was anger.

Rowledge, Surrey

When Cody had telephoned and told her that other cases where abductees were recalling their entire experiences consciously were coming to light, Jenny Thornton didn't know how she should feel. Her first reaction had been relief, since she regarded this latest development as confirmation that her own encounters had been real. It was validation, of a sort: she hadn't been lying or hallucinating.

Thornton thought back to the varied ways in which people had responded to her claims. Publicly, on TV shows or at conferences, she'd had a mixed reception. Few people had accused her of lying – although one or two hotheads had levelled this most hurtful of claims at her – but the more sophisticated sceptics had an irritating way of pouring scorn on what she said without resorting to such tactics: '*While I'm sure she genuinely believes what she's saying* . . . ' they often began. While the reaction from family and friends had been generally supportive, she'd always had the sense that they were embarrassed at what was being said, and she'd noticed that they were liable to change the subject when it cropped up. So she'd welcomed news of Elizabeth Krone's e-mail message to Cody and felt that it might be the beginning of something important – something that would prove she'd been right all along. A little while later, she wondered whether this hadn't been a selfish thought. She'd suffered enough to know that alien contact was not generally a pleasant experience, so if people derived comfort from uncertainty – telling themselves that their experiences had been dreams of hallucinations – then wasn't this a good thing? And might there be vast numbers of abductees who knew or suspected nothing at all? Would these people suddenly be faced with a nightmare from which they couldn't hide? She hated herself for her narrow self-interest, and decided that if the price of proof positive of alien visitation was untold misery for people, then it was too high a price to ask.

Ignorance Is Strength, Thornton suddenly thought, recalling one of the Party's slogans from *Nineteen Eighty-Four*. She mused over the irony of this and was mildly amused by the realization that in some cases it was true. George Orwell had clearly known a thing or two.

House of Commons, Westminster

'Order, order!' Madam Speaker was losing her patience. 'Will Honourable Members please restrain themselves and avoid intervening from sedentary positions. The Minister is on his feet and I would ask that the House show him due courtesy. I am well aware that there is strong feeling on this issue, and I will attempt to call as many Honourable Members as time allows. But this raucous behaviour helps nobody, and shortens the time available for debate.'

'On a Point of Order, Madam Speaker—'

Blackmore looked around and noticed that one of his back-bench colleagues – he wasn't even sure he knew his name – was on his feet.

'Is it not an insult to the dead man's family for certain Honourable Members opposite to receive the Minister's statement in such a disrespectful manner?'

It was the wrong thing to say, and Blackmore cursed the man for having tried to score a cheap political point at a time like this.

'That is not a legitimate Point of Order for this Chair.' Madam Speaker clearly agreed.

Blackmore was thinking rapidly now, but there was no denying the fact that things were getting out of hand. He was honest

enough to blame himself and astute enough to realize that he had
to say something conciliatory to try and undo the damage that had
just been done by his well-meaning but naïve colleague.

'Madam Speaker,' Blackmore resumed, 'I know that the *entire*
House shares my sadness at this latest tragedy, and I wish to place
on record this Government's determination to get to the bottom
of this dreadful incident as quickly as possible.' *There, that should
help.* 'But I must reiterate that we cannot prejudge the Board of
Inquiry by indulging in premature speculation. There are tried
and tested means of investigating the loss of any aircraft and the
RAF must be allowed to carry out their inquiry without political
interference from me, or indeed from anyone else. I cannot
circumnavigate normal channels, however much we all want
answers. Answers will be forthcoming, I can assure this House,
but they will be obtained through due process.'

Blackmore sat down, judging that he had done his best to
defuse what might have turned into a party political row. He
didn't think for a moment that the House would accept what he
had just said without further comment but, with luck, he had
taken the edge off a potentially disastrous situation. Cynically, he
made a mental calculation about the remaining time that Madam
Speaker would allow and judged that she would probably call only
two or three more MPs. But one of those would undoubtedly be
Margaret Hammond, Chair of the HCDC and someone who
could, if she chose, make things extremely difficult for him – even
if they were in the same party. Sure enough, he noted, Hammond
had caught the Speaker's eye and was even now rising to her feet.
Blackmore resolved to make his reply a long one to limit the
number of others who might be called. Something told him he'd
have his hands full dealing with Hammond. Ally or not.

'Madam Speaker,' Hammond began. 'Whilst I accept what my
Honourable Friend has said about the RAF's investigation
process, and whilst I can assure this House that I have no intention
of urging any deviation from this standard practice, I must ask for
clarification on the entirely separate issue of precisely what led the
RAF to scramble aircraft in the first place, immediately before

these two incidents that now appear to have led tragically to the loss of three lives. Are we now, Madam Speaker, to believe that the primary focus of the RAF's investigation is technical? If this is the case, the question of whether or not to ground the Typhoon fleet is, of course, a matter for the service and I shall press no further on the matter. But if this is not the case; if the focus of the inquiry lies . . . elsewhere . . . then surely this House is entitled to further details of what is under consideration?'

Blackmore was painted into a corner, and he knew it. The HCDC had been strangely quiet about the whole business to date but were now letting everyone know they were going to take a proactive role. Although the HCDC was dominated and indeed chaired by his own political party, Blackmore knew he could expect no favours from them. They were a dedicated group of MPs whose job was to put aspects of military and MOD policy under critical scrutiny – which they were clearly doing. He wondered whether he should have offered Hammond a private – and perhaps classified – brief on events after the first incident and decided that he probably should have: she might have given the Government a slightly easier ride.

Blackmore had a reputation as a straightforward man and had found that the best way to deal with a particularly tricky question like this was not with the sort of prevarication that was all too common in politics but with a quiet and simple state-ment of fact.

'Madam Speaker, I should like to assure my Honourable Friend that there is no area that we are ignoring in our search for answers. We have checked the Typhoon fleet already; we shall check it again. As I have said, the aircraft were scrambled because Fighter Controllers detected anomalous radar returns. As has been made clear previously, radar is an inexact science, but I can assure this House that the matter is being actively investigated as we speak. Indeed, when I leave this chamber I shall be returning to the Ministry of Defence to consult further with the RAF.'

His answer seemed to do the trick. Although the Speaker allowed the debate to go a little longer than he had anticipated –

another four questions were taken – the points raised posed no particular difficulties and were easily dealt with.

As Blackmore left the chamber his mind turned to the seemingly never-ending list of tasks that he'd need to tackle. He'd have to update his ministerial colleagues, and decide with them who should brief the PM and the Palace – warning calls had already been placed to inform them of the loss of the aircraft. Then, perhaps, he'd have time to call in Nick Templeton and take that part of his brief that had been cut short by the news of the latest crash. From the little that Templeton had managed to say, it seemed that there might be rather more to the whole UFO business than met the eye.

Farnham, Surrey

Cody usually screened his calls, because – despite being as careful as he could – his telephone number had inevitably been passed around members of the UFO lobby and had been acquired by some of the stranger characters involved. He had thought of changing it but had decided against this option because of the work of passing the new information to the vast number of legitimate ufologists and journalists who had his contact details. In the end, he had installed another line (his third, given that his fax already had a dedicated line of its own), passing this new number to family members, close friends and a few trusted colleagues only. Occasionally he would pick up the original telephone without first checking who was calling, and this was what he did when he heard the phone ring.

'Hello?'

'Richard Cody?'

'Yes.'

'My name's Tom Stott. Me and two mates were fishing the other night when we saw a UFO.'

'Uh-huh.'

'I can give you all the details if you want. It was a massive great thing, really low. But that's not all. The three of us who saw it got visited by two RAF blokes, and one of them came from that radar base that the papers say was involved in that whole business with those two planes that crashed recently.'

'Do you know the names of these two officers?' *This is getting interesting.*

'Yeah, but there's something else. My mate's got some photos of this UFO. Do you want to see them?'

'Yes, please.'

MOD Main Building, Whitehall

On his return to Main Building Blackmore had been told that there had been no significant developments and that the Air Staff were still collating information. He knew that Templeton would be busy on this but decided to ask him in to finish his UFO brief.

As his PS ushered Templeton into his office, Blackmore wondered who the other man was. Farthing hadn't mentioned that Templeton was going to be bringing somebody with him, which was unusual for her. He could only assume that Templeton had brought one of his staff and not bothered to tell Farthing. Slightly remiss of the man, he thought. And somewhat out of character.

'Nick, hello. Good to see you again.'

'Hello, Minister. May I introduce Wing Commander Terry Carpenter from the DIS. Terry's unit works very closely with Sec(AS) on the UFO issue and carries out some other rather interesting work.'

'Oh?' asked Blackmore as he shook Carpenter's hand.

'I head up a small section called DI(MP) – that's Defence Intelligence (Miscellaneous Projects),' Carpenter explained. 'Our brief is to examine any anomalous phenomena that might benefit – or threaten – defence interests. We examine such things because the consequences of ignoring them if they work would be catastrophic. Remote viewing – so-called psychic spying – is a good example. The Americans ran three official projects on it. If it doesn't work, fine, we lose a little time and money. But if it *does* . . .' His voice trailed off. The point had been made: Carpenter felt he'd gone on a little too long for someone only present in a support role.

'And does it work?' Blackmore was clearly interested.

'Sometimes it does seem to produce better results than chance alone would allow. But, to be fair, there is a counter-view that says you'd get the occasional success through the laws of chance themselves.'

'I suppose I'd heard about old Soviet research into parapsychology,' Blackmore mused. 'I wasn't aware that we were in the same business. I think I'd like a more detailed brief on your activities once this particular crisis is over.'

'At your convenience, Minister.'

At that point one of the outer-office clerks appeared with coffee, and then retreated, closing the door behind him. Templeton resumed his brief, repeating a few introductory facts and figures about the number and types of sightings reported to the MOD.

'But far more interesting, Minister, is the handful of sightings that appear to defy explanation altogether. These are the *real* UFO sightings, and the fact that we are aware of such things is why we must raise the matter in connection with the loss of our aircraft. The Civil Aviation Authority, for example, have several reports on their files of near misses between aircraft and UFOs. In some of these cases air traffic controllers were able to verify the existence of the mystery object on radar.'

Templeton handed the Minister a file. Blackmore's first reaction was surprise at its colour: the dark red indicated that it contained information classified as Top Secret. This was the highest of the basic classification categories used by the Department, though even Top Secret information could be further controlled by use of a caveat that limited access to certain specified people.

'This, Minister, is the file on an event known as the Rendlesham Forest incident. Various USAF personnel at RAF Bentwaters/ Woodbridge witnessed UFO activity over a series of nights. The Defence Radiological Protection Service confirmed that radiation readings taken from the alleged landing site were ten times what they should have been for the area. It is also claimed – although the report wasn't verified – that a light beam from the UFO penetrated the Weapons Storage Area and struck the nuclear weapons.'

Blackmore flicked through the file, reading snatches of reports and analyses from various military witnesses and experts. He'd actually heard of the Rendlesham Forest incident: by a bizarre coincidence he knew that one of his neighbours in the fashionable apartment building where he lived was an author who'd written about the case. But it was a large block and, fortunately, their paths hadn't crossed. He could just imagine what would have happened if she'd realized her neighbour was a defence minister. Blackmore wanted to read on, but Templeton had more papers in his hands and was clearly eager to continue.

'Please take a look at this photograph,' Templeton went on, handing it to the Minister. 'This was taken in August 1990 near Pitlochry in Scotland, by a member of the public. The individual concerned passed it to a Scottish newspaper, who in turn forwarded it to Sec(AS), asking for our view on whether or not it was a hoax. It was subjected to rigorous testing by experts at JARIC and elsewhere. Good UFO photographs are rarer than you might suppose. Most of them show an object in the sky and nothing else. But this one was at low altitude, so features on the ground are shown as well. That means we can calculate height, distance from the camera and, most important of all – size. This object, Minister, has a diameter of around thirty metres.'

'Bloody hell.'

'A few more examples, if I may,' Templeton continued. 'In November of 1990 a squadron of Tornado jets were overtaken by a UFO over the North Sea. Earlier that same year, in March, the Belgians detected a UFO on national and NATO radar systems and launched two F-16s to try and intercept the object. The aircraft picked it up on their airborne radars and achieved a number of lock-ons. The object seemed to be aware of this – and broke the locks.'

This really got Blackmore's attention. 'That doesn't sound too dissimilar from the situation we're dealing with.'

'Precisely.'

'Are the Air Staff liaising with the Belgians as part of the Board of Inquiry work we're doing?'

'At my suggestion, yes, they will follow up this line of inquiry, Minister.'

'Good. Go on.'

'As another example of the sort of case that we do take seriously, a UFO was seen flying over RAF Cosford and RAF Shawbury in March 1993. The guard patrol at Cosford filed a report and the Met Officer at Shawbury got the fright of his life. He described a craft the size of a jumbo jet and firing a beam of light at the ground, maintaining the thing went over his head at a height of no more than two hundred feet. And so it goes on. Every year we have a hard core of cases – around twenty or thirty out of the seven hundred or so reports that come our way – that we can't pin down. And what we have to bear in mind is that there's chronic under-reporting of these things, either because people simply don't know who to report to or because of their fear of ridicule. So we may only be looking at the tip of the iceberg anyway.'

Templeton had clearly reached the end of his prepared brief, and the rather taciturn Wing Commander was clearly not going to leap in, unbidden, with any comments of his own. Blackmore was intrigued, though, and decided to press the DIS man.

'So what, precisely, is *your* interest in this?'

'The bottom line, Minister, is that we want the propulsion system.'

Blackmore assumed that Carpenter's short answer was due to a combination of military directness and the traditional reluctance of the DIS to offer anything more than they deemed strictly necessary. Still, the man would clearly respond to a direct order. 'Explain.'

'Take that photo in front of you,' Carpenter began. 'It shows what is almost certainly a structured craft. If that assessment is correct, it clearly deploys a technology way ahead of our own – including that of both our operational *and* prototype craft. In fact, if the reliable reports of the speed and manoeuvrability of these things are accurate, then we're looking at what might be termed quantum-leap technology. It's years beyond anything we've even dreamed about. Now, if somebody is flying this sort of thing operationally, our entire air force is obsolete. We couldn't deal with that.' His finger pointed at the image on the photograph. 'Not if it was hostile. So we want that technology for ourselves. We can tell a fair bit from the photograph – it clearly incorporates some degree of stealth technology – but we want the real thing. If we could get our hands on one, we could back-engineer it and build our own.'

'Why haven't I heard anything about this before?' Blackmore asked, a little sharply.

'Because this isn't hard fact, Minister,' Carpenter replied. 'This is an assessment of the situation worked up by a few of us in the DIS. But it's a minority view, not one supported by the great and the good. Many believe that pictures like this are clever fakes, and seek to explain everything away in terms of misidentifications and – in the case of radar – angels and anaprop.'

'Nick, do you support this assessment?'

'Yes, Minister.'

'Then will someone please explain to me why I've been asked to sign various Parliamentary Enquiries ending with the statement that UFOs are of no defence significance?' The question was delivered with more than a little annoyance. Blackmore was beginning to feel somewhat exposed.

'As you know, Minister,' Templeton explained, 'I'm new in post. The UFO issue is only a tiny part of my division's business and, frankly, when it comes to this subject the noise-to-signal ratio is pretty high. Most of what my desk officer has to contend with consists of vague reports of lights in the sky. And it's hard to concentrate on even that when you're being constantly assailed – as she is – by barking-mad conspiracy theorists who believe we've got dead aliens in the basement. Over the years most of the good material has simply been swamped by a sea of rubbish. As the Wing Commander has said, it's easy to dismiss even this if you want. Another point is the snigger factor: one mention of the word "UFO" and people switch off – their eyes glaze over and they don't want to know. Wing Commander Carpenter and I intend to change this, carry out a proper study and take the whole issue more seriously.'

'We may be too late.'

'I hope not, Minister.'

Blackmore thought for a moment before asking his next question. 'OK, we've skirted around the sixty-four-thousand-dollar question. These UFOs – your hard core of good cases – who's flying them?'

Templeton and Carpenter exchanged glances. Neither man was entirely comfortable about answering a question that both of them had previously discussed and on which both agreed. The civil servant was clearly expected to offer the reply, and duly did so. 'Minister, the modus operandi of these craft does not conform to anything we're familiar with. They do things we simply can't do and they do them in a way that seems not to have any logical purpose. Both of us – and a few others within our respective divisions – believe we do need at least to consider the possibility that these craft are extraterrestrial in origin.'

There was a silence as Blackmore pondered what had just been said. He'd not been surprised, because there had certainly been hints in the briefing, but he'd wanted to hear the man come straight out and say it – which he had, after a fashion. *Need at least to consider the possibility*, he thought. Well, that was a nice way of putting it. Blackmore wasn't convinced, but there was no denying that the briefing had covered some events that were very difficult to explain in conventional terms. He was astute enough to know that the possibility couldn't be ignored, and a good enough judge of character to know that Templeton wasn't prone to flights of fancy. The man had clearly been embarrassed to talk openly about the extraterrestrial hypothesis, even though his own brief had talked about how people's knee-jerk reaction against the word 'UFO' coloured the way in which the issue had been treated.

'OK,' said Blackmore, his mind made up. 'I want you to give this brief to CAS and tell him I want this theory considered in the two Boards of Inquiry. I also want it factored into the Air Staff's discussions about how to respond to any other radar returns like the ones we've seen recently.'

The two men rose to leave, but something at the back of Blackmore's mind that had been bothering him suddenly came into focus and he held up his hand in a way that brought Templeton and Carpenter back to their seats. 'Wait a minute. Why is the Rendlesham Forest file classified Top Secret? It may be spectacular and unexplained, but TS seems a bit steep, even bearing in mind the nuclear angle – which I thought you said was unverified anyway?'

Templeton looked decidedly awkward. 'Er, it's not so much because of the incident itself but because of what happened afterwards.'

'Oh?'

'Well, it seems that the American authorities may not have been entirely straight with us over what happened.'

Chapter Five

EXPOSURE

RAF Feltwell, Norfolk

East Anglia was an area with a concentrated military presence, which was simply a legacy of history. The east was the direction from which the aerial threat to Britain had always come – whether the Luftwaffe in the Second World War or the later Soviet threat that, thankfully, had never turned into actual conflict. Not far from the town of Cambridge lay two massive bases operated by the United States Air Force. Mildenhall and Lakenheath were nominally RAF bases with an RAF Commander, but in truth this was a fiction designed simply to satisfy the legal niceties of the Status of Forces Act. Stepping onto the bases was like stepping into small-town America, right down to the burger bars and bowling alleys.

A few miles from these USAF bases lay an altogether lesser-known facility. RAF Feltwell was another US base: it was under the control of the United States Air Force Space and Missile Defence Command. Home to the Deep Space Tracking Facility, its primary mission was to track satellites, space probes and space debris. But there was a secondary mission, the details of which were known only to a handful of the Americans at the base – and to none of the British. The secondary mission could be carried out easily because it involved little more than searching the same regions of space that one would check for satellites – even though the actual targets were rather more exotic.

The USAF colonel in charge of the base was pondering the orders he'd just received. Bob Zeckle had been expecting the call: he'd been tipped off by his opposite number at the sprawling listening station at Menwith Hill on the North Yorkshire moors, even before the media broke the story of the downed aircraft. Part of him rebelled against the thought of keeping the British in the dark. *They're supposed to be our allies, aren't they?* But that was sentimentality, and there was no room for that in his job. Like his boss at Fort Meade, Zeckle was not an evil man – though some might have thought him so, had they known the true nature of his mission. He'd thought about it himself many times over the years but had always come to the same conclusion. He justified his and his colleagues' actions by examining the consequences should their mission fail. The stakes were so high that they not only justified the work they did but made it a necessity. The sign on his office wall said it all: *Failure is not an option.* It was a glib catchphrase put up by his predecessor, but somehow he'd never had the heart to take it down. Maybe it was superstition. Or maybe it was just desperation.

MOD Main Building, Whitehall

Jacqui Connolly barged into Sue Farthing's office unannounced, looking unusually flustered.

'Is the Minister in?' she demanded breathlessly.

'Yes, follow me.'

Farthing would have been within her rights to make Connolly wait, but the Chief Press Officer was one of a handful of those who had virtually unrestricted access to the Minister. Besides, it was clear that something extremely urgent had cropped up. The two women swept into Blackmore's office and Connolly immediately handed the Minister a sheet of paper. It was a colour photocopy of the front page of the *Daily Mail*.

'They've just faxed it over, Minister. This is what they intend to run tomorrow. They've given us advance warning, but only because they want a comment from us.'

'Shit.'

Farthing was slower than the Minister, since she was having to read the headline upside down. When she worked it out the colour drained from her face. *Did this shoot down RAF Jets?* the headline read. Underneath was a photograph of a delta-shaped craft over what appeared to be a lake. Before she could offer any opinion, Blackmore turned to her.

'I want CAS and Head of Sec(AS) in here right now, together with any of the other key players we can rustle up. Jacqui, I'm going to want options from you: can we dissuade them from running this? If not, can we hit them with a Defence Advisory Notice? Now excuse me for a moment. I have to brief S of S and the PM before the *Daily Mail* fax them too.'

With that the Minister rose and left the room. It was the first time that either Farthing or Connolly had seen him so rattled: this, more than anything else, emphasized the developing sense of crisis.

Farthing stepped back into the Outer Office and started issuing instructions to the APS and the various clerks, leaving Connolly alone with her thoughts. She'd been trained as a journalist and had learned her trade on a series of local papers before becoming disillusioned with the endless flood of provincial trivia that she had to write about. After a short but unrewarding spell on a national newspaper, she'd joined the Central Office of Information. She'd risen quickly through the ranks there, becoming an acknowledged expert on news management, which is the tricky art of promoting good news and playing down bad. She'd been encouraged by the MOD to apply for the job formally known as Director of Information, Strategy and News. However, the role of Chief Press Officer was part of this job and was less of a mouthful.

Connolly had now been with the Department for nearly five years, in what was a difficult job by anybody's standard: while the military did an excellent job overall, there was inevitably a stream of bad news. Aircraft crashed, soldiers started fights in nightclubs and, since the law had changed a few years ago, a seemingly endless stream of service personnel had taken the Ministry to court, seeking damages for injury or stress. Noise from low-flying jets, the scandal of gays and even transsexuals in the armed forces, nuclear test veterans with cancer: the list of thorny issues seemed endless. Still, it was a job she loved.

But Connolly had never come across anything remotely like the situation they now faced. Without the benefit of any precedent to fall back on, she would have to rely on her instincts. The irony of somebody trained as a journalist being asked to kill a story – or at the very least put an entirely different spin on it – wasn't lost on her, and part of her secretly wished to be on the *Daily Mail* team who were clearly well-informed about the loss of the Typhoons. She could imagine the excitement in their offices. This was going to be difficult, but there might yet be a way around the situation.

Frantic calls were made, and in some cases meetings had been broken up to get hold of various senior personnel. But the Minister's wishes had been met, and within fifteen minutes most of those headquarters personnel involved in the earlier discussions about the loss of the Typhoons had assembled in the office where they were intently studying the fax from the *Daily Mail*. Connolly was not surprised to see that the Secretary of State and the Chief of the Defence Staff had arrived: there were decisions to be made that would need a ruling from the very top.

Protocol demanded that S of S chair the meeting, even though Blackmore had been running with the issue. Everyone present had received at least a basic briefing already.

Tom Willoughby was portrayed in the media as a competent but not brilliant Defence Secretary who owed his position more to his closeness to the Prime Minister's party connections than to his political ability. But he was more astute than many realized and his quiet demeanour masked a sharp intellect. It was he who began the impromptu meeting by turning to CDS and CAS and asking the question everybody wanted answering.

'Thank you for coming at such short notice. Perhaps I could

start by asking if anybody can answer the *Daily Mail*'s question. *Is that thing responsible for the loss of our aircraft?*'

The question was probably a fairer one for CAS, not least because the current CDS was an Army officer. But the military were passionate adherents to the chain of command and CDS would not have dreamt of leaving his subordinate to face the music when he was on hand to provide the only answer any of them could give.

'We don't know. JARIC are looking at the picture now, but they've only got a faxed version of *this* fax. They really can't be expected to give anything other than a tentative opinion without seeing the original photograph, the negative and the camera. I've had a brief conversation with the CO and she says there are no obvious signs of hoaxing. Frankly, that was no surprise. The *Daily Mail* have some pretty sophisticated image–processing equipment themselves, as do all the nationals. They're responsible enough to have made some fairly thorough checks on the material they have and, frankly, they wouldn't have come to us if they weren't convinced. Right, Jacqui?'

He'd glanced at the CPO because he was aware that he'd strayed into her area of expertise. Politeness and a desire to be backed up on what he'd just said demanded that he seek her opinion.

Connolly nodded in agreement. 'Absolutely. This could really blow up in their faces if it's a fake. It would totally undermine their credibility and be an absolute gift to their rivals. They are very, *very* sure they've got something solid here.'

'Can we stop the story?' asked CDI.

'Absolutely not,' Connolly shot back. 'As you know, Defence Advisory Notices don't have the clout of the old D-Notices. The system is effectively voluntary. Now, most of the responsible media abide by the rules, but it's a two-way street. We have to play fair with the press and not use the system to stamp on a story that's just difficult or embarrassing. The simple truth is that this doesn't fall into any category of information we can legitimately suppress. But there's another problem. The editor rang me, basically to make sure I was aware how serious they were about running this. The chap who approached the paper is champing at the bit to put the picture out on the Internet. He's been paid, and under the agreement with the paper he gets to put it out at ten a.m. tomorrow, if he wants, whether or not the *Daily Mail* has run it. Now, he negotiated that deal himself, and got twenty-five thousand pounds for it, so he clearly knows the media very well. To complicate matters, the *Daily Mail* are also thinking of sharing the story with *Newsnight.* That means all the other papers will run the story, but the second editions will pick it up anyway and they won't have the photo. So the *Daily Mail* may go for it, probably on condition that their editor gets on the programme. If that happens, *Newsnight* will undoubtedly want a Defence Minister to go on the programme.'

'Do we play ball?' asked S of S bluntly.

'I don't recommend it. There are plenty of cases of our not going on recently, so declining the invitation isn't the big deal it would've been a few years back. I recommend we prepare a statement here, at this meeting, and release it to the *Daily Mail.* Then we can give the same thing to *Newsnight* if they ask, and send it to the Press Office to use as a defensive line to take.'

'Could we undermine the story by issuing the statement now, and effectively scooping the *Daily Mail?*' CAS asked. 'If they no longer have the exclusive, there's less of a story, and maybe they'll drop it.'

'Again, I really wouldn't recommend it,' Connolly replied. 'The story will still run, and although we'll have got our shot in first, the media will spot at once that we've run the story as a spoiler. That'll make them suspicious; they'll wonder why we're being so defensive.'

'Let me go back to the issue of killing the story altogether,' Willoughby retorted. 'Surely we could make a case for saying that it's an operational matter, with lives at stake?'

'I don't think we could justify it,' Connolly replied. 'I don't dispute that it's an operational matter, and as lives have already been lost it's reasonable to say lives are still at stake. But that's justification for refusing to comment, not for trying to stop the piece running. Whether the story runs or not won't compromise our activities or endanger personnel; *that's* the acid test. What's more, if we try to say that the current situation is covered by a Notice, the paper will almost certainly disagree and ignore us. Then we're in the situation where we've drawn attention to it by trying to ban it'

'*Can* they just *ignore* a Notice?' asked ACAS.

'They can't *ignore* the Notices; they're an extant series of papers covering very specific topics. But they can and almost certainly would argue that the Notices simply don't cover the current situation. On that basis they would still publish.'

'I presume any attempt to use the law would be similarly inappropriate,' US of S asked.

'That's right, Minister.' Connolly was grateful that Blackmore understood the realities of the situation. 'If we sought an injunction we'd have to convince a judge that the story would harm the national interest. It's *possible* that we might get a sympathetic judge who'd rule in our favour, but I have to say it's unlikely. The story doesn't help terrorists or enemies of the state. In my view most judges would throw out our request. Seeking an injunction would be a high-risk strategy that would almost certainly rebound on us. Remember all the fuss with books like *Spycatcher* and *Open Skies, Closed Minds?*'

'Yes,' CDS mused. 'And the story's still running on the Internet tomorrow, unless we can do something about that – which I assume is equally difficult, if not more so?'

'Yes,' Connolly replied. She was about to elaborate when S of S raised his hand and cut her off.

'OK, I think we've covered all the bases here,' Willoughby said. 'I think it's clear that any attempt to suppress this story with a Defence Advisory Notice or an injunction would not succeed. Furthermore, the end result of trying to kill the piece would simply be to draw attention to it. So if we can't kill it, how can we best deal with it? Jacqui?'

Connolly felt that S of S's intervention had been timely, as the discussion had been in danger of bogging down. She was convinced that killing the story was neither justifiable nor possible, and was keen to agree a strategy for the more realistic option of simply lessening the story's impact.

'The first option is a little cheeky, but has been done before. We simply come up with something big that'll ensure that the media don't pick the story up as much as they clearly will at the moment. But that's entirely dependent upon our having something suitable up our sleeves. Frankly, I don't think there is anything at the moment, although we could always widen the net with other Government departments.' She left unsaid one thought that she was ashamed of but that was a cold fact of life in the world of media management: the hope that there would be some massive catastrophe or the death of a global celebrity that would force the story off the front page.

'What else?' Willoughby's tone and expression clearly indicated that he didn't see much hope in the first option.

'Then we're talking about a standard damage-limitation job. We manage the story as well as we can, and try to respond in a way that makes our point of view seem reasonable. We decline to put anyone up to appear in the media, and avoid giving the impression that we're rattled.'

'Let's rough something out now,' Willoughby ordered. 'It seems silly not to take the opportunity of clearing something when we're all here.'

Connolly was extremely grateful for S of S's suggestion, which would save her the time-consuming and potentially difficult task of circulating a statement and getting agreement after the meeting. She'd already jotted down a few thoughts, and was able to offer them up straightaway. 'How about something like this: "The investigations into the recent loss of three Typhoons and the tragic death of the pilots continue, and we will leave no stone unturned in our search for answers. It would be inappropriate to enter into public debate at this stage, because this might prejudge the Boards of Inquiry currently being held. We have seen the story in the *Daily Mail* and will look into the possibility of a connection with the loss of our aircraft".'

There were appreciative nods from the assembled personnel. It was clearly for S of S to respond. 'I like it,' he said. 'It's straightforward and short, which should minimize the possibility of our becoming embroiled in a messy debate, because there'll be less to analyse. I'm also clear that we don't put anybody up to go on *Newsnight* or any other programme. We'll tough it out.' He looked around the table. His decision was made, and there would be no going back on that, but he needed to keep everybody onside and wanted to see if anybody had any useful ideas. 'Anyone have any comments or suggestions?'

'I have one suggestion,' CAS ventured. 'The *Daily Mail* piece doesn't talk about a UFO. The word isn't mentioned once, and you can tell from their somewhat awkward turn of phrase – "structured craft of unknown origin" – that they're desperate to avoid using the word. They're falling over themselves to appear reasonable, and I was wondering if we might be able to undermine the story by using it ourselves. Something like "As for the *Daily Mail*'s speculation about UFOs . . ." We could even bring in the phrase "flying saucers" and really put the boot in.'

S of S looked around the table with an expression that invited views on CAS's idea. It was Templeton who spoke up.

'Until we really know why our aircraft crashed and whether there's anything to the *Daily Mail* story, I'd caution against your approach. It could rebound on us.'

'Only if our Typhoons *were* brought down by a UFO,' CAS retorted.

'Well, we really don't know—'. Templeton stopped abruptly when he saw S of S raise his hand.

'Jacqui?' Willoughby was controlling the meeting tightly, and had effectively defused what was obviously going to be a circular argument between CAS and Head of Sec(AS).

'CAS's idea has merit,' Connolly began, 'but we don't want to look as if we're being *too* clever here. It will be seen for what it is – an attempt to undermine the story by trivializing it. Again, the impression will be that we have something to hide.'

'But surely the UFO angle will be played out anyway, on the

Internet?' It was ACAS, backing up his boss but making a valid point nonetheless.

'But there's always wild speculation on the Internet, on all manner of defence issues,' Connolly replied. 'We wouldn't and couldn't respond to all the bizarre stories and allegations that appear. But, bluntly, the Internet doesn't matter, because even where there is an accurate, well-sourced piece it's lost in a sea of rubbish. The *Daily Mail* is different altogether. What they say matters.'

'I agree. Thank you, Jacqui.' Willoughby's decision ended the debate but there were other issues to address. 'Now, when this story runs, someone's almost certainly going to ask questions in the House. We need to make sure we're ready for anything Parliament or the HCDC throws at us. I assume we can simply expand and update existing material?'

'Absolutely,' Templeton replied. 'I'll be doing that immediately after this meeting.'

'Good. Thank you, ladies and gentlemen. If there's no further business, let's get to work.'

RAF Coningsby, Lincolnshire

'Nobody knows what's going on, and we're all pretty wound up.'

Isabelle Bentley had run into the Station Commander quite by chance and he'd taken the opportunity to ask her how the pilots were shaping up. She had a reputation as a person who spoke her mind and although Group Captain Robert Lindley was a CO who respected the chain of command, he also recognized the value of an informal chat with someone who could tell him what was going on at the coalface.

'But you've seen the Strike Command brief, haven't you?'

'Yes, sir, but all it really says is that they don't know what's happening. We've lost three aircraft, and nobody seems sure if there's a fault with the Typhoons or not. There are rumours that the fleet's going to be grounded, then we're told to carry on as normal. Then there are rumours that the aircraft collided with an

RPV, or were shot down by a prototype Russian craft. There's even some nonsense being spouted about UFOs.'

'Do *you* think it's nonsense?'

'Sir?'

Lindley looked straight at Bentley. 'I saw a UFO once. I was flying a Phantom back from Germany and was over the North Sea at the time. Suddenly I caught sight of something out of the corner of my eye. A few hundred metres away, on the port side of my aircraft, there was a metallic, saucer-shaped object that seemed to be keeping pace with me. I was transfixed. I watched it for about thirty seconds, then it shot off at incredible speed.' He wasn't quite sure why he'd told Bentley about the incident. He'd only ever told one other person: his wife.

'Did you report it, sir?'

Lindley shook his head. 'No. I was on my first flying tour. I didn't want anyone questioning my judgement.'

'What do you think it was?'

'I don't know, but it was like nothing I'd ever seen before or have seen since. That was over twenty years ago, so if it was a prototype I think we'd have seen the production model by now. The truth is that I don't know what it was. But I did see something, and it wasn't one of ours. So don't be too quick to dismiss talk of UFOs. Look, I'm grateful for your candour. I'll organize a briefing later today and speak to all the pilots personally. I can't promise you any answers, but maybe a frank discussion will help the situation.'

'Thank you, sir, I think it will.'

Lindley walked off, leaving the young pilot alone with her thoughts. In the normal course of business it would be quite funny, she thought. *The CO's seen a flying saucer!* But somehow it didn't strike her as remotely amusing now.

BBC Television Studios, White City

Richard Cody took a deep breath and cautioned himself to speak slowly. He'd lost count of the number of times he'd already appeared on television, but he was still a little nervous at what lay ahead. A live appearance on *Newsnight* was an unprecedented opportunity to interest the public in UFOs. But more than that, he mused, the *Newsnight* audience of around seven million viewers included a high proportion of influential people. Senior folk from the world of politics, the military, the Civil Service and the business community would be watching. This was the Establishment audience that he'd always tried to reach, but with little success. A rare opportunity to do so was now just moments away. Cody had left nothing to chance, and had prepared meticulously from the moment when he'd been contacted just a few hours before. He'd spent a long time pondering which suit to wear and must have tried on at least a dozen ties before satisfying himself that he'd found the right combination. Having negotiated the deal with the *Daily Mail* – the money being split equally between the three witnesses, having refused to take a fee himself – he had been initially surprised to hear that the paper had brought in *Newsnight*, although he soon recognized that the deal benefited everyone. The programme had sent a crew up to Norfolk to interview the three witnesses on location. Cody had been glad of that, because he'd been worried that they wouldn't be particularly articulate in a TV studio and saw the benefits of pre-recording their interview on their home ground. As it happened, they'd been very impressive, and as he and the other interviewees watched on the monitor, he had to admit that their plain-speaking, East Anglian-accented statements came across well, precisely because they were such no-frills accounts.

'OK, we'll be live in about thirty seconds, and I'll go to you first, David.' Marcus Rosental, the feared presenter of *Newsnight*, had an engaging style. Live television was quite an ordeal, but Rosental had the knack of sounding so laid-back that he put everyone at ease. Sometimes that was a deliberate tactic designed to lull a politician into a false sense of security, but mostly – as now – it was a very professional way of making contributors less nervous and therefore getting the best from them.

'So there you have it. Three men out fishing on the Norfolk Broads. Three men who claim to have seen a flying saucer. Three men who have what they say is a photograph of that UFO. David Scott, editor of the *Daily Mail*, why have you decided to put this story on the front page of your paper tomorrow?'

'We've subjected that photograph to extensive in-house analysis, and taken it to a commercial company who specialize in image enhancement and analysis of CCTV imagery for the police. As far as any of us can tell, the photograph is authentic, and shows a craft roughly fifty feet above the water and one hundred and twenty feet in diameter.'

'But presumably you paid them handsomely for this picture?'

'A fee was paid, yes, but it wouldn't have been paid if the picture didn't check out.'

'OK, but these days you can produce some pretty convincing material on a number of commercially available image-processing packages. Couldn't someone knock something like this up on a PC very easily?'

'We believe we could spot a fake. But the real story here concerns the RAF, who actually sent people round to interview the witnesses and asked for copies of this photograph and the others that were taken. The personnel were from RAF Coltishall and RAF Neatishead, and we believe there is a connection between this and the recent loss of the three RAF Typhoon jets.'

'Richard Cody, you've investigated UFO sightings for many years now, and are a respected authority on the subject; what do you think?'

'It's the most exciting case I've ever been involved with. But, setting that aside, we want some questions answered by the Government. Are they going to look at this new evidence as part of the investigation into the loss of their three aircraft? Were the RAF tasked with obtaining the photographic evidence from these witnesses? Were—'

'Well, OK,' Rosental interrupted, 'but you won't believe the Government anyway, will you? People like you think that the Government are covering up the truth about UFOs, don't you?'

'I believe they're not being entirely straight with us, yes. But don't forget, there's compelling evidence for this statement. Look at the material that's come out in the last few years as a result of the Freedom of Information Act. We've found out that there's been a cat-and-mouse game going on between the RAF and UFOs for the last sixty years. UFOs are routinely tracked on radar, jets have been scrambled, pilots have seen them and UFOs have flown directly over military bases. This isn't in dispute, don't forget. This comes from the Ministry of Defence's own files. You can go to the Public Record Office and—'

'Sure, sure,' Rosental interrupted again, 'but I assume it's just a matter of interpretation. When we talk about UFOs we may simply be talking about misidentifications of something quite ordinary, or sightings of secret military craft. On that point let me bring in Sally Roe from *Jane's Defence Weekly*. What do you make of this photograph?'

'It's fascinating. My best assessment is that it could be some sort of prototype military craft – an unmanned drone, perhaps. There are quite a lot of RAF bases in East Anglia and it's possible that something exotic was being tested.'

'But if that was the case there surely couldn't be a connection with the loss of the Typhoons?'

'I don't know. Accidents happen, but it does seem unlikely that there would be two separate incidents.'

Rosental picked up a sheet of paper and put on his glasses. 'We did ask a Defence Minister to come on the programme, but nobody was willing to appear. The Ministry of Defence did send us this statement. They say it would be inappropriate to comment on these specific allegations while the Boards of Inquiry are still carrying out their investigation, but they assure us that *every* possible explanation will be considered. Well, there you have it. Flying saucers or secret prototypes? Tragic accidents, or sinister Government cover-ups? The truth, as they say, is out there. The main headlines again . . .'

So that was it. Cody never ceased to be amazed at how quickly time spent on live television passed. He began to analyse his performance. He'd only had time to make two brief comments but he was relatively pleased. More importantly, the other contributors had all been effective and he was convinced that the segment had come out well. He felt slightly guilty that he hadn't mentioned Dr Krone's work and their theory about conscious recall of alien abduction, even though he felt there was a connection. But he'd decided that this would simply make the whole topic seem cranky, so had decided against it. He wouldn't have had time, in any case, and it would have been foolish to shift the focus around too much within such a short item.

Cody allowed himself to relax a little. He was looking forward to a gin and tonic or two in the hospitality room and a leisurely drive back in the courtesy car. He toyed with the idea of allowing himself a lie-in the following morning, but decided against it. He knew that a high-profile media appearance would inevitably generate further enquiries and requests and he didn't want to miss out on any chances to push home the message. He knew that tomorrow was going to be a busy day and, even if there were no early-morning calls from the media, his Internet message was going to go out at ten a.m. It was already set up, but he wanted to check it at least once more.

Egerton Gardens, Knightsbridge
The *Newsnight* credits were still scrolling up when Blackmore's telephone rang.

'Hello?'

'Good evening, Minister, it's Jacqui Connolly here. I just wanted to touch base with you.'

'Good evening, Jacqui. I thought it went as well as could be expected. There were no surprises.'

'I agree. I think it was good news for us in two ways. First, it was a much shorter piece than I'd anticipated. More importantly, it was on last. That means the audience figures would have been declining as people went to bed, but best of all, it's what we call the "skateboarding duck slot". Wacky stories always get put on last, even on *Newsnight*. Any piece that begins "And finally" – you know what I mean; people don't take it that seriously.'

'Excellent. Still, it'll be a busy day tomorrow: it'll be on the front page of the *Daily Mail* and whatever other papers decide to run the story.'

'That's right,' Connolly replied. 'But only the *Daily Mail* has rights to the photo, and that may discourage others from running the story on the front page because they'd be seen as competing directly with the *Mail* but very obviously coming off second-best. Furthermore, their rivals may gamble on the photos turning out to be a hoax and the whole thing blowing up in their faces.'

'OK, well, I don't suppose we can do much more this evening. Thank you very much for all your hard work. It really has been appreciated. Goodnight.'

'Thank you, Minister. Goodnight.'

RAF Menwith Hill, Yorkshire

They had been caught by surprise. Despite a multimillion dollar array of eavesdropping equipment that would have surprised – and horrified – their UK hosts, the National Security Agency facility had only found out about the *Newsnight* piece a few minutes before it ran. A series of frantic telephone calls had followed, and when the Commanding Officer placed his call to Fort Meade, he hoped his voice sounded calm. He was one of a handful of people who knew the number of Van Buren's direct line.

'Good evening, sir.'

'Good evening.' Even though it was a secure line, neither man took any chances: each recognized the other's voice, so there was no need to mention names or locations.

'I have flash traffic for you, sir. We're sending it across now. When you've seen it, you may wish to discuss the situation. I'll be standing by for your call.'

'Thank you. I'll be in touch.'

Rowledge, Surrey

Jenny Thornton was in a good mood. She'd watched *Newsnight*, and had been pleased at the way the piece had gone. It had been infuriatingly short, of course, but she knew that five minutes on

Newsnight was worth more than ten hours of ordinary UFO documentary. For a start, only the believers tended to watch programmes specifically about UFOs so it was simply preaching to the converted. But when a news programme ran a piece about UFOs, people with little or no prior interest would be exposed to it, and the message would be spread to a wider audience. But she knew that what she'd seen earlier in the evening went much further than that. *Newsnight* was not simply a news programme, it was the Establishment's news programme and, like the *Today* programme on Radio Four, things said on the show reached an audience that included most of the key players in the world of politics and the Civil Service.

Thornton was nobody's fool, and over the years she'd had long conversations with Cody and other major players in the UFO lobby about how to raise the profile of the subject with the Establishment and get the message across to the wider public. They had sometimes referred to ufology as a cause, and despite the unwelcome intrusion of cranks and cultists there *were* serious people involved, some of whom were in high places. The fear of ridicule, coupled with concerns about career advancement, ensured that these people generally stayed silent, but people like Thornton and Cody knew several MPs who were actively interested in the subject and who were prepared to table the occasional question in Parliament, even if publicly they said they were doing so only in response to requests from constituents.

It was now several hours since the *Newsnight* piece, but Thornton had recorded it and replayed the item several times. She had a vast collection of UFO programmes on video, all of which were meticulously catalogued. This was partly due to her being an abductee, but also because she had progressively been becoming more active as a UFO lobbyist. Traditionally, UFO witnesses and abductees had taken a more passive role. Their stories had been used by writers and researchers and they themselves had been wheeled out on various TV shows, more to satisfy audience curiosity than out of genuine interest. But there had been a backlash against this and some witnesses were beginning to feel exploited. Thornton didn't quite see it in those terms – mainly, she suspected, because she worked with Cody, who had always behaved honourably and fairly towards witnesses – but she'd certainly adopted a more proactive role of late, and had been writing articles and giving interviews herself, talking about wider issues than her own experience.

Cody had encouraged Thornton in this and had suggested that it might be a useful tool of empowerment – his favourite word these days. Indeed, she'd begun to work as Cody's research assistant on several projects and had become more involved in the running of his witness support group. Cody had suggested that the more involved she became in ufology, and the more she helped spread the word, the less she'd regard herself as a victim. If the aliens operated covertly, anything she could do to lift the veil of secrecy was a form of fighting back.

Thornton poured herself another large vodka and tonic and mused on this idea of covert operation. If the aliens didn't want to be discovered, and went to great lengths to keep their activities secret, then trying to expose what was going on was fine, she decided. But if they didn't care any more, and made no effort to hide what they were doing, was she really fighting back at all? It was a depressing thought, and one that punctured her previously upbeat mood. She analysed her own position and realized, not for the first time, that she knew exactly why she was still up at two in the morning. *Less time for anything to happen.* And as for the alcohol, where her intake had increased recently, she was astute enough to see it for what it was. *Anaesthetic.*

Chapter Six

THUNDER CHILD

MOD Main Building, Whitehall

Jacqui Connolly walked into the Press Office just a little before
seven a.m. and could see immediately that Bob Pilkington, the
Duty Press Officer, had had a busy night. He looked as if he'd been
through the mill. His jacket and tie were off and his shirt was
unbuttoned at the neck. His desk was strewn with papers, post-it
notes and a few empty chocolate wrappers and yet, despite the
apparent chaos, Connolly knew that everything was all right.
Pilkington was a safe pair of hands – as were all those who worked
the difficult night shift – who could be relied upon to handle
matters on his own initiative but who wouldn't be afraid to wake up
key personnel in the middle of the night if he felt it was justified.

It soon emerged that, as had been predicted, most of
Pilkington's shift had been taken up with dealing with the fallout
from the *Newsnight* piece. All the national newspapers had
telephoned demanding information, as had countless television
and radio stations, local papers and specialist aviation publica-
tions. There had been the predictable crank calls, too. Most callers
had been satisfied with the MOD's statement, which was short

enough to fit onto one sheet of A4 paper. This one piece of paper had been through the fax well over a hundred times. But some callers had not been satisfied with this and had followed up with further questions. For these, Pilkington had drawn upon the comprehensive defensive lines to take that had gone into the original news brief – and were expanding in the light of experience, as the Press Office began to get a feel for particular areas of media interest. He'd known that things would be quiet until after *Newsnight*, so he had spent the early part of his shift reading and rereading the briefing pack until he was as familiar as possible with the material.

As a result of this preparation, Pilkington's answers had been delivered with the quiet confidence that came from familiarity with the subject under discussion. Inevitably, he had been caught out a few times by obscure questions that nobody had anticipated or by technical points that hadn't been covered. But this was par for the course and he knew he'd done well. He'd be handing over to the day shift in just over an hour's time and had been writing his handover brief, filled with key points and pending actions.

Connolly tried to keep their chat short as she knew Pilkington was still extremely busy, but she needed to know about any important developments. He'd been listening to the radio and television news throughout the night, and had been flicking between the channels to watch the various breakfast news programmes. He'd also taken delivery of the papers but was still awaiting delivery of the all-important daily press summary. These summaries were prepared not by the Press Office but by a private company and consisted of a pack made up from every defence-related story featured in the national press and the key international papers. The summary was divided up under various headings, of which news concerning the RAF was one. Clearly this was going to be the biggest section in today's summary, and they'd be able to tell at a glance how well the MOD had come out of the affair.

That said, Connolly and Pilkington knew that the worst was probably yet to come. The story had featured heavily in all the nationals, although none of the other tabloids had led with it.

Although not the lead story in any of the broadsheets either, it had made the front page – in varying degrees of prominence – of the *Guardian,* the *Independent* and *The Times*. The *Daily Telegraph* had covered the story, too, but not on the front page. This meant that many media people would be waking up to the news for the first time and would themselves be following up on the existing coverage.

'What's your overall impression, Bob?'

'It's not as bad as I'd expected. The other papers didn't like the *Daily Mail* having exclusive rights on the picture, and the fact that they couldn't run the photo – when that was really the main part of the story – seems to have worked for us. Some of the main stories are written around the *Daily Mail* running the piece and don't really focus on the loss of the aircraft. There's a detectable "Have they gone potty?" theme running through some of the coverage.'

'Excellent. But the Internet story runs at 10 a.m., and we don't know what deal might have been done allowing other papers to use the photograph now the *Daily Mail* has got its exclusive.' Connolly had been worried about this, but short of asking staff at the paper, or even making contact with Cody, there was nothing she could do about it. They'd simply have to wait and see.

'Yeah, well, I guess we'll find out soon enough,' Pilkington nodded. 'But, as you instructed, our statement's gone up on the main MOD website and on the RAF site as well. We'll just do our best to ride it out, same as usual.'

Connolly had to agree. The focus would now inevitably shift to Parliament. Sec(AS) would have another busy day, of that she had no doubt. One more thing to check. 'How many bottles do you owe, Bob?'

Pilkington smiled. It was a rule that all press officers had to do their best to keep their names out of the papers and ensure that they were referred to simply as 'Ministry of Defence spokespersons'. But journalists were pushy beasts and would sometimes press for a name. Eventually, holding the standard line would become counter-productive, and the name would be duly given. The penalty was a bottle of wine for each time your name appeared in print. 'Three. But one paper called me Rob Pilkington, so I don't think that should count.'

'If you can persuade *Rob* Pilkington to pay up, fine. If not, it's down to you.'

They both laughed, and the moment provided useful light relief during what was turning out to be a testing time for everyone.

RAF Neatishead, Norfolk

Alan Whitfield was in trouble but felt he might have saved someone's life. It wasn't what he'd done but what he'd failed to do: this was why he now found himself in front of the CO. He was glad of the opportunity to explain himself when he made a full report of events to his immediate boss. Maddox and Spink had reviewed the radar tape with Whitfield, who had talked them through what had happened. The CO was frankly stumped.

'In my books that's a pretty inconsequential signal,' Spink mused. 'I wouldn't have authorized a launch on the basis of that in the normal course of business.'

'But we're not in the normal course of business, sir. Given recent events, you *would* and *should* have scrambled jets. That signal's every bit as solid as the ones that preceded the loss of the three Typhoons. I hesitated, sir, it's as simple as that. And I hesitated because I thought maybe it would go away. I did it deliberately, sir, because I didn't want to put some young pilot up against something that's already caused three aircraft to crash and three people to lose their lives.'

'I can't fault your motives,' Spink replied. 'And you were right – it did go away.'

'But it might not have, sir, and if it hadn't we'd have been in trouble because I didn't get AD assets airborne in time.'

Spink pulled out a copy of the *Daily Mail*. 'You've seen this, I presume?'

'Yes, sir.'

'What do you think?'

'I think it's for real.'

'So do I.'

Spink's statement surprised Maddox as well as Whitfield, and prompted him to join in the discussion. 'Why's that, sir? What do Strike Command say?'

'Strike Command aren't saying much, except that they're keeping an open mind and will look into it. But the phone lines have been buzzing this morning, Mike, and I've been talking to other COs. The feeling I get is that the great and the good believe in it. Remember Cosford and Shawbury?'

'1993?'

'Right. I've spoken to some of the people who were there. They've seen the *Daily Mail*, and it's absolutely freaked them out. They say that's what they saw. No doubt about it.'

'But sir,' Whitfield interjected, 'none of this alters the fact that I deliberately held back on scrambling the Q aircraft.'

Spink sighed. 'No, I suppose it doesn't. But I'm not going to hang you out to dry because of that. I might have done the same in your position, I really might. In any case, it doesn't matter now.'

'Oh?'

'It's all being taken out of our hands, apparently. The Permanent Joint Headquarters are taking over and what's more they've requested that you be seconded to them for the duration of this crisis. *Apparently* they think you might be quite a good Fighter Controller.' He smiled, and had the satisfaction of seeing that Whitfield was smiling too.

DERA, Farnborough

All those involved with the operation knew that time was of the essence. HMS *Lancaster* had finally located the area where the first two aircraft had crashed and had recovered a small piece of wreckage that had been flown to the Defence Evaluation and Research Agency site at Farnborough, using the ship's Lynx anti-submarine helicopter. HMS *Lancaster* would stay on site while commercial vessels were tasked with recovering the rest of the wreckage, and HMS *Kent* had been dispatched to the area where the third Typhoon might have crashed. But everyone knew that the recovery of what looked like a large piece of fuselage from one of the first two aircraft to go down was a real breakthrough.

Dr Barbara North, the Chief Scientific Adviser, had cut short her holiday, returned and been briefed. Various key DERA personnel from Malvern had been flown to Farnborough on a specially tasked RAF Puma helicopter. The timing had worked out almost perfectly and the scientists arrived only a few minutes after the wreckage they were to examine. Needless to say, the scientists based at Farnborough were already examining the material, as were a couple of RAF flight safety experts. The detailed analysis would take days, if not weeks, but it was soon clear that they had all they needed for an initial assessment.

Dr Lisa Kaminsky lifted the phone and patched a call through to CSA.

'We have our preliminary assessment.'

'Yes?'

'The fuselage shows signs of having been struck by an extremely powerful heat source. I'd say the aircraft was hit by a projected-energy weapon.'

CSA was shocked at the statement but not unduly surprised. She'd been briefed on the radar data and had viewed the tapes personally – several times – with Mahmood Nahar. 'How sure are you of that assessment? I have to go to S of S and CDS with this, right after this call.'

'I'm as sure as I can be; we all are. The only things I know that could cause anything like this are the American Kinetic Energy Anti-Satellite System, or maybe the MIRACL ground-based laser which, as you know, is another American anti-satellite system. But the damage we've got here goes beyond KE-ASAT or MIRACL. It's more focused and higher-energy. This is like – well, like something out of a science-fiction film. I'm sorry, I don't know what else to say.'

'Don't apologize. I'm grateful for your assessment. But stay on it, and let me know the moment you have anything that may be of interest. I mean *anything*, OK?'

'OK.'

'Have you seen this morning's *Daily Mail*?'

'No.'

'You should. You *really* should. Goodbye.'

'Goodbye.' Kaminsky was puzzled by CSA's cryptic comment. Although she'd been far too busy to read the papers, she headed off to find a copy of the *Mail*.

RAF Buchan, Aberdeenshire

If Sue Harding had been on duty it probably wouldn't have happened. She would almost certainly have hesitated – as Whitfield at Neatishead had – when the blip appeared on the radar screen. No Fighter Controller who had seen an aircraft under their control disappear from the screen was ever the same, and Harding would have thought twice before putting more pilots in harm's way when the enemy – if there *was* an enemy – was unknown.

But this was another day, and Flying Officer Lewis Jackson was on duty. Young, keen and eager to make an impression, Jackson had followed unfolding events with a relentless interest and within three minutes of his having seen the unidentified blip on his screen, a pair of Typhoons from RAF Leeming was in the air. Jackson called his boss in: within minutes a flash signal had been sent, calls were being made and duty staff were being briefed.

Jackson was feeling the pressure but didn't show it. He hated people looking over his shoulder at his screen, but could hardly say anything when one of those people was the Station Commander. Staff at Strike Command and Main Building were screaming for information but while others dealt with the stream of calls as best they could, Jackson did his job, talking to the pilots only when he had to, knowing that they had enough on their plates without having to deal with a talkative Fighter Controller. He gave information on the object's position, altitude, speed and heading, managing to keep his voice calm even when the intruder changed course and headed straight for the Typhoons.

'Sector Control to Charlie One and Two, I'm still tracking the uncorrelated target which is now on an intercept course with you. Speed is still circa Mach 3 and I have no IFF.'

'Charlie One to Sector Control, I acknowledge that. We are now tracking the object ourselves. Estimated time to contact is now six minutes.'

Jackson wondered whether the man he was talking to would be alive when the six minutes were up. The aircraft were still unarmed because the MOD was flapping over changing Rules of Engagement, but they were carrying something unusual that might make a difference. Gun cameras were a throwback to a much earlier age of flying, but even in the high-tech world of the early twenty-first century there was no substitute for a good visual image.

The waiting was unbearable. But the pilots were clearly too busy to give a running commentary, however much the Air Staff might have wanted them to.

Ten minutes later they had their answer. Those following events at the Control and Reporting Centres saw it on their screens, and confirmation was soon given over the radio.

'Sector Control, this is Charlie One. Charlie Two is down. Her aircraft was destroyed and she didn't eject.' The pilot's voice was choking with emotion. He'd just seen a friend killed but he was still a professional and knew he had to get the information out, in case the hostile craft came back for him. 'I have the film and the craft has disengaged. But, in case I don't make it back, I can tell you it's not from around here.'

Everyone knew what he meant.

Farnham, Surrey

It seemed to Cody as if seven a.m. must be some kind of magical time before which nobody dared call and after which every researcher for every conceivable media outlet felt they could legitimately phone him. Between seven a.m. and eight a.m. he had taken over a dozen calls and had already done two pre-recorded radio interviews and a live one, all of them over the phone. He'd been sounded out about doing a television interview on a breakfast show the following morning, and had given his provisional agreement. He hadn't logged on to his computer yet but knew there would be numerous e-mails to wade through.

Cody had vowed to himself that he'd wait until ten a.m. before logging on and would send his own e-mail first, as he'd agreed with the *Daily Mail*. He'd been tempted to call the paper and ask whether he could send his Internet message early, reasoning that they wouldn't mind now their own story had run. He'd resisted the temptation, partly because he doubted whether the people he'd been dealing with would be in anyway, and partly because he also doubted whether a couple of hours would make much difference. He decided to pour himself another cup of coffee and continue to watch the television.

Cody made a mental note to call Jenny Thornton and to e-mail Dr Krone. Both would want to know how *Newsnight* had gone: he'd alerted both to his appearance, and to the *Daily Mail* piece. He was sure that Thornton would have stayed up to see *Newsnight*, and he'd already faxed a copy of the *Daily Mail* article to Krone. Things were hotting up – and Cody was beginning to feel that they were getting out of hand.

MOD Main Building, Whitehall

One of the constant problems of Government was that so much of its activity was reactive. It seemed that everything happened in response to some unpredicted event and that those within Government spent all their working lives responding to media enquiries, Parliamentary questions, approaches from the National Audit Office or the Public Accounts Committee.

The Ministry of Defence typified this: most officials felt that when they weren't trying to placate the HCDC they were trying to fend off the Treasury, who always seemed to be looking hungrily at the defence budget, eager to redirect money to popular, vote-winning areas like health and education. The Permanent Joint Headquarters typified the struggle to break away from this mindset and do something proactive. While others had been preparing press briefings or briefing ministers on this latest crisis, they had been tasked with concocting a plan to deal with the threat, whether it turned out to be real or imagined.

Staff at MOD Main Building had drawn up a draft Operation

Order, and now it looked as if it really was going to be authorized. This would take the form of a directive to the Chief of Joint Operations at the PJHQ, passing operational control to him, notifying him of the assets that would be placed under his control, and informing him on the Rules of Engagement that would apply. It was an attempt to seize the initiative, and it had been top of the agenda at a discussion of nearly all the senior military and civilian staff at the MOD, who had gathered in one of the historic conference rooms. Word had just come through of the loss of a fourth aircraft, and those who had not been briefed by Staff Officers soon heard from those who already knew.

It was S of S who opened discussions. Although the most recent tragedy was uppermost in people's minds, he was determined to take the meeting through the other developments first so everyone had the full picture.

'Good morning, ladies and gentlemen. As you know, a fourth Typhoon has now gone down. But before I come to that, I need to update you on some other matters. I'm sure most of you have seen the *Daily Mail* this morning. The latest assessment from JARIC is that the photograph's for real. Furthermore, we've received word from the DERA people at Farnborough, where a fragment of wreckage from one of the first two aircraft we lost has just been analysed. The wreckage makes it clear that this was *not* an accident. The aircraft was brought down by a technology considerably more advanced than even the new US anti-satellite devices. Whatever is involved, this weapon's not one of ours – and it doesn't belong to the Russians, either. Some of you may be aware that there have been some recent briefings on previous incidents involving unidentified aerial craft. I'm also aware that there's been what I suppose might be termed canteen gossip about UFOs. Frankly, as crazy as it sounds, I don't think we can avoid the issue any longer. In the absence of any other plausible explanation, I believe we have to consider the possibility that we are dealing with extraterrestrial technology.'

The meeting erupted and, contrary to the normal protocol, questions were shouted at S of S while other conversations sprung up between the various attendees.

'So it seems,' Willoughby continued, raising his voice, 'that we now have our own confirmation of the *Daily Mail* story. Staff at JARIC have viewed the gun-camera footage taken by the pilot who survived this latest encounter and have provided an initial assessment to CSA. Essentially, the craft appears to be the same as the one on the front page of the paper. Quite apart from validating the assessment of this first photograph, it gives us one of our own to look at. The testimony of the surviving pilot, coupled with our own imagery, puts it beyond doubt that we are dealing with a structured craft and that this craft downed at least one of our aircraft, and almost certainly the other three. I will now hand over to CDS who will outline what response we propose to make.'

'Thank you, Secretary of State. Against this possibility, PJHQ have drawn up some contingency plans. I am minded to accept this and pass operational control to them – with overall policy control, of course, being retained here in Main Building. We have decided to issue a directive to CJO: the code word that came off the computer was Picture. I felt, however, that we needed something more – *purposeful*.'

There were appreciative nods from around the table. In the normal course of business, code words for new operations were selected randomly, tumbling off the computer without thought of the relevance of any particular word. There were advantages in such a system. With an entirely random code word it was inconceivable that any clue would be given about the nature of the operation. Thus the Falklands conflict had been 'Operation Corporate', while the Gulf War had been 'Operation Granby'. The American system was different: while it was easy to discern the nature of any US operation from its code word, this was not a problem if the accompanying security was handled carefully. Thus the Americans had called their Gulf War operations 'Desert Shield' and 'Desert Storm'.

'I have therefore decided,' CDS went on, 'that this project will be known as Operation Thunder Child.'

The personnel present were a cultured crowd, and all immediately recognized the name of the naval vessel from the classic H. G. Wells novel *The War of the Worlds*.

'We're nailing our colours to the mast somewhat, aren't we? It's practically an admission that we're facing an extraterrestrial threat. Is that really what we're saying?' It was CDI who had asked the question.

'We're certainly facing an unknown threat and, as S of S has already said, it's hard to think of any viable alternative. But all mention of this operation will be at Top Secret UK Eyes Only, so it won't matter what we call it. It's a lucky code word, for internal consumption only.'

'Not *that* lucky,' ACAS observed wryly. 'The *Thunder Child* was sunk.'

'Yes, but it *was* the most effective human response. It's time to find out what we're up against. Please look at the draft signal in front of you.'

The various attendees read through what had just been put on the table, one copy each. The signal made chilling reading.

FROM: MODUK
TO: PJHQ
COPY TO: HQSTC
SUBJECT: OPERATION THUNDER CHILD
TEXT: FROM CDS TO CJO, COPY TO AOC-IN-C HQSTC. FOLLOWING RECENT UNCOR-RELATED RADAR TARGETS IN THE UKADR AND THE LOSS OF FOUR TYPHOON AIRCRAFT, YOU ARE AUTHORIZED TO ASCERTAIN THE NATURE AND LEVEL OF ANY THREAT AND TO TAKE ANY NECESSARY DEFENSIVE ACTION TO PROTECT YOUR ASSETS. ROE ARE ALPHA DELTA THREE. ALL THUNDER CHILD DATA AND COMMS ARE TOP SECRET UK EYES ONLY. GOOD LUCK.

This was only the summary, of course. There was more detailed appendix material covering a wealth of technical data, contact procedures, and assets that had been assigned to the operation. Over the next hour these were debated at some length, and although there were no significant disagreements on the detail, there was one fundamental point that caused some difficulty.

'I'm not entirely convinced of the wisdom of passing operational control to the PJHQ. Why don't we retain control here, in Main Building? After all, that's where all the key players are. I can understand putting the PJHQ in charge for a peacekeeping op, where procedures are straightforward and where there's precedent to follow. But here we're facing an unknown threat and it seems to me that *we* should run the show.' It was CAS who had articulated what a large number of those around the table had been thinking.

'No.' CDS's tone of voice made it clear that there was no room for negotiation: a nod of agreement from S of S reinforced the point. Many correctly guessed it had been agreed in advance. 'PJHQ will run the op from Northwood, free of political concerns. They will be focused entirely on the military issues, leaving us to set the overall policy and worry about the presentational aspects of all this.'

'So what's the plan?' asked CDI. 'What can we actually *do* about what's happening?'

'The only meaningful response is to bring one of these craft down,' CAS offered. 'Aside from anything else, that would clear up – for once and for all – the mystery of who or what we're actually facing.'

'That's an act of war,' CDI replied.

'And shooting down four of our aircraft isn't?' CAS replied, a little harshly.

CDI pointedly turned to CSA. 'Do you buy into this idea about extraterrestrials?'

'On the basis of the analyses from DERA and JARIC, yes, I do,' she replied. 'It doesn't tally with my personal beliefs, but as a scientist I have to go where the data takes me. Although this has yet to be confirmed, radar analyses of all these incidents suggest that whatever downed our aircraft moved off vertically, at incredible speed, and exited the atmosphere.'

'Then answer me this,' CDI shot back. 'If we're really dealing with extraterrestrials, shouldn't we be trying to *communicate* with them, rather than risking war with a civilization that may have at its disposal other destructive technology that we can only guess at?'

S of S picked up the theme with his next question, again directed at CSA. 'How might we establish this communication – radio signals, I suppose? What about using Jodrell Bank?'

'Although Jodrell Bank is the prime site for radio astronomy and does listen for extraterrestrial signals, it's a passive system. It couldn't *transmit* a signal. We could try using the facility at Goonhilly Downs, though,' she ventured.

'But that's insecure,' CAS pointed out. 'I think any communication would have to be secure, and for that we might use the RAF/NATO satcom facility at RAF Oakhanger.'

'Or the naval shore-station SCOT system,' offered the First Sea Lord, eager to remind those present that the Navy too had a part to play.

'What would we say, and where would we send the message?' S of S wanted to know.

CSA thought for a moment. 'To start with, we'd broadcast something unmistakably artificial, like a sequence of prime numbers or perfect numbers. That would just be an attention-getter. What we did next would depend on the response; maybe they've learnt our language – they probably found us originally by homing in on our radio broadcasts – so we could always try sending a message in English, asking them to cease hostile action and requesting that they talk to us.'

'OK,' S of S interjected, 'there are some good ideas here, but I'm going to have to wrap things up now. Barbara, I want you and the scientific staff to work up a separate report on options for communication, and any suggestions you may have for consulting the wider scientific community about this, although I have to say I'm not minded to bring in civvies at this stage. Now I've got to go to the PM with this, and then straight over to the Palace. CDS's Directive will be sent, but it'll need approval from the *very* top.'

Farnham, Surrey

Cody picked up the ringing telephone, fully expecting it to be another journalist. He'd done several down-the-line interviews for radio stations that had picked up on his involvement with the piece on *Newsnight* and the story in the *Daily Mail*. The familiar voice of Jenny Thornton reminded him that he mustn't let media appearances compromise his actual investigations. It was a lesson that many others in the UFO lobby had yet to learn.

'I saw *Newsnight*,' Thornton explained, 'and I just wanted to say that I thought the piece came across really well. You were great, as usual.'

'Thanks. That means a lot, coming from you.' Cody wasn't exaggerating; it was a tribute to his own professionalism and lack of ego that positive feedback from abductees and UFO witnesses was more important to him than any praise he might receive from media people.

'Isn't it typical of the Government, though, refusing to say anything?' Thornton continued.

Although dissatisfied with the official position on UFOs, Cody wasn't as much of a conspiracy theorist as Thornton. While Thornton believed in an active cover-up, Cody simply felt that the Government had its head in the sand on the issue, refusing to take it seriously through fear of the ridicule that might be heaped upon any official who associated themselves with the subject. Put bluntly, there were no votes in it. But Cody shared Thornton's frustration at the Government's response to the current situation. 'Yes, it's par for the course,' he replied. 'They don't mind appearing when there's good news, or leaking something if they think it's in their interest. But the moment the heat's on, nobody's available to be interviewed and we get some bland platitude.'

'Well, they can't wriggle out of this one.' Thornton said.

'No. No, they can't,' Cody agreed. Then he remembered something else he'd meant to ask. 'Did you see the *Daily Mail*?'

'Yes, it's amazing. That photo really freaked me out, I can tell you. You're sure it's for real?' Cody had told her that the story would be appearing, but Thornton hadn't seen the photograph until she'd bought a copy of the paper. Even though she was pleased to see a UFO photo on the front page, she knew that the UFO lobby ran the risk that they'd end up with egg on their face if the picture was subsequently exposed as a hoax. Such things had happened before.

'I'm convinced,' Cody replied, reassuringly. 'We really put it through the mill. But the witnesses were genuine; I could tell. And don't forget, none of this is happening in isolation. It's the links with the RAF's losses that got this story on the front page, as much as the image itself. I told you that the RAF sent people to interview the witnesses and get copies of the photos, so it's not just the likes of us talking about the connection – they've as good as admitted it themselves.'

'Yeah. Anything new on the Internet?'

Cody thought for a moment before replying. Thornton was clearly referring to Elizabeth Krone and the whole business of consciously recalled abductions. He felt awkward about this because he'd not mentioned it on *Newsnight* or in the *Daily Mail*. He'd even steered clear of the subject in his subsequent radio interviews, making a conscious decision to avoid mentioning abductions at all. 'Not a lot,' he replied, 'but to tell the truth I haven't had a chance to log on this morning. I'm going to call Dr Krone later today, but I've been focusing mainly on this UFO story because I think it's our best chance of convincing people that something's going on. I'm sure there is a connection between this new development and with abductions, but if we bring too many different strands in we run the risk that people will lose interest. The UFO story is more tangible, because people can look at that photograph and they'll talk about it. It's our strongest card, and we should play it.' Cody stopped suddenly, realizing that he was lecturing her. 'I'm sorry, Jenny,' he added, 'I don't mean to downplay what's happening to you, it's just—'

'I understand.' It was a testament to Thornton's intelligence that she really did. 'You don't have to tell me how wacky it sounds. I know it would weaken our case to bring it in and I want you to know that I don't have a problem with your leaving it out.'

'Thanks.'

The conversation continued for a few more minutes. Thornton said that although she hadn't had any new abduction experience she'd been doing a lot of thinking about why she – and others, it seemed – hadn't been given the usual instruction to forget their encounter.

'As you know,' Cody ventured, 'there are several cases in the literature where the aliens have made mistakes. People have been put back with their nightclothes on back to front – that sort of thing.'

'Yeah, but this seems more fundamental, like a deliberate change in policy. And I keep coming back to this business with the RAF. UFOs, abductions, suddenly it's all out in the open. It's almost as if . . . well, as if they don't care about hiding any more.'

After saying goodbye, Cody replaced the receiver carefully and went into the kitchen to make himself a coffee. As he drank, he mulled over what Thornton had said. Her final remarks had really struck a chord with him. It was a pretty good analysis. *What the hell was going on?*

RAF Feltwell, Norfolk

'Shit, look at *that*.' It was hardly an in-depth analysis but it didn't need to be. The duty officer had been monitoring a particular region of space with a combination of optical and radar sensors, having been tasked to do so by Fort Meade. Within moments the young USAF officer had summoned the CO. Colonel Bob Zeckle arrived a few minutes later.

'Do we warn the Brits, sir?'

'No. May God forgive us, but we don't.'

RAF Fylingdales, North Yorkshire

The space-tracking radar systems at the Ballistic Missile Early Warning Centre at RAF Fylingdales didn't have the deep-space capability of RAF Feltwell. But they could pick up objects on a ballistic trajectory and could detect various objects at orbital distance from the Earth, ranging from satellites to the small pieces of space junk that were a growing hazard to the space programmes of the various nations that were now in the business of launching satellites and space probes.

There could be no mistaking the data. A series of frantic telephone calls followed. But the objects that were being tracked were so fast that by the time the calls had reached the Signals Units and Control and Reporting Centres, targets were being picked up on conventional radar systems.

RAF Coningsby, Lincolnshire

'Go go go!'

Isabelle Bentley hadn't been on Q. But when it became apparent what was happening, every Typhoon pilot on base had been ordered into the air. She had run to her aircraft, which had been surrounded by various ground crew who were frantically making checks on the airframe. She had inspected the plane herself, climbed into the cockpit, made her pre-flight instrument checks and then had waited for Air Traffic Control to give her clearance to take off.

As she taxied the jet it struck her that she was going into a potential combat situation. For the first time since the order had come through to the crewroom, logic overtook adrenalin, and she was forced to consider the possibility that she might be dead within the next ten minutes or so. It was not a pleasant thought and she knew she had to put it to the back of her mind if she wanted to function at peak level – which might itself be essential to her survival.

'Delta Seven, you are cleared for take-off, over.'

'Delta Seven acknowledges.'

The Typhoon surged forward, racing down the runway until it reached take-off speed. Bentley flexed her gloved hand before easing the joystick back and guiding her aircraft gently but firmly into the sky. She knew there were others ahead of her, notably the two pilots who *had* been on Q, fully suited-up and sitting in their aircraft on the end of the runway.

Once the ATC personnel had steered Bentley out of the controlled airspace surrounding RAF Coningsby, she heard the familiar voice of Sarah Brooking, one of the station's most experienced Fighter Controllers. Brooking was frantically marshalling the aircraft, trying to deconflict them while at the same time attempting to close the gap between the two Q aircraft and the main group. She felt that the Q jets were badly exposed, and wanted the other aircraft to catch up. She was also grappling with the problem of integrating the Coningsby jets with those from RAF Leeming and RAF Leuchars – who would intercept the intruding craft first.

Over the North Sea

The Fighter Controllers no longer needed to give any instructions. Bentley knew that although the aircraft had now been filled with live weapons, the current ROE were strictly defensive; but she had visual confirmation that the situation had moved on. She knew that nobody would have disobeyed orders and realized that the intruders must have attacked the first wave of Typhoons. Her airborne radar was showing multiple targets, none of which was emitting an IFF signal. But what really struck her was the visual picture. The sky ahead was full of missile trails and she could see at least three Typhoons that were clearly out of action, spiralling down towards the sea, twenty thousand feet below. She also saw two parachutes: it was clear that the RAF had taken losses.

Bentley looked ahead again and caught a brief glimpse of a triangular-shaped vessel that was clearly one of the intruding craft. She selected an ASRAAM and fired it, instinctively jerking her joystick to starboard in an attempt to manoeuvre her Typhoon out of the way of any response. She hadn't had time to lock on to the target before launch, but hoped that the advanced high-sensitivity infra-red seeker would home in on the intruder anyway: the ASRAAM was a classic fire-and-forget missile that needed minimal guidance from a pilot, and was highly resistant to electronic countermeasures.

Bentley didn't have time to see if her missile had hit the target and when she saw another craft ahead of her – or maybe the same one, for all she knew – she loosed a second ASRAAM. She blinked hard as she saw a blue-white beam flash down to port of her jet. She assumed that she'd been fired on, and guessed that her tactic of randomly manoeuvring after launching the first missile had saved her life. She wasn't sure whether she'd been shot at by the craft she'd just engaged or by another one.

In a fluid movement Bentley banked her Typhoon and then brought it around in a tight turn that left her facing the area of sky she'd just flown through. She saw a Typhoon pass in front of her own jet, black smoke billowing from its engines. The canopy was off, indicating that the pilot had ejected, but she couldn't see a parachute.

Suddenly Bentley saw two of the intruding craft bearing down upon another Typhoon. She was part fascinated, part horrified as she saw them fire what looked like laser weapons at the jet, exploding it into a billowing fireball. The craft were almost directly ahead of her. In an attempt to vary her tactics and improve her chances of success she fired two ASRAAMs simultaneously, again manoeuvring her aircraft sharply before she could see if they'd had any effect. The tactical picture had gone to hell, and there was no useful information to be gleaned from her airborne radar. This was a close-quarter dogfight, with no time to do anything other than react instinctively to a threat or fire instantly on any target that presented itself to her.

Moments later, it was over. Bentley hadn't seen any of the hostile machines move off, but suddenly it became clear that the only aircraft now in the sky were Typhoons. Dripping with sweat inside her flight suit, her heart pounding, Bentley set a course back to base. She could see two other aircraft ahead of her, one of which appeared to be damaged. Although she wouldn't find this out for some time, nine Typhoons had been lost and four damaged. Only two pilots from the nine aircraft that had been destroyed had managed to eject. Despite some brave and skilled flying, none of the attacking craft had been brought down.

Chapter Seven

SURPRISE ATTACK

RAF Coningsby, Lincolnshire

Isabelle Bentley was sitting in the crewroom, her head in her hands, having just been told the full extent of the squadron's losses. Friends and colleagues were dead and the survivors were in a state of near shock, trying to take in the extraordinary events that had led to a tragedy beyond their comprehension. Two pilots were in tears and another was beating his fist against the noticeboard. One of the windows was broken, where somebody had hurled their helmet through it in a mixture of rage and frustration. But most of them, like Bentley, were sitting alone, trying to come to terms with what had happened.

Bentley had seen aircraft go down, but had been so focused on her individual struggle for survival that she'd only taken in snatches of the wider battle. What had started off as an organized engagement had degenerated into a confused mêlée. She was replaying recent events in her mind, asking tough questions about her performance and mostly wondering whether her late arrival had played a part in the outcome. If she'd arrived with the rest of her colleagues, would it have made a difference? Could it have tipped the odds in their favour? Might somebody now dead have survived, or would she herself have been killed?

The questions tumbled forth in a rush of self-doubt about her own performance. In truth, Bentley had fought as bravely and skilfully as any of her fellow pilots but, like all true professionals, she was analysing her own mistakes and wondering what she could have done better.

The CO strode into the room, grim-faced. He had flown Phantoms and then Tornado F3s in his day, notching up scores of hours on Combat Air Patrol in the Gulf War. But the Iraqis had never tested the F3s, and he'd never fired a shot in anger or been fired on. He knew that this put a gulf between him and the pilots he was now facing and that, rookies though they were compared to him, they had experienced something that he couldn't hope to understand. As it happened, he had some good news.

'Jim and Sharon have both activated their PLBs, and a Nimrod is en route to drop dinghies. It looks as if they made it.'

There were no cheers from the assembled company, who were too physically and mentally shattered to do more than break into relieved smiles. They were all grateful to learn that two of their fellow pilots had ejected safely and survived the loss of their aircraft, but the scale of the tragedy had left them all stunned, and a wild show of joy would have been somehow inappropriate.

'The bad news is that the newly set-up Thunder Child team at PJHQ are screaming for immediate debriefs.'

'Great – just great,' someone offered. But they knew what was required and filtered through to the office where secure telephone links would connect each of the pilots to the group of very senior personnel in Main Building and at the PJHQ, all of whom were desperate to hear their stories first hand.

MOD Main Building, Whitehall

'*Nine* aircraft? *Seven* dead?' Martin Blackmore could scarcely believe what he'd just been told. But CAS did not often make errors: the Minister knew he'd heard correctly.

'Yes, I'm afraid so.' CAS started to say something else, but found himself totally at a loss. This was a situation without precedent, and the other faces in the room looked equally disbelieving. A hush fell over the assembled Ministers, Chiefs of Staff and key officials. Although operational control would still be retained by the PJHQ, everybody knew that the crisis no longer involved just the MOD. There was speculation that the Cabinet Office would be stepping in to coordinate the Government's response to events and that the Prime Minister – who was even now at the Palace – would head up a War Cabinet to run the show from Number Ten.

Secretary of State swept into the room, looking unusually but understandably stressed. He had the look of a man who had been too long without sleep – as did most of those present at the impromptu meeting. He spoke.

'We have lost nine more Typhoons in the recent engagement with what we think were five intruding craft. Seven pilots are missing, presumed dead, but we have two confirmed survivors who managed to eject in time. Another four aircraft have been badly damaged. I have to brief the PM in ten minutes, and I need to make a statement to Parliament as soon as possible, preferably before the press get hold of this. Before I do any of these things I'd like to know what the *hell* is going on.'

It was CDS who decided to answer. 'It looks like we have alien contact. And it's hostile.'

'I refuse to believe in the extraterrestrial hypothesis,' CDI interjected. 'Just because we see technology more advanced than our own, that doesn't mean it's alien, for goodness' sake. We might easily have said the same thing about a stealth fighter in the Seventies, when, believe me, there *were* prototypes flying.'

'But surely *your* intelligence apparatus would warn us of such a development?' Blackmore countered, with more than a trace of sarcasm.

'Not necessarily. I'd be the first to admit we could've missed something. Let me run a scenario past you. It's the Russians. They've made a quantum-leap discovery in propulsion systems and projected-energy weapons, and produced a handful of new aircraft. We all know what's going on in Russia right now: the economy's still in ruins, the civilian Government looks increasingly shaky, and millions of ordinary people haven't been paid their wages for months. There are hard-liners in the military who long for a return to the old ways, and this might be their opening gambit – precipitate a limited conflict with the West, then step in when the civilian Government can't cope.'

'But we've already looked at that scenario,' CSA replied. 'It's inconsistent with the data. These craft appear to actually exit the atmosphere after these engagements.'

'So what?' CDI retorted. 'Is it so difficult to envisage some sort of terrestrial aircraft that can do that? It's a logical progression from space-shuttle technology, and not a million miles away from the HOTOL craft we've been looking at.'

S of S looked at CDS for comment. As the UK's senior military officer, CDS's was the opinion that S of S should take, but it was clear that his subordinates were undecided. CDS himself was in a difficult position: CDI's argument had merit and he couldn't dismiss it out of hand, not least because he didn't want to under-mine the man's authority. 'Both scenarios are viable: it's therefore premature to go firm on either, although I personally favour the extraterrestrial hypothesis. I therefore believe we should say to Parliament and the press that we have lost the aircraft in hostile action to an unknown aggressor, and are currently assessing our response.'

'Jacqui?' The Chief Press Officer had been expecting but not looking forward to the question.

'Yes, Secretary of State,' she replied, 'I agree with CDS's view. We can't say anything else. This line is very risky, and we'll be accused of all sorts of things, but there is precedent for falling back on a simple "no comment" when dealing with current operations where lives are at stake. It'll leak, though. From the pilots and the radar operators—'

CAS was off his feet in an instant, a look of anger on his face. 'Now just hold on a moment—' He paused briefly and thought it through. Instinct had caused him to leap to the defence of his people but he was intelligent enough to realize he'd spoken too soon and honest enough to admit it. So many people had been involved that *somebody* was bound to say something. It wasn't a question of loyalty, only of simple human nature. 'Yes, I see it. You're right.'

'We need to decide immediately what our response should be if we detect more intruders.' CDS pointed out. 'As things stand, unless orders are changed, we'd scramble aircraft with orders to intercept. The consequences of such a move may be catastrophic, and our losses have seriously degraded our AD capability in any case.'

'We can't risk another battle on the scale of the one we've just had. I can't justify sending people to their deaths like that.' S of S replied.

'If we order our people not to respond, we effectively capitulate and cede control of the UKADR,' CAS retorted. 'Furthermore, we leave the mainland UK wide open to an attack.'

'Not necessarily.' All eyes turned towards US of S. 'If attack was the aim, why didn't the intruders press home their assault? They had a decisive advantage, and breaking off has served only to give us time to regroup and plan. Now, I'm not claiming to be an expert on military tactics but that makes no sense to me, and suggests their strategy has never involved a conventional attack.' Blackmore had everyone's attention now. Even though he was straying outside his area of expertise, he was getting appreciative nods from CDS and CAS who clearly followed his line of reasoning. 'I'd almost go as far as to say that what we've seen to date is designed to slowly chip away our AD force, or force us out of the north-east approach area.'

'But then you'd be playing into their hands by making no response to any further action,' ACAS suggested. 'You'd give them exactly what they want.'

'I agree.' Blackmore replied. 'But in doing so, we'd have a better idea of who they are and what they want. We can track them, to a certain extent. So let's see where they go.'

'Stand the AD force down,' S of S ordered. 'And declare a total air and sea exclusion zone around the area. I have to go to Number Ten but when I come back I want to discuss options for bringing one of these craft down. It's a proportional response, whoever they are, and we can't carry on just reacting to developments. It's time we went on the offensive.' With that, S of S swept out of the room, leaving some of the military officers thinking that the man had more steel in him than they had suspected.

Rowledge, Surrey

Jenny Thornton was paralysed but not scared. She'd had a long talk with Richard Cody about the latest developments in her continuing series of abduction experiences. He'd convinced her that the most frustrating thing about her previous encounters was that induced amnesia meant that she could remember snatches of her experiences consciously, but that the actual details could only be recalled through hypnotic regression – which muddied the waters. Her own lack of certainty disempowered her.

But total conscious recall of her last experience meant Thornton was better able to deal with the situation. She was clever enough to realize that Cody was trying to reassure her, but sufficiently perceptive to see that there was truth in what he said. If she couldn't stop the experiences, she might at least come to terms with them.

Now, just a few hours after Thornton's last talk with Cody, the visitors were back. Against Cody's advice, she had secreted a kitchen knife under the bed. But it was a pointless gesture: the hypnotic block might have been absent, but the paralysis with which she was controlled was as unrelenting as ever. The room filled with blue-white light and three figures appeared, as if from nowhere.

'*We mean you no harm.*'

It was a platitude she'd heard dozens of times before, and it was usually followed by pain and fear. 'Fuck you.' She wasn't sure whether she'd said it or thought it, but the creatures seemed to understand. To her immense pleasure, they flinched.

'*Your leaders are playing a dangerous game. You must warn them. We mean you no harm.*'

'What game? Who should I warn?'

They interfere with the plan. It is for your benefit. Warn Thunder Child.'

Before Thornton could ask who Thunder Child was, the figures were gone. She reached for the phone, and called Cody. He'd know what to do.

MOD Main Building, Whitehall

Blackmore found himself at something of a loose end. S of S and the PM would by now be at the Palace, while Min(AF) and Min(DP) were briefing the Commons and the Lords respectively. Somebody more vain or insecure might have been annoyed by this development but Blackmore was untroubled. He was the junior Minister and, although he'd made the initial running, he knew that S of S and the Ministers of State would step in and take over at some point. Parliament would not expect news of this magnitude to be delivered by the Under-Secretary of State. Far from being put out, he was pleased to have the time to discuss some of the many unresolved questions with officials. He'd summoned Nick Templeton and Terry Carpenter, who had been following up lines of enquiry of their own.

'An issue that worries me, Minister, is the lack of input from the Americans.' It was Templeton who began. 'They know we're losing aircraft, and you'll recall that we asked them whether they had anything in their inventory that was anything like these triangular craft we've encountered. They said no. Fair enough. But what really concerns me is that we were passed no warning about this last attack.'

'Hold on, though,' Blackmore interrupted. 'We only cottoned onto this by chance, because of some perceptive work by this Whitfield chap.'

'Initially that's true, Minister. But in the last attack it was obvious to everyone at Fylingdales and all the rest of the UKADGE that there were inbound objects. Yet we heard nothing at all from the US authorities, not even after the event. RAF Fylingdales is only part of the BMEWS. There are two other sites, at Thule in Greenland and at Clear Air Force Base in Alaska. All data is correlated, so controllers have access to an overall picture. So if we saw it, the Americans *must* have seen it. There's more.'

'Go on.'

'The Americans also have something known as the Deep Space Tracking System. It monitors satellites, and as such might have been able to give us some warning of this attack. There are three bases, spaced around the world to give all-round coverage. One's in America, one's in Japan – but one's right here in the UK, at RAF Feltwell.'

Blackmore said nothing for a moment. 'You realize what you're saying?'

'Yes, Minister. The US may very well have seen this attack coming, but not passed on the warning.'

'Wing Commander?'

'Yes, Minister, I support Nick's conclusions.'

'OK. Before we go anywhere with this, I want to return to something you told me a while ago. You said that the Americans didn't tell us everything about this sighting near RAF Wood-bridge, but we didn't have time to follow it up. Now, what did you mean by that?'

Templeton looked uncomfortable. 'Well, first they waited two weeks before letting us know, contrary to SOPs. Next, we got a one-page memo from the Deputy Base Commander but none of the witness statements from the three-man patrol who saw the metallic craft during the first night's activity.'

'But, to be fair, it *was* the dead zone between Christmas and New Year when this happened.' It was Carpenter who offered up this case for the defence. 'And as for knowing the SOP for a UFO sighting, well, I bet there are quite a few people in the RAF who don't know.'

'There are other considerations, though,' Templeton went on. 'Numerous witnesses have now spoken out in public and have testified that the Weapons Storage Area was hit by light beams, that various threatening debriefings took place, and that all sorts of strange people were showing up at the base totally unannounced and taking away films and photographs. None of this material ever found its way to the MOD. Nobody within the MOD was ever briefed. It all gets very murky: shortly after the incident a lot of the trees in the area concerned were cut down by the Forestry Commission – we don't know why or on whose authority, and all the files have gone. We might reopen the investigation, but it would cause a lot of comment and, frankly, we've got better things to do.'

At that moment there was a knock on the door and CAS and ACAS appeared, looking quite pleased. 'Minister, we have a plan that we believe stands a good chance of bringing one of these craft down. Let me explain . . .'

Farnham, Surrey

Cody was getting frustrated. He wanted to speak to somebody in Sec(AS) and had accidentally dialled the answerphone that had been installed a few years back to ensure that Sec(AS) staff didn't have to take calls in person from those members of the public who wanted to report a UFO. The move had been criticized at the time as an insult to witnesses and a contradiction of the policy on open Government. Although those responsible for introducing the answerphone had been quietly moved on, the machine remained, much to the irritation of serious researchers.

When Cody finally managed to get through to the desk officer, he was told that Nick Templeton – to whom he'd spoken twice, and who'd been quite helpful – was unlikely to be able to call him back for a while. Cody had seen the news and knew why. He decided to take a chance and relay something that Jenny Thornton had told him, even though he didn't really know what it meant.

'Tell him I have a message for Thunder Child,' he said.

'I'll tell him that, sir. Thank you very much. Goodbye.'

The line went dead, and Cody wondered whether he'd done the right thing.

RAF Coningsby, Lincolnshire

Ever since the disastrous engagement with the mystery craft, the base had been a scene of frantic activity. The alert condition had gone to the highest possible state, effectively putting RAF Coningsby onto a war footing. Some Typhoons were in Hardened Air Shelters, while others were dispersed widely around the base, camouflaged and protected by grim-faced RAF Regiment personnel armed with the Rapier tactical anti-aircraft guided weapon system.

On paper, the RAF had more than enough AD aircraft to cover the UKADR. As Typhoons had been introduced, Tornado F3s had been withdrawn, with the aim of maintaining 232 airframes. The reality was rather more depressing. At any given time large numbers of aircraft would effectively be out of action because they would be undergoing first-, second- or third-line maintenance. An airframe on first-line maintenance would probably be in one of the hangars, with various parts removed for testing. These aircraft could be restored to active service within a few hours. But for second- and especially third-line maintenance, the aircraft might well be off-base with contractors, wings off and insides stripped out.

What this meant was that at any particular moment the RAF had far fewer operational aircraft than most outside observers might suppose. The precise numbers, of course, were classified, but it didn't take a genius to realize that the loss of any operational aircraft had a disproportionately high impact on the RAF's overall capability. Even more crucial was any loss of pilots, and it was now obvious to most within the RAF that their AD capability had been eroded significantly by the recent catastrophes. The response to this had involved a restructuring of the entire force, with pilots being swapped between squadrons and airfields to maintain an even mix of numbers and experience at all three Typhoon bases.

'Hello?' Isabelle Bentley had spotted an unfamiliar pilot who she correctly deduced had come from Leuchars.

'Hi. My name's Stuart Coultart. I was with 43 Squadron at Leuchars. I've been reassigned to fill the gap after—'

'Yes, I know.'

'Do you buy this story about the Russians?'

'That's bullshit,' Bentley replied. 'I've *seen* them and they sure as hell aren't Russians.'

'Yeah. Where are you going?' He'd noticed she was in her flying suit, which struck him as strange because nobody else was.

'I don't know. The CO asked to see me and said he had a mission for me. I can't say I'm that enthusiastic.'

'Good luck.'

'Thanks.'

MOD Main Building, Whitehall

'He said *what*?' Templeton could hardly believe what he'd just been told by the Executive Officer in Sec(AS)2a.

'Thunder Child, Nick. He said Thunder Child.'

'What did you say?'

'Nothing. Just that I'd pass the message on. I don't think my tone of voice gave anything away.'

'Has our security been compromised already?'

'Apparently so.'

'Leave it with me. Thanks.'

RAF Coningsby, Lincolnshire

'Isabelle, come in.'

'What's this all about, sir?'

'Somebody said you were the best pilot on the base and I believed them.'

'Sir?'

'I have a mission for you, if you want it.'

'I want it, sir. What's the mission?'

'It's payback time.'

MOD Main Building, Whitehall

Martin Blackmore was surprised to see Earl Sutton, and even more surprised when he asked if he could have a word alone. Somewhat reluctantly Blackmore dismissed Sue Farthing and ushered the man into his office.

Earl Sutton had just come from the House of Lords where he

had delivered a bland statement about the recent losses. The session had been stormy, but that didn't explain the man's obvious discomfort.

'What is it? What's the matter?' Blackmore asked.

'There's no easy way to put this,' Min(DP) replied. 'It's all this talk of UFOs and extraterrestrials. I've kept this to myself because I haven't known what to think. I've sat on it out of embarrassment – it's easier to tell myself that I'm having bad dreams or hallucinations. But I can't hold back now: it may be relevant, and I could never forgive myself if I was concealing information that might help us in our current peril.'

'What are you saying?'

'I believe I may be an . . . an *abductee.*'

RAF Coningsby, Lincolnshire

Bentley felt as lonely and as isolated as she had ever felt in her life. The CO had been through the plan with her several times and she'd confirmed she understood it. Like all good plans, it was simple – and it had even been tried before, although under different circumstances. Essentially, they would send up a C-130 Hercules transport to see if they could draw out one of the intruding craft. Bentley would fly as close as she dared to the lumbering plane so that on radar her fighter wouldn't show up at all.

The plan was based on a series of assumptions that Bentley didn't much care for: that the intruders used radar and that they wouldn't fire on a transport aircraft were two that sprang to mind. But the French had tried this tactic before – in Bosnia, in an attempt to assassinate Ratko Mladic with a 500lb bomb. The ruse had worked up to a point, and the Serb air defences hadn't spotted the Mirage fighter-bomber until it had peeled away from the transport aircraft it had been tucked in behind. Only faulty intelligence had saved the rogue Serb General blamed for numerous atrocities: his house had been flattened, but he hadn't been there.

Now Bentley had been tasked with a similar mission and

although she liked the idea of using the C-130 she didn't like what had been suggested next. Instead of engaging the target with ASRAAMs or BVRAAMs, it had been suggested that she should open fire with her cannon. At first she'd protested, but she'd soon come round to the CO's way of thinking. After all, common sense dictated that if what you were doing wasn't working you should try something else. Well, she'd fired missiles at these craft before, as had a number of her colleagues, only to find out they'd been ineffective. Initial analysis from Fighter Controllers suggested that the missiles hadn't hit and that the attacking craft had somehow managed to make them lose their lock. No one knew how this had been done, although some electronic counter-measures device was suspected. The Thunder Child team, now acting for the War Cabinet, had recommended this plan and felt that a concentrated burst of cannon fire stood a better chance of success. The PM had apparently just authorized the mission and had sent her a personal good-luck message.

Old War Office Building, Whitehall

Blackmore had been surprised to learn that a member of the DIS was trained in hypnotic regression – and rather disturbed to discover that he'd used the technique on abductees before, under a false identity which he'd used to infiltrate a civilian UFO group. Blackmore wondered whether this had been legal, although he knew that the DIS were careful about such things. Nonetheless, even if it was legal, he was sure it wasn't moral.

Blackmore and Earl Sutton had adjourned to Terry Carpenter's office, where the Wing Commander had insisted that he should be the only one allowed to ask any questions during the initial session. They had spent some time exploring Earl Sutton's conscious recollection of events and had decided to focus on the most recent.

Blackmore listened in fascination as Earl Sutton described what had happened on the drive back to his country house the evening after he had made his first statement to the House of Lords about the current crisis. He told how he had reached a deserted stretch of the A361, just past Beckhampton, where he'd seen a ball of light that appeared to be following the car. At first he'd thought it was just the headlights of another car but had soon realized the light was airborne. He then reported experiencing a strange feeling of disorientation, after which he remembered no further details of his journey. What he *did* remember was that he had arrived home over an hour later than scheduled. Carpenter wanted to explore what – if anything – had happened in this period of missing time.

The blinds were lowered and the door was locked from the inside. A member of Carpenter's staff was positioned in the corridor outside, to further ensure that nobody disturbed the hypnosis session. Blackmore watched in fascinated silence as Carpenter began his routine with soothing words of comfort.

Over the North Sea

Normally, two aircraft would only ever fly so close together if they were taking part in an air display, or when one of them was refuelling and the other was a tanker. Bentley had performed both manoeuvres, of course, but they were usually carried out in as short a time as possible. Flying so close to the giant Hercules for so long was an unnerving experience, and one that required unceasing concentration. A collision could prove fatal for every-body. Bentley knew very well that the crew of the Hercules faced the same dangers as herself. In the event of hostile action from intruders there was no guarantee that they would confine their attention to the fighter. The large, slow-moving transport aircraft was a big target and was equipped with only a few basic defensive systems such as chaff and flares, neither of which seemed to offer much hope of protection against a projected-energy weapon. For this reason the normal crew complement had been reduced to two, the minimum needed to fly the aircraft safely. There were no restrictions on radio traffic – indeed, it had been actively encouraged, on the basis that they *wanted* to be detected. But nobody would say anything over the air to indicate that *two* aircraft – not one – were present. Bentley would monitor her own airborne-radar system, but it was difficult to do so while concentrating on keeping a distance of just a few metres between her jet and the C-130. Now they knew what to look for, the Fighter Controllers stood as good a chance as she did of acquiring any target. As it happened, they didn't have long to wait.

'Charlie One, this is Control. You have unidentified traffic inbound on your position. ETA is four minutes. Over.'

'Control, this is Charlie One. Message acknowledged – thanks. Over and out.'

Bentley stayed off the air, but ready for action.

Old War Office Building, Whitehall

The hypnotic-regression session had been going on for nearly forty minutes, but to Blackmore's frustration nothing of any interest had emerged yet. Carpenter had spent some time going through a relaxation technique in which he had invited Earl Sutton to choose a location where he felt safe, comfortable and relaxed. He'd chosen a Caribbean beach, and Carpenter had then run through a soothing monologue in which the Minister was encouraged to imagine that his limbs were getting progressively heavier. Blackmore supposed this was the real-life version of the stage cliché about getting very sleepy, but without the swinging watch and the showbiz hypnotist's strange, drawling accent.

Carpenter spent further time establishing the scenario. As a sign of his professionalism he had a large-scale road map to hand on which he marked in pencil the features that the Minister mentioned.

'. . . travelling down the A4, two or three miles past Marlborough. Milk Hill's on the left, and on the right I can see Silbury Hill.'

'Uh-huh.'

'There's the roundabout, up ahead. I take the left-hand exit, picking up the A361. Ten more minutes and I'll be in Devizes. The road is completely deserted now, not a car in sight.'

Blackmore found all of this tedious, wishing that Carpenter would get to the point. But Carpenter had explained to him why the session had to be conducted in this way, so that there could be no suggestion that Carpenter had led the witness. Although there was scientific disagreement about the true nature of hypnosis, most agreed that during it the subject's will was repressed and the hypnotist became a central figure to them, one whom the subject might subconsciously want to please by coming up with the information they thought would be welcome. Blackmore noticed that Carpenter's questions were all neutral ones, such as 'What can you see around you?' as opposed to leading ones such as 'Can you see anything strange?'

'Hold on, I can see something in the rear-view mirror: another car, quite close behind. Wait a minute . . . *wait a minute* . . .'

Over the North Sea

Bentley's interceptor radar had confirmed the presence of the craft that the Fighter Controllers had spotted. Her heart was beating faster now and the adrenalin was flowing. This was a moment of extreme danger: she still had to maintain a close yet safe distance between her aircraft and the Hercules, while on top of that she had no choice now but to assess the data from her radar – something that was made almost impossible because of the distortions caused by her proximity to the giant transport aircraft.

Bentley made some rapid calculations about when to break away from the huge aircraft that was – she fervently hoped – shielding her from whatever optical or radar sensors the intruding craft might be using. The only bonus was that there was now radio silence: no message could be sent overtly to her, of course, but even a message ostensibly for the Hercules crew could prove a fatal distraction. And yet, as she had reminded herself repeatedly in the past few minutes, there was no way to be certain what detection systems – active or passive – the intruder possessed. Everything was speculation.

It would be ideal to acquire the craft visually before breaking away, Bentley told herself. But she knew this might not be possible. The bulk of the Hercules meant she might have to break away to get a clear view. And that was assuming the craft co-operated by slowing down sufficiently for her to have time to react.

Old War Office building, Whitehall

'It's not a car. My God, what the hell *is* that thing? It's vast!'

'OK, now try to remain calm and remember that you're safe now. What you can see and feel is actually in the past, so it can't hurt you. What happens next?'

Blackmore shot a worried look at Carpenter; despite the DIS man's attempts to calm Earl Sutton, the Minister was clearly in a state of some distress. Carpenter grimaced and held up both his hands, palms towards Blackmore. He didn't say anything, but the meaning was clear: *I know it's unpleasant, but we must carry on.*

'There's something wrong with the car; the engine seems to be . . . wait, it's cut out. I'm coming to a halt. I've pulled up at the side of the road, on the narrow grass verge. I'm getting out, and – my God, there it is. It's . . . it's amazing.'

'Describe it, please.'

'It's triangular, like a slice of pizza but maybe a little raised in the centre; maybe more diamond-shaped. It's about a hundred and fifty feet in diameter, and there are three red lights on its underside, one at each point of the triangle. There's a bright white light in the centre – I think that was the one that nearly blinded me when I was on the road. That light's fading now. It's gone out. Only the red lights are visible, and they don't seem to be as bright as they were. The triangle's hovering about fifty feet above the ground, just to the side of the road. There's very little noise – just a faint, low humming sound. Part of me wants to run, but this is just awesome. I have to watch. I *have* to.'

After that, there was a pause. Carpenter, ever the patient professional, said nothing. Blackmore was concerned for his ministerial colleague. He wouldn't really have said that they were friends, but they got on well enough – and there was no denying the courage of the man in coming forward and reporting his experience the moment he saw its relevance to the current crisis. It was clear from his facial expression that he was recalling or even reliving some new development of a decidedly unpleasant nature.

'There's a bluish beam of light and it's just hit me. I feel groggy, as if I had a hangover. It's coming from the underside of the craft, where the white light was before. Oh my God! *I'm floating up off the ground towards the damned thing.'*

Over the North Sea

Bentley knew that she would have to engage her target soon. Her airborne radar showed that the craft was just moments away. The signal revealed it was almost directly on their position and had slowed its speed to match theirs. Although she'd been using her instruments, she'd also been looking directly out of the cockpit to maintain a close – but not too close – distance between her Typhoon and the Hercules.

Bentley had hoped to get a visual fix on the target by now but hadn't succeeded so far, much to her frustration. Still, at least she now had a fair idea that it *was* there, shielded from her view by the Hercules. The plan was to engage as soon as possible and not give the target time to spot her before she spotted it. It might well attack the Hercules anyway, whether it noticed her fighter or not. She flexed her gloved hand and made ready to peel away from her escort.

Old War Office Building, Whitehall

Earl Sutton's anguish was plain to see, but they had reached what was surely the central part of his abduction experience. Carpenter had said little, and Blackmore – as instructed – had remained silent throughout, even though he had plenty of questions of his own and rather resented being ordered around by a Wing Commander. But he was astute enough to see that Carpenter was playing it correctly, avoiding the use of any leading questions.

'I'm lying on my back on some sort of raised platform or table. I seem to be almost paralysed, although my eyes are open and I can blink them. If I really try I can move my head just a fraction, but that's it. It's dark and there's a horrible smell, like rotting leaves and damp cardboard. The whole place is oppressive and somehow deeply – *corrupt*. I don't know why I said that – it just felt like the right word.'

Blackmore and Carpenter exchanged a glance.

'There's something in here with me.' Although there was no

overt panic in Earl Sutton's voice, the flatly delivered statement carried with it a sense of palpable menace. 'I can see two figures, although only faintly, as if it was foggy in here. One's off to the left and is very short. I can just make out a face; someone wearing a big pair of black sunglasses, maybe. The other figure's taller, and in front of me. Coming closer now, so I can see a little better. There's a uniform, and what seems to be a patch on it, with some letters or words or something.'

'Can you read it?'

'Yes.' He did so. Immediately Carpenter burst out of the room and grabbed a secure telephone to place a flash call to the Thunder Child team at the PJHQ.

Over the North Sea

With a fluid movement of her arm, Bentley eased the joystick firmly to port, moving her aircraft clear of the Hercules in less than two seconds. As had been planned, the Hercules then went into a banking turn and started to descend.

For a moment Bentley saw nothing and feared that her quarry had escaped or, worse still, that it had followed the Hercules. But then she saw the craft, below her and to her starboard side. It had slowed to a virtual hover, which would make things much easier. She quickly manoeuvred into an attacking position and prepared to open fire with her cannon. Before she could do so, her radio suddenly burst into life.

'Charlie One, this is Control. Abort, abort, abort. Over.'

'Control, this is Charlie One. Order acknowledged. Over and out.'

Further words failed Bentley as she broke off her attack without firing a shot. Her first thought was to get to safety as soon as possible, but then she reminded herself not to take any action that might leave the Hercules exposed. If she cleared off, the transport aircraft might have to take the consequences – and she wasn't going to let that happen. To give the Hercules time to make good its escape – and to give the intruder something else to think about – she decided to circle the craft.

Part of Bentley still wanted to attack, to get vengeance for the friends and colleagues she'd lost and some points on the board for the RAF. She wished that the order had come through just thirty seconds later, by which time it would have been too late. That was when it struck her that the last-second cancellation of her mission might actually have *saved* her life: if she'd attacked and been unsuccessful, she might have been dead by now.

In carrying out her circling manoeuvre Bentley got her first really clear look at the craft she'd been about to attack. It was beautiful, she decided. As she took in its size and shape, she was struck by the sheer power of the thing. It was just hanging there in the sky and, as she wondered about the energy expenditure involved in achieving this, she realized that it was in nobody's interest to get into a shooting war with these people.

Suddenly, Bentley became aware that the craft was changing shape. It was elongating at the edges, as if it was being stretched. A few seconds later it had gone; its departure had been so rapid that at first she thought it had literally disappeared. She only just registered that the craft had actually moved off at incredible speed – upwards. She changed course again, and began her journey back to base. The whole encounter had taken place so swiftly that the Hercules was still visible some distance away, at a lower altitude.

RAF Coningsby, Lincolnshire

Bentley had rehearsed what she was going to say in advance, cautioning herself not to get angry with either the Fighter Controller or her CO. But she'd certainly have plenty to say to the people at the PJHQ and Whitehall, if she got the opportunity.

Immediately she landed, Bentley was taken to see the CO as technicians removed from her aircraft the gun-camera footage that had recorded the entire flight.

'Why, sir? Why was I given the abort order seconds before I engaged? It could have been fatal,' Bentley demanded icily.

'I'm sorry, Isabelle, but we had no choice. We found out there might have been Americans on that craft.'

Chapter Eight

DIPLOMATIC MANOEUVRES

Cabinet Office, Whitehall

'Have you any idea what you're saying? Any idea at all?' The Foreign Secretary, Richard Chandler, transfixed his opposite number in Defence with a look of incredulity, as if the man had gone stark raving mad.

'You've heard the evidence,' S of S retorted. 'May I remind you that people have died and there are strong indications that our American friends may be involved.' Willoughby had allowed a trace of sarcasm to enter his voice when he used the word 'friends'. This seemed to have the effect of infuriating the Foreign Secretary even more.

'I'm sorry, but if one of your ministerial team gets hypnotized, thinks he's on a spaceship and then says he sees someone wearing an American Air Force uniform, that doesn't constitute legitimate grounds for calling in their ambassador. Not in my book, anyway.'

The meeting was clearly getting out of hand rather quickly, and the Deputy Prime Minister held up her hand for silence. 'Please,' she began, 'let's not allow ourselves to be sidetracked here. We simply don't know enough about regression hypnosis; all the scientific evidence suggests it's not entirely reliable. But the loss of our aircraft and the deaths of our pilots are real events that have a real cause. It's this mystery that we now need to resolve, and it may be that the Americans can help us with it.'

'I will not accuse their ambassador of anything on evidence as flimsy as this.'

'I'm not asking you to. Invite him in, talk him through what's happened and ask him what he thinks. Say that the PM may be asking the President for material assistance on this matter. See if you can smoke out any information about what's going on at RAF Feltwell, and why they didn't spark. I have no idea whether Earl Sutton's recollection under hypnosis was a real and accurate memory, but we have to cover all the possibilities here.'

'All right, I'll do it.'

Willoughby leant forward over the table and handed Chandler a dark red folder. 'You might want to read this beforehand,' he said, as Chandler took the top secret file on the Rendlesham Forest incident. 'I think you'll find it . . . illuminating.'

Whitehall
Shortly after the taxi negotiated Trafalgar Square and turned along Whitehall, Cody caught sight of the Ministry of Defence Main Building and saw that the demonstration against the Government's handling of the current crisis was in full swing. The demonstration was much larger than he'd anticipated. It had been arranged hurriedly and was being held with the permission of the police, but things looked as if they might get out of hand. Crash barriers had been erected, and Cody had noticed several police vans parked in some of the side streets off Whitehall.

Cody had known about the demonstration as soon as it had been planned. Several people had asked him to attend and perhaps say a few words. Organized by some of the more strident voices in the UFO lobby, word of the event had circulated rapidly via the Internet. The media were clearly very well represented, but Cody knew that ufology was still a fringe subject and deduced correctly from the large number present that most of the attendees were ordinary people who had probably never had any interest in UFOs before recent events.

The demonstrators were on the south side of Whitehall, opposite Downing Street and no more than twenty or thirty metres from the South Door of MOD Main Building. Cody strained his eyes trying to read some of the placards being waved, but could only make out two. One said 'Give peace a chance' while the other read 'I love ET', with the word 'love' represented by a red heart.

Cody asked the taxi driver to turn left into Horseguards Avenue so that they could avoid the crowd. It wouldn't do to be seen going into Main Building at a time like this. Some conspiracy theorists already portrayed him as a Government agent, simply because he was a well-dressed, well-spoken man with moderate views. He didn't want to reinforce such suspicions – even though he had a momentary wish to be seen sweeping into the building by some of the UFO hotheads, just to relish the expressions on their silly faces. But that was a self-indulgent notion; to act on it would have been totally unfair to his fellow passenger, who was uneasy enough in any case.

Jenny Thornton had been having a rough time lately and had telephoned Cody in tears the previous night. She was claiming total recall of her abduction experiences, but with some frightening new twists. Judging by material on the Internet, the same thing was happening to others and Cody had spoken to several of the top researchers by telephone, even setting his alarm for three a.m. in an ultimately successful attempt to speak to Dr Krone in the United States. Five of Krone's regular 'support group' of abductees had contacted her with similar accounts and she was as sure as she could be that they had not spoken to each other first. More interestingly, she and other researchers were getting new cases every day, and there was already a large backlog of telephone messages and letters claiming comparable experiences. Cody trusted a scientist like Krone more than he did many of the charlatans involved in abduction research, but just about *all* the investigators were now getting cases of total recall.

Cody had gone through a list of alternative explanations and come up with only three that might hold water: an intricate hoax on an unprecedented scale, some sort of mass hysteria – or a real phenomenon involving precisely what the witnesses claimed. Cody was sure that the third option was the correct one, particularly when looked at alongside the RAF's Typhoon losses. For the first time in over fifty years of active research into UFOs, Cody was scared by what he was seeing. Really scared.

It had been Cody's idea to seek an audience with Head of Sec(AS) and tell him about what was going on in the world of UFO research. He hadn't thought there would be much chance of Templeton agreeing to a meeting so he'd been agreeably surprised when his call had been returned – by Templeton himself, not by his PS. He cast his mind back to the call he'd placed originally, when he'd first asked for the meeting. There had been a definite pause after he'd used the phrase 'Thunder Child'. Had there been a trace of alarm in the desk officer's voice, or had that just been his imagination? Or wishful thinking? Cody didn't know, but decided he'd have to play it carefully and hold the possibility in reserve.

Cody had doubted that Thornton would want to attend, since she had expressed some fairly vitriolic opinions about the MOD and Sec(AS). Indeed, when she'd said that she *was* prepared to attend he'd wondered if this was a mistake and whether she might become emotional or aggressive and so jeopardize his chance of having a serious discussion with Templeton. But Cody dismissed his own doubts and reminded himself that she had more right to put her case than he did.

Cody paid off the taxi driver. Thornton and he began to walk up the steps to the imposing North Door of the MOD's massive headquarters building. As they did so, they could clearly hear the noise of the demonstration, even though it was taking place at the other end of the huge building, out of their line of sight. 'Yo, yo, UFO – people have a right to know!' the crowd were chanting, while someone with a megaphone – Cody thought he recognized the voice – did their best to whip them up into a frenzy of anti-Government, anti-MOD feeling.

They had a point. If First Contact really was happening, Cody could well understand the confusion and fury of those who wanted to hold out the olive branch. But, without a hint of arrogance, he also believed that he knew more about the history of ufology than just about anybody else still alive. And, although Cody could understand the crowd's sentiments, he believed them to be unjustified. The media were screaming about a war – but he was convinced that there had been an undeclared war going on for over fifty years: this, he felt, was just its denouement.

Cody couldn't know that his assessment was almost identical to that of Edwin Van Buren of the NSA.

RAF Coningsby, Lincolnshire

'What's the story, Isabelle?' asked Stuart Coultart, the ex-43 Squadron pilot.

'Yeah, tell us, Izz,' somebody else shouted out. Ever since Bentley had been chosen for the aborted attack on one of the alien craft it had been assumed that she had the CO's ear. Some of the crueller wags on the base had suggested it was another part of his anatomy, but that particular rumour – which was totally untrue – hadn't reached her yet.

'Well, we're not grounded but we're not flying, either,' she replied.

'You what?' There were puzzled looks on the faces of those in the crewroom.

'Officially, the Typhoon force is operating as normal. There's actually *less* reason to ground the fleet now, because we've found out – the hard way – that our losses haven't been due to any design fault but to hostile action.'

'So what happens if we detect another of these . . . things?'

'We sit on our arses, doing fuck all. The Control and Reporting Centres all have instructions to report any anomalous contacts and to plot them, but . . . well, the bottom line is that we won't be launched. Not unless they look as if they're coming over the mainland.'

A chorus of derisive noises issued from various mouths.

Everybody knew what it meant. They were conceding most of the UKADR.

'So why isn't the boss telling us this?'

'Because it's top secret and he's been ordered not to. He ordered me in to his office and told me about his bad habit of talking to himself. Then I just *happened* to hear him mulling over what he'd just been told by the PJHQ, as he pondered the call he'd taken on the secure phone. Get the picture?'

A few people were smiling faintly. They got it, all right. The CO had found a way to follow the letter of his instructions, but still get word to his pilots.

'We're not completely out of the game, though,' Bentley added. 'They're going to be gathering as much intelligence as possible on these things, and that'll mean the AWACS aircraft getting involved.'

'So what?' someone asked.

'Think they'll be going up without a fighter escort?'

Foreign and Commonwealth Office, Whitehall

Richard Chandler was feeling decidedly apprehensive about his meeting with the US ambassador. As Foreign Secretary it was his job to forge good diplomatic relations with as many countries as possible. He had had some notable success recently in re-establishing formal diplomatic ties with two countries that had previously been regarded as sponsors of international terrorism. Although he wondered privately if the countries had *really* changed, it had certainly been a coup for his personal standing, and many political commentators were talking of him as a potential Prime Minister at some stage in his political future.

Now Chandler faced one of the most difficult and unlikely tasks of his career: meeting with the most senior American diplomat in Britain and practically accusing him of playing a part in the violent deaths of British citizens. It was the sort of conversation one occasionally had with representatives of the more unpredictable players on the world stage but not one you wanted, or expected, to have with somebody who was supposed to be your friend and ally.

To make matters worse, the PM had insisted that the Secretary of State for Defence should attend the meeting – and Chandler had an idea that diplomacy was not at the top of Willoughby's list of priorities. He'd been briefed by his own FCO officials and had then received a further written brief – together with an oral one – from several MOD officials, service and civilian. The PM had also given him some very definite parameters for his discussion with the ambassador. As a result, Chandler was feeling decidedly overbriefed and had hardly had time to skim through the file he'd been given on the Rendlesham Forest incident – about which the MOD contingent had expressed disappointment, much to his annoyance. How many hours did they think there were in a day, for goodness' sake? They'd given him a summary but they wanted him to see the details for himself.

Ten minutes later, the American delegation had arrived. Peter Rudzki, the ambassador, was accompanied by Bill Jackson, the Defence Attaché. With them was a third man whom Chandler didn't recognize. He was introduced as a Mr Kaufman from the NSA, and was present – so the ambassador had explained – to offer some help and advice on what he described as 'your current predicament'. It had been agreed that the discussion would be in private and would not be minuted so, once aides had distributed teas and coffees, they withdrew.

'Good morning, and thank you for agreeing to see us at such short notice,' Chandler began. 'As my officials indicated when they made contact, we are interested in any advice or assistance your Government feels able to offer us concerning the loss of our Typhoons. You already have copies of the dossier we prepared on these incidents. Perhaps we could use that as a starting point for our discussion?'

Rudzki looked calm but serious as he launched into his opening statement, which was as carefully scripted as Chandler's had been. The art of diplomacy – even between friends – had very precise rules.

'May I say first of all that the President has asked me to convey her *personal* sympathies to all those who have lost loved ones in these incidents. We as a nation share your sense of loss at these tragic events, and stand ready to offer such advice and assistance as may be deemed appropriate.'

'I'm grateful for those kind words. Please thank the President and assure her that her message will be passed on as you request. Perhaps we can now turn to one or two specific ideas about how best to take matters forward. Before we do so, however, I would be grateful for clarification on one point that has caused us some difficulty . . .'

Willoughby suppressed a desire to groan. Why did the Foreign Secretary have to talk in such a roundabout fashion? He knew it was the language of diplomacy but he still wished Chandler would be a little more forthright. The mandarins had obviously got to him and indoctrinated him in the fine art of FCO fence-sitting.

'Engaged as we were in life-or-death conflict with an unidentified enemy,' Chandler continued, 'we relied heavily on our various radar installations – the so-called Control and Reporting Centres. But we were also getting important data from the Ballistic Missile Early Warning Centre at RAF Fylingdales, on their space-tracking radar. So we were wondering why the Deep Space Tracking Facility at RAF Feltwell hadn't picked anything up or, if it had, why the USAF Fifth Space Surveillance Squadron didn't pass on a warning – or even an assessment after the events.'

Willoughby experienced a wave of gratitude towards Chandler and felt renewed respect for the man. He'd been impeccably polite, but there had been no mistaking the steel in his voice. Whether or not the Foreign Secretary really believed any of the darker suspicions being discussed in certain quarters of the MOD, he had played his part brilliantly and had put their American visitors firmly on the spot. They conferred rapidly, in whispers that the British delegation half caught.

'I'm shocked.' It was Rudzki who spoke. 'We thought they had. Our view is that it wouldn't have made any difference to the final outcome, but I agree you should have had word.' He didn't put his DA on the spot by asking him to comment, but he shot him a glance that made it pretty clear that he would appreciate a comment from his military expert.

'I'm as surprised as you are, sir,' Jackson drawled, in an accent that was clearly as Deep South as you could get. 'But I give you my word right now that we're gonna find out why the dog didn't bark.'

'Mr Kaufman?'

The ambassador had turned to the NSA man and specifically invited him to speak. Now that *was* interesting, Chandler and Willoughby both thought. There had been no need to seek any input from Kaufman – indeed, there was no obvious reason for Kaufman to be present at all. Men like Rudzki didn't make mistakes and they didn't do things without good reason. Rudzki was a skilled diplomat and was clearly sending them a message: the ambassador and his DA didn't like Kaufman and felt he had something to answer for. Could Feltwell be an NSA facility? Was *that* what Rudzki was trying to say?

'I share your grief,' Kaufman ventured. 'I, too, will initiate enquiries to see whether anyone in the NSA might have made a contribution, although, as you know, the primary focus of our mission lies elsewhere.'

It had been a bland statement, delivered without emotion or conviction. But they had reached an impasse and, short of accusing him of lying, Chandler was at a loss as to how to take the matter forward. Willoughby had a trump card to play, though; one that he had not shared with Chandler; who he had feared might try to veto it, by going straight to the PM if necessary.

'I'm grateful for your assurances,' Willoughby said, 'but I'd like now to move to another issue. Information has come our way about the activities of a certain Captain Landau, who we believe may be a USAF officer. Now, this information is unverified but I'd like to take this opportunity to ask if any of you are aware of this individual and could comment on work that – we believe – may have involved activity in UK airspace.'

Chandler shot Willoughby a look, the meaning of which was clear enough. *Who the hell is Landau, and what activities are you talking about?* But, even before he glanced at his ministerial colleague, the Foreign Secretary knew that Willoughby had said something important because Chandler had caught something in the faces of his American visitors. Looks of puzzlement from Rudzki and Jackson, but something else from Kaufman. Panic, perhaps. He recognized the name, though, that much was certain. All politicians knew how to read faces, and Kaufman was either too unversed in diplomacy or simply too surprised to control his expression.

'The look on your face suggests that you recognize the name,' Chandler ventured, as he stared at the NSA man. The Foreign Secretary hadn't a clue what was going on, but he played the part beautifully.

'I don't know the details of every mission,' Kaufman replied, his composure regained. 'I must withdraw, and seek guidance from my superiors.' With that he rose and walked out of the room, leaving his own colleagues stunned.

When the door had closed, it was Willoughby who spoke first. 'We are currently following up a number of different theories about the craft that have been attacking our jets. Some of us believe they are a new aircraft or RPV of some sort, while others favour more exotic solutions. Whatever the origin of these things, we have recently received some information from a reliable source that indicates an American has been on board one of these craft.'

'I don't know what to say,' Rudzki replied. 'I'm shocked. I'm angry, dammit. If you're telling me that one of our own people has had a hand in this whole affair, I— I'll have Kaufman removed from office and put on trial. But I'll need more to go on. You'll have to share data with me, and brief me in. Then, I promise you, I'll go to the President if I have to.'

'I think you'll have to,' Willoughby said. 'Right now.' With that he handed Rudzki a thin file and asked him to step outside to read it.

When the two Americans had withdrawn, Willoughby turned apologetically to the Foreign Secretary. 'I know, I'm sorry I didn't tell you beforehand about that little stunt, but you might have objected.'

'I probably would have. But it worked, so I suppose I can't complain. Brief me in before they come back.'

'Remember the attack we launched and then aborted at the last minute? It was aborted because of something Earl Sutton said he recalled. One of the things he saw under hypnotic regression was a person in American military uniform. This person was wearing a patch with his name on: Landau.'

'If these bastards are involved in killing our people, I wish you *had* shot the damn thing down.'

'Next time we will.'

When Rudzki and Jackson returned, Chandler took up where Willoughby had left off. 'I do not know where your Mr Kaufman has gone but I would be grateful if you would find out. If he is not out of the country by midnight tonight I will declare him *persona non grata*. I'm unsure what influence you have over people like that, but I assume he answers to *somebody*. I shall be briefing the PM immediately after this meeting, and you can bet he'll want to talk to the President as soon as possible. I suggest you ensure that she's briefed, because the PM will have a *lot* of questions for her.'

Chandler gathered together his papers and made it clear that the meeting was over. A few words of farewell were exchanged – but there was little sense of any cordiality between the two nations' representatives.

MOD Main Building, Whitehall

Nick Templeton had mentioned to US of S that he was going to be meeting the man generally acknowledged to be Britain's leading expert on UFOs. Blackmore, of course, had seen Cody on *Newsnight* and had been impressed. He had an air of respectability and quiet authority about him, and was certainly no crank. But Templeton had been genuinely surprised when the Minister had said that he'd like to attend the discussion. Templeton had actually advised against it and had even enlisted Jacqui Connolly in an attempt to talk him out of the idea. They feared that Cody would seek to make capital out of such a meeting, and pointed out to Blackmore that it would send the already volatile UFO lobby into a frenzy.

But Blackmore would not be put off, even when he was told that there would be an abductee present. His instincts told him that he might learn something useful and he secretly enjoyed any opportunities to go against advice from civil servants, who, he felt were extremely able but always far too cautious. There was also the issue of 'open Government', to which he was passionately committed. So he'd overruled them, insisting on holding the meeting in his own office.

Terry Carpenter turned up with Templeton – Blackmore was beginning to think the two were joined at the hip, although he was pleased to see an unusual example of the Civil Service working so well with the military. Sue Farthing ushered Cody and Thornton into his office and withdrew.

'I hope you will forgive me for hijacking this meeting,' Blackmore said to Cody. 'I know you'd asked to see Nick but I know the UFO lobby are always complaining that we don't take your subject seriously. I wanted to assure you that that's not the case. I'm genuinely interested in what you've got to say, and I'm here to listen.'

'I'm grateful, Minister,' Cody replied. 'Although I must say it seems as if your interest is simply one forced upon you by circumstance.'

'That's true, I admit. And it looks as if we were wrong to ignore what you people have been telling us.' Blackmore really was sorry, but he was also a smooth operator who knew that a frank admission of error from a politician could be a disarming tactic on those who held the standard view that a politician would never admit to a mistake. But Blackmore cautioned himself to be wary of Cody. His impression of the man from *Newsnight* had been correct: he was intelligent, articulate and very sharp. He resolved to think of him as a retired barrister with an interest in UFOs, as distinct from just another member of the UFO lobby.

The meeting had been running for about forty minutes, during which Cody had put across some theories about UFOs, while Thornton had described some of her abduction experiences. These were what most interested the MOD hosts and, as they'd decided earlier, they asked questions designed to get the one crucial piece of information they wanted – the information that had prompted them to agree to the meeting in the first place.

'Do these entities ever give you any messages?' Templeton ventured.

'Most times, no. No messages. No information. Sometimes a word or two about how it won't hurt, or how it's for my own good. But the last time I *did* get a message. They said I was to tell the Thunder Child that he was doing something dangerous. No.' She stopped and thought for a moment. 'No, that's not it. It's not quite right. I don't know, I'm sorry – I don't write all this stuff down, you know.' She looked at Cody, apologetically. 'Sorry – I know you said I should.'

'It's OK, Jenny, you have enough on your plate without following my every whim.' He smiled. 'You're doing really well. Just take your time, though, and see if you can remember anything else.'

'OK.' There was a long pause. 'OK, they said our leaders were playing a dangerous game. Yes, that's it. They said you were interfering with some plan of theirs, and that I should warn Thunder Child. Oh, they also said it was all for our own good, but they always say that.'

'Who's Thunder Child?' Cody clearly had an agenda of his own.

'I'm afraid I can't tell you,' Templeton replied immediately. They had been expecting the question, of course.

'Oh, come on,' Cody retorted. 'We've been completely frank with you. All I'm asking is that you show us the same courtesy.'

'No, I'm sorry,' Templeton replied. 'There's no room for compromise. All information here is handled on the need-to-know principle. That overrides everything else – classification, trust, everything.'

Thornton moved to say something, but Cody leant over and cut her off. 'I'm sorry, Jenny. We won't win this one.' He turned to his hosts. 'I'm disappointed but not surprised.' He couldn't resist one parting shot, turning to Carpenter. 'I didn't catch the name of the division you work for . . .' Carpenter smiled, but said nothing.

Blackmore rose to his feet. 'I'm sorry, I have to go now. Thank you for coming in. I'm sure you'll stay in touch with Nick.'

The meeting broke up, and the visitors were escorted from the building.

'Well done, everybody,' Blackmore said. 'Thoughts?'

'Unless they were the world's best actors, they really *don't* know anything about Thunder Child,' Templeton offered. Blackmore and Carpenter nodded.

'So who told her about it?' the Minister asked.

'If we take her story at face value, I guess I'd have to say that there really *are* extraterrestrials. And they really *do* know our every move.'

It was a chilling thought, but nobody disagreed with Carpenter's assessment.

Georgina's Wine Bar, Charing Cross

Once Cody and Thornton had been escorted out of the North Door of Main Building, they decided to go for a drink and a meal, over which they would discuss the meeting they'd just had. All the pubs on Whitehall were full, but, not far from Charing Cross, they noticed a wine bar down a little side alley. Entering it, they walked down a flight of stairs, ordered some food at the bar, bought some drinks and settled down into a semi-enclosed booth that afforded them a degree of privacy. Although neither of them were familiar with the area, their choice of venue was ironic in that Georgina's was a favourite lunchtime meeting place for civil servants, especially for senior MOD personnel who regarded Georgina's as being convivial yet discreet.

'What did you make of that?' Cody asked.

'I'm not sure. They seemed sincere. I really wanted to have a go at them at one point, but I knew you wouldn't have liked that.'

'I probably wouldn't have,' Cody admitted, 'but you certainly have a right to be annoyed with them. I know how frustrating their attitude must be when you're having these experiences and they don't want to know. I know they said they were interested but, as I said, I suspect that's just something that's been forced on them. If they hadn't lost those aircraft, I doubt they'd be concerned.'

Cody excused himself and went to the toilet. When he returned, Thornton was looking pensive. He remained silent, suspecting that she had a delicate matter to raise.

'Richard?'

'Yes?'

'When we were on the sixth floor, going past all those wooden doors where all the senior people work, I passed someone in the corridor. I caught his eye, but he looked away. I – I think I recognize him.'

'From the television?' Cody speculated. For once, he was slow on the uptake.

'No. From one of my experiences. I think he's an abductee too.'

Over Northumberland

It was a cold, clear morning; one that Isabelle Bentley saw as offering perfect flying weather. Visibility was excellent, and the meteorological conditions meant that there was no dense air to play tricks with her radar – or with any of the other radars currently being monitored. Stuart Coultart was her number two and their mission was straightforward escort duty for the third aircraft in their patch of sky.

The Sentry Airborne Early Warning aircraft on which Bentley and Coultart were riding shotgun was one of the RAF's most prized assets. It was one of just seven such aircraft that the RAF possessed, of which perhaps three or four were operational at any given time. Cruising at a height of around 29,000 feet, this aircraft's job was to extend the range of ground-based radar systems, using a powerful AN/APY-2 surveillance radar and transmitting data to ground units through various digital links. The Thunder Child team at PJHQ were flexing their muscles and, although there had been a high-level decision not to fly over the North Sea any more, the RAF were not in the business of conceding control of the skies to anybody. Using a Sentry had been a logical way of maintaining a recognized air picture without actually engaging the hostile force.

Bentley felt this was false logic, and had told the CO as much. What was the point, she had said, of securing early detection of an uncorrelated target if you weren't going to do anything about it? Her view was that it simply gave you more time to feel impotent. But she'd always known that the decision to fly a mission such as this was a political one, enabling the RAF and the Government to say that standard air defence patrols were taking place. And it was true that CSA had been pressing for a mission such as this, in the hope of picking up some piece of useful data that everyone else had missed. The Typhoons were there as escorts, just in case of trouble. That said, none was expected so far away from the area of previous activity and, with all the radars looking north-east, they were confident of early detection in any case.

Bentley looked down at the massive aircraft that, like her own, was painted a dull blue-grey. Mounted on the top of the fuselage, roughly midway between the wings and the tail, was the radome that housed the aircraft's radar. It looked for all the world like a giant black Smartie with a white band running through the middle. She smiled as she recalled a story about how a man had driven into a ditch at the side of the road past RAF Waddington – home to the Sentry force – when he'd seen the radome close-up. An aircraft had been coming into land, but the only illuminated part of it had been the radome. By chance it had been the CRO who had pulled the driver, ranting about how the aliens were coming to get him, from his car. The irony of this paranoia hadn't escaped Bentley.

When her radio crackled into life she was surprised. Although there were standard com links between the Sentry, the Typhoons and the Control and Reporting Centres, they'd agreed to maintain radio silence where this was possible.

'Er, Sierra Five to Eagles Two and Three and Sector Control, we're – ah – we're picking something up at extreme range. Looks like it could be one of our friends. We're attempting a plot.'

Bentley tensed. She looked at her own radar but knew it would be blank, as would be the ground-based systems. The Sentry's equipment was way ahead of hers and, although the radars on the ground were more powerful, they were limited by the simple fact that the Earth was round. No matter, the Sentry would be feeding them real-time information before long, and they could all put their heads together and work out what they thought was going on. With an early detection it was hoped that a better plot could be established, perhaps enabling them to see where the intruder had come from and where it was going.

'We have a course change. It – it's coming our way.'

Although it had been detected at the extreme limit of the Sentry's range, nobody had any illusions about how little time they had to react to the threat. Mental calculations were being done by the various players, all of whom knew that the craft could travel at speeds of at least Mach 4, but might well be capable of more.

The Sentry did the only thing that it could and went into a steep dive, navigators frantically checking for the nearest place they could land. They were requesting additional fighter cover from Leuchars and Leeming, but it was a futile gesture: the maths simply didn't work out, and they soon realized that the issue would be decided long before any other Typhoons could hope to get close. Some aircraft were launched anyway, just in case, but everybody was too busy to pay much attention to these well-intentioned but hopelessly remote assets. Bentley cursed the fact that their position was almost exactly midway between the two fighter bases. *Maybe if we'd stayed close to one of them* . . . but then, they'd hardly expected trouble over the mainland.

Bentley and Coultart quickly talked through their options. They might have flown towards the target and engaged it at the maximum possible distance from the Sentry. On the other hand, if the intruder ignored them, the early-warning aircraft would be completely exposed. Splitting up seemed pointless, so they quickly decided to stay with the Sentry and engage the target as soon as they could.

They didn't have long to wait. The MOD had finally done

something the RAF approved of: they had effectively switched from passive, reactive ROE that only allowed pilots to shoot if they'd been attacked to guidelines that allowed them to engage a target if they assessed it was hostile and was about to commit an aggressive act. This was the hunting licence that the RAF had wanted much earlier in the game.

PJHQ, Northwood

The duty staff at PJHQ – including the newly seconded Alan Whitfield – could only watch as events unfolded. Senior officers were summoned, as if their presence could influence events. In reality they were all just spectators: calling out the brass was little more than a tonic, designed to convince everyone involved that they were doing something. There was no time for orders, and no point in giving any. The pilots had enough on their plates without a bunch of senior officers telling them what to do from the comfort and security of the bunker. The pilots knew well enough what was expected of them, and their options were so few that additional instructions were unnecessary, as well as unwelcome.

Over Northumberland

The intruder was showing up clearly on the Typhoons' radars. The Sentry had a clearer image technically, but now there was no mistaking the familiar profile of an object that had brought so much death and destruction to the RAF. There was little point in any of the Sentry crew trying to direct the battle as they might have done in a conventional engagement. In reality, there was no orthodox battle to direct, just a series of actions that might or might not prove effective.

In a piece of near-perfect synchronized flying, both jets peeled away from the fleeing AEW aircraft and activated their BVRAAM missiles. They were still picking up faint radar returns from the intruder and managed to lock on to the target an instant before the launch. Eight missiles streaked towards the oncoming craft, the pilots tracking their progress on their radars, hoping that whatever technology had rendered the missiles useless in previous encounters would not be able to cope with such a coordinated volley – especially given the tremendous closing speed resulting from the Typhoons having fired directly at a target that was already heading straight for them.

'Shit, shit, shit!'

'He's broken the fucking lock.'

The missiles were supposed to be highly resistant to electronic countermeasures, but the RAF didn't even know whether the intruder used electronics. It was all guesswork, and they were running out of options. The jets turned back towards the Sentry, trying to ensure that they didn't get too far behind the lumbering aircraft. There were seventeen people on board the AEW plane, and all but the pilot and navigator were reduced to spectators, looking at dots on screens. One dot was their aircraft, and one fast-moving dot was the hostile inbound. Two dots in between were doing their best to stop the intruder. It was a grotesque parody of an arcade game but none of them had any illusions about what would happen if the dots merged: Game Over.

Bentley and Coultart overtook the Sentry, then turned again and flew directly into harm's way. A second volley of missiles was fired, this time the shorter-range, heat-seeking ASRAAMs. An instant after they had been launched, Coultart screamed into his radio that he had a visual sighting.

Both pilots watched with a mixture of fascination and horror as the eight missiles approached the intruder and then peeled away in all directions, simultaneously losing the lock-ons that they had most definitely had before the launch. Bentley and Coultart had both ensured that after firing their missiles they had jinked their own aircraft this way and that in an automatic defensive move. It was a standard tactic, but one that was all too easy to forget in situations where pilots were tempted to follow their missiles in visually in the hope of seeing a kill. The tactic had saved Bentley's life in her previous encounter. It served them both well this time, too, because immediately after the ASRAAMs had been launched the alien craft fired a weapon of some sort in the general direction of the Typhoon's earlier position. Both pilots saw a red flash of . . .

something . . . pass by at high speed.

Gloved hands flexed and protector caps were removed from the firing buttons of internally mounted 27mm cannons. The intruder was dead ahead, and the closing speed was frightening. It was almost as if a high-speed, hi-tech game of chicken was taking place in the skies above the Northumberland countryside. Two bursts were fired and, as the craft flashed past, Bentley and Coultart had the satisfaction of seeing some of the shots hit home. Whether any damage was done was impossible to say. Still, at least it proved the craft *could* be hit and that it wasn't protected by a force field, as some of the PJHQ analysts had speculated.

The pilots threw their Typhoons into desperately tight turns, pulling muscle-wrenching Gs in an attempt to re-engage the craft before it could fire on the Sentry. Coultart's turn was the more effective and he found himself directly behind the intruder, which was decelerating rapidly. He fired another burst, being careful to avoid hitting the Sentry, and watched with amazement and satisfaction as his shots ploughed into the craft's hull, sending pieces of it flying off in all directions.

'Yessss! We can do this, Izz!' Coultart yelled, realizing for the first time that the craft was not invulnerable.

It was at this point that two things happened in quick succession. First, Coultart ran out of ammunition. Second, the intruder fired a bolt of energy at the Sentry. It missed. Bentley frantically manoeuvred her Typhoon, trying to get a clear shot at the alien craft. Coultart had broken off his pursuit and was clearly trying to ensure that his aircraft wasn't in her line of fire. When Bentley was sure of a shot that would hit the intruder without hitting the Sentry or Coultart, she depressed the red button and fired her cannon.

The shots slammed into the craft's hull, clearly damaging it but certainly not disabling it. It fired another shot at the Sentry: it was only a matter of time before it found its range – or got lucky.

Bentley cursed as she ran out of ammunition. Her options were now pretty limited, to put it mildly, and the only thing she could think of was harassing the intruder by flying so close to it that it would engage her and not the Sentry. But there was no guarantee of success.

Coultart had reached the same conclusion. Like Bentley, he had no thoughts of breaking off and returning to base, leaving the Sentry to its fate. But, unlike Bentley, he remembered that there was one more weapon left to use.

Bentley was behind the craft, trying to edge closer to it, when she saw a blur of motion from above and ahead. The choice had been a simple one for Coultart: one life or seventeen lives? Several tonnes of metal struck the intruder dead centre at a speed of around Mach 3 – but Coultart had had to stay with this 'weapon' all the way, to guide it in. There was a thunderous explosion as his Typhoon impacted with the alien craft. While Bentley looked on in horror, through eyes suddenly filled with tears, she saw the intruder start to break up and fall from the sky.

Chapter Nine

FALLEN ANGEL

PJHQ, Northwood

'Did we screw up?'

It was CJO himself who had directed the question at the stunned Thunder Child team. He had been watching events unfold from the gallery overlooking the Operations Room, deep in the heart of the bunker, and had just received a report from one of the officers on board the Sentry that had confirmed what they had seen and heard. He had watched but had not interfered, knowing as the crew of the Sentry had known that no action they could take would have altered the outcome. It was one of those terrifying, helpless moments when skilled and experienced leaders could do nothing more than watch.

Lieutenant General Ball was not looking to shift blame elsewhere: that was simply not his style. But he needed to know whether he or any of his team had made an error of judgement that had just led to the death of a brave young man. He needed to know not just because he desperately wanted confirmation that he'd done all he could to keep his people safe, but also because he might have to give further orders that could well result in similar situations. Mistakes were made and tragedies occurred, but if you could learn from them, that was one way to make a death seem slightly less pointless.

It was Whitfield who replied, answering for everyone. 'No, sir, there was no reason to believe they'd strike at us over the mainland. Nothing in their previous operating profile gave us any clue that was likely. If we're not safe there, we're not safe anywhere. Short of grounding the entire RAF I don't see any prospect of keeping our aircraft out of harm's way.'

There were nods and murmurs of agreement from the others, although CJO still entertained doubts about the matter. Had they provoked an unknown enemy? But he dismissed this thought angrily, reminding himself that this had happened not just in the UKADR but over sovereign British territory.

Hard though it was to set aside the death of a man, there were other matters to attend to and other decisions to make. The Sentry was still on site and had radioed-in locations where the wreckage of the Typhoon and of the enemy craft had fallen – several miles apart but, thankfully, in open countryside and not onto the heads of any local people. A couple of Army captains were on the phone, frantically trying to work out the quickest means of getting troops to the area and securing the two sites.

Ball looked at his map and decided that the Sentry should divert to RAF Leeming rather than attempt the longer flight back to its home base at Waddington. He was not expecting any further trouble, but recent events had shown the dangers of making assumptions based on previous experience and he just wanted to get the aircraft down as soon as possible. He told the officer who was in contact with the Sentry that he wanted Bentley's Typhoon and the other latecomers who had just arrived on station to escort the AEW aircraft in. He had no doubts about their inability to fend off an attack and couldn't and wouldn't order anyone to ram one of the enemy craft. But he assumed that, if the enemy did know about their loss, they might not know how it had occurred, and he gambled that this might deter them from attacking, if there were sufficient AD escorts on station.

It was a reasonable assessment, but Ball cursed their lack of knowledge about the enemy, recognizing that even the best estimate of the situation was based on little more than conjecture. But all that would change now. Now they'd brought down one of the craft, he hoped that all sorts of questions would be answered.

With his immediate operational tasks done and orders issued, CJO headed off for the secure video-link facility where he would now confer with Ministers and Chiefs of Staff in the DCMC in Main Building. They were, he had no doubt, screaming for an update.

RAF Feltwell, Norfolk

Colonel Bob Zeckle had just received a telephone call from an officer at RAF Menwith Hill who had briefed him on an intercept they'd recently monitored. It confirmed his own assessment of events, based on what he and a few of his staff had just witnessed on some of their radar systems. He lifted his phone and placed a call to his boss at Fort Meade. When Van Buren came on the line, Zeckle spoke quietly, but in a tone that gave away the terror he was feeling.

'Sir, we have a Fallen Angel incident.'

'What? Goddamit . . . how?'

'We don't know yet, sir. The Duty Controller – who saw the entire sequence of events – thinks there was a collision. He called me in and I saw the takedown. We'll go over the tapes again, but at this stage I concur with my controller's view. We're also trying to tap into various secure lines that we think might be used for the MOD's briefing, but my preliminary assessment is that one of their fast-jet pilots *deliberately* rammed our friends to save his colleagues who were in an AEW aircraft.'

'Poor, brave, stupid bastard.'

'Sir?' Zeckle decided it was time to raise something with his boss. 'Sir, I think we're on the wrong side here.'

'Of course we're on the wrong fucking side,' Van Buren exploded. 'You think I don't know that? But you're one of the few people who knows why we *have* to be on the wrong side.'

'They're not immortal, sir – they can be stopped. Hell, the Brits just proved that. If we levelled with them – Christ, if we even levelled with our *own* people, sir, we could—'

'We could *what*, Bob?' Van Buren cut in. His voice didn't sound angry, even though he was a man few people dared question in the way Zeckle was doing now. 'We could gamble everything on one throw of the dice? Do we have the right to do that, Bob. And would you like to make that call?'

There was a pause, as Zeckle thought through their options. 'No, sir, I wouldn't *like* to, but we may *have* to. We don't know how our friends will respond, and we don't know what the Brits might find out about our part in all this. Do we even know if our man was on board?'

'No,' Van Buren replied. 'We don't know, although the laws of probability make it unlikely.'

'Unlikely, but possible. If he *was* on board, then we'll *have* to level with the Brits – there'll simply be no other option.'

'Maybe. But we already have problems with the Brits anyway. They've asked Mr Kaufman to leave the country, and they mentioned our man by name.'

Zeckle was incredulous. 'But how?' Then he began to worry. Landau's mission was known to only a handful of people, of whom he was one. Might Van Buren think *he*'d told the British authorities? He had, after all, just spent the last few minutes trying to persuade him to brief the Brits in. Before Van Buren could accuse him, Zeckle began to blurt out his denial. 'It wasn't me, sir – even though I half think we should.'

'Don't worry, Bob. If I thought you'd been speaking out of turn, we wouldn't be having this conversation.' Van Buren paused to let the comment sink in. 'No, I don't understand how the Brits could possibly know about Landau but we'll figure it out. I think we've made a couple of errors, though. The Brits know about the capabilities of your systems at Feltwell and it was foolish of us not to pass on a vague warning. I should have anticipated this and ordered you to tip them off. It's just that I never thought our friends would come in so openly. Frankly, I don't know what they're up to.'

Zeckle didn't interrupt. He could tell his boss was thinking on his feet, assessing the situation as he went along. He went cold at the thought of the fate of the entire world hinging on the conversation they were having and didn't envy his boss the decision that he was being drawn towards.

'Another point,' Van Buren mused, 'concerns some unfinished business over your way. The ghost of Rendlesham Forest may have returned to haunt us.'

'Yes, sir.' *Shit, he's losing it.* Van Buren's voice sounded really distant now, and it was clear that he was talking to himself more than to Zeckle. But there was one more thing Zeckle needed to know. 'Sir, we assess that the wreckage has come down over land. Do we try to get in on the recovery op?'

'Absolutely not. They'd smell a rat. No, continue to listen in and see what you can find out. And just hope we don't get a call asking us to pick up our men's body.'

'If we do, they'll close us down, sir, and throw us out. Hell, I would.'

'Bob, right now that's the least of our worries. I'll talk to a few people and I'll be back to you as soon as I can. But, meanwhile, destroy all material on the project.'

'Yes, sir'. Van Buren broke the connection, leaving Zeckle to contemplate the next move. Was Van Buren going to switch sides? He hoped so, even though he knew the risks.

MOD Main Building, Whitehall

'That pilot is going to get the Victoria Cross,' CAS said, grim-faced.

Nobody raised any objections and, by collective agreement, the decision was made. A handful of people were present in the DCMC conference room, having heard CJO's brief. US of S was there, of course, and CDS. Also present were CDI, the Chief Press Officer, Head of Sec(AS), CSA and DUS(S&T). It was these last two who would now have a key part to play and, predictably, CSA wasted no time putting CGS on the spot.

'Have your people secured the crash site?'

'They're doing it now. Some of the local plods got there first and there are a few civvies around, but we're clearing them out,' CGS replied.

'What have they been told?' Blackmore demanded, just beating Connolly to the question.

'The truth,' CGS shot back. 'Well, part of it, anyway. We said that one of our Typhoons had come down, and that we were securing the crash site as part of standard procedure.'

'Hmm.' Blackmore thought about that for a while. 'Jacqui?'

'It's fine for the short term, Minister,' Connolly replied, 'but we have to come up with something more substantial before much longer. We're being crucified by the world's media, and even though we've brought extra staff into the Press Office we're not even keeping our heads above water.'

A few years ago, her remarks might have angered some of the military officers present, since men and women under their command would have been fighting and dying while Connolly sorted out her press lines. But there had been a culture shift in the forces, reflecting recent Governmental changes as well as technological advances. All those in senior positions of command had been media-trained and were well aware of the importance to any policy objective of keeping the media on-side.

Blackmore looked pensive for a moment. 'The recovery team is on its way to the crash site, and it's extremely likely that within a matter of minutes we shall know for sure whether we're dealing with something earthly or extraterrestrial. We may as well all stay here until the news comes through. When it does — well, frankly, I don't know. It'll be the PM's decision.'

'I should mention something I've done on my own authority,' CAS interjected. Heads turned. 'I've ordered a Rapier squadron from Leeming to deploy to the crash site, in case our friends want their toy back.'

'Good call', Blackmore replied, setting CAS's mind at ease somewhat.

'Minister, we have a bigger decision to make.' All eyes turned to CSA, who had been having a whispered conversation with her deputy. 'I need to tell you about Operation Fountain.' The room seemed to divide into two camps. Those who didn't know about it looked puzzled, while those who did know looked horrified.

'Explain,' Blackmore ordered.

'Minister, as you know, I have a team of scientists en route to the crash site as we speak. This is an integrated team, made up partly by my people and partly by CDI's specialists. They're all wearing full NBC suits.' CSA paused, to let the fact sink in. Even those who hadn't been consulted during the planning of Fountain could see where this was leading. 'This is because of the potential biohazard, Minister. If this craft *is* extraterrestrial, the occupants come from an entirely different ecosystem to ours. When Western explorers arrived in the New World, they brought with them diseases to which the native populations had no immunity. Many of those who went to the New World went with conquest and exploitation in mind, but disease killed many more than died in any battle. We have called our response to these recent events 'Operation Thunder Child', taking the name from *The War of the Worlds*. You'll doubtless remember what happened at the end of the book: the Martian invaders were wiped out by earthly bacteria. In reality, it would more likely be a two-way street. If humans can wipe out other humans with disease, simply because their common evolutionary paths diverged for a few thousand years, what might happen between life forms who evolved on entirely different planets?'

'But surely they'd have thought about this and wouldn't be coming here at all if we were lethal to them?' Blackmore asked. 'And what about these abduction cases? If we're to believe all of that, then there's already two-way contact between us.'

'Yes, you may well be right,' CSA replied. 'But that would be *controlled* contact; contact on their terms. This is something different, and any necessary controls may have been destroyed. Either way, I don't believe we can take the chance.'

'What can we do?' Blackmore asked. He had an idea he knew what the answer was.

'Well, fortunately this was thought through long ago, and planned for in a thorough but discreet way. The plan was originally designed to deal with the spillage or deliberate release of highly dangerous biological material. I have a team from CBDE Porton Down who are on their way to the crash site by Chinook. They will take atmospheric samples from around the site. If there is a danger, we may need to . . . *sterilize* the area.'

'With what?'

'We could try several things, starting, perhaps, with flame-throwers. But if that didn't work, or the threat to the country and even the world was critical, then we would have to consider escalating our response progressively until any threat was neutralized. In the final event we may have to consider the nuclear option.'

The room suddenly went very quiet. Blackmore resisted the temptation to object and stopped to think things through. He knew CSA wasn't mad and that she would have considered the situation logically. She could advise, but the ultimate decision was his, for the time being.

'Isn't the damage done?' he asked. 'I mean, the moment the hull was breached in the atmosphere, wouldn't any micro-organisms have scattered to the four winds?'

CSA had to admire the man: he certainly knew his stuff and asked intelligent questions. 'Yes, Minister, in a worst-case scenario that's true and there's nothing we can do. But it's possible to envisage an intermediate scenario, where there is a biohazard but where countermeasures on the main source may have an effect – especially if hull integrity was not significantly damaged in the descent. But it's all speculation, and all I'm saying is that while some factors may be beyond our control, we should try to plan for those that we can control.'

'I'll need to consult S of S, but my recommendation is that we authorize *whatever* means may be necessary. But what about the local population? What about an evacuation?' Blackmore was chilled by the realization that he'd raised this right at the end of their discussion, as an afterthought. Was it the ultimate irony of possible contact with aliens that he was losing his humanity?

'Minister, if there's a biohazard that warrants our using this sort of tactic, then those people will die anyway. Ultimately, our way may be kinder.'

Farnham, Surrey

Once he'd got home, Cody did something that he'd only thought of after he'd left MOD main building. He cursed himself for his stupidity as he accessed the Internet and called up one of the more popular search engines. He typed in the two words and waited. Sure enough, there were a number of matches for the unusual two-word combination.

Cody accessed the first site containing the words. It was one about the life and works of H.G. Wells and as soon as Cody read the context he realized what Thunder Child was. He reached for his telephone, intending to tell Jenny Thornton what he'd just worked out, but then paused. He didn't share what he regarded as the rampant paranoia of some within the UFO lobby, but he had been involved in breaking a story that the Government and military self-evidently did regard as concerning national security. Thornton and he had, after all, just met a Government minister to discuss UFOs and abductions, so people in high places *were* interested.

Cody was astute enough to realize that the MOD had probably only agreed to the meeting because they wanted to see how much he and Thornton knew. Either that, or they'd been tyring to elicit some specific piece of information – just as he had attempted a similar strategy of his own with questions about Thunder Child. Might somebody have decided that his conversations merited a wire-tap? He knew from his legal career that such things were not done on a whim, but he also knew about the Interception of Telecommunications Act and was aware that the Home Secretary was unlikely to turn down a request for a warrant, especially against the background of the current crisis. He decided to drive over and brief Thornton in person.

On his way to Thornton's house, Cody ran things through in his mind and decided that it might be worth calling Templeton to ask for another meeting. After all, he now had two pieces of important information that might serve as bargaining chips. There had been Thornton's belief that she'd seen an abductee on the sixth floor of the MOD Main Building. There were photographs of the Ministers and Chiefs of Staff on the MOD's website. It was a long shot, but he'd printed copies of these to show to Thornton in case any of them looked familiar.

But the business of Thunder Child interested Cody more. If he was right, and if this *was* the name of an MOD operation, then it suggested that the Department was sure it was facing extra-terrestrials. And yet that wasn't what they were saying in public. *Now what was that worth?* It was only then that another, more fundamental question occurred to him. *Why would the aliens give an abductee a warning to pass on to the Government when they couldn't even be sure the message would be passed on? Why not send the message direct?*

East Horton, Northumberland

About the only break that the military had had was that the crash site was so remote, Major Bannerman thought as he drove through the village closest to where the craft had come down. He'd already passed through a couple of checkpoints and knew that more were being set up on other roads to try and ensure that nobody got through.

The crash site was in a field about a mile to the north of the village and Bannerman would have been there by now had he not had new orders that all his people should wear NBC suits. He'd gone cold at the thought that there were people on-site already who had not received the order in time. What would their reaction be when the second echelon arrived in their protective kit? He knew they were alive because he was in radio contact with them. He'd ordered them to fall back in case there were contaminants in the wreckage.

Bannerman wished his driver would go faster, but the roads were narrow and a relentless drizzle limited visibility. His primary mission was to ensure that the site was secure and to await the

arrival of specialist scientific and intelligence personnel who
would study the wreckage and conduct an analysis. But he'd been
told that he'd be required to give an instant analysis himself, with
particular reference to the wreckage of the unidentified craft. He'd
picked up enough on the military grapevine to figure out that they
wanted him to say whether it was alien or not.

They were getting close now and Bannerman saw several
bedraggled and miserable-looking troops at various side roads,
waving his Land Rover through. Part of their mission – and,
indeed, part of his – was to prevent the press from getting to the
site. Bannerman didn't know how he felt about this. He'd always
been moderately interested in UFOs, and had even read a couple
of books on the subject. He was well aware that some people
believed there was a Government cover-up on the subject, but he
had dismissed such claims as nonsense. It was disturbing to think
that he was now being asked to become part of such a strategy.

Bannerman had questioned the order and been told that secrecy
was only necessary in the short term, to ensure that any political
and military decisions were not unduly influenced by public or
media pressures. Having served in Bosnia and Kosovo he could
appreciate the logic in this, although he wondered just how far he
might have to go to enforce an exclusion zone. His orders weren't
specific on that, because up until a few minutes ago nobody had
thought about the particular scenario that was unfolding. The
military had SOPs for just about everything, but there clearly
hadn't been one dealing with the downing of a UFO. This in itself
answered one of his own questions, because if the brass knew all
about UFOs there *would* have been such a plan and he wouldn't
have formed the obviously correct impression that his orders were
pretty much being made up as someone went along.

Bannerman's thoughts turned again to the issue of the media.
Initial indications were that nobody on the ground had been
killed and, again, the remoteness of the spot made it unlikely that
the crash had been witnessed. But an enthusiastic police officer
with a relative on a newspaper, or a farmer with a mobile phone
and a craving for fifteen minutes of fame could get the news out in

an instant. And although Bannerman might prevent access by road – he knew that others in his chain of command were debating the legal niceties of this – there was not much he could do about helicopters hired by the press. A nominal air exclusion zone had been declared, but this would hardly bother a freelance journalist after the story of the century. For the moment he'd have to hope the media *hadn't* found out about the crash, or that they didn't know the precise location.

The irony was that the more roadblocks were set up, the more likely it was that word would get out, as inquisitive or irked locals tried to find out what was going on and started to make calls. It was then that Bannerman began to see that the foul weather might be his best ally here, as it would deter all but the most brave or foolhardy pilot. Then again, there were plenty of those, he thought to himself as the driver halted the vehicle.

'Looks like this is it, sir,' the Corporal announced. 'From here on, we walk.'

There were about half a dozen soldiers milling around, and Bannerman could soon tell that they'd been waiting for his arrival. As he'd predicted, the sight of two men in NBC suits did nothing to improve the mood of the unprotected troops who'd already seen the site. One of them looked at him coldly. 'Anything we should know, sir?' he asked in an understandably aggressive way.

'I won't bullshit you, private: there may be a biohazard, and that's why I radioed for you to fall back and leave the crash site alone. But you should be fine. From what I understand, it's a very black-and-white situation. If there *was* a biohazard, we wouldn't be having this conversation right now.' Bannerman always found that the truth, frankly and simply put, was the best way to deal with situations like this.

The other vehicles in Bannerman's group arrived and more soldiers jumped out of the trucks. Bannerman addressed a young Lieutenant who seemed to be the most senior officer present, although the question was really for everyone.

'From what you saw, what do you think it is?'

'I don't know, sir. It's pretty beat up, and we didn't stick around when we got your message about possible contaminants. But it doesn't look like any aircraft, sir. No way.'

'OK, you and your people wait here. There'll be medics along shortly but, as I've said, I'm convinced there's no danger. If there was, you'd be feeling something by now. You're not, are you?'

'We're cold, wet and pissed off, sir, but apart from that we're just fine,' the young Lieutenant replied as cheerfully as he could under the circumstances.

'Excellent. Glad to hear it.' Bannerman turned to his contingent of troops. 'Follow me.'

They trudged through a muddy field, following the directions that the Lieutenant had given them. It wasn't long before they began to come across signs that something had come down. There were pieces of what looked like metal embedded in the soft ground and scattered over a wide area. It was impossible to say much about the origin of these but Bannerman cautioned his troops not to touch anything, NBC suits or not. Looking ahead, he could see bigger fragments of wreckage, some of which clearly belonged to the Typhoon. He felt a chill as he saw a large section of the tail, which had smashed into the base of a tree, uprooting it completely. They were walking up a very slight slope and he knew that, once he reached the top, he would have a clear view of the wreckage he'd really come to see. Despite his sadness at the death of the Typhoon pilot he couldn't help but feel a surge of excitement quite unlike anything he'd ever felt. And, suddenly, he was confronted with what he'd been sent to find.

'Fucking hell.'

There were gasps of astonishment from Bannerman's team, who had stopped dead, even though they were still some fifty metres from their objective. It looked as though the craft had come down almost completely intact and had embedded itself in the side of the slope, ploughing up the field where it had struck. Bannerman didn't know much about RPVs or secret prototype aircraft but he was fairly sure he was looking at something considerably more exotic. He called for silence and moved slowly forward. He was armed with a standard-issue SA 80 rifle, and although they were not expecting any survivors – they didn't even know if there was a crew – he wasn't going to take any chances. They were operating to a defensive rather than an offensive ROE, though. If there was anyone still alive, they were required for interrogation.

As Bannerman approached the craft, he could see that his initial assessment had not been entirely correct. The craft had actually split in two and the hull was more damaged than he'd first thought. But there was no doubt in his mind that he was looking at something alien. It was difficult for him to say exactly why this was, but the feeling of inhuman strangeness was almost palpable.

Bannerman stepped gingerly through the fissure in the hull and found himself in the interior of the craft. It was surprisingly undamaged, and there were all sorts of strange devices that he couldn't begin to evaluate lying around. And there, suddenly, was what he'd been looking for.

Bannerman stared at them, and his first thought was that he wasn't as surprised as he thought he'd have been under these circumstances. Maybe it was because he'd seen things like them before, on television. But there they were – two corpses, each no more than three and a half feet tall, their skin grey in colour, dressed in one-piece uniforms. Their heads were disproportionately large atop their spindly bodies and their eyes were huge, black and repulsive. They were obviously extraterrestrial and, judging by the way their frail, mangled bodies lay smashed against the interior wall of the craft, they were equally obviously dead.

Much as Bannerman wanted to stay and look around, he knew his duty. He went out through the gash in the hull, walked to the crest of the slope and unslung his radio. Turning to survey the craft again, staring at it intently, he spoke clearly and calmly. 'This is Bannerman. I'm looking at a craft and dead occupants that certainly aren't from around here. There's no doubt about it, sir. I can confirm we are dealing with extraterrestrials.'

MOD Main Building, Whitehall
'Well, at least we know we're not at war with Russia.' Blackmore

thought on reflection that it had been a stupid thing to say, but his comment had generated a few wry smiles, even though he doubted anyone found it genuinely funny. Still, humour was an effective way of reducing tension and letting off a bit of steam and, frankly, he hadn't known what else to say.

CDI was looking pleased. 'Minister, we have to recover that craft. We have to get it to the DERA site at Farnborough, and we have to see what makes it tick. We could learn all sorts—'

'I'm sorry,' CSA interrupted, 'but the team from Porton Down will be arriving on site within twenty minutes. They'll be running a series of independent tests that will tell us very quickly if there's a biohazard and, if so, what the nature and level of that hazard is. If there is a hazard,' she turned to look directly at Blackmore, 'I will formally ask you to authorize action under Op Fountain. But I'll need your decision before that, because we'll need to set things up, and get the assets in place.'

Blackmore thought quickly. 'You have my authorization to use anything short of a nuclear device, on the strict proviso that no civilians are killed. If they're in an area you need to sterilize, then evacuate them. If you think they may be infected – detain them. I'll see S of S right now and seek the PM's approval for the nuclear option, as a last resort.'

East Horton, Northumberland

Bannerman was beginning to get annoyed with whoever was running the operation. He'd just been ordered to pull his team out, even though they'd only been on site for a matter of minutes. He ran up to the craft where, despite his orders, a couple of the soldiers were edging closer to the fissure in the hull.

'Can't we take a quick look, sir?' one of them asked.

'No. We're pulling out anyway.'

'But we've only just got here.'

'I'm well aware of that, thank you,' Bannerman replied, his patience beginning to wear a little thin. 'However, this isn't a debating society, so *move* it.' With that he strode off, followed by a very confused and disappointed group of soldiers.

Rowledge, Surrey

The gamble had paid off. Thornton had recognized one of the photographs instantly. Cody then placed a call to Nick Templeton and told him he knew about Operation Thunder Child. He also mentioned that he knew that a very senior figure in Main Building was an abductee. In reality, neither Thornton nor Cody would ever have dreamt of revealing his name. Witness confidentiality was sacrosanct with abductees and serious researchers who would never 'out' an abductee. But, they reasoned, Templeton wasn't to know that.

'What exactly do you want?' Templeton had enquired, his voice giving nothing away.

'We want to help,' Cody replied truthfully. 'But we can help you best if you deal us in, and if we work together. There are some of us who have been studying this phenomenon for years and have amassed lots of data. Some of that information might be useful to you in dealing with the situation in which you find yourselves. We're not out to score points off you here, and if alien contact teaches us one thing, it's how much all human beings have got in common. Lives have been lost, and if we can prevent any more bloodshed then it's in everybody's interests to work together.'

'I agree with you, Mr Cody; I really do. What you say has merit, though there's more going on here than you can possibly know. But I'll consider your offer, I promise you. Goodbye.'

Thornton looked questioningly at Cody. 'Well?'

'He'll think about it.'

'Great,' she shot back, somewhat harshly. 'We've got them over a barrel – maybe we could threaten them?'

'No,' Cody replied firmly. 'No, we hold the moral high ground here and I'm not going to sink to their level.'

Thornton stared hard at Cody who, she realized, had just chastized her in his own subtle way. At first she was annoyed, but the more she thought about it, the more she realized that he was right. After all, if the Government and the aliens weren't going to act with honour, somebody had to. If you have no power, she reasoned, then maybe walking with your head held high was all that was left.

Victoria Embankment Gardens, Whitehall

'Behind me, you can see the Ministry of Defence Main Building where Ministers, civil servants and military commanders are presumably trying to make sense of recent events and decide on a response. Have we really made first contact with extraterrestrials? And, if so, have the RAF started a war with them?' The reporter thrust out his hand in a sweeping gesture, and the television camera dutifully swivelled round to follow his movement, and focus on the group of people who were standing next to him.

The reporter stepped forward, a microphone in his hand. 'OK, we're on a pre-record, not a live broadcast, so just give your comment as I pass the mike around. Keep it short and punchy.'

'The Government has been covering this up for years. We want answers – we want some bloody answers.'

'We've got a right to know, haven't we? We're all taxpayers. This is supposed to be a democracy. Why won't they tell us what's going on?'

'I don't think they know what's going on. They haven't got a clue. They're running around in that building like headless chickens right now, I bet you.'

'The visitors are our friends. They're here to help us, and if we've lost aircraft it's probably because we fired at them – Governments don't want them here, because it would show everyone how petty and stupid we are, with our wars and our . . . well, also, it would undermine world religion, the banks . . . er . . . '

There were twelve other film crews in the gardens, together with a few demonstrators and various other people who seemed to be milling around aimlessly, as if this was the place they thought they should be – though for reasons they probably couldn't articulate.

Chapter Ten

PREDATORS AND PREY

MOD Main Building, Whitehall

Five minutes after an ashen-faced Martin Blackmore returned with the news that Secretary of State had authorized the use of a nuclear weapon, word came through that the team from Porton Down had declared the area in Northumberland safe. Blackmore stepped out of the room to make a quick call to S of S and then returned to what was clearly a lively and upbeat discussion. CDI wasted no time in setting out to the Minister what he thought the next step should be.

'Study of the wreckage must be our number one priority now. We can find out about the propulsion system, the weaponry, the avionics and God knows what else. Depending on the damage, we could back-engineer the craft and incorporate some of the technology into our own aircraft, maybe. This could even us up, somewhat.'

'No,' Blackmore corrected him. 'Our number one priority is to make contact with these . . . creatures . . . and try to make peace with them. Now, how can we do that?'

'We may not have to,' CAS offered. 'Now they've lost a craft, they may back off.'

'OK, but continue efforts to make contact through secure military channels and prepare to bring in Goonhilly Downs,' Blackmore ordered. 'I've talked to S of S, and we're going to see the PM in a few minutes. We have to announce this to Parliament and the public.'

'Excuse me?' It was CDI who spoke, a trace of sarcasm in his voice.

'Do you have a problem with that?' Blackmore asked, not pleased that one of his military colleagues was questioning what he felt was a purely political decision. His adrenalin levels were pretty high, since he'd recently faced the prospect of using nuclear weapons on British soil. Understandably, he'd been appalled at the thought of authorizing so much death and destruction, however necessary it might have been. History would have remembered him as the man who had used the bomb and not as the man who'd saved the world, he thought.

'I'm wondering if release of this information to the public is wise,' CDI offered, his voice even and reasonable. 'What would the public reaction be? Might there not be panic? What might such news do to the economy? There may be wider political issues here.'

Blackmore could see that CDI was playing a skilful game. He was way outside his area of responsibility and had deliberately stressed the political pitfalls. *Time to bring him back to his own brief and see what's really on his mind.* 'Do you see any military difficulty in releasing this information?'

'Yes, Minister,' CDI replied. 'The recovery of this craft presents us with a unique opportunity. We may be the only nation on Earth to possess such a machine and if we can successfully exploit its technology it will give the UK a decisive military advantage.' He paused briefly, realizing that he'd have to offer US of S more than this if his idea was to stand a chance. 'There may be much wider benefits to the national interest,' he continued. 'I'm assuming that these craft are capable of interstellar travel. The nation that first develops such power, well . . . ' He left the thought hanging.

There were some around the table who could see the possibilities, although most felt that this sort of nationalism was distasteful.

'It won't be our decision,' Blackmore retorted. 'But I will put these points to S of S and the PM, who will consider them. I genuinely want to hear what you think about this, so please, everybody, speak freely.' Blackmore knew that he had some of the most able and creative thinkers in the country sitting around the table with him. It would be foolish not to make full use of such an asset.

'What CDI says has some merit,' CSA offered. 'But it's most unlikely that we'd be able to back-engineer such a craft. Imagine a stealth fighter crashing in Renaissance England. Could even the finest minds of the age have worked out what it was, let alone built one of their own?'

'That's right,' DUS(S&T) added, backing up his principal. 'In any case, to back-engineer even a relatively straightforward new product takes years. The situation we face now will doubtless have resolved itself by then.'

'There's another point we need to consider,' CDS said. 'The issue of the Americans. As you know, there are strong indications that the US authorities know about this. So we may not be the first to get our hands on one of these craft, after all. I suppose the notorious Roswell crash might really have happened.'

'And the Rendlesham Forest landing,' Head of Sec(AS) ventured.

Jacqui Connolly had been following the debate with a mixture of interest and disbelief. It was time for her to step in. 'If I may,' she began, 'I'd like to offer my view on this matter. I don't believe we have any right to keep this secret. We have a *responsibility* to be truthful, not just to the public but to the families of the RAF personnel who have lost their lives over the past few days. From a practical point of view we simply couldn't keep a secret of this magnitude, anyway. Too many people know about it now: the soldiers at the crash site, the team from Porton Down and the countless DERA personnel – and others – who are doubtless going to take the craft apart piece by piece. I think we need to face up to this quickly – we should announce it *before* the media get hold of it.'

'I agree,' Blackmore replied instantly. 'That will be my recommendation, although I *will* float the potential advantages of non-disclosure. As to *how* we make the announcement, search me!'

CSA spoke up. 'Actually,' she explained, 'there *are* some guidelines that may be useful. There's a procedure – the Detection Declaration, it's called – that was drawn up by various astronomical organizations involved in the SETI programme. From memory, there are eight separate principles that set out what should be done – notification of national authorities, the scientific community and so on.'

Blackmore was interested. 'Is any of this enshrined in law?'

'No, Minister, unfortunately not. It's just a voluntary code agreed between astronomers and a few other scientific groups. And the other thing is that it's not designed for the scenario we're facing now. But it still might be useful.'

'Yes,' Blackmore agreed. 'Please ask your people to get me a copy of this declaration. Anything else, before I go?'

'The entities, Minister. What do we do with them?' Head of Sec(AS) had raised an interesting point.

'We study them, of course,' CSA replied, 'just as we study the craft itself.'

'Absolutely not,' shot back CAS. 'No way. Whatever these entities are, wherever they come from, their dead are entitled to be treated with respect. Maybe treating the bodies in a dignified way might be a message of peace in itself.'

'Non-intrusive analysis only,' Blackmore ruled. He turned to CSA. 'You can take X-rays, that sort of stuff. But CAS is right, we must respect the normal rules of warfare here.'

'What we really need is a live one,' CDS pointed out.

'I have an idea about that,' Head of Sec(AS) offered.

'Let's hear it,' Blackmore replied.

Templeton outlined his plan at some length. It emerged that he'd sounded out CGS earlier and that a fairly detailed operation had been worked out between them and a few specialists. There

were sharp questions from some of those present, but the whole
thing had clearly been thought through carefully. As Templeton
explained each part of the plan, there were appreciative nods from
many of those present.

'I'm prepared to authorize the operation,' Blackmore stated.
With that, the meeting ended.

Fort Meade, Maryland

Van Buren was a man on the edge. He had played what he
sometimes thought of as a game for over fifty years and had played
it skilfully. Also, since he was a religious and highly moral person,
he played it from the highest of motives, even though he and other
members of the group – jokingly dubbed 'The Enterprise' – had
done some questionable things.

Van Buren considered the faces around him. Six of them: all
men, all aged over sixty, some in poor health. Two were from the
NSA, while the others were from the CIA, the NRO, the US
Army and the USAF. Though none were household names, they
considered themselves the most important group of people in the
world – an assessment they had made without a trace of egotism
and one that was almost certainly correct. Impassive faces, belong-
ing to grey men in grey suits who had no obvious successors.

'We were so close,' Van Buren began, his voice a mixture of
anger and sadness. 'A few more years, and we'd have perfected
their technology ourselves. Now . . .'

'What about our defensive weapons?' The question was asked
more out of frustration and desperate hope than from any need to
be told what was already known by everyone sitting around the
table.

Eyes turned to Lt General John Warren. As Commander of the
US Army's Space and Missile Defence Command he was in charge
of this aspect of the operation. 'We have a few KE-ASAT
prototypes up and running, but it's too soon to say whether we
have any degree of operational effectiveness. We can say exactly
the same about MIRACL, THAAD or the new 747 fleet. We
might throw in the Russian Gazelle and Gorgon systems – if we

could negotiate their use – but financial cutbacks mean they're barely operational in any case. My most optimistic assessment is that we'd be able to take out a handful of their scout craft, if it came to a straight fight. But we couldn't begin to dent their overall operational capability, and we have no hope of defence against their main threat. If we moved against them in any concerted way, they might take out the Hubble space telescope, the Freedom space station and all our key military satellites.'

'But that would blow their cover.'

'It's already blown,' Van Buren reminded them. 'Our latest information is that the Brits have brought down a craft and are about to go public. Our friends have not been in touch either with us or – so far as we know – with them. We have to make a very quick decision: do we level with the Brits and try to persuade them from going public?'

'I don't see the point,' Warren replied. 'If our friends wanted that, they'd surely tell them, as we were told in 1947. No, our friends have escalated this themselves, with their mass attack on the British Air Defence forces and with the removal of their usual hypnotic controls on the abductees. The Brits got lucky or got smart with their radar, and once they figured out what they were looking for, they realized they could track our friends to some extent. But why didn't our friends just back off and change their MO? Or why didn't they contact the Brits directly and warn them off?'

'There's something here that we're not seeing,' Van Buren said, 'but unfortunately we don't have time to mull it over. I agree it's strange that our friends haven't contacted the Brits to warn them off. If they still plan to do so, they're leaving it pretty damn' late. Maybe they're toying with them or maybe they're sending *us* a message – they can't be blind to our recent efforts, despite our attempts to classify them as anti-ballistic missile technologies.' Van Buren's mind was leaping all over the place as he attempted to assess the various possibilities. 'We know from the past that our friends expect us to act as their agents in this matter, but we can't talk the British Prime Minister out of going public. Only one person can do that, and unless anybody disagrees, I propose to see the President as soon as possible.' There were no disagreements. But none of the assembled company were comfortable with the decision, either. They agreed because, quite simply, they had no choice.

Downing Street

The Prime Minister had agreed with the advice that there was no way a secret like this could or should be kept. Part of this decision had been prompted by his genuine commitment to accountability and open Government, although the realization that he'd be out of office in an instant if it was proved he'd covered this up played no small part in making his mind up.

There was no established procedure for an announcement to the nation to be made. In the end it was decided that, after having gone to the Palace, the Prime Minister would address the country directly. Courtesy calls would be made to the US President, the Russian President and the Secretary-General of the United Nations. There had been some debate about whether to brief the Pope, but in the end it was decided that this might stir up bad feeling with other religions and the idea was shelved. Plans were well in hand when word came through that the US President was on the line and wanted to speak to the PM immediately, on a matter of the utmost importance. It was the kind of diplomatic language that meant 'Get him now, even if he's on the toilet with his trousers round his ankles'.

'Hilary, hello. What can I do for you?'

The President talked for three and a half minutes and the PM listened in silence. During those two hundred and ten seconds, the world became a very different place.

Rowledge, Surrey

Eight figures were silently approaching Jenny Thornton's house, skilfully crawling from the darkness of Alice Holt Forest. They were incredibly focused on the task in hand and were well equipped to carry out their instructions. Failure was simply not an option – but then, to these people, it never was.

Sergeant Jack West was in the lead. As they approached the area that he'd recced earlier it struck him that this had to be the most bizarre mission any SAS patrol had ever attempted. It had begun just five hours earlier when his bleeper had gone off and he'd driven into the base at Hereford, wondering whether he'd be in time to make the mission, what it was all about and whether he'd come back.

West was a local man and had known from an early age that he wanted to join the SAS. As a teenager he'd seen Regiment men in the local pubs and noticed the way that they all seemed to have a presence about them. Part of it came from their tough physique, but he'd known that it ran deeper than that. It was the self-assured nature, the look in their eyes that said they'd seen things and done things that were beyond the reach of most of their fellow men. They always seemed to have money in their pockets and were seldom short of female company, so when West had left school at sixteen with an undistinguished academic record, the Army had been his obvious choice.

West had been a bit of a tearaway at school, but the Army had been the making of him. He'd knuckled down and worked at it, harder than he'd worked at anything in his life. After four years he'd applied to join the SAS, but had failed Selection, much to everybody's surprise. Undeterred, he reapplied, passing at his second attempt. He'd then undergone the fearsome Combat Survival course before being officially 'badged' as a member of what most professional soldiers would acknowledge as the most fearsome, professional and genuinely elite fighting force in the world. He'd asked for and been assigned to Air Troop and had been streamed into A Squadron, where he'd seen service in Northern Ireland, Iraq, Bosnia, Kosovo – and in a number of other countries where most people would have been surprised to learn that British troops had served at all.

For this mission, West was dressed in standard camouflage gear, with a black woollen hat covering an unruly mop of black hair. As he manoeuvred his large but well-muscled frame into the small dip between the edge of the forest and Thornton's back garden, he cast his mind back to the briefing he and his team had received.

At first, West had thought it was a joke when the CO had started to explain some of the background to Operation Thunder Child. Like all of them, he'd followed the escalating crisis with interest and mounting concern, wanting to get a crack at the unseen enemy that was bringing so much death and destruction to the RAF. West and his mates could never entirely lose their inter-service rivalry, and had talked about the conflict in terms of the SAS sorting out the RAF's problem for them.

The smart money had been on Russian RPVs as the culprits and the SAS men had even got so far as discussing the possibility of being parachuted into some airbase to destroy the presumably small number of prototypes involved – even though logic told them that a cruise missile attack would be the far more likely option. They'd heard rumours about UFOs and aliens but had written them off as nonsense or deliberate disinformation. So they'd assumed they were being subjected to some sort of psychological exercise to test how far they'd accept a story – and subsequent orders – from senior commanders. Such things were not unprecedented and were meant to guard against the nightmare scenario of a senior officer carrying out an unauthorized operation with troops who blindly followed orders that ended up – for example – with the assassination of the Prime Minister. This theory had been uppermost in West's mind until CGS and CDI entered the room to carry out the briefing and emphasized that it was not an exercise.

West had still insisted on speaking to CDS or S of S – a move that had tried the patience of the two Generals but one that had filled his CO with pride. West hadn't recognized S of S's voice, but he'd carefully selected the number from the MOD directory and had been put through to a somewhat bemused man who was certainly sitting in S of S's office. Satisfied, West had accepted his subsequent briefing with dutifully suppressed amazement and had selected a fearsome array of weapons for the task in hand.

An RAF Puma helicopter had flown the SAS team from

Hereford to Odiham, from where they'd been driven to Rowledge in an unmarked truck and dropped off at the edge of Alice Holt Forest, which they'd quickly tabbed through so as to approach Thornton's house from an area of cover.

Their mission was simple: observe the property of somebody who was supposedly a 'repeater abductee' and watch for any unusual activity. Prevent any harm from occurring to Jenny Thornton by intercepting any attempt to take her from her house. Detain any entities carrying out such an act with minimum force, taking them alive if possible, while engaging any craft used in any such attempt with maximum force, bringing it down if at all possible.

West decided to split his team into two, with his Corporal, Max Otley, commanding the second group. They'd been told to maintain a watch on the property during the hours of darkness and to radio in any contacts immediately, using their PRC319 tactical radios — secure communications devices that transmitted encrypted data in burst mode. West knew that substantial forces were held in reserve but didn't know the details. He had been told not to expect any air support — correctly figuring that the MOD wasn't too keen on dogfights taking place over Surrey. The team were to find a lying-up point in the forest where they were to spend the days, and they were to say that they were on exercise if anybody stumbled across them.

The initial plan was to carry out this covert surveillance for three nights and to review the situation thereafter, perhaps bringing in other teams to watch the houses of other abductees. The names had been gleaned from MOD files and from various books and magazines. The MOD thought that many of the abductees were liars or fantasy-prone types, but apparently some sort of credibility list had been compiled. Jenny Thornton had been at the top. When West had been told about the UFO that had been downed by the RAF he'd suggested bringing Thornton in on the operation, arguing that it would be far better to place some members of the team in the house itself. But the MOD were apparently still flapping about a public announcement: at this

stage the operation had to be totally covert. The Home Secretary
had been consulted and had decided that what they were doing
was just about legal – under the unprecedented circumstances.

It was just after four-fifteen a.m. on the second night of the SAS
team's surveillance that contact was made. One of West's men
tapped him lightly on the shoulder and pointed skyward. He'd
been using his NVGs to scan the sky for anything out of the
ordinary, and had detected a very faint light source. Even as the
craft came closer, West was finding it difficult to make anything
out with the naked eye. He'd somehow expected any UFO to be
lit up like a *Close Encounters* mothership, even though the briefing
had suggested otherwise. But he realized that a black object could
operate unseen at night, provided nobody was looking for it and
provided it was unlit.

The craft descended slowly, coming to rest some two hundred
feet over Thornton's house. Both teams had weapons trained on it
but were waiting for West's orders before firing. Most of them
were carrying M16 assault rifles, although Otley had set up a
5.56mm Minimi light machine-gun. Another member of Otley's
team was the only man not carrying a weapon – much to his
disappointment. He'd been given the task of filming any
encounter and was now tracking the craft with an expensive,
tripod-mounted camera.

Suddenly, Thornton's house was bathed in a faint cone of blue-
white light, down which floated three small figures. West raised
his arm, indicating that his men should hold their fire and wait.
Seconds later, the three figures disappeared, presumably having
entered the house. When they reappeared a minute or so later,
they were not alone. They were ascending the beam of light, all
curled into foetal positions. And with them was a female figure
dressed in a white nightdress.

This turn of events was one of a number of possibilities that had
been covered in the briefing, but it was still one for which West
and his team were psychologically unprepared. Their instinct was
to take out the three small figures, but they were bunched tightly
around Thornton: although the SAS men were all excellent shots,

it was slightly too close to call. More importantly, there was no guarantee that the craft or the entities could be engaged without dire consequences for Thornton. If she was being held up by the beam of light, she might well fall if they somehow cut off the source. It was clear that they had to wait for her to be returned and mount their attack only after she was safely back in her room.

It was an agonizing wait and West did not dwell on what might be happening on the craft. He only knew that there was a helpless civilian who had been repeatedly kidnapped by intruders against whom she had had no defence – until now.

Twenty minutes passed until the figures returned in a reverse sequence of earlier events. The moment they had disappeared into the house, West gave his order and the engagement began. The Minimi opened up first and, as every fifth round was a tracer, the men with M16s had an easy job bringing their own weapons to bear and pumping rounds into the craft's hull. They were on target: the beam of light winked on and off, presumably indicating that they were having some success interfering with the craft's control mechanisms. Despite this, the vessel was maintaining its height.

Time for the big one, West thought, laying aside his M16 and picking up something a little more substantial. The standard-issue surface-to-air missile of the British Army was the Javelin, but during the Gulf War the SAS had been issued with the American-made Stinger missile and had never looked back. It was a hand-held fire-and-forget missile that was effective and easy to use.

West stepped away from his group, ensuring they wouldn't be caught up in the fearsome backblast. He acquired the craft through the optical sight and heard the tell-tale high-pitched beeping sound that showed the unit was seeking. This was followed almost immediately by the lower-pitched tone of a lock-on. It really didn't come much easier than this. He fired and had the immediate satisfaction of seeing the missile slam into the hull, exploding on contact. The beam of light disappeared and the craft lurched violently to one side, losing height as it did so.

'Two of the fuckers got back up the beam,' one of West's team shouted at him above the noise of the M16s and the Minimi. 'One didn't,' he continued, pointing at the house.

'Cease fire,' West shouted. The craft was clearly done for. It was swaying around at a low level, its hull breached and smoke billowing from its interior. West prayed that it wouldn't come down on someone's house, recalling that he'd raised concerns about bringing down a craft over a populated area at the briefing, only to have them swept aside with a bland statement about doing the utmost to prevent any 'collateral damage'. In fact, the craft crashed into the forest, creating a problem nobody had thought of: fire.

But that was the least of West's worries. Even as his comms man radioed in details of the contact, West defied the orders he'd been given earlier and raced towards the house, towards the source of the screams that all his team could now hear. He kicked in the back door and led his team rapidly through the kitchen and towards the stairs, motioning for the others to hold back and secure the ground floor.

In an instant West was up the stairs and into what was clearly the main bedroom. There were two figures in the room and, amazingly enough, neither of them seemed to notice the arrival of a very large SAS man. In the corner was a distressed woman, shaking and clearly in deep shock. She was dishevelled and her nightdress was on back to front. Blood was running down her legs from the top of her thighs: West felt awkward and somehow voyeuristic for even looking. The woman – clearly Jenny Thornton – was screaming and yet, when West thought about it, it was a scream of rage and frustration rather than of fear.

West's eyes turned to the second figure. Small, spindly and grey-skinned, with a disproportionately large head and huge black eyes, it was clearly not human. Although presumably a representative of a more advanced civilization, it seemed vulnerable and scared – cowering, almost, from the onslaught of Thornton's screams. It was wearing a one-piece outfit of some sort, which looked as if it might be a uniform.

Suddenly, moving quicker than West would have thought possible, the creature reached for a short, stubby device hanging from a belt that it was wearing. West had no idea what the object was but he wasn't taking any chances. The sound of the M16 was explosive in the small bedroom and there was no mistaking the weapon's effect on the creature. The round entered its chest and exited through its back, splattering the wall behind with organic material of some sort.

West placed his hand lightly on Thornton's shoulder. 'It's all right, you're safe now. They can't hurt you any more.'

He wasn't exactly sure if that was true.

DERA, Farnborough

Dr Lisa Kaminsky was in engineer heaven. She'd been telephoned at home and summoned back to the Space Department building at DERA's Farnborough site. Her speciality was exotic propulsion systems, but she also knew as much as anybody in the country about the new generation of projected-energy weapons that were being developed in an anti-ballistic missile and anti-satellite role.

Kaminsky's involvement with Operation Thunder Child had begun with her analysis of the wreckage from one of the RAF's downed Typhoons, but now the tables had clearly turned. Laid out in front of her in the hangar was the wreckage of a UFO that had been brought down by the RAF. She was disappointed to learn that the bodies of the occupants had been taken to Porton Down, even though she realized she would have had no meaningful opinion to offer on them. But laid out in front of her now was what was presumably a craft capable of interstellar travel – and she had the task of carrying out an initial assessment. She was under no illusions about the difficulty of such an assignment and had told CSA as much when she'd been given the job. Even a fully working model would clearly incorporate technology they could only guess at and what she had to work with was, of course, pretty smashed up. She'd explained that it would almost certainly take years to glean anything useful from the craft, if indeed that was possible at all. She had this idea – and it was not far from the truth – that certain people in the MOD thought that the scientists could wave a magic wand, say 'Oh, *that's* how it's done' and put together a fully operational fleet of craft in a couple of weeks.

Three hours later there had been two important developments. First, Kaminsky had realized that, although much of its technology was indeed beyond her, the craft certainly operated on a very basic principle that needed a minimum of control systems. Second, she'd been told to expect delivery of a considerably more intact craft within twenty-four hours.

Chapter Eleven

POLITICS

MOD Main Building, Whitehall

'What the bloody hell's going on and why haven't we made the announcement? The Press Office are being crucified, and now we've brought a UFO down over *Surrey*, for God's sake . . . ' Blackmore paused for a moment, then resumed. 'I thought we'd agreed our policy? I thought we were all clear that we couldn't and wouldn't try to hide any of this? It's already coming out, you know. There's lots of speculation on the Internet and although much of it is way off the mark, some of it is very accurate. Somebody's been leaking, that's for sure. Nobody on the Thunder Child team, because there's no policy information. Somebody in the recovery team, maybe. The media are close behind, and I've had lots of calls from MPs – even our own party are giving us a hard time on this. The Speaker has had several requests for Adjournment debates, and has indicated that she'll allow one if we don't act soon. She's been more than patient as it is.'

Willoughby held up his hand, palm towards his junior minister. 'OK, OK. I take your point, I really do. I've made much the same point to the PM, but he absolutely won't budge on this.

He's ordered me to hold off making any announcement and to maintain the line that operational factors preclude such an announcement for now because it would endanger our forces.'

'I'm sorry, but that's simply not his call. That's *your* call, taking advice from CDS.'

'Martin, you're not telling me anything I don't know. I'm as unhappy about this as you are. But the PM's assured me that he has very good reasons for the policy he's adopting, and short of calling him a liar we have to accept that. He's going to brief the Leader of the Opposition and he'll brief us as soon as he can. What I *can* tell you is this – the American President is on her way to London as we speak. She and the PM will be holding talks on the current crisis, and until those talks have taken place we are to keep quiet. Furthermore, the PM has invoked various pieces of Emergency Powers legislation aimed at actively preventing the story from getting out. Defence Advisory Notices have been issued to the media, and various Psyops measures have been put in place.'

Blackmore was intrigued by the last piece of information. 'Oh?'

'Well,' Willoughby shifted awkwardly in his chair, 'somebody, outside Government, but acting on our behalf, is busy putting out various stories on the Internet about crashed UFOs, dead aliens, live aliens, cover-ups and so on.'

'You mean *we*'re the ones leaking what happened?' Blackmore asked, astonished.

'No. We're leaking wild and totally inaccurate versions of the truth, mixed in with complete falsehoods. In that way, any bits of the real story that are leaked will be so mixed up with utter rubbish that nobody will have a clue, and serious media outlets won't touch any of it.'

Blackmore was horrified. 'Is that legal?'

'Who knows?' Willoughby shrugged. 'It's been done by somebody who used to work for the Security Service but who now runs a private company. He doesn't have any Government contracts, so it's absolutely unconnected with us. But he was in the game for years, and still maintains close contacts with his former colleagues. Every now and then, we might ask him to do us a favour.'

'Plausible deniability.'

'Absolutely.'

MOD Main Building, Whitehall

CDS was pacing aggressively up and down the room. With him were his three single-service chiefs, together with CDI. They'd filed into one of the smallest briefing rooms in the DCMC and left orders that they were not to be disturbed.

'The politicians are flapping about disclosure,' he began. 'I can't say I blame them – *I* certainly wouldn't like to announce that we've discovered alien life and that we're at war with it. But until such time as we get firm political direction, S of S has said that our job continues to be one of defending the territorial integrity of the UK. Now, I've asked CDI and CSA to prepare a short report summarizing what we know about the opposition: their strengths, their vulnerabilities, and some recommendations for following through an effective strategy.'

'Thank you, sir,' CDI began. 'We are facing what appears to be a civilization of extraterrestrial origin. The aliens are essentially humanoid and, although I'm no scientist, that does seem strange. CSA is frankly as baffled as I am by that, so I know it's not just me being thick.' He smiled at CSA as he activated a projector. Under normal circumstances a senior officer such as CDI would have had a junior assistant to carry out such a task. But Thunder Child security procedures had put severe limitations on those who could be briefed, and now three- and four-star officers were having to do their own clerical tasks.

An image of a dead alien appeared on the screen and, to CDI's horror, the slide was upside down. As he fumbled to make the necessary correction, cursing under his breath, there were good-natured laughs from his colleagues. He was pleased to see that CDS was chuckling and managed a smile himself.

The slide appeared the right way up. 'This is the most intact alien we have. As you know, it was killed at Jenny Thornton's house. There are other bodies from the Rowledge incident and the crash at East Horton. The fire at Alice Holt Forest has been put out: although civil firecrews were in attendance, the crash site was difficult to reach so we had the perfect excuse to step in under MACA rules and put out the fire by dropping water from a Puma, using a rainmaker. The bottom line is that none of the civvies got anywhere near the crash site. Both crash sites have been sanitized and both craft are now at Farnborough where a handful of DERA staff are working directly with CSA on producing an initial report. The bodies are all at Porton Down, in a secure environment. There's no evidence whatsoever of any biohazard, but every precaution is still being taken.'

'What about this woman, Jenny Thornton?' CGS asked. 'Where is she and what's to be done with her? Our security goes out of the window once she goes to the press, as she surely will.'

'She's at RAF Lyneham,' CDI replied, glancing at CAS who'd been told about this only shortly before. 'She's in the same facility used to debrief hostages like Terry Waite. She's being looked after by RAF medical staff who say she's suffering from shock but nothing else. They believe she underwent some sort of medical procedure on the ship, but they can't say what without examining her, and that's something we can't get into without breaking all sorts of laws. We've got to play this legally – and morally.' There were vigorous nods of agreement from all those present.

'She's free to leave when she likes,' CDI went on, 'and we don't particularly *want* her at an RAF base for long. Amazingly, she hasn't asked to call anyone yet but that's only a matter of time. When she does we'll simply drive her home, but for now Nick Templeton and Terry Carpenter are debriefing her, together with the SAS team – separately, of course.'

'She'll talk,' the First Sea Lord observed.

'I'm sure of it. And we refuse to comment, as we're refusing to comment on *all* the allegations being made at the moment. We're OK with that, as long as we tell no outright lies, which we won't. What we've got going for us is the sheer implausibility of her story: she was abducted by aliens and rescued by the SAS, who shot down the spaceship . . . well, it sounds crazy, and it's unlikely to be believed. I'll now hand over to CSA who, I hope, can operate a projector better than I can.'

CSA put up her first slide. 'This is one of the craft, in the hangar at DERA's Farnborough site. It's very early days but the initial assessment is that although the technology is beyond our understanding, it's comparatively simple. In other words, when we *do* figure it out we may be able to build our own. I know that's against every expectation, and we're still talking several years R & D, but there are just so few systems in the damn' thing, it really does look as if we might be able to figure it out.'

'Have your people found out anything that might help us beat them?' CAS asked, conscious that the RAF were still very much in the front line.

'No. But we think their main strength is defensive. What they had going for them was the fact that we were ignoring them because they weren't giving a radar signal that suggested a solid craft. But they *are* detectable and, although they generate only a small radar signature, they actually seem to be *less* stealthy than an F-117. Missiles – whether radar-guided or infra-red-seeking – seem to have little effect. But we've hit them with cannon fire. What this suggests is that they have a sophisticated electronic-countermeasures suite that breaks missile locks somehow. There's an outer hull that seems to be wired up to the power source. I suspect they electrify it, and that this shorts out the electronics on any incoming missile. It also appears that they can control the temperature of this outer hull, which means that if their threat receiver picks up an infra-red missile, the hull will automatically go cold.'

'And the Stinger only worked because it was fired from so close a range, before they had a chance to detect and react?' CGS asked.

'Precisely. But there's more. This outer hull may also be capable of changing colour, like the skin of a chameleon. Again, a defensive capability, designed to camouflage the craft. But if you *do* hit it, you damage it. It's not invulnerable, and simple chemistry dictates that it's got to be made of elements we know

about. There's no magic here: its hull *is* tough: but our initial
spectral analysis shows that it's made of entirely normal materials,
albeit thrown together in an unusual combination. They have
bonded polycarbonate hulls – a bit of a chemical mishmash – with
a coating of yttrium. Yttrium is a naturally occurring element
found in uranium ores. The really interesting thing about it is that
it's used in superconductors, so it backs up the idea that they can
electrify the outer hull very quickly and initiate rapid temperature
changes. Ingenious, but something we can replicate very quickly.'
She turned to CDS. 'There's no reason this can't be incorporated
into the next generation of all military kit – a really effective way
of defeating the most advanced weaponry.'

'The best way to beat them?' CDS asked.

'Get in close, and engage with basic weaponry. And here's the
other important thing. Their offensive capability is lousy.' She
glanced at CAS, who didn't look pleased at that comment. 'What
I mean,' she went on, 'is that they appear to have only one
offensive weapon. It's a projected-energy weapon that is certainly
way ahead of anything we have. If it hits, it destroys. But here's
the thing: the targeting is lousy. I don't know what they use, and
maybe they aim it themselves. But consider the fact that that it
engaged our AWACS and missed . . . how many times? You see
what I mean? *We* wouldn't have missed an AWACS from that
range.'

'What are you saying?' CDS asked.

'That they're smart. That they can do things we can't. But also
that they're not invulnerable, and that if we adapt our tactics we
can beat them, or at least hold our own.'

'Why haven't we heard from them?' CGS asked.

'I don't know,' CSA replied. 'Efforts to make contact through
secure military satellite communications systems continue, but
with no success. We can't bring in the civvies until we get the
political go-ahead to go public with the whole thing. My guess is
that they haven't been hit like this before, and that they're taking
stock.'

'But what are they doing here? What's their agenda?' It was the

First Sea Lord who had asked the question uppermost in everybody's mind.

'We don't know,' CSA replied. 'I presume it's all tied up with the alien abduction incidents, but that whole scenario is new to me.'

'I can tell you what the UFO lobby believe,' CDI interjected. 'They think it's connected with a programme of genetic experiments, designed either to create a hybrid race, or to inject fresh genetic material into their stock. As a working hypothesis it's as good as anything we can come up with.'

'Does Earl Sutton have anything to say about this?' CAS directed the question at CDI, who looked rather ill at ease. It was an open secret among the Thunder Child team that Earl Sutton had had an experience of some sort, and that information he'd supplied had proved to be accurate. But since his earlier regression there had been no new developments.

'No.' CDI replied. 'Terry Carpenter thinks he's extracted all the information Earl Sutton has. But, frankly, it doesn't really take us any further forward.'

'That brings us back to the subject of our American friends,' CAS observed. 'They clearly knew all about this, didn't they?' There was more than a trace of anger in his voice.

'Yes,' CDI replied, 'it certainly seems that way. But the President is on her way over and I can only hope that she has some answers for us. In the meantime, as you know, we're not sharing Thunder Child information with the Americans and we're even making contingency plans to ask a number of US personnel to leave the country. As you can imagine, the FCO are going into a total flap.'

'I have a number of US Exchange Officers on RAF bases and we have some of our people in the States,' CAS pointed out. 'All the services have Exchange Officers. But, even more crucially, we're deployed alongside US forces in the Gulf region, in Saudi Arabia and in Kuwait. If our Iraqi friend starts his games again we'll be involved in all sorts of joint operations under integrated command and control. What do we do about that? And what about Kosovo?'

The deployed First Sea Lord took up the theme. 'There's a naval presence in the Gulf too, and I've got a task group with the US Navy in the Adriatic. And what about staffs at NATO head-quarters? Like it or not, we're tied to the Americans on a whole range of military matters.'

'I have to believe that if the Americans know about this at some level,' CDS replied, 'and if they've been holding back from helping us – or have even been hindering us – then it's a high-level decision. If they have a covert operation around this, only a handful of people will know – look at the way we've restricted details of Thunder Child to a small audience. What I'm saying is that the people we're operating with on joint ops won't be in the know about this, so we shouldn't have any qualms about working with them.'

'I'm sorry, sir, but that's an assumption,' CAS retorted.

'Yes, but a sound one, I believe.'

'That's right.' CDI pitched in to support CDS, as the acknowledged expert on such assessments. 'This will be a political or high-level intelligence secret. You wouldn't tell the troops, because they'd talk, and they wouldn't play ball with any plan that involved allies getting hurt.'

'But they *have* talked – or some of them have,' CGS pointed out. 'Head of Sec(AS) briefed us about Colonel Corso's book *The Day After Roswell*, and about all those other US military officers who have spoken out about UFOs.'

'None of that can be substantiated,' CDI replied.

'Surely it's been substantiated by recent events?' CGS retorted.

'Not at all.' CDI's reply was a little too sharp. 'Just because we're facing an extraterrestrial foe now, doesn't mean that every-thing said or written about UFOs is true.'

CDS held up his hand for silence. 'This is interesting, but we need to move on.' He turned to CGS. 'The emphasis shifts now to the Army. I want you to liaise with CDI and get SAS teams in place at the houses of other abductees known to the DIS. Or, rather, at those houses where you can get a team in unobserved and where population density is low enough to minimize the chances of being observed, or having a craft crash onto someone's dwelling.'

'What about the rest of us?' CAS asked.

'We wait.'

Air Force One, Mid-Atlantic

It was a common belief that Air Force One travelled by itself, as if it were an ordinary civilian airliner. This, of course, was nonsense. The President of the United States was surrounded by security at all times, and the US Secret Service were hardly going to leave the world's prime terrorist target unprotected at a time when state-sponsored terrorism was rife and when jet aircraft, air-to-air and ground-to-air missiles were within the reach of a number of terrorist groups.

So Air Force One was always accompanied by a veritable convoy of other aircraft. A pair of AWACS AEW aircraft – two, in case one went u/s – provided top cover, scrutinizing the whole area, watching for intruders and staying in constant touch with a host of other aircraft. E-2C Hawkeye aircraft provided additional radar coverage for a veritable army of other escorts, including specialist B-52s carrying powerful jamming equipment and numerous F-14 Tomcats armed with a mix of radar-guided Sparrow and Phoenix air-to-air missiles and the older Sidewinder heat-seekers. There were a host of KC-135 tankers whose job was to refuel the other aircraft, particularly the fighters, that had short legs. Air Force One itself was armed with a sophisticated array of defensive countermeasures, including jamming equipment, chaff and flares.

All that was for a normal transit, but this trip was anything but normal and the usual complement of security had been quad-rupled, without most of those involved knowing why. Those who did know had advised the President not to travel at all, or to consider travelling by sea, on an aircraft carrier escorted by a naval task group in addition to the usual air assets. The President was having none of it, and had made it clear that business needed to be conducted with the British PM face to face, and as soon as possible.

President Hilary Spencer gave little thought to the vast array of military forces currently tasked with ensuring her safe passage to RAF Fairford in the United Kingdom. She was concentrating on a problem of far more importance than her own personal survival; one that at a stroke rendered trivial all the other problems she'd grappled with in the two and a half years of her presidency.

Spencer was a lawyer by profession and had entered politics comparatively late in life. A shrewd operator, she had avoided the most bitter of the infighting that had threatened to tear her party apart just a few years ago, over a whole host of issues that concerned the increasingly religious society of the first years after the new Millennium. She'd emerged as a compromise candidate, not because she had better answers to these questions than anybody else, but because she'd successfully managed to move the debate on to other issues. She'd not been expected to win the election, but the eruption of a damaging sexual scandal involving her rival had effectively torpedoed his campaign at the crucial moment and had put her in the White House.

Spencer was a fairly striking woman of medium height, whose black hair was cut into a neat bob and whose angular facial features conveyed authority rather than severity. Aged fifty-one, she was a widow – a blessing for the staff of the White House Protocol Office who would have struggled to find a role for the husband of the President. Two of her three grown-up children were at college – both studying law – while the third was a naval Lieutenant. There was no lover, and no personal scandals in her past, which gave her almost perfect credentials to lead a society where family values were so important.

The only potential cloud on the horizon was the possibility of her having to order her son into battle, in her position as Commander-in-Chief. Her critics had questioned how this would affect her military decisions and were watching her son's career intently, looking for signs of favouritism.

Until a day ago, Spencer had subscribed to the popular cliché that she was the most powerful person in the world. She did so not out of arrogance but as an intellectual exercise to remind her of the consequences that would inevitably follow any decision she made. But now there were new factors to consider: were there others even more powerful than her, and did it matter anyway?

She turned to look at the impassive face of the man sitting next to her. Her security detail had no qualms about leaving her alone with Van Buren, but they would have had, if they'd known what he'd just told the President. To them he was her friend, although Spencer wasn't so sure. She thought that it was to his credit that he'd approached her, but wasn't that a decision that had been forced on him? And, more importantly, did the fact that he had now come forward wipe away the sins of the past and mean that he was now trustworthy? That was what she really needed to find out.

'You realize that I can't rule out criminal charges?' she told the NSA Director.

'I realize that, Madam President. I've always been prepared to take the consequences of my actions. But you know the reason for them, ma'am, and it's my heartfelt belief that any technical breach of the law has been justified in the wider interest.'

It was nothing he hadn't said before, she realized, and it was a line that was clearly well-rehearsed. She had to get him away from his pre-prepared lines and persuade him to open up somehow. She'd read his dossier, of course, but it didn't really offer many clues about how to break down his defences. Her best shot was to try and use his sense of duty against him.

'If any of these Air Force people,' she began, waving her hand in a vague gesture, 'found out what you'd done, they might want to throw you out of the aircraft. They'd say you were a traitor.'

Van Buren stiffened at the word 'traitor', started to speak and then paused, recognizing the President's tactic as one he'd used himself in the intelligence business and admiring the way she'd done it so skilfully. He assumed correctly that she'd picked up the technique from her experience as a lawyer, goading those under cross-examination into an unwise rage. 'I'm holding nothing back, Madam President,' he said evenly, his face as unreadable as ever.

'I'll have to tell the Prime Minister that, in under four hours,' Spencer reminded him. 'I've had enough surprises recently. I don't want any more.'

'No, ma'am.' Van Buren glanced out of the window, as he'd done throughout the flight. He could see numerous aircraft, including the familiar and distinctive shape of a number of F-117 stealth fighters. They looked unlike any of the other aircraft in the Air Group, and although he of all people knew how vital their presence might be, the sight of them always disturbed him.

He knew why.

RAF Lyneham, Wiltshire

The facility was quite unlike any other at a military base. It looked more like a discreet private members' club and owed its existence to the Beirut hostage crisis when it had been realized that there was a need for a secure facility where hostages could be reunited with their families away from media intrusion, in an environment where they could unwind at leisure. In some ways it was little more than a glorified VIP lounge, but it was also a useful place to debrief people. It had been the logical place to take Jenny Thornton after her ordeal.

The CO, Group Captain Sandra Topp, had been nervous about having Thornton at the base and had queried the legal position, worried that what had happened was perilously close to kidnap. Templeton and Carpenter had assured her that everything was legitimate, that Thornton could leave when she wanted and that she could call anybody she liked – although this was most definitely *not* to be suggested to her. There were to be no limits placed on her freedom and she was to be treated as an honoured guest. But Topp had also been told it would be helpful if Thornton could be encouraged to stay for a while so that the MOD officials could extract as much useful information as possible.

The MOD men also wanted to try and delay the inevitable moment when Thornton would tell Richard Cody what had happened: short of detaining Cody under Emergency Powers legislation there was little they could do after that to stop him talking. Templeton had wanted to brief him in on Thunder Child, or even get him onto the team itself in some limited capacity, to buy his silence and tap into his specialist knowledge of UFOs and abductions. Carpenter had floated the idea with CDI who had dismissed it out of hand, realizing that once the politicians went public with the story it wouldn't matter what Cody did and pointing out that there was little the DIS didn't already know about these matters.

Topp had been briefed in on some – but by no means all – of the Thunder Child data several days before, since Lyneham was home to the RAF's C-130 fleet, one of which had been involved in the earliest attempt to bring down one of the UFOs. Given that she was already cleared for Thunder Child material, Carpenter had taken the decision to tell her why Thornton was at the base.

Carpenter thought that Thornton might be more inclined to tell another woman the details of her experience and had asked Topp to spend a couple of hours drinking coffee with her. She'd opened up somewhat but had had little to tell that was new to the Thunder Child team. Information about medical procedures on abductees had been widely available from the published literature, some of which was turning out to be surprisingly accurate. But although Thornton confirmed the *general* details of what was being done to her, it was abundantly clear that she didn't really know what *specific* procedures were being carried out, or for what purpose. All her talk about hybrids had been unsubstantiated by any facts, and what she claimed the aliens told her seemed on the whole to be just meaningless platitudes. *Except for a warning about Thunder Child*. Now that *was* interesting.

RAF Coningsby, Lincolnshire
'This is getting fucking ridiculous.'
   'Tell me about it.'
   'Fucking politicians.'
   It was typical crewroom banter. But there was real venom in it this time and nobody was toning down their comments just because the CO had dropped in to see how they were bearing up.

All the Typhoon pilots felt badly let down by their political masters but nobody really knew who to blame. The CO had defended S of S and US of S vigorously, but that only served to suggest that the Cabinet was divided, or that the PM was personally responsible. Fast-jet pilots who had seen combat and watched friends and colleagues die were not going to take lightly the thought that political considerations were actually compromising military operations, even though they were all bright enough to know that no military operation was ever free of any political taint.

'The enemy have been quiet for a while, but that can't last,' one of the pilots observed. 'If the Control and Reporting Centres pick anything up, do we go or don't we?'

'The Thunder Child control team will call it on a case-by-case basis, but unless we're dealing with a major incursion over the mainland my understanding is that we stay put.' The CO was far from happy with his own answer. It was correct, but it was the worst sort of compromise in military terms: however quick the consultation process was, they'd still lose time.

'People will start leaking, sir.' The comment was made without a trace of threat from an old hand with fifteen years' experience. The CO still might have chewed him out for it but he knew the man was right. Indeed, he'd heard that stories that looked suspiciously as if they came from people on the fringes of the operation *were* beginning to circulate on the Internet.

'I've been told to expect some firm decisions within six to twelve hours. More than that I don't know.'

'So we wait, and hope our friends don't show up until later?' somebody else asked.

'Yes, that's right,' the CO snapped back, losing his composure for the first time. 'We wait.'

RAF Lyneham, Wiltshire
Jenny Thornton had spent most of the day without really giving much thought to the fact that she was on a military base. It had not been what she'd imagined, and everybody had been very nice.

What had really helped was being surrounded by people prepared to listen to her and accept what she told them. Her years of involvement with ufology had implanted in her the idea that the military were the bad guys – maybe in league with the aliens, certainly covering up their activities. Unsurprisingly, given recent events, she'd found herself re-evaluating these beliefs. But she didn't want to spend the night on the base, even when she'd been told that she'd be safe there. She'd seen one of her tormentors killed, but after decades of violation she'd come to regard security as an illusion and fully expected the aliens to return. There was something else on her mind: even though she had no way of telling it had been planned that way, she realized she'd been remiss in not calling Cody. He, of all people, deserved to know what had just happened.

'Excuse me,' Thornton ventured. 'I'd like to use the phone.'

Air Force One, Mid-Atlantic

One of the AWACS had called in the contact, and Colonel Sam McAndrews was making hurried mental calculations. The blip was unidentified, but as captain of Air Force One and commander of the Air Group, he'd been briefed on this possibility. He immediately ordered his F-117s to race towards the intruder since they had the best chance of approaching it undetected. He gave a few coded orders and watched the stealth aircraft accelerate away. He saw other elements of his force take up defensive positions, knowing that all the men and women involved would willingly put their aircraft in harm's way to protect the President.

Further back, McAndrews's deputy spoke to the Secret Service agents standing outside the compartment where the President and the NSA Director were sitting. After a brief word, she approached the President.

'Madam President,' she began, hoping her voice was calm. 'We have a situation.'

Spencer insisted in going forward to see for herself what was happening, although a quick glance out of the window revealed that aircraft were being frantically repositioned. As she went forward she noticed that the aircraft was descending and her thoughts turned to the USS *Nimitz*, somewhere far below them. She wondered if she'd been wrong to rule out a sea transit.

McAndrews was not pleased to see his Commander-in-Chief, since it distracted him from his coordination of the complicated tactical redeployment. But he noticed with admiration the way that she waited for him to find the time to brief her, rather than interrupting him. 'Ma'am, we have an uncorrelated target on our heading. I've ordered the stealth fighters to intercept, and everyone else has gone to maximum alert. We're descending, and the *Nimitz* is launching everything it has, to give us some extra protection. I don't know what will happen but I strongly suggest you take your seat and strap up.'

'Thank you, Colonel. I'll do that.'

A few minutes later the all-clear came through. The target had backed off before the F-117s had got anywhere near it. The AWACS aircraft reported that the intruder had disappeared from their screens, but only after a further ten minutes did McAndrews feel he could leave his station to brief the President.

When McAndrews left, Spencer turned to Van Buren. 'It looks as though your friends had a little sniff, then thought better of it.'

'Yes, ma'am.'

Spencer watched the NSA chief closely and noticed that his hands had turned white from gripping the sides of his seat so hard. He'd been absolutely terrified.

Chapter Twelve

REVELATIONS

Porton Down, Wiltshire

With Thunder Child, as with any military operation, the maintenance of security was vital. Although Thunder Child was classified at a level higher than top secret, a number of factors meant its security was already being compromised. Foremost among these was that the information being developed was so sensational. Most secrets stay secret either because they concern technical data that very few people understand, or because the data seems to be of no general interest. The vast majority of secret documents are, in fact, mind-numbingly boring.

But Thunder Child was all about astounding revelations that were truly shattering in their global, indeed cosmic significance. Already there had been a number of leaks that clearly came from people who had been involved in some fringe areas of the operation. They knew few of the key facts and nothing of the overall picture, but some of their information was solid. This had worried those charged with ensuring that the secret stayed secret until the politicians dictated otherwise. One defensive tactic had been to swamp the Internet newsgroups with clearly bogus stories that supposedly came from military personnel. In this way, the real stories were drowned in a sea of rubbish. Another way was simply to ensure that those personnel involved in any aspect of Thunder Child were kept busy and were not allowed on leave, so limiting their possible number of outside contacts. This tactic meant that the team that had recovered the downed UFO from Northumberland now found themselves on guard duty at Porton Down, for example.

Porton Down was the MOD's Chemical and Biological Research Establishment. Like the DERA establishments, though, it had effectively 'untied' from the MOD and was now conducting its business in an increasingly commercial way. It lay on the fringes of Salisbury Plain in an area dotted with Army establishments and training areas. Its mission was purely a defensive one, since the UK had not had an offensive chemical or biological capability for many years.

But concerns about terrorist organizations and rogue states using 'bioweapons' meant that Porton Down had an increasingly important role to play. Bioweapons were known as 'the poor man's nuclear bomb' and the consequences of such a weapon being used in a major city were so dire that Porton Down was thriving, despite the protests of the peace lobby, who wrongly saw it as a Cold War anachronism.

Major Bannerman and his team had deployed at various points around the base. Their brief was to ensure that only those with Thunder Child clearance were allowed into the secure facility where the extraterrestrial corpses were being held. It shouldn't have been difficult, and existing security meant there was no danger of the public getting in.

The real problem, of course, was that CBDE employees had got wind of the fact that something big was happening – especially when they saw that CSA had virtually taken up residence at the facility. Add to that the facts that Bannerman's troops had arrived by Chinook and a massive Army transporter had turned up with a covered and secured load and it was easy to see why so much interest had been generated.

The scientists were a peculiar lot, Bannerman thought to himself. There had already been a few incidents: CBDE staff didn't take kindly to having their access restricted within their own establishment – especially when senior scientists with thirty years' experience found their way blocked by young Privates, some of whom were not yet out of their teens. Bannerman had also been warned to keep a close eye on security within his own unit and it was difficult to avoid the impression that there was a head of steam building up on all fronts. He'd already spoken sharply to a couple of soldiers after he'd overheard them making jokes about filming themselves cutting up the alien and selling the video to the tabloids.

But among the more experienced men and women Bannerman had detected something else: a feeling of real apprehension. They knew that an extraterrestrial craft had been brought down, and they also knew this meant the aliens weren't friendly. The idea of aliens might have been a joke to some, but the thought that they might be embroiled in some sort of secret war with hostile extraterrestrials was not a pleasant one, particularly for the armed forces, who might well find themselves in the front line. Bannerman had been used to dealing with Colonels, and the odd Brigadier. He'd met Generals too, of course, but only briefly. Now he found himself reporting to CGS personally and spending quite a bit of time with CSA.

CSA had her own worries. She was responsible for conducting analyses on the craft and the aliens. The good news was that the hardware was yielding its secrets quicker than she'd dared hope. She'd been receiving direct reports from DUS(S&T), who had now arrived at DERA's Farnborough site to take personal charge of the work started by Dr Lisa Kaminsky.

What concerned CSA was the lack of progress with the entities. This was why she'd decided to go to Porton Down and not to Farnborough. The real priority, she knew, was to get hold of a live one somehow and try to communicate with it. But even if this were possible, she had no idea how they would keep it. Although they had been seen operating in an ordinary house, they might, for all she knew, only be able to tolerate Earth's atmosphere for short periods. Then there was the matter of nourishment. She had no idea what the creatures could safely eat and drink. Their investigations into the dead aliens were severely limited by the order that only non-invasive examination was allowed, due to uncertainty about the death rituals of the culture they were dealing with. They'd tried X-rays, but the creature's outer skin was very tough and they weren't getting any clear images. She'd asked for permission to scrape a few cells from the skin and conduct an analysis of the DNA structure, among other things. She had yet to receive an answer to her request, mainly – she assumed – because the politicians were still debating how to release the basic information about the extraterrestrial presence. She couldn't understand the delay but welcomed it nonetheless. Even though nobody would give away details of where analyses of the craft and bodies were being conducted, it would be simple to work out who was involved. Neither Farnborough nor Porton Down needed the world's media camped outside the perimeter fence.

CSA's final worry was security. It had occurred to the Thunder Child team that the aliens might try to reclaim their downed craft and dead compatriots, if only to keep their secrets from being discovered. She understood that Rapier squadrons had been deployed around Farnborough and Porton Down to counter this possible threat, along with SAS teams armed with Stingers and all sorts of other hardware. This was fine, CSA told herself, but there was an underlying sadness about the whole situation. A civilization from the stars might have offered Earth so much, yet here they were, at war with each other. She wondered if there was a way to put things straight. Broadcasts were continuing through secure military facilities and there were hopes that the extra-terrestrials would make contact, especially now both sides had sustained losses. The recent lack of activity suggested a stalemate. Wasn't this the time to talk?

RAF Fairford, Gloucestershire
As Air Force One approached the western coast of the UK,

President Spencer floated an interesting idea with Colonel McAndrews. It was offered as a suggestion, not an order, which was a clever move and one that spoke volumes about the President's understanding of military matters. She had a tactical brain and was smart enough to realize it was a mistake to impose policy on a thirty-year veteran in operational charge of her own security.

Spencer knew she had good people working for her and was astute enough to see that they performed best when allowed to get on with their jobs. But she had to consider the wider political picture and had raised the matter of requesting additional fighter escorts from the UK. McAndrews realized it made sense and immediately called up for some support.

The RAF sent an AWACS to complement the two US AEW birds and bolstered the escorting fighter force with four Typhoons from Leuchars and a further four from Leeming. The pilots, of course, had mixed feelings about this but were glad to have something to do and realized that the arrival of the US President might well provide the answers they were all looking for. Spencer had wanted to offer a token olive branch that might go a small way towards repairing US/UK relations. She wanted, after all, to see the two air forces working together on joint operations.

Spencer had requested an initial meeting with the British PM with no other officials present. Since he was desperate for answers, he was happy to accommodate her and was eager to get down to business. The Fairford CO cheerfully gave up his office for the meeting.

When the two world leaders were alone, Spencer wasted no time in coming to the point. 'My country owes you an apology for a sin that I doubt can ever be forgiven.'

'I'm listening.' The PM's response was terse and there was real anger in his voice. Understandably, since British people had died.

'Firstly, I can assure you that I knew nothing of what I am about to tell you until yesterday. The moment I did know, I asked for this meeting so that I could explain and apologize.'

'I accept that, and I'm grateful for your prompt action.'

'It turns out that for nearly sixty years some people within my Government have known that humanity is not the only intelligent species here on earth. But please be assured that although they kept this information to themselves, they did so for the best possible motives.'

There was no visible sign that the PM was going to make this easy for her. Spencer understood his reasons but felt that if the positions had been reversed she might have been a little more gracious.

'Let me tell you a story,' Spencer began. 'In the early Forties, when the atomic bomb was being developed, the preliminary tests were conducted at Alamogordo in New Mexico. Although these tests were successful, they uncovered something that had lain undisturbed beneath the Earth's surface for millennia. I don't know how much you know about the history of human evolution, but it's known that *Homo Sapiens Sapiens* shared the Earth with *Homo Sapiens Neanderthalensis* until about 35,000 years ago when the Neanderthals suddenly disappeared. It was commonly thought that they had either been eradicated by *Homo Sapiens* in a power struggle or that they had simply been assimilated through interbreeding. Their disappearance was nonetheless odd, because the Neanderthals actually had larger brains than modern humans have. It turns out that neither of these theories was correct. The Neanderthals went *underground* and evolved in parallel with us, developing their own complex social structures and technologies.'

'I find that very difficult to believe.' The PM had not meant his response to sound so sharp and he instantly regretted questioning the President's veracity in this abrupt way.

'So do I.' Spencer had taken no offence, indicating just how much she felt she owed her British counterpart. 'But until yesterday I didn't believe in UFOs or abductions, yet we now know differently. The fact is that this planet is populated by two distinct human species. But one has generally remained hidden, only being glimpsed rarely.'

'The dwarves and fairies from our folklore?'

'Precisely. When your scientists at Porton Down examine the

entities you have recovered, you will find similarities in the DNA that will prove that these creatures are related to us. Their appearance – small, frail and pallid – is the evolutionary consequence of millennia spent underground.'

The PM set aside for a moment the fact that the President clearly knew every last detail of Thunder Child. He guessed correctly that her mention of Porton Down was not a slip but a frank admission that certain elements of the US intelligence community had been successfully following the British undercover operation's every move. 'So what's going on?'

The President shrugged. 'I'll tell it to you as it was told to me. Apparently these . . . other humans . . . are ahead of us technologically but are far fewer in number. They have been keeping a careful watch on our development, especially since the Industrial Revolution. But it's our progress in the last hundred years that has most frightened them. They toyed with the idea of contacting us but feared we would turn on them out of fear and ignorance. So their energies have been channelled in an entirely different direction.' She paused for effect, much as she had done when she'd been a practising lawyer.

'Oh?'

'Their scientists are brilliant theorists. Many years ago they began to believe that faster-than-light travel might be possible. They realized that if viable interstellar travel could be developed they might be able to find a new home and leave the Earth before they were discovered and destroyed. Initially they were constrained by simple logistics and by fear of discovery should they develop such a technology. But our mining activities increased the chance of detection every day – indeed, many of the communities nearer the surface moved deeper underground. And then, as I've said, an underground atomic test exposed part of a community. Indeed, it destroyed much of one of their cities and was seen as an act of war. You can imagine the American reaction. At the height of the Second World War, the most secret project in the entire country is struggling to develop the atom bomb. Then, suddenly, they are confronted with these strange entities. The

"Neanderthal" leaders were horrified, threatening to share their technology with the Axis powers unless their secret was kept. Much of this technology concerned bioweapons and demonstrations of these were held – they were certainly not bluffing about their offensive biological capability. The Manhattan Project team felt they had no choice but to go along with what was being proposed, including assurances that the secret would be kept from political leaders. To cut a very long story short, responsibility for keeping this secret and liaising with these creatures was ultimately passed to the National Security Agency.'

'So you're telling me that UFOs are piloted by these creatures, and are prototype interstellar craft?'

'That's right. They accelerated their space programme and that's why, from the late Forties onwards, thousands of people have reported seeing strange craft in the sky. Of course, most of these were misidentifications but some were not. There were even a few crashes–'

'Roswell?'

'And others. Anyway, the NSA was told that they had to stop word of any of this getting out. This they did, with a combination of disinformation and active suppression of evidence. I don't condone the telling of lies and I'm certainly not happy about having been kept in the dark. But I can understand why it was done, with the threat of a biological holocaust hanging over us.'

'But why the recent aggression? What's changed?'

'Two events combined to bring about the new state of affairs. A few years ago the "Neanderthals" finally perfected interstellar travel and were able to start their search for a viable new home planet. This new means of travel is virtually instantaneous and they were very quickly able to explore hundreds of worlds. Soon they found somewhere and began to make plans for a total evacuation from Earth. Their plans were well advanced, actually in the final stage, when your RAF changed its policy and decided to have a look at the sort of borderline radar return that was usually written off as spurious. You can imagine how this looked.'

The PM nodded, struggling to take it all in and wishing that he'd insisted on bringing some MOD specialists with him – although he wondered whether they'd be any better than him at making sense of this shattering information.

'They clearly took it as an act of war. To them it must have seemed like we were gearing up to attack them just as they were preparing to make their collective leap away from Earth. Now, they haven't been in touch with us recently, but the NSA had been told years ago that they should do *anything* to protect the secret. That's why they've been uncooperative. That's why no warnings were given from our facilities in your country. The NSA feared that unless they fulfilled their original remit they risked a biological Armageddon. They were sending a message to these creatures by keeping silent, showing them that we *hadn't* reneged on the deal.'

'Why didn't the "Neanderthals" simply come to us and ask us to stop? Why get into a shooting war?'

'I don't know. But, from what I understand, their thought processes are radically different to ours. Don't forget, they've evolved separately from us in a very different ecosystem for tens of thousands of years. They're fearful, even paranoid – perhaps not without justification when you consider how we surface-dwellers seize upon differences in skin colour or religious belief as an excuse for the most appalling atrocities and prejudice. Perhaps they think we don't like the idea of another human species evolving out in the universe while we remain trapped here on Earth.'

'How do abductions fit in?'

'They're a key element in a worldwide programme to infect people with a biological agent. It's introduced into the body in a dormant state and as such is completely harmless. But the "other humans" have a *second* biological agent that they could release into the atmosphere and that would act as a catalyst on the first. The disease would then take hold of the abductees who would spread it into the general population. How much do you know about diseases?'

'A fair bit. I've been briefed on biological warfare because of the terrorist threat from people like Bin Laden and the AUM Shinrikyu cult.'

'Good. The agent is a virus, not dissimilar from Ebola. As you may know, Ebola Zaire has a ninety per cent kill rate, but it isn't airborne and it has a short incubation period – meaning that people die before they can spread it. But imagine a strain that *is* airborne and has a *slow* incubation period so that those infected don't even feel sick for several months.'

The PM's expression indicated he understood only too well the implications. 'So will they use this weapon?'

'We don't know. One scenario put forward by the NSA is that they will use the weapon *whatever* we do, simply because they fear that we will copy their research, find them and wipe them out. Anyway, the bottom line, and the reason for my visit, is to ask you – to *implore* you – to do nothing further that might antagonize these creatures.'

'I'd like you and Van Buren to tell this to some of my people. I certainly can't evaluate on my own this data or any of the options we'll need to talk through. And, of course, it's not my sole decision anyway.'

The President shot the PM a quizzical glance.

'This country is still a monarchy, you know. I may be PM, but I'm still a Crown servant.'

MOD Main Building, Whitehall

Jacqui Connolly looked as if she hadn't slept for days, which wasn't far from the truth.

'Minister, we've got a *big* problem.'

Blackmore sighed inwardly. Everything was a big problem at the moment, and he was feeling increasingly cut out of the major decisions. First, S of S was taking over more of the Thunder Child work, although even *he* was exasperated at the way the PM had then stepped in and was now running the show. Blackmore knew the President was in the UK and had hoped this would lead to a resolution of the current crisis. And yet he'd just received word that Operation Thunder Child was suspended until further notice, and that no action was to be taken in the event of any further airspace violations.

S of S was at RAF Fairford with the PM, and Blackmore had had to tell an exasperated CAS that the RAF were out of the game for the time being. He'd sought clarification on what to do if there was an attack on Porton Down or Farnborough – possibilities that had been causing him some concern and against which some defensive measures had been taken – only to have his head nearly bitten off by the normally placid Willoughby, who had told him in no uncertain terms that all forces were to be stood down. Then Connolly told him something that really stopped him in his tracks.

'We've had a call from *Newsnight*. They plan to interview Richard Cody and Jenny Thornton tonight about claims that soldiers shot down a UFO near her house and then took her to RAF Lyneham.'

'What about our Defence Advisory Notice?'

'They say they don't accept its validity and couldn't possibly drop the story unless *they* were convinced it was in the national interest not to run it.'

'That's not their decision to make, surely?' Blackmore shot back, his tone a mixture of anger and incredulity.

'I'm afraid they *do* have a point.'

'Great. Maybe we should have confided in Cody and appealed to his loyalty. Why didn't he come to us first? Oh hell, what do *you* recommend?'

'There's a chance that they won't run the piece anyway. It's going to be highly speculative and I'm wondering whether it's just an attempt to get us to open up. But I think it's fair to say *Newsnight* wouldn't be going out on a limb on the basis of unfounded stories. They must have something more substantial, and indeed they've hinted as much.'

'Cody got his meeting here on the basis of the fact that he'd used the phrase "Thunder Child",' Blackmore mused. 'We know there have been some leaks, but could he have some documentation?'

'He might. I honestly don't know,' Connolly replied wearily. 'We're going to have to respond one way or the other within the next hour or so. But they're not going to show us what cards they're holding.'

'I'm going to have to kick this one upstairs, Jacqui.'

RAF Fairford, Gloucestershire

After the President and Prime Minister's private discussion there had been a short break, after which the President brought Van Buren into the office. The PM brought S of S, CDS and CSA and, once the introductions had been made, he invited S of S to speak.

'Madam President, Mr Van Buren – the PM has briefed me on your discussions and I have consulted with my colleagues here. There are several areas where we would be grateful for clarification – and we have a number of very specific questions.'

'Fire away.'

HMS *Churchill*, The North Sea

The Navy had not thus far been key players in Thunder Child. True, HMS *Lancaster* had been involved in operations, taking part in SAR ops for various downed pilots and searching for and recovering wreckage. Although any detailed knowledge of the operation had been limited to the captain and a few of his Lieutenants, rumours of varying accuracy had inevitably circulated among the 170 crew members. By and large, though, the men and women on board HMS *Lancaster* knew little more than any reasonably well-informed person who'd been following the developing story in the media. But another ship was about to find itself right at the explosive centre of the unfolding drama.

When RAF Fighter Controllers spotted an all too familiar sight on their scopes and called in the raid warning, nobody thought to tell the Navy. Frustrated military officers monitored the target's trajectory but they were under strict instructions not to launch Typhoons unless the craft looked as if it was going to come over the mainland. It was a hard call because nobody had any real idea about what the intruders' motives were. A sudden course change, coupled with acceleration to the maximum speed they'd observed to date meant that a launch might suddenly become imperative. So the crews were sitting in their aircraft, prepped and ready to go.

CAS had been lobbying ministers for a decision and was furious that they had reverted to defensive ROE that gave the advantage to any aggressor and meant his pilots could only shoot back if they were already being fired on. In the absence of any shooting by the alien craft the RAF's mission – should a launch be authorized – was to intercept any intruder and try to head it off by flying in front of it. This tense manoeuvring – reminiscent of Cold War battles between Phantoms and Bears – was fine, given a level playing field, but CAS regarded it in this context as a nonsense, considering the speed and manoeuvrability of the opposition.

It was only when the craft came to a virtual standstill midway over the North Sea and started to descend that a horrified Fighter Controller remembered that HMS *Churchill* had been enforcing the maritime exclusion zone until it had been ordered back to port at the same time as the defensive ROE were issued. But the ship was still very much in harm's way and although a hurried warning was transmitted, by the time it arrived, the craft had already been picked up on the ship's own radar system.

Realizing that the ship was badly exposed, CAS decided to launch Typhoons on his own authority, ordering them to go to the *Churchill*'s aid. But, even as the decision was made, everybody knew that the maths simply wouldn't work: the Typhoons wouldn't get there for some time and if the ship was attacked it would be on its own.

HMS *Churchill* was the first of the Navy's Common New Generation Frigates, which were replacing the Navy's old Type 42 destroyers and were deployed in a seaborne air defence role.

Commander Julian Parry-Jones ordered General Quarters, his people rushing to their duty stations and ensuring that hatches were closed. Having been briefed on Thunder Child, he had a clearer idea than most what to expect, but decided that the crew would respond better if they thought they were facing a threat for which they'd actually trained.

Accordingly, Parry-Jones informed his team that they were to
prepare for an attack by a sophisticated new prototype aircraft.
He'd posted lookouts and readied weapons, but the defensive
ROE meant there was little else he could do except wait. He toyed
with the idea of launching the Merlin helicopter, but it was an
anti-submarine platform and had no anti-air capability anyway.
He ordered the ship to maximum speed and initiated a series of
radical turns intended to make it as difficult as possible to hit.

'It's right on us, sir!' screamed the radar operator. On deck the
various lookouts yelled and pointed at the craft coming at them
out of the sun, firing a stream of incandescent light-beams. It all
happened too fast for them to get a clear look at their attacker,
but the effects of the beams were obvious enough as they struck
the sea alongside the ship. Huge areas of water were vaporized,
sending the surrounding waves rushing into the gap with a
deafening roar. Huge columns of spray were hurled skywards,
leaving none of the witnesses in any doubt that they were
fighting for their lives.

'Signal Northwood that we are under attack by an unidentified
hostile craft, and that we are engaging the enemy,' Parry-Jones
ordered. Then, to his Weapons Officer, 'Fire at will.'

In the dim red light of the operations room, a small group of
men and women were desperately trying to coordinate a defence
against a target that simply wasn't behaving in any way that they
understood. The Principal Anti-Air Missile System was engaged
and missiles duly streaked out towards the target, only to go wide.
To make matters worse, none of the ship's close-quarter defensive
systems would work, mainly because there was no incoming
missile to which they could lock on. Highly automated systems
were not working at all and ops room staff were frantically using
manual-override facilities to free up their weapons, only to find
that they were no more able than the computers to find the
inbound missiles they assumed they were facing.

'Projected-energy weapon,' somebody yelled out helpfully,
telling the Weapons Officer that there was no hope of engaging
the weapons being fired at them and that, if they didn't take out

what they assumed was the aircraft launching the attack, they were finished.

'Coming round for another pass. Weapons free!'

'Brace, brace, brace!'

The ship took hits along its length that destroyed most of the superstructure and killed most of those on deck. Secondary explosions ripped the ship apart and as the fatally injured Parry-Jones gave the order to abandon ship, blood spouting from a head wound, his last thought was the hope that at least some of his people might get off alive.

RAF Fairford, Gloucestershire

The UK contingent had retired to consider what they had just been told. The PM turned to ask for opinions but CSA leapt straight in.

'Prime Minister, I'm very sorry to say this, but in my opinion there are a number of problems with what we've just been told.'

'I know it sounds implausible, but–'

'No, I'm sorry, Prime Minister,' CSA shot back, neither noticing nor caring that she'd just interrupted the PM. 'Not implausible: *impossible.*'

'Explain.'

'The whole scenario just doesn't work. It's true that there are underground cave systems all around the world, but mining companies constantly use sophisticated ground-penetrating radar to search for mineral deposits. Any extensive systems of caves capable of sheltering entire cities or any other kind of large communities would have showed up on the scans, and somebody would have said something.'

CDS moved to speak, but CSA carried on. 'No, wait a minute, there's more. I don't care how they say this strand of humanity has developed, I'm afraid there's no way that an organized human society could exist, let alone thrive, underground. They're not ants, for God's sake. The basic problem is food. Just about everything living on this planet needs sunlight to flourish: without photosynthesis there can be no agriculture, for one thing.

There are stacks of other inconsistencies, but they're outside my area of academic expertise. Still, from the little I know about human development the idea of humanity branching in this way seems distinctly unsound.'

'What are you saying?' The PM knew exactly what she was saying but wanted to hear it from her.

'I'm saying that we're being lied to.'

The thought was left hanging for a moment and CDS realized that he had to come down on one side or the other. 'I don't have the scientific expertise to analyse the scenario point by point,' he ventured. 'But I'd have to agree. We may have fallen for a classic counter-intelligence trick.' There were puzzled looks, so he spelt it out. 'Look, it's tempting to think of the craft and the entities as proof of what we're being told. They say to us: "Hey, there's another strain of humanity here, and they've developed this amazing technology. Look, here's one of their craft, and here are the entities." And we say: "OK, you're right." But the hardware isn't proof of what they tell us; do you see? In other words, the only *facts* we have are the physical things we've recovered. Because they're outside our knowledge or experience, it's tempting to latch on to any explanation offered as being a fact. But, in this case, it's not: at best, it's a hypothesis.'

The PM and CSA were nodding, but only half-heartedly. CDS went on: 'Suppose you know for a fact that there's a mole in the SIS, leaking information to the Russians. Then a Russian spook defects and gives you a name. You set up a sting, and your suspect takes the bait. You assume you've got your man – but have you? Suppose you'd been given a small fish to take the heat off somebody else?'

'So you're saying that a superficially attractive scenario is being dangled in front of us to distract us from the real explanation?'

'Yes, Prime Minister. Now, the scenario is coherent and fits the facts in many ways. That's what's most disturbing, because it tends to suggest that this isn't just a pack of lies, made up on the hoof – it's a structured and in many ways logical narrative. In other words, it's a pre-planned cover story.'

'Except–' CSA paused, wondering whether she dared voice her suspicion. 'Except that it must be obvious that it'll soon be exposed as a lie, so what's the point of such a short-term cover story?'

It was CDS who answered that one. 'It means that they're buying time, and that they only need a little. Something big is going to happen very soon, and after that it won't matter what was said here.'

It was then that CDS's bleeper went off, followed shortly by S of S's. They all guessed correctly that it could only mean more bad news.

Chapter Thirteen

THE EVE OF THE WAR

Downing Street, Whitehall

News of the loss of HMS *Churchill* had stunned the PM, who had immediately returned to London after thanking the President for her briefing and telling her that she would have Britain's response 'by close of play'. The President had seemed stunned and her expression had been plain to read. She'd clearly been amazed that there was anything more to consider. 'As if,' the PM had observed on the drive back from RAF Fairford, 'a thousand years of history counted for nothing and she expected us just to roll over and hand this country to our uninvited visitors.'

Much had been decided on that drive back to Downing Street and in the subsequent discussions at Buckingham Palace. Some important decisions had been made. First, the Prime Minister would appoint a small War Cabinet to take overall control of the situation. This would be political and strategic control, but he had assured CDS that such control would not cut across whatever military advice he and S of S offered. He had also made it plain that the Thunder Child team would retain responsibility for carrying out the war at the tactical level. And war it was to be, because all were agreed to carry out unrestricted warfare against the intruders, should they reappear. The second decision, one that the PM felt was long overdue, was to make a fuller statement to Parliament and to the public. So far, by bringing the Leader of the Opposition in on Thunder Child and by citing operational necessity he had managed – just – to avoid a constitutional crisis and had ensured that while the public, Parliamentary and media pressure had been savage, all their actions had been legal and would stand up as such.

A major unresolved issue concerned the Americans. Nobody suggested that the President had lied – or had committed an 'inappropriate act', as CDS had quipped – rather that she was being lied to. But aside from the theory that it was designed simply to buy time, the motive for the falsehood defeated them, especially when it was bound to crumble when subjected to any degree of scrutiny. Nonetheless, the Prime Minister had instructed S of S and CDS to draw up plans for ceasing all joint operations with US forces and for requiring the Americans to vacate all British bases. He had also told a dumbfounded Foreign Secretary to prepare for a possible decision to expel all American diplomats from Britain, and simultaneously recall the British ambassador and her staff from Washington. Despite the seriousness of the situation, the PM had almost smiled at the thought of the Foreign Secretary explaining *that* one to the FCO mandarins.

The PM had been drafting his statement to Parliament when an aide interrupted and suggested that he turn on his television.

BBC Television Studios, White City

'Good evening,' Marcus Rosental began, introducing the lead item on *Newsnight*. 'Crisis, what crisis? That seems to be the attitude of the Government towards a situation that has baffled defence analysts and intrigued the world's press. It is now a matter of public record that thirteen RAF Typhoon aircraft have been lost to hostile action, with eleven pilots killed.

'Despite these unprecedented events, the Government and the Ministry of Defence remain tight-lipped. We are told that to disclose further information would compromise national security, and yet a photograph of one of the craft many believe have been responsible for the RAF losses has appeared on the front page of the *Daily Mail*, and has now been syndicated around the world. A Defence Advisory Notice has been issued, asking that the media refrain from reporting these matters. Although this is a voluntary system, editors do not normally go against a request. We are not in the business of endangering lives, but in the face of a total lack of evidence that disclosure would put any of our armed forces at risk, we have decided to challenge the secrecy. We have done this only after having consulted a number of defence experts, including General Sir Malcolm Penny, former Chief of the General Staff, to whom I'll be talking later in the programme.

'I'll also be talking to Linda Task, an Opposition MP not content with what she sees as the platitudes offered by a Government she considers increasingly autocratic and arrogant towards Parliament. But first, a report summarizing what we know and what has been alleged, including – just in – an unconfirmed report of a British warship ablaze and sinking in the North Sea.'

This last item had just been relayed to him by his producer and as the red light on the camera he'd been facing went out, indicating that the pre-recorded report was now being shown, the normally unflappable Rosental gave the production team a questioning stare, hoping to extract information that they simply didn't have. His two guests were just as confused as Rosental, and exchanged puzzled glances. It was all they could do.

MOD Main Building, Whitehall

'Shit.' It was hardly the most eloquent analysis of the latest development, but Jacqui Connolly's comment summed matters up perfectly. She turned to US of S, looking for guidance on the Department's response to the inevitable flood of calls to the Press Office that would certainly now ensue. As they were in the Minister's office rather than the DCMC, they had both been taken by surprise by the *Newsnight* reference to an attack on a ship. They hoped it was just another wild rumour but they knew that *Newsnight* checked their information very carefully.

The biggest surprises for Blackmore and Connolly had come during a pre-recorded interview with Jenny Thornton. As expected, she'd described how soldiers had come into her house and had been involved in an attack on a UFO and its occupants. The *Newsnight* researchers had tracked down locals who'd heard gunfire and seen lights in the forest, and then the programme showed pictures of the place in Alice Holt Forest where the craft had been brought down.

Thornton had made it clear that she was grateful to the soldiers and had then explained how she'd been debriefed at RAF Lyneham. The first surprise had come when she'd produced some stationery from the CO's office, stationery that she apologetically admitted having stolen to prove she'd been there. Then the camera had cut to Richard Cody, who'd sprung another surprise. Not out of bitterness or anger, he'd explained, but simply in an effort to force public acknowledgement of the events, Cody would – on behalf of Thornton – be initiating legal proceedings against the MOD for trespass and criminal damage. In that way, he had explained, the MOD would no longer be able to hide behind its 'No comment' policy and would have either to confirm or deny the specific allegations. Cody graciously and shrewdly said that he very much doubted that Ministers or officials at the Ministry were involved in a cover-up, and then explained how he and Thornton had met Blackmore, Templeton and Carpenter and had found them extremely helpful.

Connolly only just managed to avoid reminding US of S that she'd specifically advised against their meeting Cody and, much as she wanted to dislike the retired barrister for the move he'd just pulled, she had to admire his style. He was, without question, a smooth operator.

The final surprise had come at the end of the piece, when Rosental had read out a press release from Number 10. Apparently the PM was going to address Parliament tomorrow morning and follow that with a broadcast to the nation. The statement went on to say that while he wasn't going to respond to the specific points raised in the *Newsnight* broadcast, any more than he had responded to any of the other media stories, he hoped that his statement would clarify recent events.

Although Blackmore and Connolly had been mystified at this, they were relieved, because it actually took the pressure off them. Connolly hurriedly told the Press Office that they were to hold their line and refer callers to the PM's statement the following morning.

Blackmore tried to raise the PM or S of S, who he correctly assumed were at Downing Street, but was told that they weren't available. Now he was at a complete loss about how best to use his time. His first impulse was to go to the DCMC to follow developments and to try and confirm whether there was any truth to the rumour about the attack on one of the Navy's ships. But then he found himself becoming increasingly angry at having been kept in the dark by the PM and others over recent developments and decisions. He had a mobile phone and a bleeper, after all, and he didn't think it was asking too much to be briefed.

Shrugging off his brief fit of pique, Blackmore headed over to the DCMC, speculating about what he'd find and wondering if he might even get back to Egerton Gardens later for a couple of hours' sleep.

Bradbury Lines, Hereford
Jack West's life, like those of all who had been involved in any aspect of Operation Thunder Child, had changed beyond all recognition as a result of his recent experience. His physical appearance hadn't altered, but those who looked closely into his eyes realized something was different. There was a knowing look there, as if he had suddenly acquired the wisdom of a man many times his age. This look came, of course, from what he had been told by the Thunder Child briefers and, above all, from what he and his men had seen and done at Jenny Thornton's house. Combat was always memorable, but combat of that kind was a life-changing experience. West's perspective on existence had been irrevocably altered: the world in which he now lived was not the same one he'd inhabited a few days before.

Still, as far as regular military routine went, West and his team had had a relaxed time of it. They'd been sent to RAF Lyneham to be debriefed, simply because that was where Jenny Thornton had been sent. They'd been kept apart from her, though, so after their debriefing West and his team had retired to the bar, got drunk and taken the piss out of any RAF personnel curious enough to engage them in conversation. And yet they'd still remained professionals: on the only occasion when one of his men had mentioned flying saucers, West had grabbed him by his lapels and left him in no doubt about what would happen if he continued his story.

The usual command structure had disappeared and to his amazement West had found that he was still mainly reporting direct to GCS and CDI. He assumed that his CO had been briefed but he hadn't seen him during his stay at RAF Lyneham. Once the initial debriefings had been completed, and once Jenny Thornton had been returned to her home, there had been no reason for their stay to continue, and they'd been put on notice that in due course they'd be flown back to Hereford.

By this time the SAS team had got beyond the usual inter-service rivalry and befriended quite a lot of the RAF personnel, who'd correctly guessed that their presence was somehow connected with the current crisis – and incorrectly figured that a few drinks might loosen tongues. It didn't work out that way, but they'd certainly had fun, playing a game known as 'Carrier Deck Landing' in the Sergeants' Mess bar. Beer was spilt on the bar surface and participants took it in turns to launch themselves at it, arms outstretched to imitate an aircraft. Whoever travelled the greatest distance won. They'd played another version called 'Emergency Carrier Deck Landing' where the rules were exactly the same, except that players had to stuff their pockets with wads of tissue dipped in lighter fuel and set them alight. This caused great hilarity, and by the end of the evening some firm friendships forged in flame had been made.

After the lull, the storm. On his return to Bradbury Lines, the SAS's Hereford headquarters, West had been separated from his men and ushered into the CO's office. There he saw the by now familiar figures of CGS and CDI, together with two others who had been involved with his debriefing, Terry Carpenter and Nick Templeton.

'Your mission, should you choose to accept it . . . ' CGS had begun, with a carefully calculated line that achieved its aim of lightening the oppressive mood and bringing smiles to the faces of all concerned. By the time they'd finished outlining a plan that West considered bold but foolhardy, he was beginning to wonder whether it really was a case of 'Mission Impossible'. He was also wondering why he'd accepted it.

Downing Street, Whitehall
The PM was looking in astonishment at the telegram that he had just read for the third time. It was a short message, and the meaning seemed straightforward enough. In a sense, it was the sheer outrageousness that troubled him more than anything else and caused him to look for hidden meaning. He read the words a fourth time.

THANK YOU FOR SEEING ME AT SHORT NOTICE. MY TRAVELLING COMPANION HAS DISAPPEARED AND I'M UNSURE ABOUT HIS MOTIVES OR THE EXTENT OF HIS INFLUENCE. AM CONSULTING KEY PLAYERS AND WILL BE IN TOUCH FORTHWITH. GOOD LUCK.

The message had been hand-delivered by a very confused member of the US Secret Service, who would say only that President Spencer had entrusted him with delivering it personally.

The PM shared this telegram with S of S and CDS. 'What does this tell us?' he'd asked.

'That we can no longer trust our secure comms facilities,' S of S retorted, getting an admiring glance from CDS, who hadn't expected his political boss to be so quick to see the key message in the note. 'And that the President is assuring us of her personal veracity and trustworthiness.'

'But can we even be sure that the note is from her?'

'She'll almost certainly be in touch to confirm it is, although she'll be rather circumspect over the telephone.'

'I thought our communications were secure,' the PM observed, somewhat sarcastically.

'The trouble, Prime Minister,' CDS replied, 'is that we are far more vulnerable to our friends than to our enemies. Because we share technical data and data about frequencies, a deceitful ally can easily tap into our secure communications.'

'Including all our Thunder Child traffic?'

'Yes, Prime Minister.'

'What can we do about this?' The Prime Minister had correctly realized that to apportion blame in such a situation was irrelevant. There would doubtless be lessons for the future, but for the time being the important task was to devise a meaningful response.

'If I may,' CDS began, venturing a glance at S of S before turning and addressing his comments to the PM. 'There are a number of areas where action may be necessary. The US facility most heavily involved in interception of communications is RAF Menwith Hill. If there is some sort of cabal carrying out a policy against the national interest – the American national interest as well as our own – they'd *have* to be involved. They'd be the ones intercepting our comms.'

'I seem to recall a scandal a few years ago,' the PM mused, 'where it was claimed that Menwith Hill eavesdropped on domestic communications as well as overseas ones and listened to every telephone call in the country.'

'That's right,' S of S replied. 'It's true, up to a point, and we've had some notable successes against terrorists and organized crime as a result. Their computers zero in on what are known as *keywords*, such as 'bomb', 'target' or 'shipment', and when one of these words – or, rather, sequences of them – gets picked up, conversations are analysed by NSA personnel. There were allegations that the US used the system for commercial espionage, to pass information about tender bids from UK companies to their US competitors. Those allegations were never proved.'

Despite everything else that had happened, there was something about this that the PM found particularly repugnant.

'I will *not* have our own facilities used against us in this way,' he exploded. 'Find a way to put a stop to it. Send in an inspection team or something.'

S of S and CDS looked at each other. It wouldn't be quite that simple, of course, and there were all sorts of legal considerations bound up with the Status of Forces Act. But at least the PM hadn't ordered them to close the facility down. They'd find a way to carry out the PM's wishes. 'Yes, Prime Minister.'

'What else?'

'The Deep Space Tracking Facility at RAF Feltwell,' CDS ventured. 'They were the dog that didn't bark. We should have had raid warnings from them and didn't. QED, they must be part of this conspiracy. We'll resolve that situation in the same way as we'll deal with Menwith Hill.'

'And beyond that?'

'It's difficult to say,' S of S said. 'If we're to believe talk of a conspiracy, it can really only involve a handful of key people: successful conspiracies invariably involve just a handful of people simply because the more people who are in on a secret, the less likely it is to remain secret. Once one member of a conspiracy is unmasked, it's likely that the whole thing will collapse, because the co-conspirators will either flee or react in some other way that will betray their actions. In any case, the President will doubtless be sifting through every detail of Van Buren's life to see what she can turn up.'

The PM was still troubled. 'I still don't understand why elements of the American Establishment have been lying to their own President and pursuing an agenda of their own. It's not in their national character – they're normally so loyal and so . . . so bloody *moral*. And why throw everything away with an obvious lie that was bound to be exposed as such?'

'We've covered that one,' S of S reminded him, going over once more CDS's theory about how it was a move to buy time. 'But not much of this makes sense unless you factor in the extraterrestrial element. We cannot consider this in terms of UK/US relations, because it simply doesn't make sense. But throw in a third force, with an unknown agenda, and who knows what you get? It's possible that parts of what Van Buren told the President are true, and that the Americans have been coerced into cooperating.'

'Then why didn't Van Buren simply say so?' the PM retorted. 'Or, for that matter, why weren't *we* contacted directly and threatened in a similar way? We'd have backed off, if the threat of biological devastation had been real. I would have.'

'Ah, but that's the point,' CDS replied. 'It can't be true. Otherwise, as you say, all they had to do was demonstrate it to us and we'd have rolled over.'

'Yes, but are we seriously saying that the Americans were threatened with this and never once thought to check it out, or call the creatures' bluff?'

'No, Prime Minister: we're saying that the biological threat never existed and that, if anything, it's a cover story prepared by elements within the US to stop us from taking any immediate action. And it worked, in that Thunder Child reverted to defensive ROE and radar contacts weren't followed up.'

This was turning into a brainstorming session that all three men felt was taking them to the brink of something important.

'Then the purpose of the deception . . . ' S of S's tone of voice was speculative as he grasped for a revelation that seemed tantalizingly close, ' . . . one worth sacrificing any hope of maintaining the integrity of the cover-up, was to buy time – *something* was done when we changed our policy that couldn't have been done if we'd maintained an aggressive ROE.'

'Yes.' CDS felt this was the thing he'd been struggling with. 'Yes, but what?' He thought for a moment, and neither the PM nor S of S interrupted what could clearly be a valuable line of thought. 'Increased contacts over the southern part of the North Sea. Radar operators tracked our friends coming south. Why would they come south?'

'London?' the PM speculated.

'We'll have to check the tapes and do a more detailed analysis. But we're still missing something.'

Nobody disagreed with that.

RAF Coningsby, Lincolnshire

Word had rapidly spread that there had been key developments in Operation Thunder Child. The CO had called together all the Typhoon pilots for a briefing, which told them two things. First, they were to stand ready for an announcement from the Prime Minister tomorrow morning, and second, they were to prepare for military operations on a massive scale. The CO assured the assembled company that he really knew no more than them, but nobody doubted that he'd been given a few hints that he was now doing his best to pass on, striking a balance between maintaining operational security and keeping his people informed.

But there was no disguising some of the preparatory work that was taking place in advance of the big announcement. RAF Regiment personnel were deployed to RAF Coningsby, just as they had already been deployed to RAF Leeming and RAF Leuchars. There was simply no way to hide from them the arrival of the Rapier Field Standard C missile systems, positioned around the base perimeter. Special Forces personnel were also arriving and, although nobody had actually seen the weaponry, it was rumoured that they had a mix of Javelin and Stinger ground-to-air missiles, ready to complement the short-range air defence capability provided by the Rapiers.

The aircraft had already been dispersed and placed under camouflage nets, but a number of other measures were being taken that left personnel in no doubt that trouble was on the way. The main indicator had been the departure of non-essential personnel: it was this more than anything else that told the pilots they were, effectively, on a war footing.

One of the more interesting developments had been the arrival of some Harrier GR7 and Tornado GR1 aircraft. The Typhoon pilots all knew the logic behind this. Analysis of their previous engagements showed that their new-found enemy could deal with air-to-air missiles such as ASRAAMs and BVRAAMs because of the enemy's ability to control the temperature of their hulls and short out the electronics of incoming missiles. In this way, infra-red or radar-guided missile technology was rendered virtually useless.

Because of this, tactics were being re-evaluated and turned on their head. For decades the RAF had striven to develop ways of engaging the enemy from ever-increasing distances, thus minimizing risk to their aircrew and aircraft. Now they were facing the bizarre situation of an enemy who only seemed vulnerable in battle at close quarters and who could seemingly best be engaged with cannon fire. But there were hints that a craft could be destroyed with a missile hit if it was launched from close enough range so as not to give the enemy time to react, and for this reason the Typhoons would still carry ASRAAMs. But the emphasis now was on the cannon, and this explained the arrival of the Harriers and the Tornados.

Isabelle Bentley was excited but disturbed at these events and found it difficult to reconcile the two conflicting emotions. She'd talked about it to one of the older Tornado pilots who'd served in the Gulf War and had been assured that the feeling was natural. Nobody wanted a war, he'd told her, and nobody relished bloodshed. But when all your training was geared towards combat, it was impossible not to get drawn in and find yourself looking forward to action. She'd told him that she felt excited and scared in equal measure, and that part of her positively *wanted* to get up there and get stuck into an enemy who had killed friends and colleagues. He'd told her that this was exactly what he and his colleagues had been through over a decade ago. There was the added factor of the enemy being an unknown quantity, and probably extraterrestrial.

Bentley had explained – they'd been on their fourth bottle of beer by this time – that part of her was in awe of these bizarre craft and their presumably alien occupants and she had described her mixed feelings towards this. Shouldn't they be trying to make peace and establish contact? The Tornado pilot had said that violence was always the last option, and that the politicians would have tried to make peace because – despite their bad reputation – they were fundamentally decent people who genuinely hated the idea of warfare, regarding it as evidence of the failure of their political and diplomatic skills.

Before they'd ended what had turned into a marathon drinking session, Bentley had told her confidant something she would never have told any of her regular circle of friends, namely that she doubted her own courage. He'd told her that it wasn't in dispute, as everyone had seen her perform well in the big air battle. But she'd pressed him, only to have him tell a remarkable story about a man who'd turned his squadron back from a raid in the Gulf War because he'd judged that the AAA fire and SAM threat was too intense. There had been some rumblings about lack of moral fibre, yet it was subsequently realized that he'd probably saved the lives of six or eight aircrew. He'd subsequently gone on to distinguish himself in combat, but in retrospect it had been agreed by all the serious analysts that his decision to turn back on that first night had been one of the most shining examples of courage of the whole war. Bentley took the point, and came away realizing that there was more to courage than simply hurling yourself into combat: she'd proved she could do that, but wondered whether she'd be up to sterner tests.

As Bentley and the Tornado pilot parted company, she'd asked him about his part in the Gulf War. She'd not been surprised to learn that this hardened veteran of Kosovo and Bosnia had indeed been the pilot who'd ordered his squadron to abort their attack on the first night of Operation Desert Storm.

House of Commons, Westminster
The Prime Minister had been playing a dangerous game over the last few days. Normally the Speaker would have called him or Defence Ministers to the House to account for recent events and to explain the lack of any formal statement. Two things had saved him. The first and most important was that he had briefed the Leader of the Opposition on Operation Thunder Child, and secured his agreement to the Government's handling of the issue – both operational and political. The second factor was that the Speaker herself had now been briefed in general terms, in the presence of the Leader of the Opposition who had declared himself content with arrangements.

All had known, however, that this agreement had done little

more than buy the Government some time – a few days at the most. The Speaker, for her part, had made it clear that she had a wider constitutional duty than simply playing along with the wishes of the two main party leaders. She'd privately told them that if a statement was not forthcoming by the end of the week, she would have no alternative but to bring S of S to the House to account for his actions. If he refused to say more, she made it clear that she would have to hold him in contempt of the House. Such a state of affairs would have led to an almost unprecedented constitutional crisis, and she was therefore delighted when she'd been told that the PM wanted to make a statement to a joint session of Commons and Lords.

Much thought had gone into the wording of the PM's speech, which had been drafted by the PM and his Press Secretary, with input from S of S, CDS and Jacqui Connolly. They had stayed up late into the night to agree the text of a statement that would doubtless be analysed at great length, and would undoubtedly – because of the dramatic content – come to be regarded as one of the most sensational speeches of all time. For a number of reasons, though, the Prime Minister felt himself unable to make a definitive statement about extraterrestrials, even though there was little doubt that this was the correct explanation. 'As long as doubt remains – and it does, given the American bluff – ,' he had said, 'we must hold back from definitive statements, and leave the door open.'

House of Commons, Westminster
From Whitehall to Northwood, from Bradbury Lines to Coningsby, those who were involved in Thunder Child listened in. From Rowledge to East Horton, from Fort Meade to Feltwell, other interested parties waited to learn what would be said.

'Madam Speaker,' the Prime Minister began. 'It is with mixed feelings that I address this joint session today. As you will be aware, the last few days have seen some extraordinary developments in this country. The tragic loss of so many RAF pilots and their aircraft has now been overshadowed by an even greater tragedy. It is with a heavy heart that I must confirm to this House the loss of HMS *Churchill*, with twenty-eight of her crew dead and another forty-two injured.'

Although such statements were, by custom, received in silence, the significance of this news brought gasps and comments from all quarters of the chamber.

'Parliament has already been briefed on the loss of the Typhoons, and will recall that these aircraft were scrambled in response to radar returns picked up by Fighter Controllers at a number of RAF bases. At the time, the cause of these returns was not clear and for this reason we avoided making public comment about it. It has already been explained that the interpretation of radar data is a complicated task and that while some returns are generated by the presence of an aircraft, others can arise simply because of areas of dense air. The signals detected prior to the launch of the downed Typhoon aircraft were not particularly clear and were the subject of some debate. For this reason we resisted getting drawn into a speculative debate about what had caused these radar returns.

'To help resolve the issue, staff at the Ministry of Defence and at the Defence Evaluation and Research Agency, together with Royal Air Force personnel, conducted a number of analyses, both of the available radar data and of the wreckage from those of our aircraft that have been brought down. From these analyses it became clear that the radar returns had indeed been generated by a solid craft, and that this craft – or a number of such craft – had been responsible for bringing down our jets.

'We then followed up a number of different lines of enquiry to try and determine the origin of this technology, and consulted with other countries to see whether we were dealing with some sort of prototype aircraft. We wanted to believe that the losses of our jets had been the result of some accident that had resulted from their coming into contact with such an aircraft. But this was only one of a number of scenarios considered, and we never lost sight of the fact that our aircraft might have been brought down deliberately.'

'By who?' shouted someone from the back of the Opposition benches. The PM didn't recognize the voice and, ignoring the breach of protocol, resumed his statement.

'Alive to the possibility that our losses might be due to hostile action, we placed our forces on increased levels of readiness, refining the way in which radar data was evaluated so that nothing would be missed.

'Matters came to a head in an action that resulted in the loss of a further nine aircraft. At that point it became clear that we were dealing with a hostile attacking force. It had also become clear that these craft could fly much faster than our aircraft and could accelerate and manoeuvre in ways that ours could not. They also used various defensive techniques that, added to the capabilities mentioned earlier, put our pilots at a distinct disadvantage.

'At this point I want to pay tribute to the brave men and women who have engaged these craft. Their courage and pro-fessionalism in the face of such overwhelming odds has been exemplary, and I am sure both the Houses will want to join me in saluting these valiant and dedicated people, some of who have paid the ultimate price in the defence of the realm.'

There were shouts of 'Hear, hear' from all quarters of the chamber.

'At this point,' the PM continued, 'staff at the Ministry of Defence devised a plan with the twin aims of taking successful action against these craft and identifying this unknown enemy. For reasons of operational security, which I am sure you will understand, I shall not go into the details of this or subsequent operations, not least because the crisis is still upon us.'

There were a few more muted calls of 'Hear, hear', most of which came from his own backbenchers. The PM welcomed the brief interruption.

'It is for these reasons that we have made no detailed statements about the loss of our aircraft. While I understand that Parliament, the media and the public have been eager for more facts – and on occasion have been impatient that they were not forthcoming – a careful balance has had to be struck between freedom of information and operational security. I should also say that, as the crisis developed, we gave detailed briefings to the Leader of the Opposition and the Chair of the House of Commons Defence Committee, both of whom supported the operational decisions being made and the tight controls placed on the release of information.'

This last point had been a useful one to make, and his Press Secretary had correctly judged that mentioning the support given by the Leader of the Opposition would make it less likely that the Government would be attacked for its handling of the crisis.

'As a result of military action and some quite remarkable feats of daring, two of these craft were brought down in circumstances where they were committing hostile acts,' the PM continued. They'd agonized over that one, because the craft brought down in Alice Holt Forest had not actually been engaged in an active attack on UK forces. However, it had been decided that the procedure to which Jenny Thornton had been subjected – although not fully understood – clearly counted as a 'hostile' act. *Now*, the PM thought, *time for the big one*.

'I mentioned earlier that we had remained open-minded about the origin of these craft, and had not ruled out *any* possibility, however bizarre and unlikely. As a result of our successful military actions it became clear that one of these possibilities was the most likely explanation for what we were dealing with. It is with a paradoxical sense of both wonder and disappointment that I must now tell you of our findings – findings that we will now be sharing with the scientific community as a whole . . . '

PJHQ, Northwood
One man too busy to watch or listen to history being made was Alan Whitfield, who was poring over several days' radar data for the eleventh time. He'd been at his task for some hours and had got through many cups of strong black coffee. It had become pretty much his standard diet over the last few days, not that he'd minded. The trade of his home comforts for a place on the

Thunder Child team had been more than worth it.

Whitfield wasn't an arrogant man, but he did occasionally like to think that it was his analysis that had led to the operation. So it seemed to him somehow appropriate that he was here at the heart of the action, seeing it through to what he hoped would be a successful conclusion. He certainly thought of himself as no different from his fellow Fighter Controllers, considering it more curiosity than ability that had led to him seeing what others had missed.

His CO thought differently: Whitfield would have been genuinely surprised and probably quite embarrassed if he'd heard the glowing terms in which he'd been commended to the PJHQ prior to his move. Spink had pointed out to CJO that curiosity was the mark of a good Fighter Controller, because it marked the difference between those who simply reported what they saw and those who really *analysed* the data. He'd explained that in a combat environment a good Fighter Controller didn't just report the position, course, speed and type of aircraft but tried to get inside the heads of the pilots, anticipating their next moves and getting an overall sense of the wider tactical position.

This was what Whitfield had just been doing as he scanned the data, looking for connections and trying to spot an overall pattern that he'd been told might exist. He'd run it through his head time and time again. *The Americans had told an outrageous lie that had forced the UK to revert to defensive ROE. Why? Probably to buy a few extra hours of time, during which something of great importance was done. What?*

It was clear that intruder activity had increased dramatically during the period when the Typhoon force had been effectively grounded, but Whitfield cautioned himself that this might simply have been a reaction to the decreased threat from the RAF. It was maddeningly difficult trying to make sense of the data: the craft were so nearly stealthy that the radar returns were only transitory. But he had painstakingly cross-referenced data from the Control and Reporting Centres with data from RAF Fylingdales, which had helped somewhat. He'd also designed a computer program that enhanced the signals still further, although it increased the number of spurious returns to look at. *It's almost as if they're trying to confuse us*, he'd mused. *Deliberate false trails to hide the real ones?*

With that thought in mind Whitfield had returned to the data with fresh eyes, determined to eliminate the red herrings. He'd studied maths at sixth-form college and had a real talent for complicated equations where the key to finding the solution was often to cancel out various elements, progressively simplifying the picture until a result emerged. It was this process that he had applied to the radar data. In doing so he accepted that he was relying largely upon subjective judgement, but proceeded none-theless, on the grounds that he'd exhausted all other options. Put at its simplest, he was looking for tracks that seemed pointless, or that just didn't feel right. When he'd ruthlessly weeded out this material he had been surprised and delighted to see a pattern emerge.

Whitfield transposed his data onto a navigational chart and printed out a hard copy. He was now looking at a series of dots running over the southern part of the North Sea, towards the British coast. *Mainland incursions we've missed?* But he knew it was more than that and looked again. When realization struck him, the shock was such that he actually yelled out loud. Most of the tracks had been caused by objects coming in close and then turning away at the last moment, following the same route outwards. He used the mental analogy of a muddy path where the footprints showed how many people had trodden it and in which directions they'd been travelling. *But there were more tracks outbound than inbound!*

Whitfield plotted a course and, when he saw where it led, he remembered something that had been touched on in an earlier Thunder Child briefing document and *knew* he was right. He'd have to consult others, of course, and they might not accept his methodology. But he had to kick this upstairs quickly – because what he'd discovered changed everything.

Chapter Fourteen

THE BATTLE OF BRITAIN

RAF Fylingdales, Yorkshire

'You're not going to believe this, sir, but we've just had a flash call from the Duty Controller at RAF Feltwell, warning us of incoming traffic. We're looking at the area concerned now, sir, and running various programs to help us refine transitory signals. I've relayed this information to the Control and Reporting Centres.' The young Duty Officer could see that she'd impressed the CO.

'Excellent. Well done,' he acknowledged, striding into the ops room and looking at the data as it came in. The CO didn't interrupt the duty staff: he trusted them to do their jobs and knew they'd perform at their best without having their concentration broken. But there was no way that he could distance himself from this: he stood back, looking at the screens and making some mental calculations. In a few minutes a pattern emerged and one of his officers delivered his assessment, just as the CO had figured it out for himself. He lifted the secure phone link to the Thunder Child team at PJHQ, punched one of the pre-programmed buttons and got through to CJO's Principal Staff Officer. Once he'd explained why he was calling he was put straight through to CJO.

'Sir, we have indication that a major raid is under way.'

'Who's the first target?'

'We are.'

PJHQ, Northwood

CJO thought about that and weighed up the tactical situation. The possibility that RAF Fylingdales was going to be hit was not entirely unexpected. Some of the PJHQ tacticians had theorized that the previous incursions had been intended to gauge the capability of the UK's air defences. They had also suggested that the next step would be a systematic attack on the AD assets, to try and degrade them as much as possible. Such a move made sense tactically, and was a strategy that the RAF could understand. In anticipation of such a move, elements of 16 Squadron RAF Regiment, normally based at RAF Honington, had been deployed to defend the site.

But the Thunder Child planners had faced a logistical nightmare in trying to decide where best to deploy their forces. Numbers had been cut right back over the past few years: because of what strategists had seen as the virtual elimination of any real threat of an invasion of the UK mainland, SHORAD had not been considered a priority. The sudden appearance of this new threat was a tactical nightmare, because usually threats could be anticipated and countermeasures devised. Now, however, the assets were stretched very thin.

Rapier squadrons had previously been deployed to Farnborough and Porton Down to guard against any attempt to seize back or destroy the captured craft or the alien bodies. But these squadrons had just been moved to cover the Control and Reporting Centres, leaving SAS squads with Stingers and Javelins to plug the gaps. Boulmer, Buchan and Neatishead were all now protected by a mixture of Regiment personnel and SAS but, like Fylingdales, they suffered from the obvious problem that their prime assets were immobile. While aircraft could be dispersed, the primary radar heads could not. If the main radars were knocked out, there were, of course, various secondary systems that could be brought on line. But these mobile systems lacked the power of the primary radars and simply didn't have the range of the assets they'd be replacing.

This highlighted the problem of how best to deploy the AEW aircraft. The RAF had just seven, of which two were now airborne at any one time, with the others dispersed from their normal base at RAF Waddington and deployed at Coningsby, Leeming and Leuchars, so as to collocate them with the Typhoon squadrons assigned to protect them.

The solution might have been to call upon the Americans for support and the fact that a warning had been received from RAF Feltwell was seen as a good sign. But CJO knew only too well that the US position was far from clear: although the PM was apparently negotiating with the President, no support could be counted upon from a nation that, until a day ago, had been perceived as on the side of the aggressor.

Support from some of the other NATO nations was a possibility, but that was something the politicians had only just started to investigate. CJO wondered, briefly, whether the politicians might have looked into this sooner, but decided they could hardly be blamed for not asking for help when nobody had really known the nature and level of the threat. For the time being, Britain was on her own.

RAF Fylingdales, Yorkshire

As the CO replaced the receiver he realized that there was little for him to do now but wait. He reflected that this was the hardest part of warfare, but one that generations of military personnel had endured. It was a sign, he supposed, that he had done all he could do. Non-essential personnel had been sent home and those pieces of equipment that could be moved had been secreted in various underground storage areas that he fervently hoped were secure. His defensive forces had been dispersed around the base and the air raid warning was now sounding. Like CJO, though, he knew that this facility, more than most, was ridiculously vulnerable. The famous 'golf balls' – as the old radar had been known because of the way they had been enclosed in white, circular structures — were gone, replaced in 1992 by the Solid State Phased Array Pyramid. The problem was that this structure was nine storeys high and might as well have been painted like a large fairground target. It couldn't be moved, it couldn't really be camouflaged and if it was hit, the base would effectively be hors de combat.

The CO decided to look in on his people, cautioning himself to be very careful about disturbing anybody at a critical moment. He wanted the men and women under his command to see that he was there with them, sharing the danger and coordinating the defence of the base, but he was only too aware of the reception he'd get from Regiment or SAS personnel if he interrupted them while they were trying to track and engage an incoming target.

There was also the small matter of his personal safety. While the CO was quite prepared to accept the dangers of doing his job, he had no wish to take any unnecessary risks. He was a brave man but, like everyone else still at their post, he was scared too. Intelligence suggested that the UFOs — he supposed they were allowed to call them that now, after the PM's broadcast — possessed just one offensive weapon, but all that really meant was that that was the only one *witnessed* to date. He was encouraged by the news that the SAS had successfully downed a craft with a Stinger, but he worried that the opposition would have learnt from that and might adapt their tactics accordingly. There was no way of telling what other weapons they might have. Still, although the projected-energy weapon was clearly powerful, it seemed that its targeting was inaccurate.

As the CO headed off to show his face, he wondered about the Typhoon force and the other aircraft he knew had been newly designated as air defence machines. They'd try to engage the enemy as far out as possible, before they had a chance to make an attack run. But what he didn't know was how many craft were involved in the attack, or whether the RAF would have any hope of bringing some down and thinning the numbers out before they arrived at their targets. It was possible, he told himself, that all the intruders would be destroyed before they could attack any British bases, or that the RAF would at any rate inflict such damage that the entire attack would be aborted. But he suspected that this was wishful thinking, and from what he knew about the crafts' speed and manoeuvrability he guessed that the pilots would find it hard enough even to intercept the attacking force, let alone successfully engage them. Then there was the question of what tactics the opposition would use. They might come straight through any RAF aircraft and press an attack on his base or they might stop to engage the Typhoons, progressively eating into the AD force until it was stretched so thin that it was unable to plug the gaps.

But these were questions for others to worry about. While the CO might play through the various options, he knew there was nothing he could do to influence the outcome. They'd prepared for the worst-case scenario – and he couldn't shake the thought that this would be precisely what happened.

RAF Buchan, Aberdeenshire

Sue Harding had never been so stressed in her life, as she and her team of Fighter Controllers struggled to make sense of the data that was now pouring in. She'd received the tip-off from Fylingdales and had very shortly afterwards seen for herself, as her screens had filled with transitory signals. She'd cleaned up the picture somewhat with the new computer program that had come from PJHQ, who even now, of course, would be receiving this data in real time and deciding how to respond.

Harding wouldn't have any real degree of operational control, but that could change depending upon how things went. For the time being, though, she knew that she was just one link in the AD chain, although an important one. Indeed, from studying the data she could already see one thing she'd anticipated and feared – they, too, were going to be hit. She'd seen the distinctive and welcome sight of the Rapier launch vehicles and several soldiers swaggering around with various hand-held SAMs, but didn't rate their chances, even though she'd told her people that she was confident they could beat off any attack. Harding wasn't given to falsehoods but felt this was a justifiable white lie that just might make things easier for the young and presumably very scared people under her command. The only consolation was that the busier they were, the less time they'd have to worry about their fate.

PJHQ, Northwood

Whitfield's first thought had been to wonder whether the PJHQ itself might be hit. How much did the enemy know about their command-and-control systems, he wondered, and did they have weapons that would be effective against the Bunker? This had been anticipated, of course, and various SHORAD assets had been deployed around Northwood just as they had been deployed around other sensitive sites.

But, unlike most military bases in the front line, Northwood was located in a suburban area, and this had raised the matter of what to do about evacuating civilians who lived close to it. It had been decided to move only those nearest to the base and in the event this had proved to be fairly easy, aided no doubt by the fact that it was impossible to disguise the presence of the Rapier Fire Units. People could figure that one out for themselves, and most needed no additional persuading when asked to leave their homes. But Whitfield realized that, while getting civvies out of harm's way was fine, they might only have drawn attention to the importance of Northwood in doing so. Nobody knew what intelligence or surveillance capabilities the enemy possessed.

Whitfield was therefore understandably relieved to see from the initial data that it looked like Northwood was not going to be hit. He suppressed his elation, reminding himself that friends and colleagues had not been so lucky. He'd been part of a three-person team that had been responsible for amassing the data and briefing CJO and his most senior advisers. This was where the PJHQ came into its own, because although staff at the DCMC in Main Building would be receiving the same data and briefings in real time, operational control was now vested in CJO, who shouldered the enormous responsibility of making decisions about the tactical response to the attack and ordering the disposition of forces. Ministers or Chiefs of Staff might, of course, intervene, and there was always the possibility of the PM issuing direct instructions, but this was unlikely. Once the political decisions had been made, which they had, everybody knew that it was foolhardy to interfere with the operational control of an ongoing engagement.

CJO had taken the briefing in silence and listened to the recommendations. He'd raised a couple of points, asking to look again at some of the raw data, but had soon made his decisions and issued his orders. There was precious little time for debate: ultimately he, like all commanders, had to have faith in his subordinates. He knew he'd assembled a good team and he could find no fault with their analysis. He knew that aircraft would now be taking to the skies and attempting to engage the enemy at a distance, before they could get to the mainland, or launch attacks on the sites that clearly had been targeted.

RAF Coningsby, Lincolnshire

As one of the pilots who had most experience of the threat they were now facing, Isabelle Bentley was in the first wave of jets to take off. As she'd accelerated down the runway she'd noticed that some of the fire rescue units and field ambulances were already deployed alongside the runway and some of the taxiways. She wasn't sure how she felt about that. While it showed that the base was as ready as it could be, she worried that it might send the wrong message to the stream of pilots who would see the vehicles. *Some of you are going to be hurt. Or worse.* That was the message they sent.

Bentley had thought about it, of course. She'd decided that if she was going to die she'd rather do so in a mid-air explosion that ended her life in an instant. What she really feared was what terrified every pilot who had ever flown – burning to death, trapped in a damaged aircraft from which she was unable to escape. She'd given the matter a lot of thought and had tried to run through the various possibilities. She'd asked herself many times whether she'd have the courage to choose death rather than permanent disablement or disfigurement, but had been unable to decide how she'd react. She knew that people would cling

desperately to even a futile life, against all odds, and suspected
that she'd do the same. But what if this involved the risk of a slow,
agonizing death as distinct from a quick passing? Would there be
time to choose – and what if she made the wrong choice?

Bentley was angry at herself for allowing these thoughts to
distract her now but was unable to set them aside completely. She
had a tightness in her stomach that she knew came from fear. She
suddenly felt quite small and vulnerable, and her thoughts turned
to her parents and her sister. How would they react if she didn't
come back? Would they be proud or angry? Or both? How often
would they visit her grave? How many tears would they shed? It
was at this point that she realized her own eyes were watering: she
bit her lip and turned her thoughts back to the task in hand. She
was the professional once more. Tears were dangerous, since they
impaired vision – something that all the computerized control
systems in the world could not supplant.

As Bentley's Typhoon nosed its way into the sky, she gazed
ahead and saw that three other aircraft were in front of her. There
would be dozens more following, but she'd be among the first to
encounter the enemy. She closed up, awaiting further instructions.
She'd have her airborne radar, of course, and her JTIDS system
would give her access to data from the Control and Reporting
Centres and the AEW aircraft. But she reminded herself that the
pilots' final briefings had suggested that these were the very assets
most likely to be targeted. So her JTIDS system might not be
receiving data at all if they couldn't blunt the attack.

Bentley knew, as they all knew, that their Typhoons were not as
fast or as agile as the UFOs. But she also knew that they entered
the atmosphere sufficiently far away from the UK coast to allow
for an interception to be made – maybe because they hoped to
come in at a point as far from any radar system as possible – or,
possibly, because they *wanted* the AD aircraft to have time to
launch so that they could lure them into combat and pick them
off.

There had been much debate about how best to arm the aircraft.
Many of the pilots had wanted to carry no missiles at all, believing

that the previous engagements had shown they were useless against whatever countermeasures the UFOs used. They'd wanted to trade a capability they saw as ineffective for what they thought was the very real advantage of the increased speed and manoeuvrability that would come from carrying a lighter load. But the analysts had ruled this out. They believed that there was still a chance that a sufficiently large volley of BVRAAMs just might get lucky. And, since those missiles would be fired long before the RAF fighters got anywhere near the enemy, arguments about speed and manoeuvrability were politely and tactfully brushed aside. As for the ASRAAMs, it was pointed out that the SAS had successfully brought down an intruder craft with a Stinger, so the pilots had simply been told to engage at closer range. Bentley was one of those who had no problems with this line of thinking. However effective the cannon might be, she didn't fancy relying on it alone in a dogfight with wave after wave of UFOs.

As they crossed the coastline and headed out over the North Sea, Bentley was unable to avoid thinking about something else that scared her: the thought of crashing in the sea and being unable to escape from her aircraft as it slipped beneath the waves. Then there was the possibility that she'd have to eject over the sea. She had a parachute and a survival suit, but there was always the fear that she would become entangled in the chute and be unable to inflate her lifejacket. She'd done the drills in the station pool, like all pilots, but there was a world of difference between that and a real-life ditching where she might be wounded and in shock. This was another load of concerns that she could do without, so she counselled herself to run through her checks and use her instruments and her eyes to gauge her position, to see if any adjustments were needed.

Harding Manor, Devizes

Jack West was frustrated at the way in which the timing had worked out and had asked whether his mission might be postponed so that he could help in the defence of one of the bases that were now, apparently, about to be hit. He'd argued that he'd led the only team to successfully engage a UFO with a Stinger and wondered whether he might be more productively deployed to straightforward SHORAD duties.

It was pointed out to West as tactfully as possible that it had been the tactic itself rather than his leadership that had downed the craft. He might have pushed the point had it been made by anyone other than CGS, who told him to have faith in his fellow SAS soldiers, who were all capable of firing Stingers and Javelins. CGS had gone on to stress that West's mission could well be the most important engagement of this battle.

As they pulled into the drive of Earl Sutton's residence, West was surprised to see that what he correctly assumed was the Minister's car still parked in the driveway. He'd queried this and had been told that the Minister had asked to take part in the final briefing. Although Earl Sutton had already been extensively debriefed, it was possible that useful information might be gleaned from such a move, so his request had been allowed. The operation could, after all, only be carried out with his agreement. In any case, he was still a Government minister and not the easiest of people to turn down.

West, Templeton and Carpenter were ushered into the drawing room. When the four men had seated themselves, Templeton began to go over the finer points of the plan. West decided that he might, after all, enjoy this mission, which would involve him spending his days in a most luxurious house, making full use of its amenities. He was far too professional to think of sampling anything from the extensive drinks cabinet or wine cellar, but his soon-to-be absent host had given him free rein over what looked like a sumptuous larder. Then there was a games room, complete with full-size snooker and billiards tables, an extensive library of books and videos – although he doubted that he and Earl Sutton shared the same tastes – and a huge flat-screen television with access to several hundred channels from all around the world. West knew that the Earl had been widowed two years ago and that his two daughters had both married – into good families, no doubt – and fled the nest several years before that. Although Sutton lived alone, West imagined that the Minister enjoyed his life here and doubtless had a stream of visitors from other members of the country set. It would be fun, he thought, to swan around the house all day.

The downside, of course, was a mission from which there was a very real chance West wouldn't come back. But he'd been asked to undertake the task and had been told that he was almost certainly the most suitable candidate, not only because of his all-round soldiering ability but because he was one of the few people to have come up against the aliens in combat. As such, he was less likely to have an adverse fear reaction and was therefore reckoned to have a better chance of completing the mission successfully than somebody coming to Thunder Child operations for the first time. When it had been put to him like that, West realized he had no choice but to accept the mission. To have refused it would have been to expose somebody else to a higher degree of risk than he would face.

West had already seen schematic diagrams of Sutton's house but now carried out a detailed survey of his own, asking a few questions as he went. When he'd first heard details of the plan, he'd been pretty sceptical, especially when he found out that it had been devised by a civil servant and not a military officer. But CGS and CDI had clearly been impressed with it, had added a few of their own ideas, and had proceeded to sell the idea to West, who'd gradually come to appreciate its subtlety. Before they'd left Bradbury Lines he'd been issued with kit – some standard items and some decidedly non-standard ones. Then he'd been given a short training course in a technique quite unlike any he'd ever encountered previously, before being driven to Devizes for the start of his mission. He'd been told that there was no back up – although unbeknown to him the house *was* under very discreet surveillance. But the two SAS personnel watching the premises were doing so from far away, with orders not to interfere and not to use their radios under any circumstances.

When West declared himself fully satisfied – not just with

tactical matters but with practicalities like the location of keys, the fuse box and the water main stop valve – Earl Sutton, Templeton and Carpenter wished him luck, shook his hand and left him to begin his mission. West had smiled when Templeton had reminded him not to answer the door or the telephone, thinking that it was the sort of comment one made to a five-year-old. In fact, they'd thought hard about communications, weighing the respective merits of the telephone, a standard-issue PRC319 radio or a mobile phone. In the end they'd settled upon the mobile and agreed some innocuous-sounding codes for any of the communication-worthy situations that they'd thought might arise. There were not many of those, West realized. Either the plan would work or it wouldn't. Even if it worked, he'd be very much on his own.

Over the North Sea
Bentley was now part of a wave of twenty Typhoons that made up what she thought of as the first line of defence. She saw from her equipment that a sizeable enemy force – there looked to be between thirty-five and forty craft but it was difficult to be sure – lay directly ahead, at a distance of about ninety miles. They were coming in comparatively slowly, but the closing speeds meant that they'd be in amongst them in a matter of minutes. It would soon be time to launch the BVRAAMs.

The Typhoons were each fitted with the maximum load of six BVRAAMs, and it was hoped that they might have some success against the enemy. But, again, current military doctrine had been challenged by previous unsuccessful attempts to use the RAF's newest and most sophisticated weapon against this new enemy. The PJHQ analysts felt that the weapons had failed because the opposition had been given too much time to react. So, paradoxically, a weapon that was specifically designed to be launched as far away from the target as possible was to be launched a little closer this time. And, in a further twist, it had been decided to use their Skyshadow ECM pods in an attempt at some electronic jamming to interfere with whatever countermeasures the UFOs might use. Of course, none of this could stop the enemy charging their hulls or altering the temperature – which was how DERA thought their defensive systems worked – but it *might* just deny them a few of their tricks.

Bentley removed the safety cover from her firing switch, revealing the red button that would, when pressed, send the missiles on their way. She fought the urge to launch the missiles at a range that was already considerably shorter than the optimum recommended. When the prearranged distance was reached, she thumbed the button and waited for the missiles to detach. In a few seconds she saw them streaking out in front of her, racing away at a speed of around Mach 5, as part of a veritable flock of such projectiles now closing on the approaching craft.

The 'fire-and-forget' missiles accelerated away, using active radar homing to lock on to their targets. The problem with this was that, as everyone by now had realized, the UFOs were semi-stealthy. They seemed to utilize a system that enabled them to appear one moment and disappear the next, so far as any radar system was concerned. For radars simply trying to acquire the intruders this was manageable because, although the signals were transitory, they could be followed. But for radar-guided missiles the signals proved more of a problem: once the target disappeared, the missiles had an annoying habit of losing their lock altogether. Once the lock was lost there was no guarantee that a missile would reacquire its target, even if the UFO was no longer stealthy.

The analysts had debated that one at great length, wondering why the UFOs switched from stealth to non-stealth mode rather than remaining completely stealthy at all times. They had decided, again, that it was a tactic aimed at drawing out the RAF and forcing them to deploy their weapons. It seemed to be designed with the express purpose of enticing the RAF to use all its most sophisticated hardware, slowly reducing the numbers of advanced weapons in their armoury and thereby degrading and diminishing their capability.

Bentley watched the missiles streaking towards the opposition and prayed that they would have some success. But as the lethal cloud approached the tightly bunched UFOs, the enemy craft adopted a tactic that hadn't been seen before. The projected-energy weapons that had been deployed with such devastating effect against the Typhoons in the last engagement were now being utilized defensively. Missile after missile was exploded by the energy beams and Bentley noticed something that nobody had anticipated: the missiles were so tightly bunched that when one blew up it tended to take out others around it. She cursed this latest development.

The final result was confusing, to say the least. Bentley's instruments suggested that the surviving missiles – and the numbers were unclear – had now intersected the path of the approaching enemy craft, which had suddenly accelerated rapidly. She thought that a very small number of hits might have been recorded, but they were so bunched up that it was impossible to tell. Again, this didn't make sense from a tactical point of view. Logically, the craft should have dispersed when fired upon so as to present a more difficult target. Bentley tried to figure out what was going on. It was almost as if the opposition was prepared to accept limited casualties in order to preserve a pre-planned attack formula. She asked herself why that would make sense and came up with no answers. She reminded herself that if the intruders were alien, they might play by completely different rules anyway. With that thought in mind she told herself to stop analysing every move. Like every good pilot she recognized that her performance would suffer if she lost her concentration in pointless speculation about enemy motives. She'd have to leave that to others better qualified than herself. Her job was to concentrate on reacting to the immediate tactical situation, not to try and figure out the wider strategic implications.

The Typhoons had been flying on a fairly straight course. Bentley decided that this probably wasn't a particularly bright move, given that the opposition hadn't been entirely stupid to date. She began jinking her aircraft first one way then the other, not in response to a specific threat, but against the possibility that such a threat would materialize. All the time she was maintaining a visual lookout for any threat or any sign of the enemy.

Suddenly, Bentley saw an explosion out of the corner of her eye. She was puzzled for a moment until she realized that what she was seeing was the destruction of a Typhoon, blasted out of the sky by the projected-energy weapon the UFOs used. There were no aircraft ahead of her and because of this she was unable to see what countermeasures her fellow pilots were taking. She assumed that, like her, they were simply throwing their aircraft around in desperate attempts to present more difficult targets to any aggressor – although since they were unsure about the nature of the weapon the UFOs used she wasn't certain this would do any good. The Thunder Child analysts had ruled out the possibility that the weapon was a laser, on the basis that some pilots had apparently been able to manoeuvre their aircraft out of harm's way during the previous big engagement. Some of the scientists at DERA had suggested that the weapon fired superheated pulses of plasma towards a target, at speeds that didn't entirely rule out evasive action. Bentley felt that if there was a chance of dodging she'd try it, and continued to throw her aircraft around brutally. She was encouraged to see smoke trails ahead of her and nearly yelled out loud when she realized that this could only mean that some of the BVRAAMs had found their targets. But there were only three such trails that she could see – and she could now make out the dark shapes of enemy craft moving inexorably towards her.

Bentley had two ASRAAMs on the outer part of each wing and was determined to make them count. She had no idea whether any of her BVRAAMs had found their target and although she hoped so – especially as she was sure she'd been among the first to fire – she knew that the odds were against it. Most of the missiles had clearly been defeated by the countermeasures and had failed to achieve lock-on.

Pilots could sometimes forget that when two fast aircraft were flying towards each other, the closing speed could be phenomenal: even experienced fliers could be caught out. Bentley wasn't completely taken by surprise but she was stunned by just how quickly the enemy was upon her. One moment they had been dots on the horizon, the next they were swarming around her. She fired both her ASRAAMs at one of the craft, but saw them miss as the UFOs accelerated towards her position and then passed behind her field of view. She turned her Typhoon rapidly, but even as she pulled Gs she realized that she wouldn't be able to catch the opposition. Worse still, because of the way that the intruders had accelerated so rapidly, most of her fellow pilots hadn't been able to fire their ASRAAMs for fear of hitting their comrades.

Once Bentley had turned through 180 degrees and found herself almost at the back of a pursuing pack of Typhoons, she realized just how desperate their position was. Even at top speed they obviously had no chance of catching an enemy that had clearly accelerated to its maximum speed. Worse still, her course change revealed that the UFOs had not been firing their projected-energy weapon in an entirely defensive mode. As she flew back in the direction she'd come from she saw smoke trails beneath her that indicated a number of Typhoon pilots had not been as lucky as she had. The first wave of intruders had cut straight through them, with only two or three attackers falling victim to the vast number of missiles that had been launched. If the enemy's targets were indeed Fylingdales or the Control and Reporting Centres, then they were now on their own. Although the AD aircraft had, quite literally, given it their best shot, they were out of this particular game.

RAF Fylingdales, Yorkshire

Although she knew the value of early warning, Corporal Jane Vatch wished that somebody would kill the klaxon that had been sounding for the last few minutes. As one of the SAS personnel guarding the establishment, she had been glad of the advance notice of an attack, but needed now to concentrate on meeting the threat. Her Sergeant had deployed to an area of high ground where he thought he might stand a better chance of spotting any inbound craft, while she had positioned her team close to the giant radar itself.

Although the CO had told Vatch that she was the last line of
defence, they'd both known that was a harmless piece of fiction. If
an intruder craft got anywhere near where she'd placed her people
the radome would almost certainly be taken out, and her real role
would really be little more than that of trying to even the score
somewhat. There *might* be a moment of enemy vulnerability
during a final attack run and analysts suggested that, as the crafts'
targeting capability was weak, they might reduce speed immediately before firing. But as Vatch had surveyed the position,
looking for the best places to deploy her team, she'd realized what
everyone on the base had always known – the massive and
immobile radar was virtually impossible for any determined
aggressor to miss.

Usually, around 110 people worked in the structure, the centre
point of which was the nine-storey pyramid that housed the radar.
This number had been cut right back to the absolute minimum
needed to operate the facility: once the klaxon sounded, even these
personnel had evacuated to more secure parts of the base, together
with staff from other support facilities that were potential targets.

Vatch was about one hundred yards from the pyramid, sharing
a field with the three men under her command and some sheep.
She had been proud to be selected for this mission and was
determined to do well. Women had been eligible to join the SAS
for a few years now, but the great physical strength required still
kept out all but a handful of the most determined applicants. She
still felt that women like her were somehow on trial, and this
made her even more keen to impress. But it wasn't all about brute
strength, of course. It was also about *mental* toughness, leadership
skills and tactical awareness.

It was this last skill that was being tested now. Vatch had given
some thought to positioning her members of the platoon. She
wanted the four of them spread out so that at least one of them
might get a shot from close range. The other reason for dispersing
her people – aside from presenting a more difficult target if they
themselves were attacked – had to do with the mechanics of firing
a Stinger. Essentially, its operator couldn't engage a target directly

overhead because the angle was too steep and they'd be in danger of being burned by the backblast. So the angle of attack had to be sufficiently shallow to ensure that they were in no danger of being taken out by their own weapon.

They'd received word that the main body of alien craft had passed through the vanguard of jets sent to intercept the intruders. Information was sketchy, but it appeared that the RAF had got a few hits in but had taken some losses themselves. There was a second group of RAF aircraft closer in, but there was no reason to suppose they'd fare any better. The enemy had apparently now split into separate groups and were heading for a number of targets, including the key Control and Reporting sites as well as Fylingdales itself. As ever, the data was unclear because of the transitory nature of the radar signals these craft generated, but it seemed as if five craft were heading their way.

Vatch had no idea how long this war – if that's what it was – would last, or of how many other times she might be called upon to defend a site such as this. But she was fairly sure that, because they were fighting with maximum radar coverage, this first day presented them with their best chance of inflicting serious losses on the enemy. Since radar sites were now the prime target for attack, it was inevitable that subsequent actions would have to be fought with a seriously degraded radar capability. They *had* to make it count today, she knew.

Vatch knew, too, that she wouldn't be able to rely on any air support. The RAF were deployed elsewhere, having been detailed to try and intercept the intruders on their way in. She knew that other elements had been held in reserve to try an attack on craft returning from the raid. An air exclusion zone had been declared around the base, because although the Rapier and Stinger missiles both contained IFF systems that should prevent them from locking on to friendly aircraft, no pilots particularly liked putting this to the test by flying in an environment rich in missiles, 'friendly' or not. It was far better simply to declare that *anything* flying in your area was hostile, and Vatch knew that all her colleagues felt the same. It would be a devastating catastrophe to be responsible for a 'blue on blue': even if the equipment turned out to be at fault, she knew that anybody who fired the fatal shot would be inconsolable. They didn't need the distraction of such worries and were happy to fight this one themselves.

In the foreground, Vatch saw and then heard Rapier missiles being launched. That could only mean that RAF Regiment personnel had detected a hostile inbound on their tracker radar. She watched the missiles streak upwards, trying to see what they were aiming at. She now had her Stinger up and ready, its tracker unit giving out a high-pitched whine as it searched for a target, although she would only fire when she heard the lower tone that would indicate she'd achieved a lock-on. She was peering through the optical sight, trying to acquire one of the craft, when she saw more Rapiers being launched. But she'd seen no explosions in the sky, which could only mean that the missiles had missed.

Suddenly, much faster than she'd expected, Vatch saw a massive diamond-shaped craft flying towards the base. It was firing steady pulses of light down at the ground, at the rate of about one per second. Simultaneously, she was rewarded by a low growl from her Stinger's seeker unit. An instant later she pulled the trigger and the missile shot skywards with a roar.

Vatch was far too much the professional just to stand there watching and a moment later she had a second missile ready. But, as she frantically searched for another target, there was a thunderous explosion that threw her to the ground. As she picked herself up she turned to find out what had happened, knowing only too well what she would see. The massive pyramid containing the radar had clearly been struck full on by an energy beam from the craft and had suffered massive damage. It was ablaze, and this interfered with her Stinger's chances of acquiring any of the intruders, which were nowhere to be seen. Although her Stinger's seeker unit was again growling furiously, it had clearly only acquired the nearby fire.

Vatch cursed to herself and scanned the sky, but didn't spot any new targets. Clearly somebody else had, though, and from the other side of the base she saw a mixed volley of Stingers and

Rapiers streaking skywards, away from the burning radar, presumably chasing after the now departing intruders. Again, she saw no explosions and realized in frustration that not one of the enemy craft had been shot down.

Vatch waited for several minutes more, nervously scanning the sky for any sign of a further raid. But she saw nothing: with the enemy's primary target gone, there was clearly no need for a follow-up attack. Although so much about their tactics and motives was unknown, it seemed unlikely that they would return simply to engage the SHORAD units or the SAS soldiers.

After a few moments the klaxon sounded the all-clear and Vatch ran towards the pre-agreed rendezvous point to take stock of the situation. Incredibly, it emerged that there had been no casualties: neither the base personnel nor the defending RAF Regiment and SAS people had sustained any wounds or fatalities. But it also seemed that, despite the large number of missiles that had been fired, nobody had scored any hits. They'd done everything right, and yet the primary target they'd been defending had been destroyed without loss to the enemy.

PJHQ, Northwood

CJO was having a difficult job keeping up with what had turned out to be a multifaceted attack with a number of entirely separate components, all of which had come into play almost simultaneously. Information was crucial to all commanders, but information overload was almost as dangerous as a lack of awareness about the developing tactical and strategic position. CJO's subordinates tried to shield him from as much of the unnecessary data as possible, but like all commanders who have themselves seen combat – as CJO had in the Gulf War – he distrusted executive summaries and preferred raw data. This exasperated his briefers, who felt that *they* were more than able to sort through the material and pick out the key points.

The information was coming in steadily, and it was clear that the RAF had taken a pounding, with Buchan, Boulmer, Neatishead and Fylingdales bearing the brunt of the attacks. The

Fylingdales radar had been completely destroyed, its capability reduced to zero for the foreseeable future.

The Control and Reporting Centres had been hit hard, and while CJO was encouraged to learn that repairs were already under way, their effectiveness would be unclear for a while. Although mobile Tactical Air Control Centres would be deployed to plug the gap, CJO knew only too well that although these secondary radars were powerful, they were no substitute for the out-of-action primary systems. There was no getting away from it: the entire AD system was operating at greatly reduced effectiveness.

CJO was pleased to note that casualties had been light, though. There were no reports of any deaths among ground forces, all of whom had had warning of incoming raids and most of whom had been moved well away from the most likely targets. One of the Rapier squadrons deployed to defend RAF Buchan was claiming a hard kill, reporting that one of the attacking craft had been hit and had crashed into the sea a mile or two from the coast. This was unconfirmed so far, although an RAF Sea King SAR helicopter from RAF Lossiemouth was en route to the area to check if anything could be seen.

Elsewhere the news was not so good. The RAF had fought a desperate battle over the North Sea, but it was feared that six aircraft had been lost and a further two damaged. There had been unconfirmed reports that two pilots had ejected, and a Nimrod that had been stationed at Coningsby against this eventuality was en route and tracking signals from two PLBs. The only other good news was that neither RAF Waddington nor any of the Sentry aircraft had been attacked, although CJO had no illusions about that – if the enemy pressed this assault on the RAF's AD assets, they'd clearly be next.

The big surprise was a report that RAF Feltwell had been hit, presumably having paid the price for passing on the raid warning. CJO wasn't sure how to react to that one. A valuable link in the early-warning chain had presumably now gone, but he wondered whether the political benefit would outweigh this. Had the Americans now come in on the operation, and would the fact that they'd taken casualties stiffen their resolve and force them to pitch in decisively?

CJO didn't know what luck the politicians were having in trying to unravel the mystery of the American involvement with the whole business, but he could see straightaway that the Feltwell attack was his priority. He tasked his team with finding out as much as possible. He had to brief the PM and the War Cabinet in a few minutes and needed to get them some firm data. He was doubtful about the wisdom of integrating any US forces into Thunder Child operations until he could be certain they could be trusted. But with the Americans on board they *might* have a chance. Without them, even though all British forces had performed well, CJO had no such illusions.

Rowledge, Surrey

Jenny Thornton sat alone in her living room, pondering the empty bottle of wine that lay on the floor in front of her and seriously wondering if she should open another. A few weeks ago she'd have leapt at the prospect of confirmed alien contact and the opportunity it presented for her and those like her to vindicate themselves after years of ridicule. No more self-doubt, and no more snide implications of lies, hallucination or even mental illness. But then she'd recalled an old proverb that she'd heard somewhere. *Don't wish for something too hard – you may get it.* How true that was, she told herself. Robbed of the possibility that her experiences were all in the mind, and confronted with the fact that even the Government and the military seemed powerless to prevent these things, she faced a decidedly uncertain future.

Thornton had discussed things with Cody, of course, and with other members of the witness support group. They were all in sombre mood. For a long time now, some abductees had clung to the idea that the aliens were benign and were here to guide humanity into a new age. Thornton had always dismissed this as nonsense but had been too polite to call it that and not sufficiently sure of her own ground to state categorically that there *weren't* people out there having positive contact experiences. But recent events had shown that this New Age interpretation was wrong. People claiming benign contact were either lying or mistaken. Cody had confided privately to her the possibility that some abductees were subconsciously deluding themselves with a New Age fantasy that represented their best and only protection against the horrors that they had endured.

There had been constant media speculation about the nature of the enemy and of the battle that was even now being fought in the skies of Britain. There was much talk of how the RAF was in the front line, and Thornton certainly had nothing but admiration for the people who were fighting and in some cases dying in their attempts to fight off the intruders. But, as she turned this over in her mind, she realized the commentators were wrong, and that it was she – and the other abductees – who were really in the front line. From what she understood, the military were certainly putting up a brave fight. But there was no getting away from the fact that they were late arrivals in this particular war. She had been fighting this enemy for years.

Chapter Fifteen

ENDGAME

Harding Manor, Devizes

Despite his earlier plans for the ways he'd spend his time in Earl Sutton's country residence, West had spent much of the day watching television. He wasn't doing it for entertainment but to get information on the developing crisis. Virtually every serious channel was broadcasting special programmes dealing with the British Government's announcement that they were at war with an unidentified enemy. In the event, the PM had refrained from saying that this enemy was definitely extraterrestrial, because of the possibility – however remote – that the American cover story had been true, or that the creatures recovered might really have been genetically modified humans.

Governments, West knew, never liked to make definitive statements, because they had a habit of blowing up in spokespersons' faces if subsequent events cast doubts upon the first analyses. But the PM had been forced to float the idea and, the moment he had, everything had gone crazy. West vaguely remembered the furore that had erupted in the summer of 1996 when NASA announced that they had evidence – subsequently disputed by other scientists

– that there had once been bacteriological life on Mars. That was nothing compared to the impact of the PM's announcement, not least because of the small matter that the UK, for some inexplicable reason, now found itself at war with these entities.

West's interest was twofold. First, he was keen to keep up to date with any new announcements or analyses that might help him with his mission. This was difficult, because there had been very little official comment since the PM's announcement and any serious speculation was drowning in a sea of nonsense. He was constantly switching between BBC 1 and CNN, but wasn't really hearing anything of any operational use.

The other thing that West wanted was news of how the military operation was going and, specifically, of how his friends and colleagues were faring. He'd been ordered to attempt to communicate only in cases of extreme emergency, so there was no way he could access the official military channels of information that would normally be open to him. So he was in the same position as the public, except that his interest in finding out how things were going was a little more personal. Still, he'd been told that he was on the *real* front line and that his mission gave him a chance to really make a difference.

West knew that Defence Advisory Notices had been issued and that the PM's announcement had contained a specific plea to the media to report matters in a responsible way that wouldn't compromise ongoing operations or endanger lives. This meant that details of deployments and defensive measures should not have been given and West was furious to see that some of the media simply didn't understand where the line was drawn. A shot of a Rapier FSC launcher deployed at RAF Buchan had made him particularly angry and he'd sworn loudly at the television set.

As nightfall approached, West looked at the various briefings he'd been given and went through the technique that Carpenter had taught him. He went to bed and lay there for a while. As he'd been instructed, he resisted the urge to stay awake, although this was difficult. Only the fact that he was exhausted, mentally and physically, enabled him finally to fall asleep.

RAF Coningsby, Lincolnshire

The crewroom was a hive of activity as returning pilots anxiously sought news of friends, debating at length and with understandable passion the outcome of the engagement. Despite some optimistic news of PLB signals being detected, several fliers were sure they'd seen aircraft explode in mid-air with no sign that the pilot had managed to eject in time.

The confusion was heightened by the fact that they'd been a mixed force, with Typhoons from Leeming and Leuchars joining the fray. Other aircraft types had also taken part in the engagement, so none of the pilots were entirely sure how many losses had been sustained. Pilots from individual squadrons could simply look around and see if anybody they knew was missing, but they couldn't tell which fliers from other bases hadn't returned. Further complicating matters were those damaged aircraft that might have diverted to other airfields to land.

The question of whether the RAF had recorded any kills was equally confusing. Although films from onboard cameras had already been removed for analysis, the consensus was that the fighters had scored few hits, bringing down perhaps just three of the craft. But as these kills had supposedly been the result of hits by BVRAAMs, even these claims were based on a mixture of dubious radar data and wishful thinking, since the missile strikes had occurred before any of the pilots had visually acquired the UFOs. One or two of them claimed to have seen smoke trails from downed intruder craft, but Bentley wasn't the only pilot who wondered – however much she wanted to believe the claims – whether they'd simply seen their own missiles. Pilots were notoriously over-optimistic with their kill claims, but after some debate they agreed that they simply wouldn't know for sure until the radar tapes and long-range TV camera images had been analysed.

Ground crews were rushing around outside, frantically refuelling aircraft. This was a task made more difficult by the aircraft having been dispersed around the airfield to present a more difficult target if Coningsby itself was raided. But flash

signals from PJHQ indicated that the intruders had withdrawn
and radar screens – the surviving ones, anyway – were clear. Not
that any of the pilots believed that happy state of affairs would
last.

'They've gotta hit us soon,' one of the new arrivals observed to
nobody in particular.

'Yeah,' somebody else replied, half-heartedly.

After the initial debriefings, the pilots were allowed, in small
groups, to grab a quick shower and some much-needed food and
drink. But at any given time, most of them were being held at a
moment's notice to return to the fray and protect whatever target
might be attacked next – possibly their own base. Some pilots
were on Q, sitting in aircraft that were fuelled and ready to go.
Additionally, and as part of the more aggressive ROE that had
been adopted, four aircraft were flying CAP missions out over the
North Sea, supported by a VC10 K3 refuelling aircraft from 101
Squadron at RAF Brize Norton. That had presented the tacticians
with a dilemma, because sustained attacks on the tanker force
itself – as well as the predicted but yet-to-materialize strikes at the
AEW aircraft – could prove an easier way of degrading the RAF's
operational capability. But, as ever, there was so much speculation
and so little hard data to go on. The enemy's motives were still
unclear and, although information about their capabilities and
tactics was slowly being pieced together, nobody even knew what
their numerical strength was. This meant that planners were
unable to say whether or not taking out a few of the craft would
have had any effect whatsoever. If the intruders had vast numbers
to play with, they could afford to take a few losses while slowly
wearing down the RAF. But if their numbers were comparatively
few, then any losses might dent *their* operational capability and
make them think twice about further attacks.

The pilots had all sorts of questions for their commanders. They
wanted to know what progress was being made on the political
front and whether the Government had managed to get any
scientists to come up with some way of making contact with the
enemy. They were also desperate for information about the

Americans, and in particular for news of whether any material US support would be forthcoming. Others were pushing for intelligence about what DERA were doing with the craft they'd recovered and whether any useful data had been obtained. Although the more experienced pilots knew better, some of the younger ones had the mistaken idea that DERA would simply be able to strip out and replicate some useful offensive or defensive gizmos and incorporate them directly into the RAF's own aircraft. The reality was that although DERA staff were working around the clock, there was no way in which back-engineering could deliver the goods by when the pilots wanted.

Downing Street, Whitehall
'So what do we do now?' the PM demanded. 'Do we just go on reacting and reacting until we don't have any assets left?'

The question had been meant to be rhetorical – the PM had a habit of working things through out loud – but Willoughby felt he had to offer something. 'We keep our defences up, we make good the damage that's been caused and we continue to try and find ways to counter these creatures.'

CDS nodded his agreement, but the comment – which was really little more than a statement of the obvious – elicited only a grunt from the PM.

CDS then decided it might be a good time to brief the PM on something he'd only just relayed to S of S, while they'd been crossing the road from Main Building to Number Ten. 'CJO tells me that one of his people has worked up an analysis of their activities. It seems there may be a pattern to all this, and one that might indicate motive.'

'Yes?'

CDS looked sheepish. 'He said he'd come in to brief us direct, when they're sure.' Seeing the PM's expression he quickly added a caveat. 'He says this could be the breakthrough we've been looking for and that he'll be over by 2300. Secure or not, he didn't want to put this out over any comms system.'

The PM accepted this news without comment before briefing

his senior advisers in on the latest political developments. 'I've spoken again to the President, who's consulting the Joint Chiefs. They *want* to help, but she'll need political approval before pitching in. You know how twitchy the Americans are about taking casualties in somebody else's war.'

'Doesn't the attack on their facility at RAF Feltwell make it their war too?' Willoughby asked, not unreasonably.

'Apparently there's a debate about whether these entities would understand that the base was anything other than British.' The PM's voice was scornful and sarcastic, so those present felt comfortable making noises of anger and frustration themselves. 'To be fair,' the PM continued, 'the President is clearly doing her best, but I can't overstate the extent to which her administration has been paralysed by the revelation that the NSA was involved with this. As you know, Director Van Buren and a few of his key subordinates have disappeared, together with a few other officials here and there – mainly in the NRO. Investigators are going to have a tough time piecing it all together, because all of these people were too experienced to leave many tracks. And, just to add icing to the cake, there's an inter-agency turf fight to run the investigation going on.' There were sighs of frustration from the assembled company, followed by a pause.

'Any chance of support from NATO or the UN?' the Deputy Prime Minister asked.

'The UN Security Council will meet in emergency session tomorrow, as will the NATO Military Committee,' the PM replied. He'd been having a busy day, handling many of the most delicate calls himself, in an attempt to bypass the usual bureaucracy. The result was a rare situation that only ever arose in times of national crisis when leaders made deals direct with other leaders: he was now briefing his subordinates, rather than vice versa. 'That's as much as we could have expected, but I very much doubt they'll decide to make any forces available in the absence of firm information about who our enemies are. Most of the unofficial soundings we've taken have resulted in messages of moral support and sympathy but no indication that anything more material than this will be forthcoming. "It's not our fight" seems to be the message we're getting. Don't underestimate the public and media angle here: many people think we're the bad guys, and have implied that we started this. Governments aren't going to want to come in on our side when that's the sort of message they're getting from their own people. They'll spin it out and wait to see how things develop. But there's very real fear there, too. There's a sense that if these people really *are* aliens, they may have much more effective hardware up their sleeves than anything we've seen to date. Nobody wants to go up against an enemy who might be able to wipe you out.'

'We don't, either,' Willoughby observed, bitterly, before a question occurred to him. 'Anything from our own civilian scientists yet?'

The PM handed over to the Deputy Prime Minister on that one. 'No. But just about every radio observatory in the world that can is firing messages into space. But nobody can agree on what to say or how to say it, so mixed messages are going out. Frankly, I wouldn't hold out any hope there: as you know, the military have been broadcasting sequences of prime numbers since the earliest days of Thunder Child, with no joy yet. There's no reason to suppose that the messages aren't being received and understood, because the opposition seem pretty well informed about us in every other respect. It's just that, for whatever reason, they're choosing not to reply. This being the case, I doubt that the civilian scientists will fare any better.'

The meeting ran on for another fifteen minutes. Just before it broke up, Willoughby – who had consulted CDS – decided the time had come to brief the PM on the activities of Sergeant Jack West. The meeting listened in silence to what S of S told them. It was a bold plan but, given how little anybody knew about the opposition, nobody had any idea whether or not it would succeed.

Harding Manor, Devizes

Lights. Figures. A strange, floating sensation. Was this a dream or the real thing? West cautioned himself to do nothing for the time being, and began to go through his drills. He was sure this meant he was awake, although he knew that people often dreamt of the last thing they'd been thinking about before going to sleep. But he'd seen a light, and Carpenter had explained how turning on a light was the test of whether you were dreaming or not. It had to do with levels of activity in the brain, apparently. If you were dreaming, you wouldn't be able to turn on the light. Or so the theory went.

West told himself not to resist what was happening, even if he could. Not yet, anyway. For the time being, he had to act the part of Earl Sutton; if the Earl had been unable to speak or move during his experiences, West would have to pretend to be similarly helpless.

Before West had gone to bed, he had put in the special contact lenses that Carpenter had given him. The DIS man and Templeton had both agreed that this might degrade the control that the entities had over him. The abduction literature was full of references to bluish-white beams of light – indeed, West had seen one himself at Thornton's house. So lenses that filtered out light at the blue end of the spectrum might block an important element of the control mechanism that incapacitated the abductees. There would be a price to pay in terms of his overall ability to see clearly but they'd felt this was an acceptable trade-off. West ran it through in his mind, certain now that he wasn't dreaming. But his eyes were still closed, and he wasn't sure whether he should risk opening them or not. Earl Sutton had said that he'd been fully awake during these procedures, with his eyes open, and the consensus had been that it wouldn't matter if West opened his eyes. But they'd debated whether this might be a tell-tale sign that he wasn't under full control and had decided that if he was removed and taken onto a ship he'd keep his eyes shut at least until he was on board. The problem was that he wasn't sure *where* he was, because of a general feeling of light-headedness.

Just as West was trying to decide when to open his eyes, he became aware of another problem. He could hear something. Straining his ears, he realized that a voice was speaking, but extremely quietly. There was something soporific about the voice and West assumed there was someone in the room with him. He'd been told that the technique used to control abductees – and, indeed, to induce their amnesia at the end of each kidnap session – was nothing more mysterious than hypnosis. The irony was that researchers had used regression hypnosis to try and uncover memories of abductions for years, when all the time it looked as though the entities themselves used hypnosis to suppress the memories in the first place.

But this wasn't what West had been briefed to expect, this was more like . . . he thought for a moment, then he had it: *subliminal messages*. He was listening to a recording. It made sense, he told himself. Immobilize the subject with the lights – they weren't quite sure how this worked yet, but it probably had to do with interfering with signals in the brain – then subject them to subliminal messages to keep them on the straight and narrow. Ufologists used misleading terms like *mind control*, but in a way they were right – it *was* mind control, of a sort. The only difference was that there was nothing spooky about it at all – most of the techniques were well understood and a standard part of any interrogation procedure. West had learnt about much of this on a Conduct After Capture course, which was another reason why Carpenter and Templeton thought he'd already have useful skills for this mission.

'That's not Earl Sutton.' *An American voice!* The briefing had covered this eventuality, but–

West snapped open his eyes and threw himself instinctively to the side, rolling his body as he moved away from the direction of the voice. He fell about three feet to the ground, and in an instant had taken in his surroundings. He had just rolled sideways off a raised platform that stood in the middle of the archetypal round, white room to which the briefing had suggested he'd be taken. He'd seen the real thing before, of course, although only after his Stinger missile – and the subsequent crash of the UFO – had done its work. They'd taken him to the DERA site at Farnborough specially to familiarize him with the layout of the craft. The only difference was that this room was humid and dimly lit, almost as if he was in a Turkish bath.

There were four figures in the room with him, two human and two decidedly not so. The voice had come from a man in military uniform with a name patch on his chest. *Landau. I've heard of you*, West thought. One of the beings moved directly in front of him. *Quicker movement than I'd expected*, West reflected as he found himself staring at a small rod being waved in his face. He could see a white light and assumed this was the controlling device that was sometimes used to incapacitate abductees. Templeton had speculated – acknowledging that he was not the first to do so – that these were the magic wands of human folklore, and that the entities were the 'little people' reported over hundreds if not thousands of years in a remarkably cross-cultural way. West swept the device aside and brought his right hand down on the being's neck in a sweeping motion. *No time for subtlety.*

Another of the beings darted into West's field of vision. Clearly they hadn't realized that their toys didn't work any more. Then he heard a different voice – another American, and obviously panicked. 'Shoot him.' This was getting serious.

There had been much debate over what equipment West should take on the mission. Everyone had agreed that the more items he took and the bulkier these were, the greater the possibility that he'd be rumbled before the transfer. But the mission objective meant that he obviously needed to go in armed – a decision that the latest turn of events had clearly vindicated. In the end he'd opted for a 9mm semi-automatic Browning pistol and ammunition – two clips, each carrying eighteen rounds. This had been strapped to his chest, under the T-shirt he'd been wearing.

Keeping low and on the move, West snapped in the first magazine and brought his weapon up, scanning for a threat. But before he could spot Landau in the gloom, a shot rang out, catching West in his side and spinning him around as he fell. The bullet had only grazed him but the shock of the impact had caused him to drop his pistol, which went sliding across the floor. Fortunately, he had another and more potent weapon at his disposal. The other advantage was that he was now alongside the raised platform: it lay between him and Landau, who was clearly firing from another section of the craft, using the doorway as cover. Because of this obstacle, and because of the gloom, Landau clearly hadn't spotted that West had lost his pistol.

'Give it up,' came the American's voice. He was out of sight, of course, to one side of the doorway. A man like Landau clearly wouldn't make the mistake of silhouetting himself. It wouldn't matter. West removed another object from his belt, pulled the pin, and sent the grenade on an arcing curve across the room and through the doorway. He'd taken cover behind the platform but, even so, the noise of the explosion in the confined space was deafening. He located his pistol and scooped it up in a fluid motion, running forward through the doorway.

Landau was dead, having taken the full force of the grenade blast. Another man, older and smartly dressed, had been hit in the arm, and was trying to stem the blood flow. West assumed that as this one had told Landau to shoot he'd be unarmed himself, but took no chances and searched him roughly.

Having satisfied himself that the man was indeed unarmed, West turned his attention to the control room. Three of the creatures were struggling with what he presumed was the drive mechanism: it seemed to be faltering, presumably due to damage from his grenade. Certainly the craft was lurching around violently, and although he couldn't see outside, it was clear they were losing height. His original mission had been to capture an operational craft, complete with its crew, but the presence of the Americans had complicated matters, and he'd had no option but to use his grenade – which his briefing had made clear should only have been a weapon of last resort. He wasn't sure why the creatures were ignoring him. Either it was because they'd figured out they couldn't control him or it was because their priority was to avoid a fatal crash – something that suited West just fine. His first action on realizing he was on the craft had been to activate his PLB, the final item he'd been carrying – and he fervently hoped that the Thunder Child team would, as planned, be tracking his progress. As soon as the craft was down, military personnel – hopefully SAS, but naturally that depended on where they landed – would be flown to the area to take charge of the craft. He hoped he'd be alive to greet them.

MOD Main Building, Whitehall

CJO swept into S of S's office and delivered the news that the assembled company had waited up for. 'It's Bentwaters,' he announced. It was a place that had come up many times in the Thunder Child background briefings on UFOs and everyone in the room immediately saw the significance. 'They – whoever they are – still have a presence there. Much of their activity has been aimed at hiding that from us.'

'The underground facility?' S of S ventured.

'It's got to be,' CJO replied.

'We have to get this to the PM *right now*,' said S of S, moving to the door. He turned to CDS. 'I assume we attempt to take the facility?'

CDS nodded his agreement. 'I recommend we use Special Forces for the assault, with air cover only if they request it. We can position the Typhoon force well out to sea to intercept our friends if they move in, which I assume they will.'

'What if the attack fails?' S of S wanted to know.

CDS thought about that for a moment. 'It's the PM's decision – and yours – but if the assault fails I recommend we pull our people back and send in a low-level air attack. We could use Tornado GR1s armed with laser-guided Paveway III bombs, and utterly destroy the place.'

Over the North Sea

The news had come through just after 0330 hours. Ground forces were moving in on a site in Suffolk, and this was bound to provoke a response. The RAF's job was to run interference on the craft that would almost certainly appear as soon as the attack was detected.

The pilots had been stunned by this latest turn of events, but the information they'd been given wasn't detailed enough to have sparked off anything more than the usual wild speculation. The pilots' favourite theory was that another one of the craft had crashed there, perhaps making a forced landing after one of their earlier missile hits. But the fliers had somehow sensed it was something bigger than that – something decisive.

Bentley was airborne again, wondering if this was the time when her luck would run out. The klaxon had sounded fifteen minutes previously, and wave after wave of aircraft had taken to the skies. Fighter Controllers had marshalled them in a holding area over Norfolk before assigning them to different 'boxes' of airspace. They'd lost some of their radar capability, but that didn't matter so much if the Thunder Child analysts were correct, because they knew exactly from which direction the UFOs would be coming. Two Sentry AEW aircraft were also patrolling the skies over Norfolk, protected by a veritable swarm of Typhoons. Data from mobile T99 radars together with the Rapiers' tracker radar would also be available and would, to a certain extent, make up for the loss of capability at RAF Neatishead.

Bentley was watching her on-board systems very carefully, scrutinizing them for any sign of the enemy, when word came that they were about to have company. It was not good news. Although the data was far from clear, it seemed that this was a larger raid than the previous one, with perhaps seventy or eighty craft heading their way.

But before the intruders got to the Typhoons there would be another obstacle in their way. The Navy, still smarting from the loss of HMS *Churchill*, had a carrier group in the North Sea, with an accompanying escort consisting of three of the new Project Horizon air defence frigates, HMS *Howard*, HMS *Alfred* and HMS *Henry*. The aircraft carrier HMS *Invincible* was at the centre of this group, armed with Seadart missiles which it was hoped might thin out the attackers a bit. Additional firepower would be provided by twenty-four Sea Harrier fighter aircraft whose pilots were absolutely spoiling for a fight, and – through the intervention of the First Sea Lord – were clearly going to get one now that the Navy had been given first strike at the enemy. Bentley could appreciate the anger that the naval pilots felt at the loss of HMS *Churchill*, which had been the first of the new air defence frigates to enter service. She'd trained with some of them, and although – naturally – she felt the RAF had the edge, she had to acknowledge they were pretty good too.

Downing Street, Whitehall

'Prime Minister,' Willoughby began, 'we have tracked Jack West's position through the PLB he was carrying. It seems he has come down in Rendlesham Forest. Now that's *right* next to Bentwaters – actually it lies between Bentwaters and Woodbridge – so it's got to validate our idea that the aliens have some sort of facility there.'

The Prime Minister thought about that for a moment. The fact that people had died was a tragedy, but he felt this was somehow compounded by the fact that it had been connected with clandestine activity here on the mainland. It outraged him that this had taken place, effectively right under their noses. 'I'm going there,' he announced.

'That's not wise, sir,' CDS pointed out.

'It's not debatable.'

Over the North Sea

Bentley had just fired a volley of her BVRAAMs at the approaching craft, which she had acquired visually a few moments ago. Even before she'd fired her missiles, she'd seen that the number of intruders had been thinned out, and she'd realized that the Navy claims of a number of hard kills must have been correct. But she also knew they'd taken fearful losses: although the ships hadn't been attacked, it was reported that many of the Sea Harriers had been destroyed or damaged.

Bentley fired her ASRAAMs next and, again, performed no follow-up actions, since they too were fire-and-forget missiles. She'd been moving her Typhoon around a fair bit, trying to avoid flying on an entirely straight – and therefore predictable – course, and was now ready to try a burst from her cannon. In an instant she and the others were in among the intruder craft and she'd fired her cannon straight at an oncoming target. Last time the craft had gone right through them because the objective of their raid had been a number of fixed sites on the mainland. But this time they'd been told that the enemy's presence would be in response to ground action, meaning that the intruders would be providing cover. This meant the craft couldn't simply accelerate past the Typhoons because, for all they knew, the RAF pilots would simply follow them back to the site of the ground attack and harass the intruders' forces there. They'd have to stay and fight, taking the RAF out of the game aircraft by aircraft.

The engagement had turned into an ultra-modern version of a World War Two air battle, with individual dogfights taking place over a wide area. Bentley was still mindful of the dangers of blue-on-blue, and recalled something she'd heard in training. *A bullet doesn't carry IFF equipment, so watch where you fire it.* But visibility was good, and the RAF jets were all well separated. She depressed the firing button as a craft came into view but it flashed across her path so quickly that by the time she turned to pursue, it was nowhere to be seen. She thought she'd hit the first craft but hadn't seen it go down. She was so focused on her immediate surroundings that there was no time or scope to get a wider tactical view of the engagement. Data was available on her on-board systems but she knew her best chance of survival was now simply to use her eyes to watch out for any immediate threats. The Sentry crews were also passing data, but once they'd seen the enemy, there wasn't much more for them to do. Any information they could pass now would be no good for close combat. Thankfully, the Fighter Controllers on the two Sentry aircraft realized that and had stayed off the air for a while, although the data was on her screen for her to use if she wanted.

Bentley was suddenly aware that a lot of craft were bearing down on her position, with bolts of energy blasting towards her. Realizing that there was a difference between being brave and being suicidal, she thrust the joystick down and to the right, rolling and then turning her aircraft out of the line of fire. Now she could see another large group of the craft. They seemed to be regrouping, getting ready to use their numbers to maximum effect. A thought flashed through her mind. *They hunt in packs*. She couldn't see any other Typhoons but decided she had to try to disrupt the intruders' regrouping effort. She flew straight at the craft, engaging the lead one with her cannon. She had the satisfaction of seeing her shells hit it before it lurched to one side.

Then something strange and unexpected happened. Three of the other craft suddenly exploded in mid-air. Bentley saw a sinister black shape hurtling past her from behind and for a moment was confused at this latest development, wondering whether another alien faction had joined the fight on the RAF's side. When she realized what she was looking at, she whooped with joy. American F-117A Nighthawk stealth fighters were engaging the UFOs with air-to-air missiles, their sudden and unexpected arrival having gone undetected not just by the RAF but by the aliens. America had finally done the right thing.

Rendlesham Forest, Suffolk

Lead elements of D Squadron advanced through the trees, with half the troops moving at any one time while the others scanned for trouble, weapons at the ready. A few carried Stingers, GPMGs or Minimis, but most were armed with the SAS's favourite weapon, the trusty M16. The real beauty of the M16 was that the M203 40mm grenade launcher could be attached to the rifle, making a really effective combination weapon. Since their briefing had suggested the presence of extensive underground facilities that they might have taken room by room, this was the option favoured by most of the soldiers, who knew that the grenades would be devastatingly effective in the confined spaces.

'There, through the trees,' somebody whispered.

Sergeant Bob Crawford, the troop leader, raised his field glasses and saw what he immediately realized was a downed UFO in a nearby clearing. It looked intact and, although this was not his primary objective, he decided to move in. It was a prize too good to miss and he needed to make sure it – or its occupants – posed no threat to his team. They approached cautiously, noticing, as they drew close, two figures sitting on the clearing floor. One man was wearing a suit and the other was dressed more casually, in what looked like baggy tracksuit bottoms and a T-shirt that was stained with blood. He was holding a pistol.

'Drop the weapon,' Crawford called out, aiming directly at the man with the gun while using a tree as cover. Then something unexpected happened as he heard a voice raised behind him, from one of his own people. 'Jack? What are *you* doing here, you stupid bastard?' The man with the gun grinned. Crawford didn't know West, but clearly a number of his team did.

West rose slowly and deliberately, making sure that everyone could see he was no threat. Several of his colleagues moved forward, eager to find out what was going on. The troop leader walked forward too and looked questioningly at the smartly dressed man who was clearly in some discomfort from a wound of his own.

'May I present Edwin Van Buren, Director of the National Security Agency,' West announced theatrically. And behind me, in the craft, you'll find some even more unusual prisoners. They're in pretty bad shape after our heavy landing, but I think they're still alive. I suggest you secure the craft, though.' The two men promptly did so.

'Movement in the trees!' someone called out, as another group of men emerged into the clearing. They were wearing US Army uniforms.

'Drop your weapons!' Crawford yelled.

'You drop yours,' drawled an arrogant voice from behind the treeline.

Two groups of soldiers stood facing each other, in an obvious stand-off. 'Mr Van Buren, sir,' one of the Americans said. 'Are you OK? What are our orders, sir?'

'His orders are for you to obey your President's new Executive Order and give every assistance to the United Kingdom,' a new and instantly recognizable voice rang out. It was the Prime Minister. He hadn't managed to approach the scene undetected, of course, and was completely surrounded by a group of SAS soldiers who had been absolutely horrified that the PM was walking into a potential danger zone but had been unable to dissuade him from doing so. Some might have tried, were it not for the fact that CDS was present and seemed to be playing along. All they could do was bunch around him so he wasn't in the direct line of sight of any of the American troops.

'The war's over, Mr Van Buren,' the Prime Minister said. His voice was firm and the SAS soldiers recognized the steel in it. 'Your President has just informed me that the stealth aircraft of the Forty-Ninth Fighter Wing from Holloman Air Force Base have crossed the Atlantic and joined with Royal Air Force and Royal Naval aircraft in attacking a hostile force that was engaged in an act of war against our country. Your friends are leaving.'

Van Buren stood, motioning to the American troops to drop their weapons. Most had already done so. 'I—' Van Buren was interrupted by a low, rumbling sound that grew steadily in intensity until the ground shook. It lasted for fully fifteen seconds: the SAS soldiers all looked for its source, scanning for danger but finding nothing. A group of soldiers still surrounded the PM and CDS and they were particularly nervous, weapons pointing at the trees around them, ready for any threat that might materialize.

When the sound finally subsided, there was an eerie silence, broken by Van Buren's voice. 'Yes,' he said. 'They've gone. Now they've really gone.' There was a trace of sadness in his voice.

'Explain,' demanded the PM.

'As you clearly know, the . . . *visitors* have — had — a base here. Actually, it was a few miles out to sea, well beneath the ocean floor. Clearly it's the destruction of that facility that we've just heard. They've been here for hundreds of years, so far as we can tell, and provided they flew at night, with no lights, they were unlikely to be seen as they arrived and departed. Then all that changed, due to an accident of history.'

'Bawdsey Manor,' CDS interrupted, not liking Van Buren's condescending tone and wanting to show that he was following the plot.

'Precisely,' Van Buren replied. 'Bawdsey Manor, just a few miles from here, was where radar was first developed in the late Thirties, and suddenly it was harder for the visitors to operate without risk of detection. Indeed from time to time they *were* detected, in 1956 for example, and most notably in 1980. On that occasion we were . . . approached, and asked for help, when one of their craft developed a technical problem.'

'Here in Rendlesham Forest.' The PM's comment was delivered as a statement of fact.

'Yes. Probably no more than a few hundred yards from this spot. And that was when they levelled with us and told a few of us what was going on. They're remarkably like us in many ways. When they found the Earth, they wanted it for themselves, just as we humans have taken land and resources that we coveted from the weak throughout history. But interstellar travel isn't easy, and the energy needed for faster-than-light travel is vast, meaning that only small craft can be moved this way. Big craft can only travel at sub-light speed. One such craft is on its way, and has been for a long time. It's essentially a large asteroid, converted into a ship carrying *millions* of . . . I suppose you could call them colonists. I've been on that ship, so I know their capabilities.'

'So what was this *deal* that you made with them?' the PM asked.

'When they get here, they want to integrate into existing political systems, instead of starting from scratch. If it ain't broke, don't fix it, as they say. They told us they didn't care which political system they integrated into, but that, if we kept their secret and helped them in other ways, they'd integrate into *ours*, and not the Soviets'. To me, that seemed the lesser of two evils, so we repaired the ship that got into trouble here in Rendlesham Forest and kept their secret.'

'How come they look so much like us?' the PM wanted to know.

'Think back to *The War of the Worlds*,' Van Buren retorted. 'Terrestrial microbes would have killed them, because they would have had no resistance. So they've been gradually integrating terrestrial DNA into themselves during the so-called abductions – genetically modifying themselves until they are essentially human. This means that when the main vessel arrives, the colonists will be entirely adapted to live on Earth. Bear in mind that all Earth's infrastructure is designed for Earth-dwellers' use; any non-terrestrial species would encounter enormous practical difficulties in trying to carry out even the most basic functions.'

'Why should we believe this story any more than your last?' the PM demanded.

'Because you'll soon see for yourselves. The mother ship will be here within five years – I'm surprised, frankly, that astronomers haven't picked it up already. The visitors were evacuating their base here when you stumbled upon their activities. They had equipment here that was important to them, and it was essential that you didn't capture it – you might have disrupted their plans. They wanted to remove it, but when it looked as if you'd discovered their base they clearly destroyed it rather than let you have it.'

'But if they're that scared of our capabilities, surely it shows you were wrong to think we couldn't resist? And, indeed, we've just shown we *can* mount a successful defence.' The PM's point seemed reasonable to the various soldiers who were listening intently, as their fundamental beliefs about humanity and its place in the universe were turned on their heads.

'Against scout ships. The heavy stuff is only sub-light capable and isn't here yet but, again, I've seen it and I can tell you we wouldn't win. We tried, though, we really did. First with the Strategic Defence Initiative, then with MIRACL and KE-ASAT, but the timing was wrong. We made great progress, but the systems simply weren't going to be operational in time. We might dent them, but unless we can win, there's no point in even fighting. But why *should* we fight? The creatures you've seen are genetically engineered drones. As I've told you, the colonists aren't alien invaders – to all intents and purposes they're human. Why fight them? Why fight a catastrophic and unwinnable war when we could simply allow them to integrate? That way, we can share their technology and join with them. We would simply be aiding the evolutionary progress of humanity.'

'We *shall* resist, you know,' the PM replied. 'And your

President tells me that America will resist, whether you like it or not. And when they're briefed on the situation, I have no doubt that all the nations on Earth will resist.'

'Then God help you,' Van Buren replied, a trace of bitterness in his tone.

'No,' the PM retorted, 'God help *you*. Because the President tells me that you are to be placed on trial for your collaboration.'

'On what charge?' Van Buren asked, his voice shaking with outrage. 'For loving my country so much that I wanted to save it?'

'The charges you face are a matter for your own Government,' the PM replied. 'But if it was my decision, well . . . perhaps crimes against humanity would be appropriate.'

Having delivered this most damning of indictments, the Prime Minister turned to leave. As he walked back towards his car – a detachment of SAS still surrounding him – he turned things over in his mind. He had come to terms with an alien presence, but not with the fact that this had led to deceit and subterfuge between allies. Wasn't the emergence of an external threat supposed to unite people and make them stand together against a common enemy? Might not revelations about hostile aliens make international quarrels less important and strengthen the perception that all the nations on the Earth were inextricably bonded together by their shared humanity?

Putting these thoughts aside, the Prime Minister turned to address CDS. There were plans to be made and defences to be organized. Until a few days ago he'd viewed humanity as an advanced species that had recently entered the new Millennium to stand on the threshold of even greater things. But now, in his mind, he saw the fragility of human existence. He lived not in the Space Age but in a house of straw. And, in the distance, he could hear the approaching wolf.